4

CHECKED OUT

Previously published Worldwide Mystery title by
SHARON ST. GEORGE

DUE FOR DISCARD

CHECKED OUT

SHARON ST. GEORGE

W✦RLDWIDE®

TORONTO • NEW YORK • LONDON
AMSTERDAM • PARIS • SYDNEY • HAMBURG
STOCKHOLM • ATHENS • TOKYO • MILAN
MADRID • WARSAW • BUDAPEST • AUCKLAND

To Marjorie Anne Souza, who loved books, horses and music. Thank you for the precious gift of unconditional love.

Recycling programs
for this product may
not exist in your area.

Checked Out

A Worldwide Mystery/September 2018

First published by Camel Press, an imprint of
Epicenter Press, Inc.

ISBN-13: 978-1-335-50672-6

Printed in U.S.A.

ACKNOWLEDGMENTS

Thanks to George Souza for keeping me straight with legal matters, Mary Souza for her medical expertise and Steve Souza for sharing his knowledge of blues music. Special thanks to Dr. Betsy Adamson, Dr. Jen Powers and Donna Goodell for advice on matters involving llamas and horses. Chloe Winston's first draft critiques are deeply appreciated as is the expert advice of Sensei Scott Redden on matters of judo and jujitsu. A special nod to Wendy Johnston, Art Stackhouse, Robert Feamster, John Higley and Huckleberry for helping Game Boy come to life. Finally, much gratitude to Jennifer McCord and Catherine Treadgold of Camel Press for a valued publishing relationship.

ONE

I WASN'T SURPRISED when rodeo cowboy Cody O'Brien vanished from Timbergate Medical Center the night before his testicle surgery, but I was surprised to hear of his death. I had known the O'Brien family since childhood, and though we'd lost touch over the years, I still felt sad for their loss.

Cleo Cominoli called me the morning after O'Brien's getaway to tell me he had been found unconscious ten miles north of town in a horse trailer parked along I-5. TMC's Life Support Unit had rushed him to the hospital, but his severe head wound proved fatal. He died in the emergency room. The incident was immediately assumed to be an accident, since horse-related injuries are common in our part of the state. Rural northern California has always been famous for its rodeos and horse shows.

"Meet me for lunch," Cleo said. "We need to talk."

I first met Cleo when I was hired as Health Sciences Librarian at Timbergate Medical Center. Cleo's position as Director of Medical Affairs gave her access to all the confidential information disclosed behind closed doors when medical staff committees dealt with patient care mistakes. She knew more about the doctors on the TMC medical staff than anyone, though some of that information trickled down to me.

In addition to managing the library, I was responsible for the medical staff's Continuing Medical Education requirements. Since Cleo's work dovetailed with mine, we'd become friends and confidants. Both our jobs required professional discretion, so we shared our information only with each other.

I assumed Cleo wanted to talk about the unfortunate runaway cowboy, and I was surprised she was free for lunch. She facilitated at least fifteen medical staff committee meetings every month. The doctors were always pressed for time and hungry, so their meetings were usually scheduled over breakfast or lunch.

"In your office?" I asked.

"No. Margie's Bean Pot. Noon."

Lunch at Margie's meant a conversation that we couldn't talk about at work. The little restaurant was across the street from the hospital, so it picked up a lot of business from TMC.

AT NOON I walked over to Margie's, enjoying the first hint of a cool mid-October breeze. Cleo had not arrived, so I helped myself from the self-serve bar, dipping out a bowl of Hawaiian Baked Beans. Fragrant aromas filled the cozy diner, and saliva pooled under my tongue. Owner Margie Sacchi believes beans are the key to longevity and claims she can serve a different bean special every day for an entire year.

"Hi, China," Margie hailed me with her usual greeting.

My name isn't China, it's Aimee Machado. I always explain that it's pronounced *Ma-SHAW-doe* to avoid the inevitable confusion with *The Mikado*. Margie calls me China because I'm half Chinese and she thinks that's cool. To hear her tell it, Asian women have it made.

Beauty, brains, and exotic looks. When I remind her I'm also half Portuguese, she says that's even better and hums a few bars of "The Girl from Ipanema," a number she plays with vigor on her accordion.

There was no use in trying to explain that although the Brazilians speak Portuguese, my father's grandparents came from the Azores Islands, a Portuguese archipelago in the middle of the Atlantic Ocean.

I chose a small table against the back wall under a large framed photo of a younger Margie and handsome, white-maned Dick Contino shaking the bellows together fifteen years earlier at the Cotati California Accordion Festival. Mellow and romantic accordion music from the Parisian bistros of the twenties flowed through ceiling speakers, providing Margie's diners with Continental atmosphere.

Cleo, the happy Italian workaholic, admitted to forty, but her stunning body and winning way with men made her age irrelevant. Cleo had never married, but she'd been engaged often. Sig Modaresi, the latest in a long line of fiancés, was a wealthy dentist and loopy for Cleo. Their engagement had lasted five years, but smart money said he'd never get her to the altar. The medical staff jokesters had already saddled the poor guy with a nickname, and I had to admit it presented Cleo with a dilemma. If she did marry Sig, she'd have to retire or be known ever after as Mrs. Sigmoidoscopy, which is a diagnostic method of examining the colon.

I watched Cleo dip soup from the self-serve bar and scan the room for hospital employees who might overhear us. Finally she slid into the chair opposite me.

"Looks good." I nodded at the steaming bowl she placed on the table. "What is it?"

"The special. Meatball soup with kidney beans."

"Okay, enough small talk. What's up?"

"This is strictly off the record," she said. I'd never seen her so tense. Her shoulders were hunched up nearly to her ears.

"Of course. So tell me."

"It's big. At least I think so."

"What is it?"

"Sig's prostate."

"Sig's prostate is big?"

"No. Well, yes, but that's not the problem. I mean, it's a problem, but not *the* problem."

I waited.

Cleo sucked in a deep breath and blew it out on her soup. "He's scheduled for prostate surgery."

"Oh, no. Not with—"

"Yes. Dr. Poole."

"How did that happen?"

"He didn't ask me. His family doctor referred him to Poole, so it was a done deal when Sig finally told me."

"Does Poole know Sig's your fiancé?"

"'Fraid so. He told her, so of course she'll blame me if he tries to back out. Besides, none of the other urologists on the TMC staff will take him on if he does," Cleo said. "Poole's so darned intimidating, I think they're all afraid of ticking her off."

"Then what are you going to do?"

"I don't know yet, but we'll have to act before Sig's surgery date."

"We?"

Cleo's eyes filled. "Please, Aimee. Siggy's loud and bald and fluffy, but I love him to pieces and we have a great sex life. You've got to help me. We can't let Dr. Poole turn him into a eunuch."

"You can't be serious. I agree that Poole is aloof and intimidating, but that doesn't mean she's going around castrating men just for the fun of it."

"Doesn't it?" Cleo scooped a meatball into her spoon, stared at it, then dropped it back into the deep crimson broth in her bowl. She looked a little green.

Cleo's reaction to Sig's impending surgery seemed unwarranted, but I had learned it was wise to take her seriously.

"Okay, one step at a time," I said. "When is Sig scheduled?"

"He's being admitted on Halloween night for surgery the next morning."

"That's what…two and a half weeks from now?"

"Right."

"Have you tried to talk him out of it?"

"Yes. But Poole's got him thinking it's a matter of life and death."

"Is it?"

"Cancer, you mean? That's the thing. Poole's not saying, but Sig's convinced he's going to die if she doesn't operate."

Cleo's reaction was so extreme there had to be something she wasn't telling me. She facilitated every one of TMC's peer review committee meetings. All of their findings and corrective actions were kept in padlocked file cabinets in her office. She also kept confidences brought to her outside committee by nurses who observed suspicious behavior both on the patient floors and in the operating room.

"You know something, don't you? Something about Poole that you're not telling me."

Cleo glanced quickly around the room. "Nothing I can confirm, but when a patient leaves the hospital against medical advice the night before his surgery, it raises an enormous red flag. There was an incident several years ago at the last hospital where I worked. One of the surgeons was performing unnecessary surgeries, and eventually the OR nurses got suspicious. Word got out to the rest of the nursing staff, and one of the floor nurses started warning the surgeon's patients away. After a third patient checked out against medical advice the night before surgery, that nurse was exposed and fired."

"What about the surgeon? What happened to him?"

"Nothing. He's still there performing surgeries on other unsuspecting patients. That's why I turned in my resignation and moved here, three states away."

"Are you saying you think someone warned Cody O'Brien about Dr. Poole?"

"Why else would he bolt at the last minute?"

"Then you should tell Sig to get a second opinion, even if he has to go out of town."

"If I can convince him to do that and he does decide to back out, I'm afraid he'll end up like Cody O'Brien."

"Cody O'Brien was killed by a horse. Sig's not a cowboy, he's a dentist."

Cleo sniffed and said softly, "How do we know Cody was killed by a horse?"

"What? You're the one who told me—"

"All I heard is that he was found unconscious in the trailer with his horse. There was a contusion on his forehead consistent with a kick from a horse's hoof."

"Sounds pretty straightforward. Is the sheriff's office investigating the incident?"

"No, and that's what bothers me. They won't investigate unless the coroner's report shows something suspicious. In the meantime, I thought you and I could do some checking—on the quiet. We can't go through hospital channels."

"What kind of checking?" I said.

"Checking up on Dr. Poole. You were hired because you're a forensic librarian. Use your skills."

"Technically, I'm not a forensic librarian. I'm a health sciences librarian, and part of my job is building a forensic component for the TMC library. That doesn't make me a detective."

"But you're familiar with all kinds of forensic resources. Some of that must have rubbed off. I'll bet you know more than you realize about how to investigate a murder."

"Cleo, you can't believe Dr. Poole is going around killing patients who change their minds about surgery?"

Before Cleo could reply, Margie bustled over to our table. "Hello, ladies. Just dropping off our flyer. Friday night's entertainment is Code Blues."

She was referring to a blues combo made up of musicians affiliated with Timbergate Medical Center. Chief of Urology Tobias Fausset played lead guitar and sang; Edna Roda, chief nursing officer, played bass; Hospital Administrator Jared Quinn played drums and harmonica; and a popular floor nurse named Laurie Popejoy played piano and sang vocals. Margie sometimes joined Code Blues on her accordion.

I glanced at the flyer and noticed Laurie Popejoy's name crossed out. I asked Margie what that was about.

"Rumor has it Laurie Popejoy can't be in the combo now that she's not employed by the hospital."

That was news to me. I shot a look at Cleo.

"I was getting to that," she said.

Margie continued her update. "I was told they already have a new gal who plays, sings, does it all. They're thanking their lucky stars they found her right under their noses."

"Who is she?" Cleo said.

"Dr. Fausset told me when he called this morning." Margie frowned. "Let's see… I think her name is Peale, or something like that."

"Poole?" I said.

"That's it. Dr. Phyllis Poole."

As soon as Margie was out of earshot, Cleo grabbed my arm. "Can you believe that? Poole in Code Blues?"

"No, but let's get back to Laurie Popejoy. What's going on with her?"

"I was about to tell you that Laurie was Cody O'Brien's floor nurse last night. He checked himself out against medical advice at the end of her shift. She called in her resignation first thing this morning."

"And Code Blues has already replaced her? That was fast."

"No kidding. Tobias Fausset must have fast-tracked that since they have the gig here on Friday. Poole is Fausset's associate, but who knew she was a musician?"

"I wouldn't have guessed it." I frowned. "What does all of this have to do with Cody O'Brien's death? Are you thinking Laurie Popejoy said something that made O'Brien skip out on his surgery?"

"He skipped out and ended up dead. Laurie resigned immediately. The timing is too suspicious to dismiss as coincidence. I don't like it one bit, and I won't rest until I know whether Phyllis Poole's involved."

"Come on, Cleo, don't you think you're overreacting because of what happened at that other hospital?"

"Maybe, but we don't know what lengths Poole's capable of going to when it comes to protecting her reputation and keeping her medical license. Meanwhile, she's not getting her hands on Siggy, whether you help me or not."

TWO

BACK IN THE LIBRARY, I pondered Cleo's far-fetched theory. She seemed convinced Sig would end up neutered if he went under Dr. Poole's knife. If he backed out of the surgery, she feared he'd end up dead—like Cody O'Brien. Granted, Dr. Phyllis Poole was an ice maiden obsessed with making her mark as a surgeon, but I thought it was more likely Cleo was overreacting where her darling Sig was concerned.

What troubled me most was Laurie Popejoy's abrupt departure from TMC. I had to admit the timing was peculiar. Laurie's reputation as a nurse was impeccable, and her ebony beauty and sultry vocals had made her the star of the Code Blues combo. The chemistry between Laurie and Tobias Fausset when they performed duets was palpable.

Dr. Poole's success in wheedling her way into Code Blues wasn't a big mystery. She was an associate in Dr. Fausset's urology practice. If she really was a gifted musician, she was an obvious choice to replace Laurie. But no matter how talented Dr. Poole was, Code Blues would not be the same.

A call from TMC administrator Jared Quinn interrupted my musings. He said he was on his way to the library. He didn't say why.

Quinn and I had been thrown together under unusual circumstances a couple of months earlier when the wife of the library's medical director disappeared and turned up dead. He and I had shared some personal details about our pasts during that challenging time, but now we'd retreated into a more professional camaraderie.

That was good, since my romantic relationship with Nick Alexander had gone into a tailspin a few months earlier when Nick's boss, a wealthy philanthropist named Buck Sawyer, asked him to recruit a second pilot, the best he could find. The pilot Nick recommended was not only an ex-fighter pilot, she was Nick's ex-girlfriend, Rella Olstad. The Nordic beauty was blond like Nick, and nearly as tall as his six feet. They must have been a stunning couple when they were dating. I tried not to think about that, but it wasn't easy.

Nick and I were still dealing with a misunderstanding over his current relationship with Rella. We had been limping along for more than a month, both of us aware that we were not back together but we were not really apart. We were in limbo.

Nick faded from my thoughts as Jared Quinn advanced toward my desk. My tiny octogenarian volunteer, Lola Rampley, called him Rhett Butler behind his back. I'd read the book and seen the movie. Clark Gable without the moustache? Close. Quinn had a wicked smile, the kind women pay money to see, but he was still off limits. I had sworn to never, ever, date at work. Especially not the boss.

"Hello, Aimee. How are the llamas?"

Quinn thought my living in a studio apartment above my grandparents' llama barn was quirky and exotic, but I looked upon it as a financial necessity. It was rent free, and I was still strapped with school loans and credit card debt.

"They're fine, thanks. What brings you to the library?"

"I'm here about the surgery department's next CME program." He took a wrapped peppermint from the candy dish on my desk. "Do you know if Vane's picked a topic?"

Dr. Vane Beardsley was medical director of the library and chairman of the hospital's Continuing Medical Education Committee. Quinn signed my paycheck, but Beardsley was my supervisor and liaison to the medical staff. In addition to managing the hospital's library and developing the forensic collection, Dr. Beardsley and I were responsible for keeping the medical staff in compliance with CME requirements. If our doctors didn't address their problem areas by attending mandatory CME programs, the hospital's accreditation could be jeopardized.

"There is one possibility," I said. "The Quality Assurance Committee submitted a request for a special urologic surgery case review. When it's finished, they want all the urologists on staff to appear together as a panel in a CME program. Indications for surgery, expected outcomes, complications, that sort of thing."

"I haven't heard about that. Was it discussed at the last CME Committee meeting?"

"No, the written request came in this afternoon's mail." I pulled the letter from my inbox. It had been dictated by Dr. Ruben Frye, chair of QA Committee, and signed *Cleo Cominoli for Dr. Frye.* Cleo often signed letters for busy committee chairs, but coming on the heels of my lunch conversation with her, this one raised a red flag. Surely she wouldn't have faked this letter.

"Has Dr. Beardsley seen this?" Quinn said.

"He's out again today, but I called him at home, and

he said to go ahead and schedule it since we don't have anything else planned. We have to do something for this month's mandatory surgery department program."

"What prompted QA Committee's request? Are the urologic surgery stats out of line?"

"I'll let you know after I talk to Rocky." Rochelle Taylor, known by everyone as Rocky, was TMC's Quality Assurance Coordinator.

"Sounds good. And don't wait for Beardsley. You'd better get started on this yourself." Quinn tapped a finger on my desk. "You know, that patient who checked out against medical advice was scheduled for a urologic procedure. I'd like to know what spooked the guy. Do you recall his name?"

"Yes, it's Cody O'Brien. I grew up knowing his family. His sister and I were friends as children."

"Oh, I'm sorry. Have you talked to the family?"

"No, we've lost touch over the years."

"Well, it's bizarre how he checked out AMA then died the next day—from an accident in a horse trailer, of all things."

"Umm." I thought of Cleo's paranoid suspicions.

"Make sure you include his case in the urology review. Maybe it'll give us a clue about why he bolted." Quinn twisted the wrapper off his mint. "What's the date for that meeting?"

"October thirty-first. It's a Wednesday night, week after next. I'll get started on it right away."

"Good." He walked over to the partially filled shelves labeled *Forensic Collection*. "How's this coming along?"

"It's been stalled without Dr. Beardsley to approve my suggestions, but I've been in touch with the major medical schools and crime labs across the country, and I've come up with a recommended list of resources. I'm trying to arrange meetings with the key law enforcement agencies and hospitals in the far northern counties we're hoping to serve."

"Is Beardsley making contact with the people you need?"

The expression on my face gave him his answer.

"Ah," he said. "That would be *no*. Do you want me to light a fire under him?"

"I don't really need him. I just need a title with more clout than *Librarian*."

"Use my name. I'll sit in when you get the meetings set up. Meanwhile, keep me posted." He popped the mint into his mouth. "Say hello to the llamas." He flashed his Rhett Butler smile and left.

I wasn't thrilled with the timing of a CME program designed to address problems in the Urology Department. Officially, Dr. Beardsley was in charge of arranging the CME programs. Since his wife's death two months earlier, he'd been passing all the routine work off to me and rubber-stamping whatever I came up with, but I'd never organized and facilitated an entire CME event on my own. Beardsley had cut back on his surgeries, made perfunctory visits to the library only a couple of times a week, and expressed little interest in how I was managing both our jobs.

Two weeks was scant time to arrange the program, but I had to make it happen, even with Cleo determined to discredit Dr. Phyllis Poole, one of TMC's highest-grossing urologists. In spite of Cleo, this patient care review had to be impartial and follow protocol. I put in a call to Tobias Fausset, Chief of Urology, leaving a message with his office manager, who assured me the doctor would call back right away. I knew better than to hold my breath. Dr. Fausset was easy on the eyes and nice to be around, but elusive as smoke in the wind when he didn't want to be pinned down.

My brother, Harry, had promised Amah he'd come to dinner that evening, so I closed the library at five o'clock and headed home. Our grandparents' Highland Ranch was in Coyote Creek, a community eight miles east of Timbergate. Most of its residents raised livestock on working ranches, but there were a growing number of executive homes perched on oak-dotted hilltops with million-dollar views of Lassen Peak and Mount Shasta.

Grandpa Jack and Amah were in the former category, with livestock consisting of eight llamas and a flock of turkeys. Their house was a rambling but inviting relic from the forties, with rockers on the front porch and a sunny veranda in back.

Harry, an architect and commercial building contractor, is two years younger than me and a lot richer. He's a volunteer jujitsu instructor at the dojo in Timbergate and always stays at least one rank above me. I'm a third degree black belt and Harry is a fourth.

A couple of months ago a local police investigator tried to pin the death of Dr. Beardsley's trophy wife on my brother. I had a run-in with the real villain in that scenario, who eventually came clean.

Still a bachelor, Harry was rarely free for dinner, so I was sure Jack and Amah would be cooking his favorites: Jack's freshly caught rainbow trout and marinated zucchini, and Amah's shoofly pie.

After work I drove out to Coyote Creek and down the lane to my little studio apartment above the llama barn.

Inside I checked the old-fashioned answering machine Jack had installed when I moved in. I had told him I didn't need it, but he insisted I have a backup landline. My only message was from Jack. "Dinner's at six."

I changed into jeans and a T-shirt and walked up the lane to the main house, stopping on the way to offer treats to the llamas. As soon as they heard me shaking grain in a bucket, I was surrounded. I managed to give each of them a handful without starting a spitting war.

My petite Amah, my father's mother on the Portuguese side of the family, was setting the dining room table in her *company's coming to dinner* mode, just a tad slower than a hummingbird. She's pushing seventy, but she out-hikes me every summer and races around like a teenager the rest of the year. Jack, still a strapping six feet in his early seventies, was in the kitchen combining the secret seasonings that made his fried trout so delicious. Harry had just pulled up in his Jag. Amah raced to peer out the front window, and I heard a little intake of air.

"Oh, he's brought someone and my hair's a mess. Here, you finish." She shoved a handful of silverware at me and sped down the hall to primp in the bathroom.

Harry hadn't brought a woman to meet the family since his fiancée broke off their engagement four years ago. His successful career and dark good looks made him the best catch in town, but we'd pretty much given up on seeing him settle down. I opened the front door, eager to see what remarkable creature had prompted this landmark event.

Harry stood on the porch with Keely O'Brien, Cody's younger sister. The last woman I'd have expected to see with my brother.

"Hi Aimee, you remember Keely, don't you?"

Keely was my age, but she had lived a troubled life and it showed. Dark circles bruised the tissue under her eyes, and her designer jeans hung on a nearly skeletal frame. I tried to hide my confusion. "Of course. Keely, I'm so sorry about your brother."

"Don't be sorry on my account." She dropped a cigarette on Amah's porch and ground it out under a snakeskin sandal with a five-inch heel. "I haven't spoken to him for more than two years."

That shocked me. When we were kids in dance class together, Keely worshipped Cody. He was the younger of her two half-brothers, five years older than Keely and a star athlete. I looked to Harry for an explanation. Why had he brought her here? They had dated a couple times in high school, but that had been years ago.

"James is flying in from New York at seven o'clock tonight," Harry said. "I'm driving Keely to the airport to meet his plane, so I figured she might as well come to dinner first." James, the oldest in the O'Brien's clan of half-siblings, lived in New York City.

"Forgot to renew my driver's license," Keely said. "I'll get it back in a couple weeks." She'd most likely lost her license over a DUI, if rumors of her longstanding cocaine and alcohol problems were true.

"Come on in," I said. "Dinner's almost ready."

Harry led Keely to the dining room and I followed behind, still puzzled. The municipal airport was only five miles from Jack and Amah's place, so Harry's explanation made sense, except for the part that didn't. Why was he doing this? I'd heard Keely was dating Tucker Pottkotter, a farrier and part-time hunting guide who worked as an apprentice in her father's taxidermy business. Why wasn't Tucker driving her to the airport?

Harry anticipated the question. "I ran into Tucker at the gym this morning and he asked me to drive Keely out to meet James's plane." Harry and Tucker weren't even good friends, but it was like my brother to help someone out if he was asked.

"Tuck's working late tonight," Keely said. "He and Daddy are keeping crazy hours. They have three different hunting outfitters who want full-body mounts. And there's another guy who wants his dead horse mounted like that old-time singing cowboy guy did."

"Are you talking about Roy Rogers and Trigger?" I said.

"Yeah, I guess so. Daddy said they were famous for some reason. Anyway, except for the horse, they have to get everything done in time for the SCI convention, and now Cody's dead and he's still getting all the attention." Keely sniffed and dabbed at her nose with a Kleenex. "I might as well be freakin' invisible."

SCI stood for Safari Club International, an outdoorsmen's organization that held its annual convention every January in Reno. Keely's father, Seamus O'Brien, owned a lucrative taxidermy business. The top hunting and fishing guides in the west always came to him first. A trophy-winning mount in one of their booths at the SCI show could translate into big money. Hunting guide outfits competed fiercely at SCI, hoping to attract wealthy sportsmen looking for the perfect hunt.

Our conversation had come to a standstill when Amah reappeared, her short dark hair primped and her cheeks blushed.

"Hello, Keely," she said. "I'm so sorry for your loss. How's your father doing?"

"He's keeping busy with his work. He seems sad, but he's been pissed off at Cody for years about wasting his life on the rodeo circuit, so it's kind of hard to tell what he's feeling now." At that, Amah excused herself to help Jack in the kitchen.

After we had all settled in at the dining room table and filled our plates, Amah tried another tack. "How is your mother, Keely?"

"Depressed as hell since Daddy dumped her." Amah winced, but Keely went on. "I keep telling her to suck it up. It's been almost two years. Besides, he dumped someone else before he married her, and she lasted a helluva lot longer than any of the others. What did she expect?"

Each of Seamus O'Brien's children had a different mother. The first wife had long since relocated to the East Coast where her son James lived, and Cody's mother had died of an overdose the year after Seamus divorced her.

"Is your mother still in Timbergate?"

"No. She's getting pretty decent alimony so she bought a place in Tahoe."

"That must be nice. Do you visit her often?" Amah said.

"Not really. She's always running around with some stud from the casinos. I think she's afraid I'd be competition."

Jack gave Amah a meaningful look. *Change the subject.*

At that point Amah gave up on conversation and got very interested in her trout, so I decided to give it a try.

"I understand your father's new wife is quite a

hunter." I looked to Jack for confirmation. "Didn't you write about Echo O'Brien shooting a trophy blacktail last fall?"

"I might have," he mumbled, modest as usual about his prolific career as an outdoor writer.

"Yeah, she's a hunter all right," Keely said. "Sniffed out Daddy's money and tracked him down like a blood-hound." She gripped her knife and made a savage cut in a sourdough roll. "Echo's five years younger than me and she thinks she can boss me around. She'll get the picture pretty soon."

Harry had been unusually silent, but at this point he put in his two cents, trying to salvage the mess Amah and I were making of dinner conversation.

"Are you still singing, Keely?"

"A few local gigs." She brushed her nose with her napkin. "I'd have a recording contract by now if dear, departed Cody had put in a word for me back when I needed him. His own sister, and he wouldn't use his connections. Said I wasn't tough enough for the music business."

"It's pretty brutal, from what I've heard," Harry said.

"Cody didn't give a crap about that. He was just making excuses. He was so obsessed with DeeDee he didn't want to bother with me."

Cody's late wife, DeeDee Dakota, had been a superstar in the trick riding world a few years back. She and Cody were the sweethearts of the rodeo circuit until DeeDee died after a trick riding accident.

Amah got busy dishing up her shoofly pie with scoops of vanilla ice cream while Harry and I cleared the dinner plates. Keely asked directions to the bathroom.

She returned sniffing, dabbing at her nose with a tissue.

Harry and I exchanged knowing glances.

After Harry and Keely left, I helped Amah clean up. We chatted about how my parents were doing since they retired to the island of Faial in the Azores. Dad was still teaching jujitsu, and Mom, with her nursing degree and her fluency in four languages, was enjoying a part-time job at the hospital in Horta, the island's port city where they lived.

Later, I walked down the lane to the barn. I was looking forward to some alone time in my studio apartment, which was now a cozy little home.

The message light on my answering machine was winking when I got inside. I punched the play button.

"Aimee, this is Laurie Popejoy. Call me back as soon as possible. It's urgent. Don't tell anyone about this call."

THREE

WITH A JOLT, I recalled Cleo's story about the whistle-blowing nurse. I tried the number Laurie had left, but she didn't answer. I left a message asking her to call back on my cellphone. Her call had come in at eight o'clock, while I was visiting Jack and Amah. Laurie was young, pretty, and single. At nine o'clock she might have gone out, but the urgency in her voice seemed at odds with her going clubbing.

I tried Laurie's number every ten minutes, but the result was the same each time. No answer. I kept calling without success during the late television news and eventually caught myself dozing. At midnight I stepped out on my deck to take a last look at the star-filled sky. While I breathed in the clean, cool air of approaching fall, I counted eight llamas kushed for the night. Amah's cat, Fanny, issued a short meow-purr and ran up the steps to my deck. She had started sleeping in my apartment shortly after I moved in. Fine with me. She was big, loud, and gutsy. A fine bodyguard. I crawled into bed and worried about Laurie Popejoy until sleep finally came. It lasted until my phone rang at two o'clock in the morning, jarring me awake. I groped for it.

"Laurie?"

"No, it's Cleo. Are you awake?"

"I am now. What's going on?"

"Laurie Popejoy." Cleo sounded both sleepy and agitated. "She called me earlier, looking for you. I was at Siggy's and didn't check messages until now. I just got home."

"Did Laurie say what she wanted?"

"She said to tell you that what happened to Cody wasn't an accident."

"Did she say why he checked out or why she resigned?"

"No, and nothing about Poole, either."

"Did you try to call her back?"

"No. I thought I'd call you first to see if you'd heard from her." Cleo's voice tightened with stress. "Aimee, I'm worried Laurie's in big trouble. She left the message at eight o'clock. That's six hours ago."

"She must have called you right after she called me. I've been trying to reach her, but she doesn't answer. I don't understand why she wanted to talk to me instead of the police."

"I can think of two reasons. Your knowledge of forensics and your black belt."

"Neither of those qualifies me to help her, but she's smart and levelheaded. She would have gone to the police if she thought they were a safe option."

"What do you think we should do?" Cleo's yawn traveled through the line. "Sorry, I'm running out of steam."

"There's nothing we *can* do tonight. One of us will probably hear from her tomorrow."

"Let's hope she decided to go to the police."

I HAD JUST fired up my search engine at work Wednesday morning when Cleo called to ask if I'd heard from Laurie. I told her I hadn't.

"Maybe we should call Edna Roda. She might know if Laurie's in some kind of trouble." Edna had been Chief Nursing Officer at TMC for ten years. She kept tabs on the entire nursing service of a 250-bed hospital. I'd been in my job just over two months, so I hadn't had a chance to get to know her well. She had visited the library a few times since I was hired, but she was hard to read and I wasn't sure I'd earned her respect.

"I don't know if that's a good idea," I said. "Laurie explicitly said not to tell anyone about her call. We don't know why."

"I'll get back to you on that," Cleo said, and hung up. Apparently someone had come into her office. Our conversation was over.

Later that morning, I wondered if some kind of karmic energy was in play when Edna Roda made one of her infrequent visits to the library.

"Hello, Aimee. How are you?"

"Fine, thanks, and you?"

"Too busy, I'm afraid." She took off her glasses, huffed a breath on each lens and wiped them with the edge of her sweater. After repositioning them, she peered at me with an analytic gaze. "The better to see you with," she said. She broke into a broad smile that lit up her handsome, Margaret Thatcher face.

"Is there something I can do for you?" I asked.

"As a matter of fact, there is. I received an email from you a few weeks ago with an article attached about forensic nursing."

Oh, boy. Was she going to tell me I overstepped? I was constantly looking for ways to promote library services, and once in a while I pushed a little too hard.

"I do recall sending that," I said, "but if you'd rather I didn't—"

"Oh, no. Please don't misunderstand. I appreciate a heads-up about anything that could be of value to our patients. In this case, I am aware of the emergent field of forensic nursing, but with my heinous workload, I haven't had time to explore the possibilities it might offer to TMC." She glanced at her watch and sighed. "Never enough time, which is why I'd like your help finding all you can for me on the subject."

"I'd be happy to. As I recall, the most comprehensive program in forensic nursing is at Cleveland State University's nursing school. The field accounts for about thirty percent of their MSN program, which is one of the reasons I felt you'd be interested."

"Yes, well, that's a little far away for our nurses. Can you see what training programs are available online?"

"I can do that."

"Well, then. You'll let me know when you have something for me? I don't want to seem pushy, but the sooner the better."

"I'll start right away."

"Thank you." Again, the elegant smile. I watched the purposeful rhythm of her stride as she walked toward the exit. Did I dare ask her about Laurie Popejoy's abrupt departure? While I hesitated, she pushed the door open and went on her way.

I switched gears and went back to the search I'd been planning before Edna dropped by. I wanted to know more about the O'Brien clan. I started with DeeDee Dakota.

I spent a few minutes on a website called rodeotrick-riders.com, where I found a bio on Dakota, born Deirdre

DeGraw in Coffeyville, Kansas. She was Rodeo Queen her senior year of high school, took a pass on college, and focused on her trick-riding career. She met Cody O'Brien at a rodeo in Tulsa, Oklahoma, eloped with him two weeks later, and her career took off. Within a year, DeeDee was the brightest trick-riding star on the rodeo circuit.

DeeDee had been fatally injured two and a half years ago during a performance of her signature trick, the Back Drag. The stunt required DeeDee to place a foot in a loop on either side of the saddle, bend over backward lying over the rear of the horse until her hands touched the ground, and then pull herself into an upright position. The website said the trick was the most dangerous in the business, because the rider's hands weren't in control of the reins and because the galloping horse could accidentally kick the back of her head. When DeeDee tried to come out of the pose, the saddle twisted down under the horse's belly and DeeDee's head was thrust into the path of flying hooves.

Now Cody O'Brien was dead, also from a blow to the head by a horse. Two victims of the animals they no doubt loved. Tragic coincidence? I was not a firm believer in coincidence alone. Was there more here for me to know?

DeeDee's accident had happened at a rodeo in Dunnsville, Idaho, so I searched online for archives of newspapers in the area. I found an article saying DeeDee had been alert and responsive at first, but slipped into a coma the next day at a small private hospital near the rodeo grounds. Cody insisted she be flown to Timbergate Medical Center, where she died without regaining consciousness.

I recalled Cleo telling me that committee peer review of all in-house deaths was mandatory. She had been working at TMC back then. Maybe she would remember something about DeeDee's case. I thought again about Cody O'Brien's flight from TMC. Could that somehow be related to what happened to DeeDee?

I needed more information on both patients. Cleo could get the minutes for me, but due to privacy laws, the Health Information Office would not let me access DeeDee's medical record. After two and a half years, it was likely that her chart and other pertinent information had been relocated to the basement archives. Almost everything in the archives was sensitive, and I wasn't authorized to enter without an appropriate escort. That would be Cleo.

I made a mental note to ask Cleo to retrieve the minutes—and DeeDee's medical record, if possible.

I had to shove Edna's request for forensic nursing information to the back burner and focus on my more immediate problem involving Dr. Fausset. I needed his cooperation to put together the Surgery Department's CME program focusing on urologic surgeries. Proposing an educational program addressing his particular specialty implied that there was room for improvement. Since he was chairman of the Urology Department, he was bound to be defensive. His having to deal with me instead of the truant Dr. Beardsley wasn't going to help matters.

"Hello, Aimee, remember me?" A deep voice, vaguely familiar, pulled my attention from the computer screen. A man who looked about forty walked in. He was dressed in faded jeans, scuffed cowboy boots, and a gray plaid Pendleton shirt. As he walked toward my desk, his broad smile told me he expected a warm welcome. His wavy hair was reddish-brown and his face was familiar, but the name wouldn't come.

"I'm sorry," I said. "You have the advantage."

"Come on, Aimless, you're breaking my heart."

No one called me Aimless except Harry. How did this guy know that nickname? Then it struck me. *James O'Brien.* Cody and Keely's older brother. He used to drive Keely to and from the dance studio where we took lessons when we were eight years old. He was eighteen then, and my infatuation with him was sweet misery. It didn't help that he flirted with me shamelessly, telling me that when I was all grown up he was going to marry me. I stopped believing him when he moved to New York right after my thirteenth birthday. I cried every night for a week. Seeing him now, I felt a flush of pleasure warm my cheeks.

"James, I heard you were back. I'm so sorry about your brother."

"Thank you. It was a shock for all of us." He opened his arms. "Hey, don't I rate a hug?"

"Of course." I walked around my desk and tried for something tepid and platonic.

"You call that a hug?" He wrapped me in his arms with the warmth of a long lost lover, rocking my body back and forth. Then he kissed the top of my head. I felt myself melting, and when he released me, I stepped backward, unsteady on my feet. The man smelled like dessert. Lemon meringue pie.

"How long will you be in town?"

"As long as it takes," he said. "This hit Dad pretty hard, and Echo's no help. She's acting like Cody's death is no big deal, since he and Dad were estranged for the past few years. Keely's no better."

"Your father really needs you right now, doesn't he?"

"It seems that way." He cocked his head to one side. "Look at you. All grown up."

"Even better," I said. "I went back east and finished school. I'm now a Master of Library and Information Science."

"Quite a mouthful. If you shorten it to *MLIS*, it sounds kind of like Aimless." I threw a peppermint at him, but he ducked and laughed. "Seriously, though, I heard you were in New Haven for a couple years. Why didn't you ever come down to one of my shows?"

"I didn't know you were producing on Broadway until I moved back to California. Then I heard you'd switched to off-Broadway. How's that going?"

"Good. Not as intense as Broadway, and not as risky."

"I think my Grandpa Machado auditioned for one of your productions. He's been taking acting lessons since he retired."

"Tony Machado. Yes. *The Gin Game*. He got the part. Maybe you can fly back and see the show."

"I doubt it. I'm pretty busy these days." *And broke*, but he didn't need to hear that.

"Do you see much of Keely?" James asked.

"Not really. We sort of lost touch."

"I guess you don't have much in common." He was no doubt alluding to her drug problems and dropping out of high school. We shared a moment of awkward silence.

"What brings you to the hospital? Are you here about Cody?"

"That's the main reason, of course. I wanted to talk to the people who saw him last. His doctor, nurses, that sort of thing. I don't suppose you dropped in on him the day he was admitted?"

"No. His name wasn't on the admission list that morning. He must have been admitted in the afternoon. I didn't know he was here until it was too late."

"I see." His obvious disappointment made me wish I *had* seen Cody—that I had some comfort to offer this man hoping to understand his brother's death.

"You said Cody was one of the reasons you're here. What are the others?"

"Just one other. You, little Aimless. I figured since we've been engaged all these years, it was time I saw how you turned out. Looks like I got lucky."

"Thanks, but since I was only eight when you asked me to marry you, we should probably call off the engagement."

"Fair enough," James said. "I assume you get a lunch hour. How about joining me?"

"I wish I could, but I have to attend an annual employee in-service on infection control."

"Are you contagious?"

I laughed. "Not that I know of. It's routine for all employees, along with other precautions like TB tests."

At that point, Lola wandered in and walked up to James, who stood a foot and a half above her. She studied his face for a moment.

"Young man, you look just like Burt Lancaster. Are you any relation?"

James grinned. "We're both Irish, so there's always a chance, I suppose."

Lola rattled off the URL of a genealogy website and

suggested James get to know his ancestors. Then she excused herself and went to work sorting medical journals.

James nodded toward her, his eyes twinkling. "Think she'd go to lunch with me?"

"I don't know. Why don't you ask her?"

James gave me a look. "Rain check?" He pulled a card from his pocket and picked up a pen from my desk. "Call me or text me." He circled the number.

I took the card. He planted a quick kiss on my cheek. "See you, Aimless."

When the door closed behind him, Lola winked at me. "Hubba," she said.

FOUR

I CAUGHT MYSELF thinking about James throughout the afternoon. That distraction wasn't welcome, especially since two far less pleasant ones were already competing for my attention. One was Laurie Popejoy. Why would she leave urgent messages for Cleo and me and then not answer our calls? The other was Cleo. Would she help me access DeeDee Dakota's medical record and the minutes documenting her death review?

Meanwhile, I had an actual job to do. First and foremost, I had to develop a CME program addressing the care of urologic surgery patients at Timbergate Medical Center. The patients were to include Cody O'Brien, who checked out against medical advice and ended up dead. I had assured Jared Quinn I could pull the program together in two weeks.

Still, taking a rain check with James was a good idea. He was my first big crush, and a girl never really gets over the first one. Well, maybe if she marries him, but otherwise probably not. I figured James might remember something key about the circumstances involving the death of Cody's late wife, DeeDee.

I dialed Cleo and asked if she could take an afternoon break for a brainstorming session. She agreed and suggested we meet at Margie's for tea and bean cake.

At our usual table, I brought Cleo up to date on my visit

from James. She barely acknowledged my news before starting her drumbeat about saving Sig from Dr. Poole.

"Fine," Cleo said. "James O'Brien is in town. Big Apple producer returns to his humble roots. How is that going to help Siggy?"

"I don't know, but I'll do my best to find out what James knows about Cody's last night among the living."

"Poole must have done something that spooked him," she said. "Why else would he check in, then check out?"

"Something obviously happened that night, but we can't blame it on Poole without knowing more." I pushed my plate aside. "How can we identify everyone who was in Cody's room that night?"

"His medical record, up to a point. It will identify everyone who was involved in his care, but anyone could have entered his room without being noticed. He wasn't in a critical care unit, so his visitors probably weren't restricted."

"Would it show which nurses were on duty that night other than Laurie?"

"Of course." Cleo dabbed her lips with a napkin.

"What are the chances of your getting a look at his medical record?"

"I don't know. I could probably sneak a peek. I'm not supposed to have access to patients' charts unless it's committee business, but the staff in the records room gives me a lot of latitude."

"When can you do it?" I asked.

"Depends whether anyone's suing TMC over Cody's death."

"Why, have you heard something?"

"Just a rumor so far, about a request for a legal photocopy of his medical record."

"Is it the O'Brien family?"

"Don't know," Cleo said. "And it would only restrict access to the chart for a couple of days. I'll see what I can do. Meanwhile, do you have any other ideas?"

"Finding Laurie Popejoy is priority, but apparently that's not going to be easy. In the meantime, I've been doing some research on DeeDee Dakota."

"Where's that?" Cleo's mystified frown almost made me laugh.

"Not *where*, who. DeeDee Dakota was Cody O'Brien's wife. Dakota was a stage name. She died after a trick riding accident in Idaho a couple years into their marriage. It troubles me that both the husband and wife were killed by their horses. Doesn't that seem like an unlikely coincidence?"

"It's pretty unusual, but certainly possible, considering their occupations. Did the wife die in Idaho?"

"No, she died at TMC."

"When was this?"

"About two and a half years ago. You probably facilitated the Intensive Care Committee meeting when her death was reviewed."

"I suppose, but the name isn't ringing a bell," Cleo said. "What does her death have to do with anything?"

"My question exactly. Probably nothing, but I want to find out. Can we get access to her medical record?"

"I can't guarantee it. If it's that long ago, it'll be archived." Cleo pulled out a pen. "If Dakota was a stage name, do you know what name she was admitted under?"

"Her legal married name would have been Deirdre O'Brien. Couldn't you at least glance through her record and any minutes from the committee if you found it in the archives?"

"What would I be looking for?"

"I don't know, maybe you'll see something that reminds you of the case—triggers some kind of memory of the committee's discussion."

"That was quite a while ago, Aimee. Besides, this is supposed to be about Dr. Poole. She wasn't on TMC's staff back then. How could this trick rider's case possibly involve her?"

"I don't know, but I just don't buy coincidences." I checked the time. "We need to get back to work. If you can't get her chart, at least get the minutes of her death review."

"It might take a few days. I'd rather sneak in and out without being seen." Cleo massaged her temples. "Give me a time frame—at least a window. The review could have been up to a month after she died."

"The accident at the rodeo in Idaho was in late April, two and a half years ago. She died here almost three days later. Does that narrow it down enough?"

"That helps, but isn't that early in the year for a rodeo? What if it got rained out?"

"Not a problem. It was held in an indoor arena."

"Shows what I know about rodeos. In any case, it's probably going take more than one try to locate the file. That storage room is an inexcusable jumble. No one ever puts things back where they belong."

At that point Margie stopped by with her usual friendly reminder. "Code Blues Friday night. Are you coming to see the new gal?"

The new gal. Dr. Phyllis Poole.

Cleo opened her mouth, but before she could answer, I said, "I'll be here. What time do they start?"

"Seven thirty. They play until ten. I hear it's going to be sexy and romantic. Better bring a hot date."

As if I had a long list of hot dates waiting in the wings. I thought of dragging Harry along so I wouldn't have to go alone, but my brother never lacked for dates on a Friday night. No way would he be available.

I gave Cleo a questioning look. "How about it? Want to come and watch Poole's debut?"

"Sorry," she said. "Siggy and I have other plans."

Date or no date, I had to be there. I wanted to see how the various members of Code Blues handled their first gig without Laurie. I didn't relish showing up alone, but then James O'Brien's rain check came to mind.

Back at work I called Tobias Fausset about the CME program. He wasn't available, so I left a message.

Next I called the Quality Assurance office, where I had better luck. Rocky Taylor confirmed that TMC's urologic surgery outcomes had slipped over the past several months. Nothing that would raise eyebrows in most hospitals, but not up to TMC's usually high standards. More complications, even a death. One of Phyllis Poole's patients. A man. Rocky didn't seem surprised about the CME program, so I figured it was legit, and not something Cleo had manipulated. I told Rocky that Quinn wanted Cody O'Brien's chart included in the review.

"Seems like there wouldn't be much to review," she said. "Didn't he split the night before his surgery?"

"He did, but Quinn's interested in the indications for surgery."

Rocky hesitated a moment. "Did you know an attorney subpoenaed a legal photocopy of O'Brien's chart? Maybe that's why Quinn wants to rush the review."

"I heard the rumor, but not from Quinn. That definitely explains his hurry."

Rocky agreed to email all the stats we would need, and we ended the call. The subpoena would complicate my efforts to see Cody's chart. In any case with lawsuit potential, the medical record was copied immediately by the hospital's records room staff before a legal photocopy service from outside was allowed to copy it for an attorney.

The library was empty, so I put a sign on the door and hiked over to the fourth floor of TMC's modern tower, where the administration suite was located. Varsha Singh, Quinn's executive assistant, looked up from her computer. With her glossy black hair and elegant East Indian features, she looked more like an exotic model than a California-born soccer mom with four adolescent children.

"Is he in?" I said.

"For you, probably." She punched a button on her phone and announced my name. After a pause, she smiled up at me. "Go on in."

"Aimee. What brings you?" Quinn stood behind his desk. After a month or so on the job, I'd gotten over being distracted by his disarming smile and rugged good looks, but I still enjoyed the view. He stepped around his desk. "Coffee?"

"No thanks. I have to get back, but I have a question about Cody O'Brien, and I wanted to ask you face to face."

Quinn tapped a sheet of paper on his desk. "You heard about the subpoena, right?"

"Right. Why didn't you tell me about it when you were in the library this morning?"

"You're not going to like my answer." Quinn got up

and came around his desk toward me. He gripped my shoulders with both hands and steered me toward the small couch across from his desk. "Let's sit for a minute."

I sat at one corner of the couch, and he took the other. "Okay, let's hear it." I was pretty sure I knew what was coming.

"You told me about your family friendship with the O'Briens. I figured if you knew the O'Brien clan was filing a wrongful death suit against TMC, at the very least you'd be stuck in a conflict of interest that could affect your job." Quinn got up and walked back to his desk. "I don't want to lose you, Aimee. You're a superb employee. Please tell me you'll stay neutral in all of this. If I hear otherwise, I'll have no choice but to put you on administrative leave. Do you understand?"

His words hit me like a slug to the stomach, and I lost my breath for a moment. Quinn was supposed to be more than my boss. We were friends, and we'd been allies during a difficult time a few months earlier involving the death of Dr. Beardsley's wife. I managed a response.

"I understand."

"Good." Quinn continued. "I was informed as well by the O'Brien's attorney. Apparently she wanted to make sure your job doesn't offer you any access to O'Brien's medical record."

"I don't see how I can include Cody's chart in the urologic surgery review if I don't have access to it."

"Cleo can take care of that."

That was good enough for me. "Okay," I said. "That should work."

Back in the library, I opened an email saying Tobias Fausset planned to drop by the library after his four o'clock surgery. I checked the time—three thirty—then glanced at the TMC surgery schedule. Nothing for Dr. Fausset. A call to his appointments clerk confirmed he was doing the surgery as an outpatient procedure in his office. He would drop by the library as soon as he could after he finished.

An hour later, my notes on the CME program were taking shape when I heard the library doors open. I looked up, expecting Dr. Fausset, and instead saw Phyllis Poole advancing toward my desk, white coat flapping and Kabuki-white face scowling. Twin dots of color in her cheeks were the only sign that blood actually ran through her veins.

"Where's Beardsley?" she said.

"He doesn't work here in the library, but—"

"I know that. I just came from his office. That silly girl hasn't a clue where he is. I certainly hope you'll be more helpful."

"I'll try. What is it that you need?"

"I need to talk to Dr. Beardsley." She placed both hands, palms down, on my desk and looked me in the eye. "Now."

Instead of reacting in a way I'd savor in the moment and regret later, I kept calm by imagining how she'd look lying on the floor with my knee on her chest. Good thing "the gentle art" disciplines the mind as well as the body.

"Dr. Beardsley is still taking personal time," I said. "He's asked not to be disturbed."

"Then who's responsible for this CME program I'm hearing about? I want to know why TMC's urologic surgery cases are under attack."

"I've been authorized to carry out his duties until he returns."

"You? Since when are you qualified—"

"Hello, Phyllis," Tobias Fausset's rich bass broke in. He walked up to Poole and wrapped an arm around her shoulders. "Code Blues rehearsals start at seven. Will you be there?"

Poole might have been smacked in the face with a magic wand, her transformation was so complete. Her eyes widened and her complexion brightened to a delicate shade of pink. The smile she offered Fausset proved there was fire inside this woman that had nothing to do with her work.

"I'll be there," Poole said. The seductive timbre of her voice made me blush. I cleared my throat in case either of them wanted to be reminded why they were in the library.

"Aimee," Dr. Fausset said, "I'm told we have business. I have ten minutes."

"You're not going to wait for Beardsley?" Poole said.

"That isn't necessary. I'm sure Aimee can handle the preliminaries. Why don't you finish up at the office? I'll see you at seven."

"If you're sure."

"I'm sure." His words were smooth and sweet as chocolate mousse, and the intimate way he looked into her eyes suggested he was sure of any number of things.

"Seven, then." Watching Phyllis Poole's retreat, I marveled at the graceful sway of her hips. Something I'd never seen before. Tobias Fausset was watching, too.

Fausset's calm, efficient approach let us work out the details of the urologic surgery review and CME presentation in record time. In half an hour I closed up and headed home.

FIVE

That evening I helped Amah and Jack with llama worming and pedicures. Amah and I kept the animals as calm as possible while Jack emptied a large syringe filled with milky fluid down each of their throats. Next, Jack trimmed the toenails on their split hooves with a pair of sharp shears. The cria's hooves were still small, so she was exempt.

I scrubbed off the dust and perfume of the barnyard with a quick shower in time to help with dinner. Amah and I put together salad and garlic bread while Jack seared steaks on the grill.

Over a dessert of peach pie à la mode, I tried again to offer them a rent check.

"No, sweetie," Amah said. "Put it toward your school loans."

"Or use it to pay off your new tires," Jack said. "You're not paying rent until you're out of debt."

"By then you'll want a place of your own," Amah said. "It can't be ideal for you living in a barn out here in the foothills."

"It's not so bad." I got up and gave each of them a hug. "I'm still a country girl deep down."

Jack huffed a little cough and glanced at Amah. "You're welcome as long as you want to stay. You've been a big help watching things around here when we're gone."

The truth is I loved living in Coyote Creek. It was

only a ten minute drive to Timbergate, and I'd become attached to my homey little apartment over the barn. With Mom and Dad living in the Azores, and Grandpa Machado and his wife Tanya in New York, Amah and Jack were the only family Harry and I had close by. Although they were vibrant and active, they were getting older. I liked that we were there for each other.

I walked down the lane toward the barn with a full stomach and a sense of peace that lasted only until I checked my message machine. One message. I hit the PLAY button.

"It wasn't Game Boy." A woman's voice whispered the words. Then silence.

Game Boy? What kind of message was that? A wrong number? Curious, I replayed it. The second time, listening carefully, I realized the voice was Laurie Popejoy's. She sounded distraught or exhausted, and the Game Boy reference made no sense. Was it some kind of code? What could this second message from her mean? And where was she?

My knee-jerk reaction was to call Cleo, but I hesitated. She was so wound up over Cody O'Brien's death and so freaked out about Phyllis Poole operating on Sig, she couldn't be objective. I needed Harry's impartial take on this. He was much better at thinking outside the box, and he'd always been a whiz with Game Boy.

Harry wasn't answering, so I left a message telling him to call me. I hadn't told him about Laurie's disappearance, so it would take some explaining to bring him up to speed.

That left one more call. I stared at the card James O'Brien had given me that morning in the TMC library. I wanted to be at Margie's Friday night to observe Phyllis Poole and Tobias Fausset. A date with James would look less suspicious than dropping in alone. For James that would be some thrill: a hot Broadway producer living it up at Margie's Bean Pot with a hospital librarian. It had seemed like a good idea at the time—before I heard about the O'Brien lawsuit against TMC. Still, I could kill two birds with one date. I made the call.

"James here. Talk to me." His quick answer took me by surprise. "Hello?" James said again. He sounded impatient, but still polite.

"James, it's Aimee Machado."

"Aimee, great to hear from you." Definite change of tone. "I hope you're calling to collect on that rain check."

"I am."

"So when can we get together?"

"Friday night. There's a thing." Suddenly this seemed like the worst idea I'd ever had.

"Friday night is good. What's the thing?"

"A blues combo from the hospital. They're playing at a small restaurant."

James laughed. "A hospital blues combo? Did I hear that right? What do they call themselves, The Arrhythmias?"

"Close. They're called Code Blues."

"Clever. So, young lady, are you inviting me out on a date?"

"I guess I am." No big deal, since he would soon be back in New York. With any luck I'd find out what was behind the O'Brien's lawsuit before the evening was over.

"Excellent. Tell me when and where to pick you up."

I couldn't bring myself to tell James I lived in my grandparents' barn. "Let me meet you there around eight o'clock. I have a family commitment earlier."

"All right," James said, "and speaking of family, I'd like to get copies of Cody's hospital records. What's the protocol there?"

Why was he asking me about Cody's medical records when they had already been subpoenaed? I kept my response neutral, remembering Quinn's warning.

"I'm not sure, but I'll see what I can find out for you." I gave James directions to Margie's and finished the call so I could leave another message for Harry, a call he didn't return before I went to bed. Laurie's mysterious message about Game Boy had me tossing and turning most of the night.

HARRY CALLED MY cellphone the next morning while I was driving to work. I answered anyway, avoiding eye contact with glaring motorists while I told him about the strange message.

"Game Boy?" he said. "You called me because some ditzy runaway nurse left you a message about Game Boy?"

"She's not ditzy. She's smart and level-headed."

"Then why call me?"

"She sounded distressed. I think she's in danger. Just meet me somewhere and let me explain."

"Come to my job site at noon and bring lunch. It better be good. And expensive."

As soon as I reached the library, I called the Health Information department with a hypothetical, not identifying myself as a TMC employee.

The clerk rattled off a practiced answer. "We provide a copy of the deceased patient's hospital record only to the person named as next of kin on the death certificate." She emphasized that there were no exceptions.

Was Cody's father the official next of kin? Would

Seamus cooperate with James and request the records? I made a mental note to ask James about his relationship with his father, even though I knew none of that would matter if the record had already been subpoenaed.

Harry's favorite food is practically anything edible, but he said expensive, so I picked up two Big Macs and stopped off at a dessert shop for a caramel pecan cheesecake.

I hadn't seen the Timbergate Mall project for several weeks, and it now rose three stories high, a magnificent skeleton formed of beams and girders. It looked as if Harry's most ambitious childhood Erector Set creation had come to life. A small group of men and women in dust-powdered work clothes and yellow hard hats sat in the shade of a portable canopy talking and laughing while they munched food from lunch boxes and poured coffee from thermos bottles.

Harry appeared in the open doorway of his job site trailer as I pulled up and parked. Wearing a dark green polo shirt, creased khakis, and immaculate suede boots, he seemed immune to the dust and grime of the construction site.

"Hey, Aimless, what did you bring?"

"Big Macs and cheesecake."

"That's it?"

"I'm on a budget. So are you going to let me in or not?"

"What kind of cheesecake?"

I pushed my way inside the trailer, once again marveling at his perfectly organized home away from home. A custom-built rack held dozens of rolls of blueprints. His laptop sat open, displaying a spreadsheet. A high-tech printer rested on a nearby table. Books on architecture filled a shelf over his settee.

He moved a blueprint off his drafting table to make room for the food.

By the time we had finished our burgers, I'd brought Harry up to date on Laurie Popejoy's disappearance and her phone messages. I filled him in on my visit from James O'Brien and our impending date. I even mentioned Cleo Cominoli's growing fears for Sig's fate if he went under Phyllis Poole's knife.

Harry cut two slivers of cheesecake and licked the knife. He stuffed the remaining cheesecake in his mini-fridge and brought our dessert to the small table.

"Why are you getting involved in all this? It's none of your business."

"Cleo asked me—"

"Cleo's boyfriend is a grownup. He can make his own decisions. If he needs an operation, it's up to him to decide who's going to do it."

"But he doesn't know what we know about Poole."

"What do you know?"

That stopped me. What did we know?

"We know she was going to operate on Cody O'Brien and now he's dead." Hearing myself, I realized I sounded as paranoid as Cleo.

"So what?"

"So why did Laurie Popejoy turn up missing right after Cody checked out against medical advice? And why is she calling me saying it wasn't Game Boy? What's that about?"

"How am I supposed to know?"

"You're the Game Boy expert. I thought it might mean something to you."

Harry reached for his laptop. He typed a few keystrokes, nodded at the screen, and gave me a pitying look. "And you're supposed to be the research whiz."

I got up and looked over his shoulder. He had pulled up a website for Cody O'Brien. There, under a picture of Cody and his horse, was a caption: *Former bull rider Cody O'Brien pins hopes for a new career on his palomino cutting horse, Game Boy.* The text of the accompanying article, written two weeks earlier, mentioned injuries that had finished Cody's career as a bronc rider but didn't go into detail about his injured testicle.

Harry pointed halfway down the screen. "Did you see this?"

I looked where he pointed. Cody bought the horse at auction for two hundred thousand dollars.

"Holy horse flesh," I said.

Harry printed the page and handed it to me. "Game Boy is a horse. A hell of an expensive one. Now what?"

"That's what Laurie meant. 'It wasn't Game Boy.' She knows Cody wasn't killed by his horse. She must know what really happened to him. What if she witnessed something? Maybe Cody's killer is after her and she's hiding out."

"You're doing a lot of speculating. If she knows something, why doesn't she go to the police?"

"I don't know, but she's called me twice. What if she's in danger? I can't ignore that, but I can't reach her."

Harry got up and rinsed our cheesecake plates in his small sink. "What are you planning to do?"

"Find Laurie. But I need your help."

"Why me? Why not Nick? Why don't you give him a call?"

"I don't know.... Nick and I aren't...we're not—"

"I know what you're not. Nick keeps me informed. I don't have time and Nick's available. Call him."

"Why would he be available? He's usually tied up for days at a time, flying Buck Sawyer off to some exotic destination."

"Buck and Delta are in Greece for three weeks on a second honeymoon." Harry picked up his hard hat—a hint that our lunch was over. "Nick's free. Call him. Unless you're afraid you'll weaken and fall into his arms."

After he stopped laughing, Harry looked out the door of his trailer. He whistled, and a foreman came running. After they conferred for a few minutes, the man ran back to his crew.

"I'd better get back to work," I said.

"Me, too." Harry gave me a hug. "I'm sorry, but I'm working almost around the clock here. If you need boots on the ground, call Nick. I can only help if it's something quick and simple like the Game Boy connection. I suggest you find out where that horse is. Maybe it'll tell you what happened."

"I can't talk to a horse."

"Nick's good with horses."

BACK IN MY OFFICE, I wrestled with Harry's suggestion. Nick *was* good with horses. He was good with a lot of things, but we hadn't resolved our stumbling block to living happily ever after. That obstacle was his working relationship with Rella. I still struggled with doubts about their feelings for each other. Until I conquered those doubts, it wasn't fair to either of us to pretend I had.

Most women would see dating other men as a reasonable alternative, and Nick had even asked me if that's what I wanted to do. I had told him no; all I wanted was to regain the trust I'd had in him before Rella entered our lives. Besides, Timbergate wasn't exactly brimming with eligible bachelors. Jared Quinn, TMC's administrator, was one of the most eligible men in town, but he was my boss, and would remain on my off-limits list.

My musing brought me around to James O'Brien and Friday night. A date, but not really. Even so, I could see how it felt to be a single woman again. Then I remembered the O'Brien family's pending lawsuit and changed my mind. Definitely not a date. James was going to have some explaining to do.

I spent the afternoon and evening hoping to hear from Laurie Popejoy, but she did not call again and did not answer my calls. I wondered if she had decided to go to the police. I considered going to the police myself to report her missing, but what would I tell them? A woman suddenly quits her job, leaves a cryptic message about a horse that didn't commit murder, and then doesn't return my calls. I'd go straight into the flake file along with all the other crackpots. Plus, if the police were involved and the story got into the news, Laurie's identity could be revealed, putting her in even greater danger.

Meanwhile, I'd saved her messages, but I had no idea what to do with them. Could calls on old fashioned cassette tape message machines be traced? I didn't have a clue, but Nick might. He seemed to know a lot about that sort of thing. It wouldn't hurt to ask.

I sent him a text with a terse message just before I went to bed. "Call me."

I could almost hear Harry chuckling. *Shut up*, I thought.

SIX

I PUNCHED IN Cleo's number as soon as I got to work Friday morning.

"What's up?" she asked. "Any more calls?"

"No. How about you?"

"No."

"Have you had a chance to look for DeeDee's chart?"

"I tried early this morning, but either it wasn't there, or it was misfiled. I told you, that place is a mess, and I only had a few minutes to look for it. I'll go back again first chance I get."

"What about the minutes of her death review?" I asked.

"Sorry, struck out there, too. I couldn't find any mention of Deirdre O'Brien in death reviews during the month after her death."

I ended the call, saying I'd touch base later. Quinn had already threatened me with temporary, if not permanent, loss of my job if he heard I was poking my nose where it didn't belong. So I got to work. First I followed up on Edna Roda's request. A few minutes of searching located Duquesne University, based in Pittsburg. Edna was excited to hear about the school's online forensic nursing program. I wished her luck getting funding approved. With that simple task out of the way, I tackled the more complicated and time-consuming chore of putting a CME program together.

As the day wore on, my thoughts wandered to my

evening with James O'Brien and my wardrobe. What message did I want to send? A classy outfit that said *Look, but don't touch*? Or a little black something that might loosen his tongue? I wanted to know everything about the O'Brien clan, including the motivation behind the lawsuit. I decided to go with the little black something. *Tell me all your family secrets, James.*

When I reached the employee parking lot after work, Cleo was waiting by my car, shifting her weight from one foot to the other.

"Hi," I said. "Do you have news, or do you need to pee?"

"Both, but the news is, Laurie Popejoy was definitely Cody O'Brien's nurse the night he left the hospital. He checked himself out against medical advice while Laurie was busy with the change-of-shift report. No one saw Laurie after she reviewed her patient notes with the nurse coming on duty, and no one realized Cody was missing until after Laurie left the hospital. Apparently, he filled out an AMA form and left it on his hospital bed."

"But someone must have known. Doesn't the form need his physician's signature?"

"Yes, and a witness. O'Brien signed and dated the patient line, but the rest of the form was left blank."

"Do you think Laurie gave him the form?"

"Seems likely, but my source couldn't confirm that."

I mulled over Cleo's information on my drive home, convinced Laurie was involved in the mystery of Cody's death and wishing she would call me again.

The old message machine in my apartment indicated no new calls. I wondered why Laurie hadn't called my cellphone until I realized the old landline number was the only one she could get by calling Information.

TMC's HR department had my cellphone number, but they couldn't give it out without my permission.

I raced through my evening chores, throwing hay, cleaning and filling watering troughs, and inspecting dung piles to make sure none of the llamas were showing signs of digestive problems. All the fresh droppings looked like large, shiny coffee beans—a good indicator that everyone was healthy.

With that out of the way, I barely had time to shower and dress for my date with James O'Brien.

Margie's Friday night crowd was warming up to a recorded Miles Davis rendition of "You Go to My Head" when I walked in a few minutes after eight. Spicy aromas and heady perfumes mingled in the air. I spotted James at a table near the back wall. He wore classic New York casual attire: black slacks and a long-sleeved cashmere pullover in charcoal-gray that probably cost as much as every stitch of clothing in my closet.

James waved me over and appraised my black dress. "Nice," he said. "Let's plan our wedding."

"Let's get reacquainted first. I don't even know if you're single."

"I am now." For a fleeting moment the merriment left his eyes. A bad divorce, I guessed.

"I made it to the altar once," James said. "I might tell you about it after a few more beers. What about you?"

"Same answer as yours. Single, that is. Except I never made it to the altar."

"But you came close?"

"They say close only counts in horseshoes." I regretted my words immediately, since James had been told that his brother's death was caused by a blow from a horse's hoof.

A young waitress with bobbed brown hair and enormous false eyelashes stopped by our table. "Hi there," she said. "Care to try our complimentary fried favas flavored with Spanish paprika?" She placed a bowl on our table. "A Margie's snack special. They're yummy."

James ordered another beer for himself. I asked for a soda and surveyed the growing crowd while I munched a fried fava. The waitress was right. *Yummy.*

"Looks like a good turnout." I reached for another bean.

"Have you heard this combo before?" James asked.

"A few times. They have a new female vocalist tonight. Looks like they're starting soon."

Lights came up on a small elevated stage. Phyllis Poole emerged from a corridor in the back of the restaurant. I couldn't see her face, but I recognized the pale flesh and white-blond hair hanging straight to her shoulders. She wore a glittering red strapless dress that accented curves never seen in her everyday work clothes. She seated herself at the piano and lifted her face up to the spotlight. I heard myself gasp. Her transformation was stunning. She wasn't Mary-Kay-makeover pretty, but radiant—her face was supermodel gorgeous.

"Damn," James's jaw dropped. "Who is that?"

"She's the new one. Vocals and piano. You might want to close your mouth."

"Sorry. I see beautiful women at the theater every day, but her face is made for a spotlight."

"Hey, don't apologize. I was shocked for a moment, too. I see her at the hospital all the time without makeup. I had no idea she could look like that."

Poole's fingers flew across the keyboard, filling the room with boogie-woogie as she glanced toward the corridor and smiled. The other musicians emerged and took their places on stage: Quinn at drums and harmonica, Edna Roda on bass, and Tobias Fausset, who sang and played lead guitar.

The combo slipped into a mellow rendition of "Driftin' Blues," with Tobias doing the vocal. A few couples leaned together on the tiny dance floor, swaying to the sensual sounds.

The next number featured Poole on piano and vocal in a jazzy version of "What a Little Moonlight Can Do." Ella Fitzgerald must have willed her voice to this normally pale, uptight woman. What had Ella been thinking?

Next, Tobias Fausset took the mic again and crooned "I Almost Lost My Mind" to Poole's piano accompaniment. The lyrics flowed from Tobias like dark honey, setting the crowd's pheromones flying.

"Ivory Joe Hunter," James said. "Great song." He took my elbow and led me to the dance floor. With no room to maneuver, he wrapped his arms around me and pulled me close. We swayed in place, and I tried to keep my pelvis a cautious distance from his. If anything on his anatomy was stirring, I didn't want to know about it. I couldn't manage a discreet interrogation if I let my hormones short-circuit my brain.

After the dance we sat sipping our drinks, neither of us finding anything to say. We weren't the only ones. With their first four songs, the combo had tapped into the universal urges and longings blues are made of, and the audience was mesmerized. By the time they finished the set we would be lucky if any oxygen was left in the room.

So far I'd learned nothing from James about the

O'Brien clan, Seamus in particular, but the evening was young. I excused myself, hoping a walk to the restroom might clear my head. I was still processing Phyllis Poole's astonishing transformation. I'd figured her for a pale and poor substitute for Laurie Popejoy and assumed she had somehow coerced Tobias Fausset into adding her to the combo. *Wrong.* Tobias would have been nuts *not* to use her in Code Blues. Laurie Popejoy had been talented, but Phyllis Poole's presence on that that stage was like white lightning.

The more I learned about Dr. Poole, the more I wanted to know. Who was this woman? How many ways was her life entangled with that of Tobias Fausset? Was their relationship based solely on medicine and music, or was Cleo on the right track? Were Laurie Popejoy and Cody O'Brien collateral damage in some greater scheme cooked up by Poole?

I dropped my purse on the vanity counter and fished for a notepad and pen. The music and the dance had been distracting, and I was afraid I'd forget some vital detail. Just as I put pen to paper Edna Roda walked in.

"Hello, Aimee, are you writing a review?" Her smile held a hint of amusement, but I saw curiosity in her eyes.

I jammed the pen and pad back into my purse. "Shopping list," I said. "I remembered something I need."

"Birth control?"

My mouth dropped open. "No, I—"

"Relax. It was a joke. We've been told our music puts people in the mood. What do you think?"

"It's incredible. You're all so talented. Are you on a break already?"

"No. Poole is doing a couple of solo numbers. What do you think of her? How is she filling Laurie's shoes?"

"She's exceptional." I waited to see if Edna had more to say about Laurie.

"Of course, Laurie was exceptional, too." Edna hesitated. "I wish she hadn't…. Ah, well, we can't make people's decisions for them, can we? Wish her well for me, if you're in touch."

Edna ended our conversation by slipping into a stall. The lock slid in place. The subject was closed. When I heard the papery *whish* of a seat cover being pulled from the box on the wall, I left. *If you're in touch.* Did she know Laurie was trying to contact me?

Back at our table, James sat munching a fava, his fingers dancing on the tabletop to Poole's jazzy rendition of "Hit the Road, Jack."

"Ah, there you are. I wondered if you'd escaped out the restroom window."

"No, sorry. I met someone I know and we started talking."

Poole's number ended, and Tobias announced a ten minute break. The combo left the stage and congregated at a table in back of the room. Time to pump James about his family.

"Has your family decided on arrangements for Cody?"

James squared his white napkin on the table and picked four fava beans from the bowl. "Here you see the family, or what's left of it." He put one bean on the napkin. "That's me." Two more beans went down. "There you have my father and his oh-so-charming wife, Echo." He placed the last bean on the table.

"Keely," I said.

"Right." He lifted the napkin and dropped the beans

back into the bowl. "You'd think the four of us could sit down calmly and discuss the situation, but you'd be wrong."

"Why?"

He shook his head. "No one agrees with anyone about anything in the O'Brien family. That's why I live in New York."

"Has Cody's body been released?"

"That's part of the problem. There's been some delay. I hate to think of him lying in a cold drawer somewhere. Dad thinks he's already a ghost rider in the sky, and Keely thinks he's burning in hell."

"What does your dad's wife think?"

"Echo? Who knows? She sits around sipping sherry and asking if anyone wants a Valium."

I didn't think I'd get a better opening so I charged ahead. "James, there's something I need to ask you. I hope you'll be honest with me."

"Sounds serious. What is it?"

"Is your family suing the hospital?"

"What?" He looked genuinely puzzled. "What makes you think that?"

"A subpoena. It was on Quinn's desk this morning."

"Jesus, I don't believe this." He reached out and touched my arm. "Aimee, I swear, I don't know anything about a lawsuit, but you can sure as hell believe I'm going to find out."

The waitress appeared at that moment with another beer for James and a soda for me. I was about to protest when she said they were compliments of the combo. I looked behind us at their table and saw Jared Quinn lift his bottle toward us. On the way back to the bandstand, he stopped at our table.

"Aimee, glad you could make it." Quinn nodded at James.

James stood, I performed the introductions, and the men shook hands. I prayed they weren't playing *let's see who can squeeze the hardest*. If Quinn lost, he'd have trouble holding a drumstick in that hand for the rest of the evening.

Quinn glanced toward me then turned to James. "O'Brien? Any relation to Cody O'Brien?"

"Yes, he's…was my brother."

"James is from New York," I added. "He's here to help with arrangements."

"Damn sorry for your loss. Let me know if I can help." Quinn caught my eye for a moment and sent a silent message. *Why was I on a date with the enemy?*

"I think you can, actually," James said. "I was hoping to get a copy of Cody's medical record." The last thing Quinn would have expected to hear from James, considering the subpoena, but he covered his surprise well.

"Give me a call first thing Monday." Quinn was already walking backward, making his way to the bandstand. "Aimee has the number." I knew I'd be answering to Quinn first thing Monday morning.

"Thanks, I'll do that," James called after him.

James and I had one more slow, sensuous dance during the combo's second set, but I needed to distance myself from him and from the evocative music before I sent the wrong message. Nick and I were trying to repair our fragile relationship, and James was only a tempting diversion. I still hoped I was on a path that would lead back to Nick, so I made lame excuses about a headache, long day, long week.

James didn't argue. He walked me to my aging green

sedan, holding my elbow like a proper gentleman until we reached my car.

"Aimee, I promise you I'll get to the bottom of this lawsuit. As soon as I do, I'll let you know."

I wanted to believe him. I let him pull me into a warm bear hug.

"This should have been a perfect date, little Aimless. Thanks for inviting me." He pressed his lips to my forehead in a kiss as chaste as a pope's blessing.

"Your boss must think I'm jerking him around. Will you explain that I didn't know about the subpoena?"

"I'll tell him first thing Monday."

"Great. If I can get the family to withdraw the suit, I'd still like a copy of Cody's record."

"They'll only release a copy to the person named as next of kin. That would probably be your father, but you might bring it up when you talk with Jared Quinn."

"I'll talk to him and my father. First I have to see where Dad stands on the lawsuit issue. In any case, I can't think why he wouldn't agree to request a copy of Cody's record, but that's not all I want. I want to know why Cody left the hospital the night before his surgery."

"I'm not sure anyone knows the answer to that. Most likely he got anxious thinking about the procedure. If Dr. Poole explained what she was going to do, it might have spooked him. She's notorious for her appalling bedside manner."

"I think it was more than that."

"Why?"

"When he called me in New York that night from the hospital, something was bothering him. I tried to reassure him, but he said it wasn't about his operation. He wanted me to fly out as soon as I could. He said when I got here he'd explain, but I was too late."

My pulse quickened with that bit of news. So there *was* something troubling Cody, but if not his surgery, what could it be? "Maybe your father knows."

"I thought of that, and I plan to ask him, but not while he's still trying to get his mind around Cody's death."

I smiled. "I remember meeting your father years ago when Keely invited our dance class to a swimming party at the ranch. Is he still larger than life?"

James took a deep breath and gazed out at the passing traffic, illuminated by street lights. "I'm afraid not. I'm worried about his health. He's not the same man I saw when he visited me last year in New York. He was a patient at TMC back in July, but you probably knew that."

I read discouragement in the slump of his shoulders. "No, I didn't," I said. "I wasn't hired until August. Why was he admitted?"

"He said it was for a suspected heart problem, but his doctor didn't find anything. Now he's blaming his symptoms on old age, but that doesn't explain the way he's gone downhill since last year. He has pain in his abdomen, his energy's at rock bottom, and I could swear his skin is turning yellow. That can't be good."

At the mention of yellow skin, a few nasty possibilities raced through my mind. I didn't mention any of them to James. "Maybe he needs a second opinion. Do you know who his doctors are?"

"He has a cardiologist and a family doctor." James gave me their names and asked what I knew about them.

"They're both on the TMC medical staff. Good doctors, but it sounds like he needs an internist. You might suggest that his family doctor refer him to someone."

"I'll try, but I'm not sure I can convince him to see another doctor. I'm afraid he's given up on getting well. He's more concerned about revising his will."

I shook my head. "That's probably because Cody's no longer a potential heir. It doesn't mean he's expecting to die soon."

"But most wills take into account that an heir could die prematurely," James said. "If Dad wants to make a change, it must be for a significant reason that wasn't accounted for in the current version."

"Maybe he just wants to make sure. It's the responsible thing to do, isn't it?"

"I hope you're right." James opened my car door. "I'd better let you get home."

I slid into my driver's seat and rolled down the window. "Thanks for coming tonight."

"My pleasure. And tell Jack and your grandmother I plan to visit them while I'm in town. Are they still out in Coyote Creek?"

"Yes, same place."

He pulled a pen and the card I'd given him from his pocket. "What's their number?"

I gave him the number, considered 'fessing up about living on their property, but decided to let it go. Maybe he wouldn't get around to calling them.

Driving home, I tried to piece together what I'd learned from James. Cody had made an urgent call from his hospital room asking James to come to California right away. Then he'd bolted from TMC in the dark of night. Did he get cold feet? Was he afraid of Dr. Poole? Or did something else spook him?

And what about Seamus O'Brien's failing health and his anxiety about his will? His medical record might hold some answers. I wanted to investigate Seamus's health status for myself. It struck me that three O'Briens had been patients at TMC: DeeDee, Cody, and Seamus. Two were dead and the third might be dying. Would any of their medical charts hold clues to Cody's death or Laurie Popejoy's disappearance? I'd need Cleo's help to sort that out.

SEVEN

At home I glanced at the light on my ancient message machine in case Laurie Popejoy had called again. It wasn't blinking. I checked my cellphone, hoping she had managed to get my number, but my only call was from Nick.

"Hey, you. Got your text." I heard him laughing as he hung up. Not the sound of a lonely guy. He sounded happy. Happy to hear from me or happy for some other reason? I didn't like the direction my thoughts were going. I nuked a cup of leftover coffee and called him back. He picked up on the second ring.

"Hi."

"Hi, yourself," I said. I heard whining in the background and a loud *woof.* "What was that?"

Nick chuckled. "My new best friend. I picked her up yesterday. Her name's Ginger."

"You got a dog? Why?"

"I'm lonely." He laughed, and I heard another *woof.* "Why did you ask me to call?"

"It was Harry's idea. I need help with a problem."

"What kind of problem?"

"I need to find a missing person."

"Another mystery? Didn't that last scrape teach you anything?"

"This is different." His reference to my last scrape had to do with my face-off with a suspected killer a couple of months earlier. I'd survived intact, but for a moment I'd expected a bullet in the head. Nick hadn't shown up until the worst was over, and he felt terrible that he hadn't been there for me. I had promised not to play detective again.

"So who's missing?" Nick asked.

"We need to get together so I can explain."

"Okay. Where and when?"

"Can you come by my place tomorrow?" I wanted him to hear Laurie's messages.

"What time?"

"After jujitsu. Are you going to black belt class in the morning?"

"Can't make it. I have a training thing with the dog until noon."

"I'll be home from the dojo by one o'clock, then I'll be helping Jack and Amah all afternoon."

"That'll work. I can help you help them. What will you be doing?"

"Shoveling."

"Llama dung?"

"'Fraid so."

NICK ARRIVED AT one o'clock Saturday afternoon with Ginger, his newly acquired Chesapeake Bay retriever. A full grown dog about the size of a Labrador, she walked easily on a leash and seemed smitten with Nick. Amah was an instant pushover, fussing over the pretty waves in Ginger's red-brown coat. Jack observed the animal with his usual cool reserve and finally expressed his opinion.

"Nice dog."

"Thanks." Nick beamed. He had been an avid reader

of Jack's articles in outdoor magazines even before he met me. There were few things he valued more than the approval of Jack Highland.

Startled by a high-decibel howl, we all turned to see Amah's cat, Fanny, with her back in a Halloween arch, fur standing on end, and bushy gray tail straight up. With flattened ears and a malevolent glint in her yellow eyes, she hissed and spat at Ginger, who dropped onto her belly and hid her nose in her front paws.

"Shame on you," Amah told the cat. She shooed Fanny into the house and shut the door.

"You can tie the dog over there." Jack nodded toward a peach tree near the pasture fence.

While Jack and Amah tended the remains of their vegetable garden, Nick helped me shovel and haul several loads of llama droppings. I told him about Cody O'Brien's death and the subsequent disappearance of Laurie Popejoy. I mentioned Cleo's suspicions about Dr. Poole and her worry about letting her fiancé go under Poole's knife.

Nick leaned on his shovel and wiped his brow. "You think there's anything to it—the idea that this woman doctor is doing something hinky with her male patients?"

"It sounds far-fetched to me, but I've learned to take Cleo seriously. In her job she sees it all, and she's told me some stories about aberrant behavior by doctors that are hard to believe but well documented."

"Do Jack and Amah know you're meddling again?"

"Of course not. And I'm not meddling. I want to reassure Cleo that Sig's surgeon isn't a serial castrator."

"Is that even a word?"

"I don't know, but I'll look it up."

Nick laughed. "I'm sure you will."

We kept at our task for two hours, transporting our full wheelbarrows to a small fenced area where Jack stored the rich manure. Llama dung piles look like giant mounds of oversized coffee beans. The smell is earthy, but not repulsive. Jack uses some of it every spring to fertilize his garden, and the rest goes to various neighbors who prefer it to commercial fertilizers.

Amah finally announced that it was time for a break. She spread a paper tablecloth on the picnic table in the backyard under the shade of a blue oak and put out iced tea along with sliced tomatoes, marinated zucchini, smoked salmon, and chunks of crusty bread.

The temperature had climbed to a humid ninety degrees, which wasn't unusual for a mid-October day in Coyote Creek. Nick and I were hot, sticky, and covered in dust, so we scrubbed and rinsed up to our elbows in Jack's mudroom before sitting down to eat.

Whenever Nick was on the premises, Amah was on romance alert, hoping our relationship might take a turn toward matrimony. Throughout the meal her sharp hazel eyes studied Nick and me, analyzing every word, gesture, or nuance. Jack's scrutiny was less obvious, but I knew where he stood on the matter. He would never criticize my choice of men, but as far as he was concerned, Nick was The One.

After we ate Nick and I walked down the lane to my little apartment over the barn. Settling into a chair at my dinette table, he listened to both Laurie's recorded calls several times. He leaned back in his chair and stared at the ceiling for a moment.

"What do you think?" I asked. "Can we find out where she called from?"

"I doubt it. This equipment is ancient. Where did you get it?"

"The phone and answering machine are old discards Jack found in his storage shed. He never throws anything away."

"Why would she call on this old phone instead of your cellphone?"

"I've never given her either of my phone numbers. She must have gotten my landline number by calling Information."

"Well, forget about tracing her calls. You need to figure out why she called you. Are you good friends?"

"We knew each other at work, but we weren't really close. All I know is it has something to do with how Cody O'Brien died. She said it wasn't Game Boy. She knows his horse didn't kill him. She must know who did. She either witnessed it or she discovered some kind of evidence."

"Any idea why Laurie would be anywhere near where the murder took place?"

"No. I do know she was working on Cody's floor that night. Cleo said no one noticed Cody was gone until after Laurie's shift ended and she left the hospital. The nurse who took over Laurie's patients on the next shift found an AMA form on Cody's bed. He was gone."

"What's an AMA form?" Nick asked.

"It means 'Against Medical Advice.' He signed the form, but there was no signature by a physician or a witness on the form."

"You think Laurie gave him the form? That she was mixed up in Cody's escape from the hospital."

"It's possible. At least she must know something, or else why call to say the horse didn't do it? I've left a dozen messages on her phone, but she hasn't returned any of my calls. Since her second message, the one about Game Boy, I haven't heard from her again."

Nick stood and looked out the kitchen window toward the main house, checking on Ginger. I followed his gaze. Jack was standing over the dog while she drank from a water dish.

Nick turned back to me. "What do you want me to do?"

"I was hoping we could have the tape from the answering machine analyzed. Maybe there's some background noise we can identify that will tell us where she was calling from."

"I'll see what I can do, but don't get your hopes up." Nick popped the tape out of the machine. "Aimee, if she is on the run, you could be asking for trouble."

"Nick, I just want to make sure she's all right."

"Hell and damn. I might as well do this or you'll ask someone else." He dropped the tape in his shirt pocket. "Do you have another tape to load into this thing?"

I gave him another tape. "How long do you think it'll take?"

"A few days, maybe. If you hear from her in the meantime, let me know."

"Okay." I walked toward the door and opened it.

Nick sat, watching me. "Going somewhere?"

"I thought you were." I stood at the open door, feeling silly.

"You're letting flies in."

I closed the door. "So are you leaving or what?"

Nick stood, stretched, and yawned. I recognized that particular stretch and yawn. They were reliable signals that he was in the mood.

"Must be nap time," he said. "Too much good food."

"Amah's cooking will do that."

Nick walked over to me, took my hands and leaned his forehead against mine. Desire weakened my resolve. I wanted his arms around me. He pulled me close, nuzzling my neck and awakening every nerve in my body. As he leaned in to kiss me, the old landline phone rang, shattering the moment. I backed away from Nick. The phone rang again.

"Son of a gun," Nick said, in a ragged whisper.

I reached for the phone, hoping it was Laurie. Nick grabbed my arm. "Wait. Let's see if the new tape in your message machine is working."

It was Amah. "Hi, honey. James O'Brien dropped by. He's asking if you might come up to the house and say hello."

Nick cocked his head at me. "Who's James O'Brien?"

"Brother of the dead cowboy."

"Why is he visiting your grandparents?"

"He's a family friend. Didn't I tell you? We've known the O'Briens since I was a kid."

"No, you didn't mention that." He gave me a speculative look. "Anything else you didn't mention?"

"If I think of anything, I'll let you know."

Nick and I walked up the lane and found Amah, Jack, and James in the backyard. I introduced Nick and James. They shook hands, but said nothing beyond a cursory "Nice to meet you." Jack finally broke the silence by inviting Nick and James into his den. He wanted to show them brochures of Namibia where he and Amah would be on safari in a matter of days.

As soon as the men were out of range, Amah stopped

cleaning the picnic table. "Okay, young lady, what's going on?"

"What do you mean?"

"What's Nick's doing here?"

"He wanted to pick up some books and CDs he left with me." I hated lying to Amah, but I wasn't about to admit I was trying to solve another mystery. "I told him I'd be doing chores, and he offered to help."

"So it isn't a date?"

"No. Sorry."

"And James?"

"He came by the hospital to ask about Cody. He did mention that he'd like to see you and Jack, but I didn't know he was going to show up today."

"So he came by to visit Jack and me. That I believe, because he was surprised to hear that you're living in our barn, but it doesn't explain the look on his face when he saw you with Nick."

"You must have imagined that. James is just an old friend."

"I have a pretty good memory, you know. He was your first big crush, wasn't he?"

"That was a long time ago. I was just a kid."

Amah raised a skeptical eyebrow, but let it go.

A few minutes later, Nick and James appeared on the veranda chatting like long-lost buddies. Amah asked if they wanted iced tea, or maybe a cold beer. They declined, each making noises about how it was getting late and how he should be leaving. It couldn't be soon enough to suit me.

"How long will you be in town, James?" Amah asked.

"I'm not sure. Family matters are going to take some time, I'm afraid."

Jack put an arm around Amah's shoulders. "Let us know if we can help."

"You're always welcome," Amah added. "Come by any time. And we'd like to attend Cody's memorial, if you have one planned."

"I'll let you know." James turned to me. "I had a great time last night. Thanks for inviting me." He kissed my cheek in front of everyone. Amah gasped, Jack coughed, and Nick's smile had a dangerous twist.

After James left, I walked to Jack's driveway with Nick and waited while he loaded Ginger in his SUV and slid into the driver's seat. Through his open window he said, "So James is an old family friend?"

"Yes. I wanted to see Code Blues at Margie's Bean Pot last night. I hoped Laurie Popejoy might show up. I needed an escort, and James was available."

"So was I."

"That wouldn't have worked. I wanted to hear what I could about the rest of the O'Brien family. James and Keely's father is gravely ill. Seamus wants to change his will, but James doesn't think it's because Cody died. He thinks there's some other reason."

"Ah, the plot thickens," Nick said.

"You have no idea. I found out yesterday morning that the O'Briens filed a wrongful death suit against TMC. Last night James claimed he knew nothing about it."

"You believe him?"

"I think so. He asked Jared Quinn how to get a copy of Cody's medical record. Why would he do that if he knew the record had already been subpoenaed?"

"To cover himself and keep you guessing what he's up to?"

"Possibly, but I'm more concerned that Laurie Pope-joy knows something that has put her in danger. I won't stop worrying until I hear from her again."

Nick started his engine. "You're not going to let this go, are you?"

"How can I? She called me twice. I have to know why. What if she's been abducted?"

Nick turned off his engine and opened his passenger door. "Sit with me. We need to talk."

I got in the car, stifling the impulse to cross my arms like a kid resisting a parental lecture. "I'm listening."

"Aimee, I understood your taking risks back when Harry was in trouble, but I didn't like it." He put up a hand. "I know, it's your life and I don't have veto power over any of your decisions, but that doesn't prevent me from speaking my mind."

"I appreciate your concern, but I have to make sure Laurie's okay and that there's nothing going on at the hospital that puts patients at risk. I'm not going to do anything dangerous. I'm not a particularly brave woman. I don't cut into people on operating tables like Phyllis Poole or fly fighter jets over hostile third-world countries like Rella Olstad."

Nick shook his head. "You're comparing apples and oranges, lady. Don't sell yourself short. You don't work your way through a master's program or earn a black belt without courage and grit."

"But those are things I could do without leaving terra firma or taking another person's life in my hands." I struggled with how to explain myself. "Nick, all I'm really good at is digging for information and coming up with answers. That's why I became a librarian. Call it an addiction, if you want to label it. Once I'm confronted with a problem, I *have* to stay with it until it's solved."

Nick sighed. "And where do you suppose this addiction came from?"

That stopped me for a moment. "I don't know. I've been this way all my life. Even as a kid, my friends always came to me with their problems—help with their school work or maybe finding a lost pet. Just simple stuff, but I loved the feeling of helping and making people happy."

"You're not a kid now. The stakes are different."

"That's my point. A man I once knew has died, and his death could mean other lives are at stake. Two people I care about have asked me for help. I can't ignore that. I'm sorry you don't approve, but I have to see this through."

"All right, then." Nick took the answering machine tape out of his pocket. Ginger sniffed at it. "How about we go to the missing nurse's home and knock on the door? Chances are we'll find her there, safe and sound. Do you know where she lives?"

"I'll find out." I got out of the car.

"When you do, call me. Do not go alone." I closed the door and drove away, with Ginger riding shotgun.

EIGHT

SATURDAY NIGHTS WERE AWKWARD. Nick and I were still working out the kinks in our relationship, so by tacit agreement, we had been spending them apart, and neither of us asked the other for details. I got through my evening by borrowing *Foul Play* from Amah's DVD collection. She said it was a comedy about a librarian, so I shared a bowl of goldfish crackers with Fanny while I watched a young Goldie Hawn being stalked by a killer in a closed and darkened library. *Thanks, Amah*.

THE TEMPERATURE SUNDAY morning was seventy degrees—perfect for a five-mile jog on the country road that ran past Jack and Amah's property. The long, hot summer with its bleached and empty sky had given way to a few strips of gauzy clouds above the mountains to the east. A cool breeze spread the pungent aroma of wild grasses through the branches of the blue oaks and gray pines dominating the landscape.

On the home stretch, I stopped at Coyote Creek's Four Corners Market for a cold bottle of green tea. I spotted Keely O'Brien and Tucker Potkotter in the check-out line with two loaded grocery baskets. Keely's hair was tangled and dark at the roots, and her wrinkled Montgomery Gentry T-shirt hung loose on her frame. Tucker's skintight muscle shirt lived up to its name, showing off his biceps and an impressive six-pack. I'd heard Tucker had moved into Keely's house in the O'Brien compound in Coyote Creek and wondered if they'd gotten engaged.

I started to duck into a different line before I could be spotted, but then the urge to hide from Keely nipped at my conscience. We'd been good pals long ago, and she had just lost her brother. I walked over with my bottle of tea and stood in line behind them.

"Keely, how are you doing?" I said.

She plastered on a phony smile. "Great." She gestured toward Tucker. "You know Tuck, don't you?"

"I think we met once at the gym when I was there with Harry. Nice to see you, Tucker."

"Same here." He nodded at me and looked away.

"Go ahead and ask," Keely said.

"Ask what?"

"About James. You know you want to." She lifted her chin, challenging me. "I heard you asked him out."

"Oh, that. It wasn't really a date." Sure, I was curious about James, but Cody's death had renewed my interest in all of the surviving members of the O'Brien family.

Keely ignored my protest and went on. "His wife won a Tony a couple of years ago. So did her co-star. James was the director. He didn't win. The bitch hooked up with the co-star, and James left her and the production. It's still playing on Broadway. I keep hoping it'll fold, but he did too good a job putting it together."

"I hear he's producing off-Broadway these days."

"Right. The divorce was final about a year ago. She cleaned him out, in case you're wondering if he's rich." Keely's basket was next in line for the cashier. "Anything else you want to know?"

I didn't like hearing that James might be strapped for

money, but I wasn't about to pursue that topic in front of everyone in the grocery line.

"Not really," I said. "James is a great guy. I hope you get to spend a lot of time together while he's here."

"Yeah, he's a great guy all right. Won't even give me a walk-on in one of his precious productions, and he *owes* me. That makes two big-shot brothers who never gave me a freaking break. It looks like James is more interested in being your escort service than spending time with me." She grabbed a *National Enquirer* off the rack and tossed it in the basket.

Keely's rudeness wasn't pretty, but at least it made sense. She thought I was competing for her time with her big brother—now her only brother—and nothing I said was going to change her mind. She said he owed her a role in one of his productions. Poor James. I could imagine the can of worms that would open, considering Keely's addiction problems.

When their bill was totaled, Tucker didn't make a move to pull out his wallet. Keely put the purchases from both carts on a charge card she extracted from the back pocket of her jeans.

I paid for my tea and followed Keely and Tucker outside where a woman who had to be Seamus O'Brien's current wife leaned against the front fender of a shiny black Hummer with a license plate that read: TAXDMY2. She held a cellphone to her ear, and her pouty lips were pulled down in a frown. Keely had said Echo was young, but I wasn't prepared for what I saw. Dressed in designer jeans, spike heels, and a tube top that stretched across breasts the size of cantaloupes, Keely's stepmother was nothing if not eye-catching. Her long, thick hair was chocolate brown and shiny, the same color as her exquisitely lined and shadowed eyes. Her tan torso was an expanse of bare skin that started just below the tube top and ended where her low riders barely covered her pubic region. A tattoo of a snake adorned the flesh near her hipbone, its head dipping down and disappearing into her pants.

She put her phone in her purse and walked to the back of the Hummer, where Keely and Tucker were loading the groceries. She snapped her fingers in Keely's face.

"Hand it over."

Keely batted her hand away. "Knock it off, bitch."

Tucker stepped between them. "Hey, ladies, let's not make a scene, okay? Give her the damn card, Keely."

Keely reached into her pocket, pulled out the credit card and flicked it in Echo's face. It fell to the ground between them.

"Pick it the hell up," Echo said.

Before Keely could reply, Tucker reached down and grabbed the card. He handed it to Echo. "Here you go."

She held his gaze with her eyes while she slipped the card into her cleavage. "Thanks, Tuck." She turned a defiant glare toward Keely. "Are you finished yet?"

Keely slammed the back gate of the Hummer. "No thanks to you, *Mommy*."

Tucker climbed into the driver's seat. Echo sat in front on the passenger side, and Keely took a backseat behind her. Taking the backseat seemed to be a way of life for Keely.

I watched them drive away with Keely's words about James's divorce running through my mind. James had mentioned that Seamus wanted to change his will, but he didn't volunteer anything about his own interest in his father's estate. I couldn't help wondering how much he knew about the current will. Keely said James lost a major chunk of his assets in his divorce. Living in Manhattan wasn't cheap. If James was deep in debt, he might be counting on that will right along with the rest of the O'Briens.

On the last mile of my run, I pondered Laurie Pope-joy's phone calls and her subsequent disappearance. She had me convinced that Cody's death wasn't an accident, but Cleo's suspicions about Dr. Poole seemed unfounded, unless the doctor was truly a psychopath. I wasn't convinced of that.

Back at my apartment I checked the old answering machine again for messages and found nothing. I decided the best use of Sunday afternoon would be to scope out Laurie Popejoy's home. I took a quick shower, ate a handful of trail mix, and called Cleo to ask if she knew Laurie's home address.

"I might have it. Hold on a sec." She came back right away. "She sent me a Christmas card last year and I kept the return address so I could send one back to her." Cleo read off the address and I recognized the name of the street.

"Thanks, I know where that is."

"What are you going to do?"

I told her Nick's idea about dropping by Laurie's house but didn't mention that I was going to make an early reconnaissance run on my own. My plan was to park near Laurie's address and watch for any sign of her coming or going. Nick couldn't object to that. I was about to pull out of Jack and Amah's driveway when I spotted Harry's red Jag signaling to turn in. I backed up to give him room. He parked and walked over to my car, motioning for me to lower my window.

"Where're you going?"

"Nowhere. Shopping." Guilty answer. Harry knew I was dissembling.

"You're not going snooping alone."

"Fine. Come with me."

He glanced toward Jack and Amah's front door. "Sorry, I promised to help Jack install their new air-conditioning system."

"How long will that take?"

"All day and then some. My crew will be here in five minutes to start the ducting." Harry had his cellphone in his hand, punching at it with his thumb. He held it to his ear for a moment, then handed it to me. Nick was on the other end. I glared at my meddling brother, who repeated his directive in a whisper. "You're not going snooping alone."

"Harry? What's going on?" Nick asked.

"It's me," I said. "I'm on Harry's phone."

"Why?"

"Because my brother's a pain in the rear. I didn't call you, he did."

I told him I had an address for Laurie and asked if he wanted to help me check it out.

"Definitely, but it'll have to wait until this evening. I'm busy 'til then." He was busy. That left a lot to my imagination.

We agreed to meet in the parking lot of Harry's office at seven thirty. I had nothing planned for the rest of the day, so I volunteered to help with installing the A/C. I quickly became the designated gofer for the crew, but it didn't keep me from chewing over my conversation with Nick. And recalling how we used to spend Sunday afternoons.

When Harry and his crew broke for dinner, I helped Amah put out a spread consisting of grilled venison burgers, Greek salad, and strawberry trifle. After dinner, Harry and his men went back to work and I left to meet Nick, heading west toward Timbergate and into a lavish pink sunset back-lighting the deep velvet peaks of the Yolla Bolly Wilderness.

Nick was already parked at Harry's office. I let myself in the passenger door of his SUV, determined not to ask what had kept him busy all day.

"Where's your dog?" I asked.

"Home. So where does this woman live?"

"She's at 456½ Jefferson Street."

"What's the half about?"

"That means it's accessed from an alley. I checked."

"Of course you checked. You're a librarian."

The sunset had faded to twilight when we reached the address, a large two-story Victorian painted blue with white trim. A shabby sign out front read *Apts. Reasonable. No Pets.* The building sat on a southeast corner under a canopy of liquidambar trees. Nick turned right and slowed, watching for an alley entrance.

"There," I said.

"I see it." He turned right into the alley. Behind the apartment house was a small single unit that appeared to be converted servants' quarters. Nick backed out of the alley, drove half a block down the street, and parked. He took a small flashlight out of his console.

"Ready?" he asked.

"Why are you parking here?"

"I'd rather not draw the attention of her neighbors in the apartment house."

"Why not? If she's not home, maybe someone will know where she is."

"We don't know what kind of neighbors she has. Let's try it my way first."

I followed him up the street and into the dark alley. He aimed his flashlight beam at a tiny yard—a patch of fenced lawn lined with geraniums. Stone steps led to the front door. The number on the door frame confirmed the address as Laurie's. The porch light was out and full dark enveloped the little house. No light burned inside.

Nick rang the doorbell and leaned in to listen. "It's working," he said. We waited. He rang it again. We waited a minute more, listening, hearing no sounds from inside.

Nick whispered close to my ear, "Let's go around back."

At Laurie's back door, Nick put his arm out, motioning me to stop. In the beam from his flashlight, I saw what he had already seen. The frame was splintered, and the door was ajar.

NINE

NICK PUT A finger to his lips. We both listened but heard
nothing except the hum of light traffic half a block
away, mingled with the rustle of leaves in the trees surrounding Laurie's little house. Somewhere farther away,
a car horn honked and a dog barked. Nick pushed the
door open wider. I tapped his shoulder and he flinched.

"What?" he whispered.

"Are you going in?" I whispered back.

"Yes. Do you want to wait in the SUV?"

"No."

He pulled two pairs of vinyl gloves from his pocket
and handed one to me. "Put these on."

"Mind explaining why you carry—"

"Not now," he whispered.

While I slid my hands into the gloves, he stepped
inside the back door. It opened into the kitchen area. I
followed him through into the small living room, afraid
of what we might find, but more afraid of what might
find us. In the glow of his flashlight, we scrutinized
the space and saw nothing suspicious. A short hallway
opened into a bedroom on one side and a bathroom on
the other. I hovered in the hallway and watched while
Nick entered her bedroom. The bed was still neatly
made and a laptop sat open on a desk across the room.

"No sign of a struggle in here," he said when he
emerged. He crossed the hall and entered the bathroom.

"Ah," he said. "Here's something. An open window onto the alley. She could have escaped through here when the back door was being forced."

"So maybe she got out before the intruder got in."

"That might account for the place being untouched. He wasn't looking to take anything. He just wanted her."

"She must be scared out of her mind. We have to help her."

I followed Nick back to Laurie's bedroom, where the laptop sat open. A charging cord for a cellphone sat next to it. Nick picked up a small notepad and pencil from the desk and put them in his pocket. He crouched down and trained the light beam under her bed, but came up with nothing.

Back in the kitchen, Nick opened the refrigerator, sniffed an open milk carton and winced. Following his lead, I looked under the sink for a garbage container. I opened the lid, and the smell that hit my nostrils made it clear the garbage hadn't been emptied for several days.

"Look at her mail." I pointed to a pile of envelopes on the floor below a mail slot in the front door.

"Looks like it's been accumulating for a while." Nick spread the mail out. "Bills, flyers, ads, catalogs. Nothing personal." He pushed it back into a pile.

"Her last shift at work was Monday," I said. "That's a week ago tomorrow. It looks like she hasn't been back here since that night."

A sudden gust of wind set a shrub rattling against the living room window. The broken back door slammed against its frame.

"We'd better get out of here." Nick started toward the door.

"Shall we take her laptop? There might be something on it that could help us find her."

He hesitated. "Better not. What if she comes back for it?"

While we stood undecided, a siren wailed on a nearby street.

"Ah, hell," Nick said. "Let's go."

We left through the back door, leaving it just as we'd found it, and hurried to the car. The siren continued, but grew fainter as it pursued a lawbreaker in a distant part of town.

Nick drove to a sandwich shop where we were the only customers. We ordered coffees and sat in a booth. He took the notepad and pencil from Laurie's apartment and began rubbing the pencil lead against the blank top sheet of the notepad. I saw faint outlines begin to form and recognized my name and landline phone number, but there was another word I had trouble making out.

"She must have torn off the page and taken it with her," I said.

"Or the intruder did."

"Nick, if the intruder has my home phone number, he could track me to Jack and Amah's address. They could be in danger. I have to warn them."

"Maybe we can hold off on that," Nick said. "They're leaving on that safari to Africa the day after tomorrow. How long will they be gone?"

"Three weeks. Good point. All we have to do is keep them safe for a couple of days without telling them what's going on. Otherwise they'll worry about me and cancel their trip. Jack's waited all his life for this, and with me ranch sitting, he and Amah can finally enjoy a worry-free vacation. I couldn't stand to disappoint them."

"Then here's the plan," Nick said. "I'm flying them to San Francisco the day after tomorrow to catch their flight to Africa. I'll ask if I can stay in their guest room tomorrow night, since we're leaving early the following morning."

"That takes care of tomorrow night. What about tonight?"

"Call Harry. Fill him in and ask him to think up an excuse to stay over with them. I'd do it myself, but I have something else to take care of." I didn't ask what his something else might be.

Nick drained the last of his coffee and set the cup aside. "You might want to stay somewhere else at night while your grandparents are away, at least until we know if this character might come looking for you."

"I should be safe in my apartment. No one would think of looking for me in the barn."

"Not true. If you're burning your lights, it'll be pretty obvious someone's living out there. Why not sleep over at Harry's until we get this sorted out?"

"No. I won't do that. I'm supposed to be ranch-sitting in exchange for free rent. I can't leave the place unprotected every night."

"Then Ginger and I will sleep in the main house until your grandparents get home."

I knew it was futile to argue. "Okay. The cockatiel and Fanny can stay in the bunkhouse with me, but you have to babysit Jack's king snake."

"Fine with me," Nick said. "The bird's loud and that cat's crazy, but I get along fine with snakes. Now can we get back to what we were doing? There's another word on this notepad."

"What is it?"

"I don't know. I thought you might. It looks like the first letter is a D or a P." He used the pencil again, gently coaxing the indentations to reveal themselves.

"Looks like *Pat*," he said.

I studied the page. "*Pat*. You're right. It says *Pat*, but there's something else at the end."

He took another look and went to work again with the pencil. After a minute, he cocked his head and said, "Huh. Looks like a question mark."

"Let me see." He was right. I saw the same thing he did: *Pat?*

"So who's Pat? Someone who works at the hospital?"

"No one comes to mind, but it's a pretty common name."

"Check it out. Considering all the staff members and doctors who work there, you're bound to find at least one named Pat."

"I'd probably find more than one. How am I supposed to know which one Laurie meant? And why is this Pat's name on her notepad, along with my name and phone number?"

"Maybe she wanted you to get in touch with Mystery Pat." Nick tucked the pencil and notepad in his pocket. "Maybe Mystery Pat knows what's going on."

"Or maybe Laurie's hiding out with a friend named Pat."

"If she is, let's hope it was Laurie who ripped off the page and not the person she's running from."

Nick walked over to the counter and asked for coffees to go, bought two peanut butter cookies, and stuffed a few bills in the tip jar. He handed me my coffee and a cookie. "Let's go."

NICK PULLED INTO the parking lot at Harry's office and lowered his windows to catch the cool night breeze.

We sat eating our cookies and sipping coffee until a cat jumped on the hood of Nick's SUV with a muffled thump and stared at us through the windshield. Nick tapped the glass, and the stray dropped down and ran off under a hedge.

"Poor cat. I'll bet it's hungry."

"Tomcat," Nick said. "I'll bet it's not looking for food."

I wrapped the last half of my cookie in a napkin and stuffed it in my purse. "Let's get back to Laurie Popejoy. I'm going to work on finding out who Pat is, but we need to do more than that. Do you have any other ideas?"

"A few. Too bad we don't have Laurie's laptop."

"You're the one who said to leave it."

"I know," Nick said. "But I wish we'd had time to take a look."

"I wonder why the intruder didn't take it."

"He was chasing after her. I doubt he had time."

"But he didn't go back for it, either."

"Either he didn't think of it, or he didn't need to."

"You mean he might already have her?" I thought of Laurie gagged and bound somewhere. Or worse, Laurie's body buried in a shallow grave in the foothills. I flashed on Dr. Phyllis Poole replacing Laurie in Code Blues. How far would the doctor go for a place in Tobias Fausset's combo? Or in his life?

"The intruder may not have Laurie yet," Nick said. "If he's lost her trail, he might decide to come back for the laptop. But we're guessing, and we have little to go on except a lot of assumptions."

"True. But I'm convinced Laurie's in trouble. And I'm not sure it's a man who's after her."

I reminded him of how Dr. Phyllis Poole's life had intersected with Laurie's. Laurie had been Cody O'Brien's nurse the night he checked out AMA. She was the last hospital employee to see him before his scheduled surgery the next morning with Dr. Poole. Laurie had also made hot, urgent love to Tobias Fausset in their onstage duets, which led to speculation at the hospital about their private relationship. I described Dr. Poole's obvious infatuation with Fausset.

"You think she'd kill for love?" Nick asked.

"I don't know, but I'll bet she'd play dirty."

"Then you concentrate on identifying Mystery Pat, and I'll follow up on your answering machine tape. Maybe something will turn up there."

We sat a moment in silence until the evocative whistle of a freight train sounded in the distance. A lonesome cry in the night. It triggered a need to connect with Nick, if only for a moment. I reached out and touched his hand where it rested on the steering wheel.

"Thank you for coming tonight. And for helping in spite of your reservations."

He gave my hand a quick squeeze and released it. "Don't thank me. It's not like I have a choice."

He didn't explain his remark and I didn't ask, for fear we would enter into territory we weren't ready to explore. I got out of Nick's car and into mine. He followed me until I reached the exit toward Coyote Creek; then he flashed his headlights and headed off in one direction while I went in another. *Going our separate ways?* I told myself it was only temporary. We'd work things out.

I stopped at the Four Corners Market in Coyote Creek to pick up a few groceries. While I was there I put in a call to Harry from the parking lot and filled him in. He agreed to come by Jack and Amah's and stay the night. He said he'd come up with a reason, and I knew whatever it was, they'd believe him. He'd been a master of the innocent face and the little white lie ever since we were kids. His subterfuge worked on everyone except me.

In my apartment I found a message blinking on the answering machine. Not Laurie, but Amah. I called her back and feigned surprise when she told me Harry's condo had been sprayed for termites and he was spending the night in their guest room.

I put Ivory Joe Hunter on my portable CD player and took it out on the west-facing side of my little deck along with the last half of my peanut butter cookie and a cup of instant decaf. I didn't know much about blues, but the mystery surrounding Laurie Popejoy's leaving TMC and dropping out of the Code Blues combo triggered my interest in the genre. I hoped the music might inspire me somehow.

While Ivory Joe played piano and sang, I searched my memory. Had I met anyone at Timbergate Medical Center named Pat? And what did that scribbled name mean to Laurie? Was it a friend offering Laurie a safe place to hide? Or was it Cody O'Brien's killer?

Footsteps on my stairs and a knock on my door set my heart pumping. I sat still in the dark. Would a killer knock?

"Hey, Sis. Where are you?" *Harry*. He'd walked down the lane from the main house.

"I'm in back on the deck. Come around."

With a bottle of beer in one hand and a sandwich in the other, he strolled around the corner of my little deck and leaned against the rail. "They bought it. The termite thing."

"Of course. They'd believe you if you said you'd been abducted by aliens."

He plopped down into a chair next to me. "So have you figured out who Pat is?"

"Not even close. Any ideas?"

"The only Pat I know is a seriously hot electrician. She moved to Kansas last month."

"I'm sure you'll get over it."

"I already have. Want to talk about *your* love life?"

I answered too quickly. "I don't have one."

He chuckled. "I heard different. According to Amah, you're juggling Nick and James O'Brien. What's that about?"

"Wishful thinking on her part. There's nothing going on with either of them. James is an old family friend whose brother has just died. I can't just turn a deaf ear if he needs someone to talk to. And neither Nick nor I want to move ahead until I'm comfortable with his working relationship with Rella, so just let the two of us work it out."

He gave me a long look. "I know that's your official story, but I'm beginning to think Rella is an excuse."

"What do you mean?"

"You were with at least two other guys before you met Nick. I'm pretty sure they had ex-girlfriends too, but you never went through the kind of BS that's going on with Nick. You always seemed to be in charge, and as I recall, you were the one who did the dumping without shedding a tear."

"I didn't dump anyone. I was younger then, and those relationships ended because they weren't serious."

"So what are you saying? You don't want a serious relationship with Nick?"

I stared down at the floor of the deck, avoiding his penetrating gaze. "I don't know if this will make sense to you—I'm not sure it does to me—but I'm afraid of how I feel about Nick. I didn't realize it until the incident with Rella in Paris. Even though I believe now that nothing happened between them in that hotel, my reaction at the time was a level of shock that seemed to stop the world. I'll spare you the details, but believe me when I say I won't put myself through that again."

"What makes you think you'll need to? Do you really think Nick's going to cheat on you if you get back together?"

"All I know is that Nick is the only man I want to be with, and I'm afraid to be with him. It makes no sense, but somehow Rella has become the face of that fear."

"Whatever you say, Sis. I just hope you're doing the right thing. Nick's a patient guy, but I can't believe he's put up with your indecision this long. He's not going to wait forever."

Harry bit into his sandwich. I sipped my coffee and finished my cookie. A cool breeze sent a shower of oak leaves rattling down across the deck and a shiver across my bare shoulders.

"Time to go in," I said.

"Right, it's getting late." Harry drained the last of his beer and stood up. "I'd better get back to the house. The folks will be going to bed soon."

"Thanks for coming. If you think of—"

"I know. Mystery Pat. I'll let you know if I come up with anything."

I went inside and crawled into bed, avoiding thoughts

of Nick by thinking about Laurie Popejoy's broken door and wondering about the name on her notepad. *Pat?* Too bad we left the laptop behind. We might have found Mystery Pat in Laurie's emails. Then I thought of Cleo. This whole thing had started because of her darling Siggy's iffy prostate. If Nick wouldn't go with me to steal the laptop, I had a hunch Cleo would.

TEN

Quinn didn't beat around the bush. When I got to work Monday morning, he was waiting for me in the library, parked in the chair at Lola's desk.

"Did you and your litigious date enjoy the music last Friday?"

"I knew you'd be upset, but I can explain."

He got up and glanced at his watch. "All right. What the hell you were doing at Margie's with one of the O'Brien clan after I told you they were suing?"

It occurred to me that I should start a swear jar. Quinn's *hells* and *damns* and other profanities would add up pretty fast.

"Okay, here's the thing…" I said. "Before you told me about the lawsuit, I had already decided to invite James to go with me to Margie's. I know the family, and he's a friend of mine, as you recall. It still seemed like a good idea. I thought I could find out why they decided to sue."

"Go on. What did James tell you?"

"Nothing. He swore he didn't know about it. He said he'd look into it and get back to me."

"And you believed him?"

"I had my doubts, but he had already asked about getting a copy of Cody's hospital record before I brought up the suit. Why would he ask me about that if he knew the record had already been subpoenaed?"

Quinn scrubbed a hand against his chin. "If you see him again, be damn sure you come to me with anything he tells you." Another *damn*. Another quarter. If I worked for the man long enough, I could pay off all my loans and buy a new car.

"Pat?" Cleo dropped her spoon beside a steaming bowl of Margie's Chocolate Chili and dabbed at the corners of her mouth with a paper napkin. "That's all you got from your home invasion caper with Nick? The name Pat?"

"It was written on the same notepad as my name and phone number. Do you have any idea who that is?"

"You mean someone at TMC?"

"I don't know, but it seems likely."

Cleo stared at the restaurant's acoustic ceiling. "I can't think of any men, but there are three women. There's a Patty in Dietary, and Pat and Patricia in the business office."

I cut off a bite of my bean burrito and dabbed it in a pink puddle of mixed salsa and sour cream. "Do you know if any of them were Laurie's friends?"

"I doubt it, and I'm afraid if we start asking people if Laurie is hiding out in their attic, they'll think we're nuts. Or worse, they'll spread it around. If it gets back to the wrong person, Laurie will have an even bigger problem."

"I thought of that. I have a plan, but I need your help."

Cleo sighed. "You're going to tell me something I'd rather not hear, aren't you?"

"You want this whole thing resolved before Sig's prostate surgery, don't you?"

"Of course."

"Then here's what we need to do." I told Cleo about the laptop Nick and I left behind at Laurie's little cottage in the alley.

"You left it? Why, for heaven's sake?"

"That was Nick's call."

"So what's your plan?"

"We're going back for it."

"You and Nick?" Cleo said. "How'd you change his mind?"

"Not Nick. You and me."

"No thanks." Cleo drew back. "I'm not cut out for sneaking around in dark alleys."

"Remember, this whole thing was your idea."

"Okay, okay. I'll do it. If Phyllis Poole is a nut case or a kidnapper—or something worse—we have to know before she takes a sharp instrument to Sig's manhood."

"Or anyone else's. I'll pick you up tonight around ten o'clock. If Laurie is home—which I seriously doubt, since her back door is broken—we'll say we stopped by to see how she's doing. If her place is still the way Nick and I left it last night, we'll take the laptop."

Cleo pushed her chili away. "I'll be ready."

"Be sure to wear something comfortable. Dark colors."

"Good idea." Cleo looked down at a piece of paper with scribbling on it. "Now let's get to work on some hospital business that could help us get a handle on Dr. Poole."

"You're talking about the Surgery Department's CME program?"

"Of course. The urologic surgery case review."

"I'm still suspicious about the timing of that particular topic. You engineered it, didn't you?"

Cleo squared her shoulders. "It's a valid and timely topic. That's all you need to know."

"It's scheduled for October thirty-first. That's the night before Sig's surgery. Why don't you ask him to postpone?"

"I already have. It's been put off for a month."

"Too bad we can't postpone the rest of Poole's cases."

Cleo peeked at her phone. "We need to get back. For now, just tell me you're making progress with the review. Did you get all the stats from Rocky in QA?"

"She sent them this morning."

"Has Dr. Beardsley been around? He should be looking at them."

"Dr. Beardsley might as well be hiding out with Laurie Popejoy. I haven't seen his face for at least two weeks. He's dropped everything in my lap."

"Is Dr. Fausset okay with you handling the CME program on your own?"

"He seems to be. Dr. Poole is another story, but so far she's willing to go along with whatever Fausset wants."

"No kidding," Cleo said. "Poole has the mother of all crushes on that dark, delicious hunk...in case you haven't noticed."

"It's hard to miss."

We split the tab and walked across the street to my building. I was about to head into the library when I realized I hadn't told Cleo about Seamus O'Brien's failing health. I gave her the nutshell version of what James told me about the O'Brien patriarch and asked if we could get a look at his medical record.

"Another chart? I don't know. That's really pushing our luck. I have no good excuse to be snooping in any of them."

"Your excuse is protecting Sig's manhood, remember?"

Her shoulders slumped. "Yeah, and losing my job in the process. What's Seamus O'Brien got to do with anything?"

"I'm not sure, but I want to know if he's terminal."

Cleo blinked. "Whoa. You think he's dying?"

"I think we need to know. If he is, there's going to be a fortune up for grabs."

"What's the connection to Poole? Do you think Seamus is one of her patients, too?"

"That's something else we need to know."

Cleo headed for her office in the main tower. A couple of hours later I was scrutinizing statistics for the CME program on urologic surgery deaths and complications when Jared Quinn dropped by again.

"Aimee. How's it going?" His mood had improved since our morning meeting.

"It's going okay. What brings you here again?"

"I want to make sure you remembered to include Cody O'Brien's medical record in the urologic surgery review."

"It's been earmarked, but it will only be reviewed for indications for his planned urologic surgery, not for the trauma death in ER."

"That's right," Quinn said. "His death in the ER is a separate issue. It'll be reviewed later by the Emergency Department once the coroner's report is ready."

I understood Quinn's reasoning. In the case of a lawsuit, it would be good to be able to testify that Cody's abrupt departure from the hospital the night before an acutely needed surgery had been addressed in a timely fashion and proper actions taken by the hospital staff. Quinn would be on the stand if that came to pass.

Quinn sat in the guest chair next to my desk. "Your boyfriend called me this morning. Not long after our little talk."

"Nick? Why would he—"

Quinn chuckled. "No, sorry. Bad joke. You have too many boyfriends. I was talking about James O'Brien. Your date at Margie's last Friday."

"Oh, James. He's not—"

"Not the flavor of the week?"

"Never mind. Did you ask James about the lawsuit?"

"No, but he brought it up, basically said the same thing he told you. Looks like your instincts were correct. He's trying to convince his family to drop it. No final decision so far."

"Were you able to tell him what he wanted to know about Cody?"

"Hardly," Quinn said. "He wants to know if his brother's death was accidental or foul play. I told him I spoke to the coroner yesterday, and so far there's nothing to warrant a homicide investigation, but he hasn't ruled on the manner of death. I told your friend I'd keep him informed."

I'd seen enough death certificates in my training to know that the cause of death section involved a chain of events leading to an immediate cause of death like heart failure. I also knew there was a separate section for manner of death. That included half a dozen options, but the two I was most curious about were *Homicide* and *Accident*. Which one would be checked when Cody's certificate was complete? I hoped the coroner wouldn't settle for *Could not be determined*.

"I thought the first responders were convinced he was kicked by Game Boy." I wasn't ready to tell him about Laurie's mysterious calls until I knew more about why she'd called me.

"Game Boy?" Quinn looked puzzled.

"Game Boy is his horse. If Cody was kicked in the head, is there any doubt it was accidental?"

"Apparently not, but the coroner is taking his time with this one because Cody was a public figure, and he was also Seamus O'Brien's son. Seamus has a certain standing in the community. The coroner doesn't want to make a hasty decision that will come back to bite him."

"Then there is no active investigation by law enforcement?"

"Not so far. There doesn't appear to be a reason, but the coroner's ruling could change that."

"Have you seen Cody's chart?"

"I dropped by the Health Information office to have a look." I envied him. As TMC's administrator, he had greater access to patient records than the administrative department heads.

"Were there any photos of Cody's wound in the chart?"

"I didn't see any," Quinn said, "but he died so soon after arriving that he wasn't treated for the head trauma. The EMTs' paperwork was all in there. I saw EKG tracings, notes about IV lines…all their standard stuff. Most of the documentation was from O'Brien's pre-surgery admission the day before. ER documented that his body was moved to our holding morgue to await transfer to the coroner."

"What did you think about indications for surgery? Did Poole's notes satisfy you?"

"They seemed appropriate, but I'm not a doctor. I want that record reviewed by every urologist on our medical staff."

"Every urologist except Dr. Poole, of course."

"Of course," Quinn said. "Medical staff members don't review their own patient care."

"Right. I'm familiar with the protocols for chart review."

"Sorry, I keep forgetting you're no longer a greenhorn. After the death certificate is complete, we'll see that O'Brien's case is reviewed by the Emergency Department." Quinn stood and gazed around the room.

"You have your regular library chores, plus building the forensic collection, and now this CME program. That's a lot on your plate. Are you sure you can handle it without Beardsley around?"

"So far, so good," I said, "as long as I can count on Lola for the routine stuff."

"All right, then." Quinn tapped his fingers on the edge of my desk. "Poole's a scrupulous surgeon; however, she sometimes agrees to take on extraordinarily complicated cases. I'm curious to know if her peers agreed with her planned approach in this one."

So was I, but I wasn't about to tell Quinn about Cleo's theory that Poole wasn't man's best friend when she had a scalpel in her hand.

After Quinn left, my focus shifted back to my conversation with Cleo about Seamus O'Brien. If the patriarch was terminal, I could imagine Echo and Keely competing for the lion's share of his estate. James said Seamus was in a hurry to change his will right after Cody died. I wondered when Seamus had first contacted his lawyer. Was it before or after Cody's death? If he started the process while Cody was still alive, maybe he had been contemplating divorcing Echo.

Too many variables leapt to mind. It was pointless to pursue them until I knew more. I could ask James who his father's lawyer was, but I wasn't ready to tip my hand to James just yet. I forced my mind back to the work I was being paid to do.

Cleo called half an hour later. "I have news."

"I'll be right over."

Five minutes later, in mild respiratory distress, I walked into the Medical Affairs Office in the main tower.

"Mother of God," Cleo said. "I just put the phone down. How did you do that?"

"Ran," I said. "What's your news? I have to get back."

She handed me a piece of note paper. "What's this?" I scanned the page and saw three words: *Lyme, babesiosis* and *splenectomy.*

"I just finished writing up an Infection Control Committee report to be forwarded to the Centers for Disease Control in Atlanta. They follow diseases caused by the Lyme tick, and Seamus O'Brien was one of the patients on the list."

"What does this mean?"

"See the columns of questions with boxes to be checked? I copied the items that were checked with a *yes* for Seamus O'Brien. I thought you'd want to do some research, see if you can get some idea how serious his case is."

"I'll see what I can find out," I said. "I think we're dealing with more than just Sig and Dr. Poole. Something's going on with the O'Briens. DeeDee's dead, Cody's dead, and if we don't figure out what's going on, someone else might die."

Cleo pointed at the notes she'd given me. "I'm going out on a limb giving you even that much. I just wanted to make sure Siggy will be safe going under Poole's knife. I didn't sign up to save the world."

"But you did agree to go to Laurie Popejoy's house with me tonight. Don't forget I'm picking you up at quarter to ten."

"I know. Dark clothes. I'll be ready." Cleo's phone rang. While she reached for it I let myself out and returned to the library. I was familiar with Lyme disease, but I had never heard of babesiosis, and I had no idea why splenectomy was mentioned. Both were listed on the CDC form, so I assumed they were important. Before I could start a MedLine search, my phone rang.

Although the temptation to ignore it was strong, conscience won out and I picked up.

"Hey, Lady. I've got something you want."

It dawned on me Nick was talking about the answering machine tape. *Laurie's messages.*

"When can I have it?"

"Dinner tonight. Meet me at Casa Loco."

"Okay. I'll be there at five thirty."

Dinner with Nick. He worried about my taking risks, but he was no more able to resist an adventure than I was. That quality came in handy when I needed an accomplice. I started the MedLine search for babesiosis. I had promised to give James the names of a couple of specialists for his father to contact, but before I could do that I wanted to learn as much as possible about Seamus O'Brien's illness. Half an hour later I suspected Seamus knew more about his prognosis than he was willing to admit to his offspring.

The patriarch's illness was dire, and it further complicated the dynamic of the O'Brien family. No wonder he was concerned about his will. James and Keely were his only remaining offspring. What would they inherit if he died? What about his young wife? Surely she would be counting on a big chunk of the estate. Did any of his heirs know how ill he really was? If so, did that knowledge play a part in Cody's death?

ELEVEN

I SPOTTED NICK waiting in the foyer at Casa Loco. The hostess took us to a low-lit booth in the back.

"Dinner at five thirty?" Nick said. "Why so early?"

"I have to be home to do chores before dark, and Jack and Amah might need help with packing. Going to Africa for three weeks means more than throwing some socks in an overnight bag." I quickly changed the subject. "So what did you get from the tapes? Anything we can use?"

"I think so. That second message Laurie left on your machine has some background noise that might help us."

"Really? What is it?" My body tensed with curiosity.

"Remember the last time we stopped for lunch at Uncle Fudd's Tavern on our way to the Tamarack trailhead? There was a cuckoo clock on the dining room wall."

"The broken one that sounded like it was being strangled every time it marked the hour?"

"That's the one. I'm pretty sure that's what was in the background of Laurie's second message to you."

"She was calling from Uncle Fudd's? But why?"

"I did some checking with a buddy who works at Hikers' World. He knows Laurie. Apparently, she's hiked into the Thousand Lakes Wilderness a few times."

"You think she's hiding out up there?"

"It makes sense," Nick said. "If the guy who's after

her doesn't know she's a backpacker, he'd never think to look for her there. And there's no cell service in the wilderness, so unless she has a satellite phone, that would explain why she didn't call you again."

"She left that second message on my machine five days ago. She's endured some cold nights if that's where she's gone."

"Maybe we should find out."

"You mean go search for her?"

"Why not? We'd know where to look." Nick glanced at his watch. "We could head up there as soon as I get back from flying your grandparents to SFO tomorrow."

"I can't. I have to work."

"Take a couple of days off. Come down with something contagious. Strep throat would be good."

"I don't know—"

"Hey, this woman reached out to you. Someone broke into her home, and now she's disappeared. It's worth a white lie to find out if she's still alive."

"You're right. I'll talk to Quinn. It's just…there's so much going on at work."

"Ask for two days. We should take a couple of Jack's llamas. I'll clear it with him. We'll need his pickup and trailer."

"Why llamas? We'd cover ground faster without them."

"We might need more emergency supplies than we can carry on our backs." Nick reached out and touched my arm. "And we might as well be prepared if—"

"You don't have to say it." I envisioned Laurie's lifeless body lying in the duff of a wilderness campsite. Jack's llamas wouldn't tolerate a live rider, but they would carry dead weight. *Laurie's dead weight.* I was more determined than ever to go back for her laptop.

That night the door of Cleo's condo opened before I rang the bell.

"How do I look?"

She got most of the outfit right with a black turtle-neck and dark skinny jeans, but her footwear was all wrong.

I pointed at her black boots with three-inch heels. "You need to take off those ankle busters and put on something you can run in."

"Wait, you didn't say anything about running."

"There probably won't be running, but we'll be walking in a dark alley. You need sensible shoes."

Cleo shuddered. "Never tell anyone I own sensible shoes."

She changed into a pair of black sneakers and grabbed a navy pullover sweatshirt while I stood at the door choking back second thoughts about my choice of partners in crime.

While I drove, I told Cleo about the sounds Nick heard on Laurie's message, and our plan to look for her in the wilderness.

"You're going to take time off *now*?"

"Unless we find her at home tonight, or something that disproves Nick's theory."

"What are you going to do about the library?"

"I'll be there tomorrow morning, and Lola can keep the library open for minimal services until noon on Wednesday. I'll be back to work on Thursday."

"You think Quinn will give you time off when Beardsley's out and you have so much to do?"

"He'll have to," I said in a forced whisper, "I have strep throat."

Cleo inched away from me toward the passenger door. "Cripes, don't breathe on me."

"Relax, I won't be contagious until tomorrow."

We reached Laurie's neighborhood at ten thirty. I parked in the same spot on the street that Nick had used.

"Here, don't turn this on." I handed Cleo a flashlight. "It's for backup, just in case."

"In case what?" Cleo said.

"In case… I don't know. You don't have to come. You can wait in the car."

"No way. You're not leaving me here alone."

We crept through the alley and I led her around to the back door Nick and I had used the night before. It stood open at the same angle, sad proof that Laurie had not returned. I trained my light on the kitchen floor, motioned for Cleo to follow me, and started a room check. The fridge still stank of old milk. The living room was still tidy, and the bathroom window to the alley was still open.

Only the pile of mail near the front door was different. Several new envelopes had dropped through the mail slot. I played my light on the one on top. The return address was a local pathology laboratory used by most of the doctors in town.

Cleo followed my light. "Timbergate Labs," she whispered. "Probably a pay envelope. Laurie moonlights there."

"How do you know that?"

"I heard it somewhere. I hear things all the time."

"Do you know how long she's worked there?"

"No idea, but she's a certified lab tech in addition to being an RN. Lots of job security there."

"Job security isn't helping her right now."

"True. So where's the laptop we came for?"

I led Cleo to Laurie's bedroom. "This is where Nick and I left it." I trained my light on the desk across from Laurie's bed.

"Well, where is it?" Cleo said.

"What the…it was right there." I pointed to an empty spot on the desk.

"You're sure? 'Cause this is starting to freak me out."

"I'm sure," I whispered to Cleo. "Positive."

"Then someone else has been here."

"Looks that way. Let's leave. Now."

She didn't needed prompting. I caught up with her standing outside my car, sucking on an inhaler.

"Since when do you use one of those?"

"It's my mother's. I forgot to drop it off at her senior residence after work today." Cleo took another hit.

"If you don't stop nursing that thing, you're going to have to get her another one."

"Maybe I will. This stuff works. I'm feeling better already."

I grabbed the inhaler and tossed it in the backseat. "No more. You don't know what's in that thing, and I need you with a clear head right now. We have to brainstorm." I pulled away from the curb and headed back across town.

"Okay," Cleo said. "You start."

"The laptop's gone. That means someone else knew about it and came back for it."

"Unless she came back for it herself."

"She fled for her life, so I doubt it. I'm betting it's the guy who's after her."

"Why did he wait so long to come back for it?" Cleo shivered and glanced toward the inhaler in the backseat.

"It must have taken a while to realize it could help him find her. Maybe he's your classic dumb thug."

"What makes you so sure it's a guy?"

"You're thinking Dr. Poole, aren't you?"

"She's the last person I'd want to meet up with in that alley. Or maybe she's the brains, and she sent the dumb thug back for the laptop." I couldn't argue with that.

We reached Cleo's condo around eleven o'clock. She promised to stay off her mother's drugs, so I let her have the inhaler. We sat on her sofa eating diet vanilla ice cream topped with diet chocolate syrup. No wonder she'd kept her figure.

Cleo set her bowl aside on her glass coffee table. "We struck out with the laptop. Now what?"

"That depends on what Nick and I find in the wilderness."

"What about Seamus O'Brien? Did you come up with anything useful based on that CDC report?"

"Maybe. It looks like he's suffering from two tick-borne diseases. Lyme is bad enough untreated, but he got a double-whammy. He also has babesiosis. And his spleen was removed sometime in the past, he's a very sick man with a poor prognosis."

"I've heard of Lyme, of course, but I've never heard of bab-whatsis."

"It's less common and more lethal, especially in combination with Lyme."

"I thought an early course of antibiotics took care of those things."

"According to what I read, healthy people with the two diseases can recover, but it can be fatal for a patient without a spleen."

Cleo hugged herself and shuddered. "Ticks are disgusting, but I didn't realize they could kill."

"The deer tick is the nasty piece of work. The problem is that they're so small they can attach and burrow under the skin without being noticed. I contracted Lyme disease when I was in library school in Connecticut. Had a big red bull's-eye rash on my right hip and so much joint pain I felt like I was a hundred years old."

"Are you cured?"

"Definitely. I got lucky, in a way. New Haven isn't far from the town of Lyme, where the disease originated. Connecticut doctors are quick to diagnose it. Thirty bucks worth of antibiotics killed off those nasty little spirochetes before they did any permanent damage."

"No lingering aftereffects?"

"Only a soft spot for deer hunters."

I followed her into the kitchen, where she rinsed our bowls and put them in her dishwasher.

"Any chance Seamus will get well?" she said.

"There's a chance, but the odds aren't good. The question is how long he'll linger before his health gives out altogether." I told her about his will and the three potential heirs: Echo, Keely, and James.

"Sounds like the vultures are circling."

"I'm afraid so," I said, "and it's too bad. Seamus deserves better."

I drove home assessing what we'd learned that evening. Laurie's missing laptop was significant, but it didn't help narrow the suspects. Her moonlighting at a medical laboratory seemed like an incidental bit of information, but I filed it for future consideration.

When I saw Nick's car parked at the main house, I recalled that he had insisted on spending the night there. The lights were still burning in the living room, so I knocked on the door. Amah opened it and pulled me into a big hug.

"Oh, my sweet girl, I'm going to miss you while we're gone. Are you sure you don't mind looking after things again?" This was their second trip since I'd taken up residence in their barn.

"Of course not."

I caught a glimpse of Jack and Nick over Amah's shoulder. They sat at the kitchen table poring over the safari brochures.

"I hear you're taking time off to go hiking with Nick." Amah's hazel eyes had that romantic, starlit glow that only Nick's presence could evoke. Hope never died in her heart for our eventual wedded bliss. She took my arm and steered me into the kitchen.

"Hi," Nick said. "Jack thinks we should take Captain and Smoke."

I wondered what excuse he'd come up with for needing two llamas on a two-day hike that could have been done with simple backpacks.

"Sounds good," I said, raising an inquisitive eyebrow at Nick.

"Don't forget to save us a slab of liver," Jack said. "And get me some good photos."

Liver? Photos? The light dawned. They thought Nick and I were going deer hunting and might need llamas to carry our kill down off the mountain. I nodded at Nick. *Okay, I'm up to speed.*

I gave my grandparents extra hugs and good wishes for their trip, and left Jack and Nick to continue their man talk about trailers, spare tires, electrical hookups, and what-not. As I drove down the lane to the bunkhouse, I was already missing my adventuresome grandmother and her crusty, endearing husband. In the morning they would be flying with Nick toward the San Francisco airport to catch their commercial flight to Africa.

I TELEPHONED QUINN'S office as soon as I got to work Tuesday morning. My scratchy, nearly incomprehensible speech over the phone seemed to convince him that I should be at home instead of spreading additional microorganisms around an already germ-infested hospital. I told Lola about my sick leave and explained that she should close the library when she left at noon. Any questions should be referred to Cleo.

"That throat thing of yours seems to come and go," Lola said. "One minute you're talking fine and the next you're all raspy."

Oops. "I know," I whispered, "but I think it's getting worse. I should probably stop talking."

"Too bad. I was going to ask you if you've seen the Irish hottie lately."

I shook my head and pointed at my throat with a shrug. Lola nodded and headed off to patrol the shelves for misplaced books and journals.

Irish hottie. She meant James O'Brien, which reminded me I hadn't heard from him since he showed up at the ranch on Saturday morning. I was conflicted about telling him what I'd learned about Seamus's illness and poor prognosis. James had a right to know, but was it my place to tell? I was conflicted, and I'd be on shaky legal ground revealing the content of a confidential hospital report.

I had an even more compelling reason to wait. I had

to keep an open mind about James. On the plus side, I saw no evidence he took part in the squabbling the rest of the O'Briens indulged in, but I was concerned about his financial situation. How badly did he need his father's fortune?

James's little sister Keely and his young stepmother Echo both lived extravagant lifestyles that depended on Seamus footing the bills. Seamus wanted to make changes in his will. Maybe James knew more about those potential changes than he'd admitted to me. Any further communication with James would have to wait until Nick and I returned from the wilderness. If we found Laurie Popejoy, or identified the mysterious Pat, that might change everything.

TWELVE

NICK HAD THE trailer hooked up and both llamas haltered before I reached home at noon. I met him at the barn where he was pulling pack saddles and panniers out of the tack room. I asked about the flight to San Francisco.

"It was great." Nick pulled out the last pannier and locked the tack room door. "They were so excited they could have flown to San Francisco without a plane."

"Do they suspect anything?"

"I doubt it. Jack talked about hunting the whole time, and your Amah was absorbed in her Kalahari Desert travel brochures."

"Good. Amah will take a million pictures. Did you happen to check the weather forecast for the Thousand Lakes Wilderness?"

"Clear for three days. Highs in the fifties, lows in the thirties."

I helped Nick load the saddles and panniers in the back of Jack's truck. "Did you bring your dog? Her nose might come in handy."

"No. I'd have to keep her on a leash, and I don't want both hands full."

"We could rig the llamas in tandem and I could lead them both."

"Not necessary. Ginger needs more training before she'll be any good at search and rescue. She's staying with Harry while we're gone."

When the tack was loaded, I ran upstairs to fill my backpack with extra socks and a pair of thermal long johns. I filled my water bladder and stuffed it into the backpack along with a few protein bars and some trail mix. After I locked my apartment, I joined Nick in the llama pen. He was brushing Captain, so I worked on Smoke. We didn't want any burrs under their saddle blankets.

Nick finished first and offered Captain a handful of cob. "Harry said he's taking care of the place while you're gone. Is he sleeping here, too?"

"That's what he said. He'll spend nights in the main house until I get back. He noticed a few things that needed fixing. Said something about a plumbing problem."

"Sounds like him," Nick said. "He'd probably rewire the house and put on a second story if we were gone for more than two days."

We loaded up and headed east toward the Cascade Range, reaching the Tamarack trailhead at three o'clock. That gave us plenty of daylight to reach Barrett, the closest lake and a hike of less than two hours. Ours was the only vehicle in the trailhead parking area, but there were two other trailheads that accessed the same lakes. Laurie could have chosen one of those.

We each saddled a llama, and then teamed up to attach the panniers to the saddles.

"Do we need to weigh them?" A balanced load was important to make the llamas comfortable on the trail.

"No, Jack and I packed and weighed them last night. They're each carrying about forty pounds. They're light, but that's because—"

"I know." Laurie's body draped over a llama made for a gruesome mental picture.

"Sorry," Nick said. "Which one do you want to lead?"

"Doesn't matter. They're pros. They'll walk for anyone."
He took Captain's lead rope. "You want to go first?"

"No, you're a better tracker. I might miss something."

"Don't count on seeing any sign that your friend used this trail," Nick said. "We don't know what kind of boots she was wearing—if she's even wearing boots. Hell, we don't even know if she's out here."

"But you heard Uncle Fudd's cuckoo clock. That's the best lead we have now that...."

I caught myself just in time. I'd been about to say now that we knew her laptop was missing. I couldn't share that bit of information with Nick unless I told him Cleo and I had gone back to Laurie's house.

"Now that what?" Nick said.

"Huh?" I played dumb, but he didn't buy it.

"You didn't finish your sentence. Now that what?"

"Oh, I just meant now that she's stopped calling me."

"Hmm." Nick gave me a skeptical look, but he let it drop.

We followed the trail as it wound up the mountain, watching the ground for boot prints—any prints—and the trees overhead for mountain lions. Soon I was inhaling dust stirred up on the dry trail by Captain's hooves. I stopped to dampen a bandana and tie it across my mouth and nose. My breath warmed the cloth, and the scent of fabric softener tickled my nose. Warm afternoon sunshine slanted through the canopy of Jeffrey and lodgepole pines, and a fickle breeze rustled the leaves of whiteleaf manzanita. The only sign of wildlife was the scattered remains of pine cones efficiently stripped of their nut meats by squirrels preparing for the coming winter.

Forty-five minutes in, both llamas stopped in their

tracks and faced right, ears erect and nostrils quivering. I followed their gaze. Thirty feet off the trail a fat, cinnamon-colored bear was digging grubs from a fallen tree trunk. The bruin gouged the soft wood with a massive paw sporting curved yellow claws at least three inches long.

The trunk of a large conifer blocked Nick's view of the bear. Guessing the usual reason for a llama to stop on the trail, he called over his shoulder, "Why'd we stop? Is someone peeing?"

"Bear," I whispered.

"What? Speak up, I can't hear you."

I pulled the bandana away from my mouth. "Bear at three o'clock," I said, trying for a louder whisper. The llamas were still focused on the shaggy beast. I half expected them to bolt.

"What?" This time he spoke loud enough to alert the bear. It glanced our way for a moment, went back to digging at the trunk, and then did a double take.

This time I didn't whisper. "Bear at three o'clock," I yelled.

Nick stepped around the obstructing tree. "Ah, hell. Here, hold this." He handed me Captain's lead rope and started waving his arms and yelling, "Hey there! Hey, scat!"

The bear stared at Nick for a fraction of a second then turned tail and lumbered off into the woods, its fur catching the sunlight and rippling in shades of copper and gold as it ran.

"Wow," I said. "The color in its coat is spectacular. What kind of bear is it?"

"Black bear, but with a cinnamon coat."

"Amazing, I've always wanted to see a bear in the wild."

"Be careful what you wish for. That was probably a young female without cubs. They're not always that people-shy."

My thoughts turned immediately to Laurie. Even if she was an experienced hiker, she'd fled her home at a moment's notice. Was she equipped to survive alone in the wilderness for almost a week?

We reached Barrett Lake without spotting any fresh footprints on the trail and found all three campsites empty. I tethered the llamas where they could graze on shoots of green grass near the shore. Nick started picking through ashes in one of the fire rings.

"See anything?"

"Just a beer can and some tangled fishing line."

The other fire rings were scattered and held no remnants of recent use. We circled the perimeter of the lake, taking our time along a shore left muddy by the receding water level. We identified bear scat, deer and mountain lion tracks, and traces of boot prints in a variety of sizes and patterns. If any were Laurie's, we had no way of knowing.

"We might as well head up to Durbin," Nick said. "It's only a thirty minute hike." It was the closest and smallest of the other lakes we planned to search.

"Are you sure? There's enough light left to get up there and look around, but it'll be too dark to move on to the others."

"No problem. Unless we find her there, we'll come back here and camp for the night. We'll wind back down to Eiler in the morning."

"What about Hufford and McGee? Aren't we going up there?"

"Not unless we have to. If she's out here, I hope she didn't go that high."

"The cold nights?"

"Right. If she isn't prepared for it...." He didn't finish his thought, but I knew what he meant. Hypothermia.

We patrolled the shore at Durbin but spotted nothing to indicate Laurie had been at the lake, so we dropped back down to Barrett to spend the night. We worked as a team to unload the llamas, setting the panniers and pack saddles aside. I staked the boys out to graze while Nick put our fishing rods together. After we pitched Nick's two-man tent, I arranged the air mattresses and sleeping bags while he collected firewood. The routine had been established during our hikes the past summer, and we fell into it without comment. We fished until we caught four pan-sized rainbows.

The sun dropped behind McGee peak to our west, bringing early twilight as we finished our trout and trail mix dinner. We brought the llamas in close, let them have a good roll in the duff, and tied them to trees near our tent. Good watchdogs in case four-legged critters decided to raid our supplies during the night.

After KP we sat on a fallen log to drink hot cocoa and watch the embers of our fire.

After a few minutes, Nick said, "Well?"

"Well, what?"

"What'll we do until it's time to go to sleep."

"Let's enjoy the peace and quiet."

He rubbed his knuckle across the back of my hand. "Remember what we used to do?" His touch sparked vivid memories, causing tendrils of sensation to flood through my body. I stayed quiet, not trusting myself to reply. A screech owl suddenly trilled out in the darkness, breaking the mood. I got up and dropped another piece of wood on the fire. "Things were different between us then."

"Then let's use the time to try and make some sense of your O'Brien puzzle."

"Good idea, but every time I try to sort through the pieces, it seems more complicated."

Nick drained the last of his cocoa. "Then let's try to simplify it. Start at the beginning. Just the facts."

"Facts. Cody O'Brien was found dead in his horse trailer with a head wound assumed to be the result of a kick from his incredibly expensive horse."

"Yet your friend Laurie said it wasn't the horse. She couldn't know that unless she witnessed what really happened or someone told her about it."

"You're right. I've been thinking she witnessed Cody's murder, but maybe she found out about it some other way. In any case, she seems sure it wasn't Game Boy."

"Which leaves foul play."

"And that's why we're here, on what is probably a wild goose chase, because you heard a cuckoo clock on my answering machine tape."

Nick pulled a small notebook and pencil from his backpack and turned on his headlamp. "You said Seamus wants to change his will now that Cody's gone, right?"

"That's what I assumed, but it was James who wondered if Seamus was planning to change the will while Cody was still alive. That would put a different spin on it."

"Hmm, how many O'Briens are there in that clan?"

"Counting the dead ones?"

"Might as well start with those."

"There's Cody, the most recently deceased, and his wife, DeeDee Dakota, who died about two and a half years ago after a trick riding accident. She was kicked in the head by her horse."

"Are you serious?"

"I'm afraid so. I'll fill you in on that later. Let's get back to the list."

Nick nodded. "Go on. Are there more deceased O'Briens?"

"There's Cody's mother."

"What happened to her? Not a horse, I hope."

"No. An overdose, a year after Seamus divorced her and married Keely's mother."

"Any others?"

"Those are all that I know about."

Nick stirred the embers and added another piece of wood. "Now let's make a list of surviving family members. Start with the oldest and we'll work our way down."

"The first wife is still alive. She lives back east."

"She's the mother of your new admirer?"

"Cut it out. James is just an old friend. But you're right. His mother's been remarried and out of the picture for decades. She must be in her late sixties by now."

"I'll put her down as unlikely. Who's next?"

"James, I guess."

We were interrupted when Captain, the older and more experienced llama, got to his feet from his kushed position and hummed a soft *mrrrr* that meant something had caught his attention. I walked over to where he stood and trained my flashlight beam into the dark forest. The light reflected back from a pair of eyes that

I hoped belonged to a deer. Nick came up behind me and trained a stronger beam in the same direction. We both watched as a small doe turned on dainty hooves and slipped into the darkness.

"Let's get back to counting O'Briens." Nick glanced at his notes. "We were just getting to your old friend James."

"He's another unlikely. He wasn't around when Cody died."

"That doesn't necessarily rule him out. He could have a partner in crime."

"I suppose it's possible," I prodded the fire, producing a gentle flame. "He went through an expensive divorce and he may be hoping to inherit something when Seamus dies, but I can't believe he would kill his brother. Cody called him from the hospital. He trusted James, had something he wanted to tell him."

"But James doesn't know what that was?"

"No. He knows his father wants to change his will, but he doesn't know why."

"Why doesn't James just ask his father?"

"I don't know, Nick. Maybe he will. Maybe he already has."

"Does James know who his father's lawyers are? Or whether Seamus has assigned anyone as his Power of Attorney?"

"That never came up, and I'm not sure I'd feel comfortable asking James."

"No, don't. If James volunteers that information, fine, but someone has already killed once, and you can't afford to make yourself a target." Flames from the fire cast meager light on Nick's grim expression. "For now, let's get back to this list. How many more O'Briens are there?"

"We're almost finished. There's Seamus's present wife, Echo, and Keely, his youngest child."

"What do you know about them?"

"From what I saw the other day at the market, Keely hates Echo and the feeling is mutual."

"Any idea why?"

"They're both used to being pampered by Seamus. I'd say jealousy is a big part of it."

"Did we miss anyone?" Nick flipped to a new page in his notebook.

"No. But there is another person close to Seamus. He could become family one of these days."

"Who's that?"

"Keely's boyfriend, Tucker Potkotter."

"Potkotter? Isn't he a farrier?"

"He was. I think he tried working as a hunting guide for a while, too. Maybe still shoes a few horses, but he's employed by Seamus now. Learning taxidermy from the master."

Nick added Tucker's name to his list. "That takes care of the O'Briens, but it isn't getting us any closer to finding your friend Laurie. Or to knowing how she's involved in Cody's death. What else can you tell me about her?"

"She was on duty the night Cody left the hospital. The next morning, on the same day he died in the Timbergate ER, she called in and resigned from her job at TMC. Now she's disappeared."

"But she called you."

"She called me, then she called Cleo asking for me."

"Then she called you again and left the Game Boy message?"

"Yes. And I think there's some connection to the hospital in all of this."

"Care to speculate?"

"Cody's urologist is a woman, and she has a thing for another doctor on the staff, someone Laurie may have been involved with."

"This is starting to sound like a soap opera. If Cody O'Brien wasn't part of this love triangle, what does it have to do with his death?"

"I wish I knew. It's just that Cody was admitted with a serious injury to his testicle, and his surgery was scheduled for very early the next morning. Laurie was his nurse that night, and by morning, Cody was dead and Laurie was gone."

"And you think this woman doctor was so ticked off about the aborted surgery that she decided to murder both of them?" I heard the skepticism in his voice.

"I know it sounds crazy, but Dr. Poole is an unusual woman. Not necessarily in a good way. She's actually pretty scary."

"Is she also pretty?"

I recalled seeing her come to life on the bandstand at Margie's. "She can be." I told Nick about Dr. Poole taking Laurie's place in Code Blues and her obvious crush on Tobias Fausset.

"But she isn't dating this Fausset exclusively?"

"I don't think so. But I think she'd like to be."

"Why don't you introduce me?"

"That's not funny."

"I'm serious." Nick prodded the campfire's dying embers. "If we don't find Laurie up here, it might be a good idea for me to get to know the infamous Dr. Poole."

I had to admit that he was probably right.

THIRTEEN

WE BROKE CAMP at first light, working with clumsy fingers stiff from the cold. Breakfast was a quick meal of high-protein trail bars washed down with instant coffee. I packed the tent and sleeping bags while Nick saddled the animals.

He poured our leftover coffee water on the charred remains of our campfire and turned the ashes with a folding camp shovel. We both knew a live ember could smolder unnoticed in the duff for more than a week, then erupt into an inferno.

I used a small rake to scatter the llamas' droppings into the underbrush, then naturalized our campsite by spreading pine needles and twigs where the llamas had raked it with their sharp toenails. Nick stood in the damp fire pit checking for any hint of warmth coming through the soles of his boots.

"Satisfied?" I said.

"It's good." He untied Captain's lead rope. "Let's scout Eiler next. If we don't see anything, we'll try the higher lakes."

I shrugged into my backpack. "Let's go. I'm freezing. If Laurie's hiding up here, she's got to be miserable." The trek generated some welcome body heat. We hiked without talking, our silence broken only by twigs underfoot or the faint hum of a commercial airliner far over our heads.

Lake Eiler was bathed in full light and appeared deserted when we arrived. It was the last of the three lower lakes on our list, and four times as large as the others. We tied the llamas to sun-bleached logs in a grassy clearing. Heads down, they ripped into the tender green shoots.

We shed our backpacks and inspected the two closest campsites. In one, the rocks from the fire ring were scattered, and what traces of ash remained were overlaid with forest debris. Nothing suggested the site had been used recently. I walked over to where Nick squatted on his haunches near the site of another fire ring.

"Anything?"

"Someone's been here recently," he said. "These ashes aren't very old."

"Can you tell how recent?"

"I'd guess within a few days, but don't get your hopes up. It could have been anyone."

I looked around. "What about these boot prints? They look pretty fresh."

"They are, but anyone could have made them."

"They're not very big." I placed my foot next to one of the prints. "Here, put your boot down on the other side." He did. It was obvious the boot print was closer to my size than his.

"Could be a woman," Nick said. "Or a kid. Or a guy with dainty feet."

"How many other prints do you see as fresh as these?"

Nick gave me a quick look—the one he uses when I have a good idea and he hasn't thought of it first.

After scouring the camp site, we agreed there was only one set of fairly fresh prints—woman-sized boots with a distinctive heel tread. Three slash lines divided the heel into four segments.

Searching the east side of the lake, we found only animal tracks. Most were made by deer, but there was one bear print, confirmed by a rank-smelling pile of scat in the grass a few feet from the shore.

"I hope she didn't cross paths with a bear," I said.

"I doubt it. Bears are generally shy. And you're still assuming these are your friend's prints."

"They might be, and they're all we have right now. Let's keep going."

"Okay. I just don't want to see you disappointed."

"I know. Laurie isn't a close friend, but for some reason, she called me when she was in trouble. I feel responsible for her."

"You have no idea why she chose you to call?"

"Not really. We've eaten lunch together a few times in the cafeteria."

"Did she ever confide in you about anything? Her job? Her love life?"

"No, we never talked about anything personal."

"There must be some reason. Does she know you're a black belt?"

"You know, that did come up. She wanted to start classes."

"Does she know you can shoot?"

"Now that you mention it, she does. We talked once about women and self-defense. Do you think that's why she called me when she needed help?"

"That, among other things." He laughed.

I frowned at him. "What's funny?"

"You don't know, do you?" He reached an arm around my shoulders. "You're a five-foot-four-inch little girl on the outside, but on the inside, I swear you're an 800-pound gorilla."

"Thanks a lot. I thought you were going to say something about my brains."

"Hey, you don't need anyone to remind you that you're smart."

"I wish I felt smarter right now. The more I try to make sense of this whole thing, the more confused I feel."

"Then let's stop talking and start walking."

When we rounded the south end and started back up the west side, the trail gave out, obscured by foot-high shore grass and dark gray lava rock. Halfway back to our starting point, we came to a grove of aspens with golden leaves shimmering and chattering in the breeze. A makeshift lean-to constructed of bleached, long-dead tree limbs sat at the base of the aspens' slender white trunks. Near it I spotted a bit of wet ash.

"Nick, look." I pointed at the wet dirt. One partial print matched the prints we'd been following.

"I see it." He dropped to a knee. "You're right. It's a match."

I reached down and picked up a charred scrap. "Look at this. It's a bit of burned paper. I can make out four numbers and they look familiar."

Nick took the paper from my fingers and held it up, turning it in the light.

"I think it's a matchbook. Maybe the numbers are part of a phone number or an address."

"That's it," I said. "The numbers are Margie's street address."

"Who's Margie?"

"Margie's Bean Pot. Across the street from the hospital. Code Blues performs there."

"Okay, slow down," Nick said. "You're going to have to translate for me."

"Laurie played piano and sang in the hospital's blues combo. I thought I told you."

"You did, but I didn't know they were called Code Blues. You think this matchbook proves Laurie was at this campsite?"

"It can't be a coincidence. She was here. We just missed her."

"Hold it." Nick's eyes narrowed. He pointed to a spot at the edge of the lean-to.

"I see it." Another fresh print. But larger than Laurie's. "It looks like someone tried to cover the prints, or sweep them away."

"Right, but they missed this one. It's as fresh as the smaller print."

"Maybe she met someone here who could help her hide."

"Or someone who overpowered her," Nick said.

"There you go again."

"Okay, have it your way. Let's assume she arranged to meet someone here. You know her—better than I do, anyway. Do you have any idea who it could be and where they would go?"

"We only have a few mutual acquaintances, and they all work at TMC."

"Anyone who might have missed work the past day or two?"

"No one comes to mind. There are more than five hundred employees at the hospital. Laurie must have friends I don't know about."

"It might not be someone from the hospital." Nick poked at the duff with a stick. "There are three trail-heads feeding into these lakes. If she and this alleged friend left before we came in, they could have used any one of them."

"I know, but the ashes are still damp. They might have been here this morning, so there's a chance she's alive, and with a friend."

"We can't assume anything, no matter how much—"

A sudden staccato blast split the air above our heads. Nick dove at me, shoving me to the ground and shielding me with his body. I covered my ears against the noise and waited for a painful, bloody death.

When the rat-a-tat barrage ceased I felt no pain, just Nick's weight on my back and pine-scented dirt filling my nostrils. I wriggled under Nick until I got my elbows propped up and my face out of the dirt.

"Get off. I can't breathe."

Nick rolled to one side and looked up into the trees. "Damn pileated woodpecker. I should have shot it."

My mouth was full of grit and pine needles. I spat, ran my tongue over my teeth and spat again. "A woodpecker made that racket?"

"*Dryocopus pileatus*. Loud as a jackhammer when they start pecking."

"Thanks for the biology lesson. If you knew what it was, why did you tackle me?"

"I wasn't taking any chances." He pulled out a kerchief and wet it from his water bottle. "Here, your nose is brown." When he held the bandana out to me, his fingers trembled. Mr. Cool had lost it over a bird.

I wiped at my face. "You actually thought someone was shooting at us?"

"A potential murder witness is on the run. She tried to contact you and now we're trying to find her. That's enough to put us in someone's sights." Nick trained

his binoculars toward the clearing where we'd left the
llamas.

"Are they okay?"

"They're fine." He picked up his pack. "If you're
through cleaning your face, we might as well head back.
You're in charge of chores at the ranch tonight, aren't
you?"

I handed him the wet kerchief. "Harry can do them if
we're late. Maybe we should check the other two trail-
heads before we go home."

"Not a bad idea. It would take them longer to hike
out if they're using the Bunchgrass trailhead. We might
intercept them on the road."

We made good time on the downhill trek to the truck
and trailer. Nick drove west on the highway until we
reached the entrance road to the Bunchgrass trailhead.
As we slowed to turn in, a black Ford F150 pulled out of
the trailhead road on our right with his blinker signaling
a left turn. The driver wore reflective sunglasses and
a billed cap in a camo pattern. The passenger, a dark-
haired, dark-skinned woman, glanced our way for a moment. The driver barely cleared the front of our truck
with a tight left turn that headed him in the direction
we had just come from. He hit the gas, and the black
truck sped off. In my side-view mirror I watched it disappear around a curve in the road behind us.

"Nick, that woman—she looked exactly like Laurie."

"Did she look distressed?"

"I couldn't tell."

"Do you think she recognized you?"

"I don't know."

A driver behind us honked and waved his arm, impatient to get moving. Nick pulled off the highway and cut his engine. "Did you see the plate number?"

"Not all of it—too much dust—but it was an Idaho plate. I saw a two and the letter C."

He took a pencil and notebook from his glove compartment. "Okay, we've got that, and it was black. I saw the four by four decal on the rear fender. What else?"

"The cab had four doors. What do they call that?"

"Crew cab. You're sure about the four doors?"

"Yes. But I don't see how any of this is going to help us. They're going the opposite direction and we don't know where they're headed."

"Looks like they're headed for Idaho, but we can't chase after them with two llamas hitched to our behind." He handed me the pencil and notebook. "Here, in case you think of anything else about that pickup. Right now, we have to take Jack's animals home."

I wanted to argue, but Nick was right. We had to go home. Even so, knowing I might have seen Laurie and that we were headed in opposite directions was unbearable.

Half an hour later, something I'd been trying to recall clawed its way to the surface.

"Idaho. That's where Cody O'Brien's wife was injured. It was at a rodeo somewhere near Boise. She was flown to Timbergate Medical Center with a brain injury and died in the ICU."

"Didn't you say she was kicked in the head by her horse?"

"Yes. Spooky, isn't it? Both of them dying the same way. Except—"

"Except your friend said Cody's horse is innocent." Nick drummed his fingers on the steering wheel. "It's been a while since I've flown to Idaho. What do you say we visit the Gem of the Mountains?"

"Really, you'd do that?"

"Might as well. I have to log a little flight time. A trip to Idaho sounds about right."

FOURTEEN

WHEN WE PULLED into the driveway at the Highland Ranch, Harry and Ginger greeted us on Jack and Amah's front porch. Ginger's tail spun in ecstasy, and when Nick bent to scratch her ears, she anointed his cheek with a few slobbered kisses.

"Any luck?" Harry said.

We filled him in and told him about our planned flight to Idaho.

"Idaho, huh?" The satisfied gleam in his eye told me what he thought of Nick and me thrown together for another two days. He readily promised to watch the ranch while we were gone. Ginger got a final pat on the head, and Harry took off in his shiny red Jag.

Nick and I split the evening chores as the sun was setting. Working in twilight, we managed to feed and water eight llamas, a dozen turkeys, a cat, a snake, and a cockatiel. We were almost home free when Nick turned his back on the turkeys to open the pasture gate.

"Look out," I yelled, but it was too late. I watched helpless from the garden as the dominant gobbler lunged at Nick and dug a spur in the back of his upper thigh. Nick came through the gate muttering under his breath. I resisted any impulse to joke about his getting kicked in the butt by a turkey. Or to point out that farm life requires its own set of survival skills—even for a fearless pilot with a drawer full of sharp-shooter medals.

Nick spent a few minutes in the bathroom of the main house with antibiotic ointment and some sterile strips. When he came into the kitchen, he wore an expression that said, *I don't want to talk about it*. Nevertheless, I had to ask one important question.

"Are you current on your tetanus shots?"

"Yes."

"Just checking."

He pulled two of Jack's beers from the fridge. I found a stash of homemade turkey burritos in the freezer. We nuked our dinner and sat in the family room, feasting on our plunder. Ginger sat at attention between us, head swiveling back and forth to see who might offer her a bite. After Nick finished his food, he gave the dog a treat and a chin scratch and then turned to me.

"How sure are you about the woman in that truck?"

"Are you asking if I'm sure enough to fly to Idaho?"

"Unless you have a better plan. Like going to the police."

"If Laurie wanted the police involved, she'd have called them instead of me."

"If she knows anything about a murder, she'll have to deal with them sooner or later."

"But she has to stay alive in the meantime. What happens if the police start talking to people at the hospital? To me, for instance. I'd have to tell them about breaking into her house, and about Idaho, and then whoever is after her might find out, too. Right now, she's probably safer without the police involved."

"Then so are you." Nick opened the slider and let Ginger out into the fenced backyard. "Who else knows you're trying to find Laurie?"

"Just Cleo Cominoli, and she wouldn't tell anyone. And Harry, of course."

"All right. Let's decide whether we're flying or not."

"I think we have to. Two and a half years ago, Cody's comatose wife was transported to TMC from a hospital in Idaho. Now Cody's nurse, who knows something suspicious about *his* death, may be headed to Idaho."

"So we're going to find out if there's any connection, but if we come up empty, that's where it ends. Deal?"

"Deal. By then, someone else might have called in the police. We're not the only people who want answers."

"That's right. One of them is your friend James."

"Yes. He wants to know why his brother died."

"I suppose your coworker at the hospital would like some answers, too."

"Cleo? Of course she would. This all started because her fiancé is scheduled to go under Dr. Poole's knife." I picked up our paper plates and took them to the kitchen.

Nick followed me, reaching out to touch my shoulder. "Hey, we're going to do this, but I don't want you getting your hopes up. What's more, if this Laurie's in danger, you're heading down the same road. I don't like it."

"I'm not giving up on her now. Finding her is the key to solving this mystery—and maybe to keeping her alive."

Nick stood close behind me with his hands on my shoulders. "If you're determined to risk your neck, I'm stuck. I don't want to be the one to face your grandparents if they come home and find you've gone missing, too."

"So we're flying to Idaho. When?"

"How soon can you get away?"

"Friday, after work. I'll try to take off early."

"Good. Where in Idaho is the hospital you need to visit?"

"It's in a small town called Dunnsville. Near Boise."

"All right. I'll check it out and file a flight plan. In

the meantime, you're going to fix me up with Cody O'Brien's intimidating lady doctor."

I'd forgotten about that. The thought of Nick dating anyone but me was bad enough, but the thought of him with Phyllis Poole, even if it was a pretense, stirred an emotion different from jealousy. It felt like fear.

"I'll see what I can do, but let's call it a night. I have to go take a shower."

"Why not stay here in the main house with me?"

I searched his face for the meaning behind that suggestion, but I couldn't read him and didn't ask.

"The barn is my home. I like it out there. And you don't have to babysit here. Aren't you still living in Buck Sawyer's pool house?"

"For the time being. Rella's still subletting my apartment while she waits for her escrow to close."

"How much longer?"

"It's unclear, but I don't really care." Nick sat at the kitchen table. "I like the pool house, and it's free. Buck won't let me pay."

Nick had saved the life of his boss's wife a few months earlier when she fell and cut herself on a piece of broken glass and nearly bled to death. After Delta Sawyer's accident, Buck began treating Nick like the son he'd always longed for and never had.

Nick pulled a small notebook from his pocket. "What's the lady doctor's name?"

"Phyllis Poole—with an E." I watched him write it down. "What are you going to do?"

He put the notebook away. "I thought I might watch some TV, have another beer. Want to join me?"

"You know what I mean. What are you going to do about Dr. Poole?"

"First, you're going to set me up with an appointment so I can get my prostate checked."

"You can't be serious."

Nick laughed so hard Ginger jumped up and nuzzled him, whining. "It's okay, girl," he told her. To me, he said, "Then you think of something."

"What makes you think she'll go out with you? If she's ethical, she won't date a patient."

"Technically, I won't be a patient if there's nothing wrong with me. Let me take care of that."

"Don't count on your charm being irresistible. Remember, she's already fatally attracted to Dr. Fausset."

"So you say. Now, give me a reason to make an appointment. Something simple that doesn't require a hands-on physical exam."

"Okay, tell her you're considering a vasectomy. The first visit should be a consult, with clothes on. If you tell her you don't have kids yet, she should try to talk you out of it."

"Sounds good. I can take it from there. How soon can I see her?"

"Right away, if I pull some strings."

"How about tomorrow?"

"I'll see what I can do."

"Good. Can you meet me at the hangar by four thirty on Friday?"

"That should work. But what about your dog? Harry agreed to watch the ranch again. Did you ask him to watch her, too?"

"No need. She'll spend the weekend with her trainer."

THURSDAY MORNING I called the office of Timbergate Urologic Associates and introduced myself to the appointment secretary as an administrator at Timbergate Medical Center. I explained that my cousin urgently needed an appointment, preferably with Dr. Poole. She scheduled Nick for late afternoon on the same day.

I fought a losing battle trying to clear my mind of the impending scene in her office. Virile Nick, all cute and bashful, showing deference to her profession.

Just as I reached the point where I was about to castrate him myself, my phone rang and saved Nick's manhood. James O'Brien was on the line. *Perfect.*

"Aimee, it's James. Is this a bad time?"

The library was empty and Lola was out making the rounds with the mobile book cart.

"No. It's fine. What's on your mind?" I'd encouraged him to have his father see an internist almost a week ago. Then I'd learned how dire Seamus O'Brien's prognosis was. If he hadn't told James, I knew in my heart I could not tell him. More medical opinions weren't really necessary based on what I'd learned about Seamus' tick-borne illness and his missing spleen.

"I wonder if we could get together again," he said. "There are a couple of things I'd like to bounce off someone, and you're the ideal sounding board."

"Is this about Cody or your father?"

"Both, I think."

If James had any pieces to the puzzle, I wanted to know about them before Nick and I left for Idaho.

"It would have to be this evening. Are you free?"

"More than free," James said. "Desperate to get away from the O'Brien clan. Shall I pick you up? We can grab a bite somewhere."

"I'll have to do chores first. The folks are in Africa for three weeks."

"Right, Jack told me about their trip the day I visited. Why don't I come by and help with chores?"

I wasn't crazy about James dropping by the ranch to take me out while Nick was there playing resident watchdog.

"That's a nice offer, but it isn't necessary. Let's just meet somewhere."

"Tell me where."

I was about to answer when I spotted Jared Quinn sauntering through the door. Of course he'd show up when I was on the phone making a date.

"Aimee, are you there?" James said.

"Yes." I murmured rapid-fire directions. "There's a steak house at the junction in Coyote Creek. It's convenient. We can meet there at seven."

"I remember a feed store there. It's a restaurant now?"

"That's it. They call it The Feed Bag. It's not as bad as it sounds. It's new and considered trendy."

"Then I'll see you there. And you might check your phone. I can barely hear you."

"Okay, see you." I hung up, hoping Quinn would give me a break. He didn't say a word. Just stood there, smiling.

"Sorry, didn't mean to interrupt your phone call. Sounds like your voice is still a bit compromised. Are you feeling better?"

I was puzzled for a moment then remembered I was supposed to be recovering from a sore throat.

"No problem," I said, affecting a slight whisper. "I was arranging to meet James O'Brien. He wants to talk about Cody."

"Hey, I didn't ask, but since you offered, let me know how that works out."

"I will. What else can I do for you?"

"It looks like Beardsley's left you on your own. He's given me notice that he's going to take an extended break. He'll be out of the country for at least a month."

"Wow, that's a shock. I expected him to be back any day."

"So did I, but it looks like we were wrong. In light of this news, it looks like I'm officially your acting supervisor again. I thought I'd better ask about the CME program. How are the urology reviews coming along?"

"I have appointments lined up with Quality Assurance and Medical Affairs this afternoon. Cleo and Rocky are working on the peer reviews, and we're on track for Wednesday night, October thirty-first."

"Halloween." Quinn smiled. "Easy to remember. Let me know if you need my help with anything." He hesitated, seeming to weigh his next words. "What did you think of the combo last Friday?"

"I enjoyed it very much."

"We weren't sure how it would go over without Laurie, but Phyllis Poole saved our bacon."

"She's certainly multi-talented," I said, wondering what other skills she possessed and whether she used them for good or evil.

"She is talented," Quinn said, "but so was Laurie. I hope she'll find another combo when she gets settled."

What was he saying? Quinn knew where Laurie had gone? I tried to keep my surprise from showing. "You know where Laurie is?"

"Only what she told Edna Roda. Laurie has family somewhere up north in Idaho. Edna was disappointed about losing one of her best nurses." Quinn gave me a puzzled look. "Why do you ask?"

"Her leaving seemed so abrupt. Do you know why she left?"

"Some kind of a family emergency. She left without notice, but called in and explained it to Edna. She said she needed to be closer to an ill parent, something like that. Laurie's a talented nurse and a fine person. I'm sure she'll do well wherever she is."

Of course he didn't know about Laurie's phone calls to Cleo and me, or what I'd discovered by sneaking into her home twice and tracking her in the wilderness. Since all that amounted to was a patchwork of suspicion and speculation, I kept it to myself. But Edna Roda told Quinn that Laurie had family up north in Idaho. That was good to know.

"Before I go, there's one other thing," Quinn said. "I don't mind acting as your supervisor for the time being, but there's been speculation that Beardsley might retire. If he does, I'm thinking about restructuring your department, and the change will affect you."

That produced a hit of anxiety. Restructuring usually implied downsizing.

"What would that involve?" I tried for mildly curious, but my question came out sounding a little squeaky. Not bad, since I was already faking a scratchy throat.

"Nothing much where your job duties are concerned, but you'd be reporting directly to me. It would be considered a promotion, and I suppose I'd have to give you some sort of raise if you were running the show by yourself. Are you willing to take on the added responsibility?"

The prospect of a promotion and a raise made me seriously giddy, but I managed to whisper a casual, "I'm sure I could handle it."

"I've been considering this for a while, but I don't want to go ahead and create the position unless you're willing to fill it." He glanced at his watch. "I've got to go. Take some time to think about it. We'll talk again. And take care of that throat."

What was there to think about? All I could do was pray Dr. Beardsley would retire.

I spent the next two hours working with Rocky Taylor in Quality Assurance to identify all urologic surgery deaths and complications from the previous twelve months. Every urologist on the staff had at least one complication. Dr. Fausset had three, but Dr. Poole was the winner hands-down. She had seven complications and the only death, other than Cody. His didn't count as being related to urologic care. At Jared Quinn's request, I'd included his record as a complication, although his leaving the hospital against medical advice the night before surgery meant I was fudging a bit in the complication category.

Truth is, administrators aren't thrilled when patients escape, and to have one escape and promptly die under unusual circumstances was a huge red flag. Quinn was covering his backside big-time on this one. Likely the hospital had nothing to do with any of it. TMC's lawyers were wary just the same.

I called Cleo Cominoli to give her an update about the case review, and she immediately went off on a tangent.

"I can't believe this. Dr. Poole's office called Sig about a cancellation in Dr. Poole's surgery schedule. They asked him to move his surgery back to his original date."

"It's back on for November first?"

"Yes, and I can't talk him out of it. Aimee, he'll be in surgery the morning after the CME program. Even if Poole's cases are out of line with the rest, she'll be able to operate for at least a month while the committees decide whether to revoke her surgery privileges."

"I thought there was something called a summary suspension that could be done immediately."

"Sure, the chairman of Urology Department can do that," Cleo said. "That's Tobias Fausset, so don't count on it."

"Doesn't anyone else have that power?"

"The Chief of Staff, who if you recall is the truant Vane Beardsley, and I just heard he's in Aruba. Then there's Quinn, who just recruited Poole into Code Blues. Fat chance he's going to pull her privileges. She'd have to be caught snorting coke in the operating room."

"Then you'll have to tell Sig to cancel it himself."

"It might come to that, but he's convinced she's his angel of mercy. I won't be able to change his mind unless I have some hard evidence of her incompetence."

"We'd have to prove it before November first. Are the charts already pulled and assigned to the reviewers?"

"As of this morning."

The charts would be divided among the urologic surgeons. Each one would evaluate the other's cases, with none having an opportunity to re-evaluate their own before the special meeting.

"Try not to worry, Cleo. We won't let anything happen to Sig."

With that angst-filled conversation out of the way, my work day was over. Time to think about dinner with James O'Brien.

FIFTEEN

THE FEED BAG was doing a brisk business Thursday evening.

I spotted James waiting for me just inside the door and said, "Sorry. Hope I'm not late."

"No, I'm early. I wanted to make sure I could find the place."

In faded jeans and a crisp white shirt, James could have passed for a cowboy, except he smelled more like lemon meringue than alfalfa. We were shown to a table and given menus. I asked for iced tea. James ordered a beer, then glanced around the room.

"I like what they've done here. Thanks for coming on short notice."

"I'm glad you called. I've been wondering how things are going with your family."

"Not well. Keely and Echo are at each other's throats when they're not falling all over themselves to cater to Dad."

"That must be hard on Seamus."

The waiter arrived with our drinks, and James waited for him to leave before responding.

"Echo and Keely's ongoing war is bad enough, but Cody's death is tearing him up. He can't accept it. Keeps asking why it happened." James stared at the label on his beer bottle as if he might find an answer there. "Dad keeps asking why Cody left the hospital. Has anyone come up with an explanation for that?"

"Not as far as I know." Unless Cleo's theory about Laurie Popejoy warning Cody away turned out to be true. Although even Cleo couldn't explain how Poole might arrange on such short notice to have Cody kicked in the head by his horse.

The waiter reappeared to ask if we were ready to order. James asked for a few more minutes, and he moved on.

"There must be a connection. Something spooked Cody. He wouldn't do something as drastic as skipping out on his surgery without a hell of a good reason."

I wasn't ready to share Cleo's theory with James. "You've met our administrator," I said. "He's a good man. If he discovers why Cody left the hospital, he'll tell you."

"Unless his lawyers advise against it."

I couldn't argue with that, and I couldn't tell James about Cody's case being part of the urologic surgery review. Divulging privileged information outside the legal protection of a medical staff committee could get me fired in a heartbeat.

"Did you ask Seamus if he knows why Cody called you from the hospital?"

"No." James lifted his glass then put it down without drinking. "I hate to bring it up. He's ill and still grieving. It's only been eleven days since Cody died."

"Maybe you should. He might know what Cody wanted to tell you."

"If he did, he would have said something by now. He believes Cody's death was an accident. I'd rather leave it at that unless we…."

James stopped in mid-sentence and looked toward the entrance to the restaurant. I turned to see what caught his eye. It was Nick, walking toward a table with Dr. Phyllis Poole on his arm.

"Isn't that your friend?"

"You mean Nick Alexander? Yes." Although *friend* wasn't exactly the right word.

"That's the woman from the blues combo, isn't it?"

"That's right, Dr. Poole. She's the surgeon who was scheduled to operate on Cody."

James shook his head. "I'm an idiot. I didn't recognize her the other night when she was wearing all that makeup."

"Recognize her? What do you mean?"

"From the hospital in Idaho where DeeDee was taken after her accident."

"DeeDee Dakota? Cody's wife?" I nearly spilled my tea. "Are you telling me Dr. Poole was involved with her care?"

"Cody called me in New York right after DeeDee's accident, and I took the red-eye out to Idaho. I sat with him at DeeDee's bedside while a parade of doctors and nurses passed by. That woman was one of them."

"That was more than two years ago. Are you sure?"

He glanced toward the table where Poole sat with Nick. "Minus the spotlight and the glamour makeup. Yep, I'm positive."

"What else do you remember?"

"Just that no one thought DeeDee was badly hurt. When they got her to the hospital, she was only supposed to be there overnight for observation. The next day she seemed fine, but they wanted to keep her one more night. The morning she was supposed to be discharged, she took an unexpected turn for the worse and lapsed into a coma. They were going to transfer her to a medical center in Boise, but Dad arranged to have her flown here to Timbergate instead."

His story matched everything I had read about the incident. "Did you come along?"

"Indirectly. Cody rode on the air ambulance flight with DeeDee, and I drove their truck and trailer home. DeeDee wouldn't have wanted her horse left behind."

I saw the sadness James felt remembering that time. Still, I had to ask another question. "Were you here at TMC when DeeDee died?"

He answered in a voice husky with emotion. "I barely made it, but I was here." He blinked, gave his head a slight shake. "It was heartbreaking. She was an amazing woman. Beautiful and brave."

It sounded as if James's feelings for his sister-in-law ran deep. I wondered how deep.

"It must have been sad for all of you."

"It was. She was one of those people you couldn't help but love."

I felt like a heel for pressing him about her when he was already hurting about Cody's death.

"I'm sorry. I've upset you by asking about her."

"I'd come to terms with that, but now Cody's death and Dad's illness are taking a toll." He fixed his gaze on the menu. "Do you see anything you like?"

I glanced toward Nick and Poole. Neither of them had spotted us, but the last thing I needed was for Poole to see me with her dead patient's brother.

"Not really. I'm afraid I have to leave."

"Why? Are you upset about seeing Alexander with another woman?"

"No, I think I'm getting a migraine. They come on fast." I picked up my purse. "Sorry to spoil the evening."

I left James alone at the table and made my exit. A discreet glance on my way out confirmed that Nick and Poole were deep in conversation. Neither had noticed us.

I pulled into the driveway at the ranch and drove down the lane to the barn, where I parked and sat for a moment. I'd agreed to see James because he'd said he had something to tell me. How important could it be? As important as knowing Dr. Poole had been one of DeeDee Dakota's care providers years ago? Not likely.

A flash of light in my rearview mirror caught my eye. A car pulled into Jack and Amah's driveway. Not Nick. He and Poole wouldn't have finished their appetizers, much less dinner. And he wouldn't bring another woman to my grandparents' house in any case, unless he'd lost his mind. My cellphone rang. It was James.

"Hi," he said. "I followed you home. I was worried about your headache—wanted to make sure you were okay."

"Thanks, that's sweet, but I'm already feeling better."

"Good. I still owe you a dinner if you're interested."

And I still hadn't heard what he wanted to tell me.

"Stay there." I took a flashlight from my glove compartment and walked up the lane. He got out and stood beside his car.

"What happened back there? I don't buy the migraine story."

"It's complicated." How could I explain my erratic behavior to James without telling him Dr. Poole may have killed his brother?

"I have time to listen. Can we go someplace where there's food?"

"There's a pizza place just down the road." I heard the lack of enthusiasm in my voice.

He ignored it. "Good. Get in. I'm starving."

At Four Corners Pizza, James ordered a white pizza and a pitcher of soda. The young girl behind the counter gave him a puzzled look.

"They don't do white," I said.

"Then what do you want?"

"What do you have by the slice?" I asked the girl.

She brightened. "Oh, combination or pepperoni."

James said pepperoni, and I said combination. We took our slices and went to a booth.

"No white pizza?" James said. "Really?"

"This is Coyote Creek, not New York."

"Damn, how do you do it?"

"Do what?"

"Live here."

"Hey, this is your hometown, too. But never mind that. You said you had something to tell me."

"We'll get to that, but first, you might explain ditching me at the Feed Bag. You said it was complicated."

"James, please trust me for now. It's true I didn't expect to see Nick there with that woman, but there's more to it. Some of it is personal and hard to talk about, and the other has to do with my job. It's confidential."

"Okay, I'll let it go…for the time being."

"Thanks. Now it's my turn to ask questions. You've been observing the other O'Briens for a few days. What did you want to tell me?"

"Damn, I hate to say it." He shook his head. "If I'm right, it's a disaster."

"James, what is it?"

He clasped his hands on the edge of the table as if he

were praying. "I hope like hell I'm wrong, but I think Echo's pregnant."

"Your stepmother?" James was right. *A disaster.*

"Please don't call her my stepmother."

"We are talking about the girl with the snake on her belly?" I recalled her dragging on a cigarette in the grocery store parking lot.

"What snake?"

"Never mind. What makes you think she's pregnant?" I almost added that it seemed impossible, considering the state of Seamus's health.

"My ex-wife was pregnant once. I know the signs even though she miscarried in her second month. We never had kids."

"I'm so sorry."

"So am I. Sorry for the lost child, but glad I'm not sharing joint custody with my ex."

"You'll make a great father someday."

"I hope to, but in the meantime, what do I do about Echo's pregnancy?"

"What do you mean?"

"Should I talk to my father…tell him I know?"

"Before you get to that, you'd better find out whether she's told him yet. She can't be very far along."

"Not showing yet," James said, "but bouts of nausea. I only know the earliest signs."

"If you noticed, your father must have, too. It's likely she told him. Think of the leverage it gives her."

"You're right. Maybe changing his will was never about Cody's death. It makes more sense if he expects to gain another heir."

"But if that's true, how long has he known?"

"My question exactly. Did Dad know about the baby before Cody died?"

"Are you going to ask him?"

James refilled our glasses from the pitcher of soda, and I realized I had yet to take a bite of my pizza. He'd eaten only half of his slice. He picked up the other half, then dropped it back on his paper plate.

"I think I have to. I don't want to hurt him, but I feel I should warn him. Once that kid is born, Echo could use it to take everything he has. I love my father too much to let that happen."

"You said you father's health has failed, but if Echo's pregnant, he must be well enough to have sex."

James hunched his shoulders and leaned toward me. "That's another thing that bothers me. When I tried to convince him to see an internist like you suggested, he refused. Said he didn't need any more doctors. Then I saw a prescription for an erectile dysfunction drug in his medicine cabinet. I suspect that was Echo's idea. She must have figured having his baby would put a lock on the lion's share of his inheritance. Apparently she decided to have his kid even if it kills him."

"Did you happen to see the name of the prescribing doctor?"

"No. Part of the label was missing and the rest was blurred, like it had fallen in water. He probably knocked it into the bathroom sink. All I could really make out was the name of the drug. When I realized what it was, it threw me for a loop. I couldn't quite believe it."

"What about the date? Did you notice if it was recent?"

"Sorry, no." James massaged his temples. A weary gesture. "So what do you think? Should I talk to Dad?"

"It's a tough call. If he already knows she's pregnant—or when he finds out—he's going to be excited and proud. You don't want to spoil that by suggesting she got pregnant out of greed rather than out of love. On the other hand, you love your father and want to protect him."

"That's about it. Echo has convinced Dad he's the love of her life. How do I rip that away from him now, when he's just lost his favorite son?"

"Don't say that. I'm sure your father loves you as much as he loved Cody. Parents love their children equally."

"In your world, and in your family, that may be true, but I live in a different world. All my father ever wanted from me was a son to carry on his life's work. In his eyes, producing plays in New York City is foolishness and worse—it's a rejection of his values."

"James, if your father is seriously ill, this could be your last chance to clear the air."

He searched my face. "Is there something you're not telling me? Is my father dying?"

"I don't know anything for sure, but you have to talk to him. It's never easy to ask the hard questions, but sometimes it has to be done." I hoped my advice sounded wise and heartfelt, because I truly meant it that way.

"I suppose you're right." James stood and dropped a few bills on the table. Sadness and confusion played across his face, making it impossible for me to believe he was guilty of any wrongdoing in the O'Brien saga.

I wondered whether I was reading the man standing before me or letting the memory of a childhood crush cloud my thinking.

SIXTEEN

JAMES AND I parted at the door to my apartment with awkward, back-patting hugs and promises to keep in touch. I stood on the deck and watched him drive his rental car down the lane and onto the street fronting the main house. As he drove away, Fanny appeared, rubbing against my leg. I let her inside and locked my door. She dove into a bowl of kibble while I clicked the remote to catch the local eleven o'clock news. I changed into a sleep tee and shorts and settled on my futon bed with a glass of milk. Five minutes into the news, I heard knocking on my door and guessed that would be Nick.

After checking the peephole, I let him in. "Why are you here?"

He flopped down in the chair at my computer desk. "Just checking in. I thought we might as well compare notes."

I realized I was still holding the milk. "Want something to drink?"

"No. I want to hear about your abrupt departure from The Feed Bag. Did your date do something to tick you off?"

"Nothing like that. I wasn't expecting you to be there with Poole, and I didn't want her to see me with James. Do you think she recognized us?"

"I doubt it. She had her back to you the whole time."

"Good, so what were you able to learn?"

"Not much. She got paged. She was on call and had to be at the hospital by ten thirty for some kind of emergency surgery. She said she could only stay long enough to finish her meal."

"Emergency surgery, but she could stay and have dinner first?"

"Hey, I'm no doctor. I don't know how that stuff works."

I wondered if the emergency was a late date with Dr. Fausset, but I didn't wonder out loud.

"She asked for a rain check."

"And you agreed?"

"I thought I should. It was slow going tonight. I was trying to be subtle. I don't think she was suspicious, but I didn't get a whole lot of information out of her, either."

"Did you get anything helpful?"

"Maybe. I'll let you decide. Apparently the O'Brien patriarch is a patient in her urology practice."

"What? Seamus is Phyllis Poole's patient? How did she happen to tell you that? It's a violation of patient confidentiality."

"I faked it. Said Seamus told me he was a patient of hers and that she came highly recommended. She said Seamus was actually Fausset's patient, not hers."

"What if Seamus hadn't been a patient there?"

"No big deal." Nick shrugged. "I'd have played dumb and said I must have been mistaken."

Fanny padded over to Nick and jumped on his lap. He stroked her fur and she squeezed her eyes closed in ecstasy.

"Nick, did Poole give any hint why Seamus is seeing Dr. Fausset?"

"No. She changed the subject. Do you have any ideas?"

"As a matter of fact, that fits with something James said. He thinks Seamus's wife is pregnant."

"Whoa!" Nick sat up and Fanny dropped to the floor. "That would definitely fit with his visits to Fausset."

"Including the prescription for erectile dysfunction medication that James saw in his father's medicine cabinet. Although I'm having trouble believing Tobias Fausset would give that to someone as sick as Seamus. I'm guessing it was purchased online without a prescription."

"Poor old guy. His wife's milking him in more ways than one."

I felt my face flame. "Nick, that's a disgusting thing to say."

"Tell me it isn't true."

"I'm afraid it is. Bearing his child gives her a lot of leverage when it comes to his will."

"Why would she need it? She's already his wife."

"That isn't a guarantee. He can divide his estate any way he wants as long as he's alive and in his right mind."

"But California's a community property state," Nick said. "If all Echo wants is his money, couldn't she divorce him and take half? That's got to be more money that she'll ever need."

"She could try, but it's not that simple. They've only been married a couple of years. Anything less than ten doesn't bode well for her."

"How do you know this?"

"I'm a librarian. I researched California's community property law for one of the doctors on staff. Take my word for it: Echo O'Brien would be a lot better off as a widow raising his child, especially if Seamus thinks it's a male heir."

Nick's brow furrowed. "Why do you say that?"

"From what James says, Seamus has always wanted a son to carry on his business. Cody was his best bet and now he's gone."

"What about James?"

"He claims he's not interested in the business and doesn't expect more than a token inheritance. Cody wasn't interested in the business either, until recently. James thinks he had a change of heart when he quit the rodeo, but he died before he had a chance to take over the reins of the O'Brien dynasty."

"So Seamus will be pinning his hopes on the little newborn. How soon can they tell if the fetus is boy or girl?"

"Amniocentesis at sixteen weeks, or ultrasound at twenty weeks. We don't know how far along she is, but I wouldn't put it past Echo to convince Seamus she's carrying a male child."

"How would she go about that?"

"Lie, if necessary. He probably won't live long enough to see it born."

"Damn, that's brutal." Nick got up from the table. "Seamus with a conniving, pregnant wife is a whole lot more than what I got from Poole."

"Wait. There's more." I told him how James recognized Poole as one of DeeDee Dakota's care providers while she was hospitalized in Idaho.

"Poole was one of DeeDee's doctors? She didn't mention that."

"You know, James didn't say she was a doctor, just that he'd seen her going in and out of DeeDee's room.

If Poole worked at that hospital, it should be listed in her credentials file. I'll ask Cleo to check that."

"Is she allowed to tell you?"

"Not really, but she will. She thinks Poole's a rotten apple, and she would do more than that to prove it."

"Good. See if she can do it before we fly to Idaho. I'll touch base with Rella so she'll know where to reach me about anything work-related while we're gone."

"What could she need you for? Isn't Buck out of the country?"

"It's part of the protocol. We're supposed to maintain contact just in case."

So no matter where Nick and I were, he had to be in touch with Rella. On top of that, he would be making a second date with Phyllis Poole. I suppressed a sigh. Now I had two reasons to work on my trust issues with Nick—both of them tall and blond, each extraordinary in her own way. I had counted on time to put Nick and me back on course after the Paris incident, but it was taking longer than I'd expected. Harry warned me that Nick wouldn't wait forever, and I knew he was right. I had to resolve my nagging doubts, but how?

AT WORK ON Friday morning, I called Cleo and told her about James seeing Phyllis Poole in DeeDee's hospital room in Idaho.

"That's impossible," Cleo said. "I've seen her CV. She was working in a hospital in New York back then."

"But James was certain he saw her. Maybe she was on a leave of absence or some kind of teaching exchange. Please take another look at her file. Maybe there's something in her CV that you missed."

"I'm pulling the file as we speak." I heard her turning pages. "Nope, nothing about her working at a hospital in Idaho."

"Does the CV show that she ever lived in Idaho?"

"No."

"Then how do I find out if she was really there?"

"I've already arranged for you to talk to Brenda Mc-Clurg. She's my counterpart at Dunnsville Memorial up there. Maybe she'll remember Poole."

HARRY GAVE ME a ride to the airport on Friday afternoon. We met Nick at the hangar, where he'd already pulled out the plane. Buck Sawyer's Mustang Citation gleamed in the slanting late October sunlight—a sleek combination of prehistoric bird and futuristic time capsule.

"Hot damn," Harry said. "How about I go with you guys?"

I poked his chest. "You're watching the ranch, Bro. Besides, you said you were much too busy, remember?"

"Some other time," Nick said. "When you can tear yourself away from your mall project, we'll do a ski weekend in Sun Valley."

"Deal," Harry said. "When will you two be back?"

"No later than Sunday evening," I said. "Keep an eye out for any sign of prowlers or intruders."

Harry glanced at Nick. "You think that's likely?"

"No, but someone else is looking for the woman we're trying to find, and whoever it is might have your grandparents' address."

Harry lifted my overnight case from the backseat of his Jag. "Aimee, did you ever get a handle on that person named Pat you asked me about?"

"No, but thanks for reminding me. Maybe we'll find someone named Pat when we get to Idaho."

I insisted on a hug from Harry and held on until he squirmed. He shook hands with Nick and drove away.

Nick did a final walk-around and stowed our luggage. We were soon airborne, lifting over oak-studded hills and rising above forested mountains as we headed east toward southern Idaho into a sky tinged with twilight. Despite the circumstances of our trip, we both took pleasure in the comfort of Buck's luxurious six-passenger aircraft. Nick said it was capable of 400 knots and an altitude of 41,000 feet, but there was no need to push it to the maximum for our relatively short flight.

We lost an hour by crossing into Mountain Standard Time and touched down shortly after dark at a municipal airport a few miles from Dunnsville. Our rental car was a tidy gray sedan.

The motel rooms Nick had reserved for us at Kitty's Koral were quaint but clean. At least mine was. The motel clerk recommended a diner within walking distance. Nick had checked the weather before we took off and got the forecast pilots like to hear. No storms were expected for the days we planned to be in Idaho, but daytime temperatures were predicted to vary anywhere from the low sixties to the high seventies.

The night air was cool on our walk to the diner, and I was glad I'd taken along a fleece-lined denim jacket. On our way I filled Nick in on my conversation with Cleo and how she'd found no references to Idaho in Dr. Poole's CV.

"Too bad. Sounds like you'll have a hard time verifying James O'Brien's story. Maybe he was mistaken."

"Cleo said the woman I'm meeting at Dunnsville Memorial might know something."

We arrived at the diner half an hour before closing and found The Roundup empty except for a bored waitress—Ursula, according to her name badge—who reminded me of our rental car: small and gray with no frills. We sat at a speckled yellow counter worn almost white from decades of use and gave our orders.

She disappeared into the kitchen and came back in less than ten minutes with our food. My burger and fries smelled so delicious I nearly drooled, and Nick gazed at his steak and onion rings with an expression of pure joy.

We had finished half our meal when the waitress asked how everything was. We assured her the food was great. She lingered for a moment, probably bored with no one else to feed, so I seized the initiative and asked her for directions to Dunnsville Memorial Hospital.

Ursula's eyes widened. "You're not sick, are you?"

"No," I improvised. "We think a friend of ours is a patient there."

She rubbed at a spot on the counter with a damp cloth smelling of bleach. "I hope your friend's condition isn't serious."

"Why?"

"I shouldn't say anything." She glanced behind her at the double doors that led to the kitchen where pots and pans were rattling.

"But you said you hoped her condition isn't serious. Is there a problem with the hospital?"

When she looked again at the doors to the kitchen, I glanced at Nick. His turn.

He used his arsenal of secret weapons: the smile, the eyes, the intimate *just between us* tone, and soon the waitress was spilling the beans in whispered tones about a scandal at the local privately owned hospital.

Rumor had it, the ER doctors there were given incentives to admit patients who didn't really need to be hospitalized. Even worse, freelance ambulance services were offered bribes to deliver patients to Dunnsville Memorial even when their medical needs would be better served at a larger nearby hospital.

"How long has this been going on?" I asked. DeeDee's stay there had been more than two years ago, but it was still within the realm of possibility that she'd been a victim of this misconduct.

"Who knows?" Ursula's reply came with a shrug. "No one noticed until a few months ago, when our mayor had a stroke. He should have been taken to Boise, but instead he was delivered to Dunnsville Memorial by the crooked ambulance service."

"What happened then?" I asked.

"He died. His wife went freakin' ballistic and it hit the news. She's suing Dunnsville Memorial and the ambulance service for a bundle."

Nick and I finished up a few minutes later, declined Ursula's offer of dessert, and left her a hefty tip to compensate for the dirt she'd dished up about Dunnsville Memorial. Maybe there would be more to come.

SEVENTEEN

BACK AT THE motel I suggested we spend some time planning our fact-finding strategy before calling it a night. I opened the door to my room and Nick followed me inside. Our rooms shared an adjoining door that either of us could choose to lock. Or not.

"I'll let you know when I'm ready to work," I said. "First I want a shower."

"I'd offer to help, but I'm guessing that's not an option." He reached out and caressed my cheek. His fingertips set off an electric tingle that traveled up into my scalp and down below my comfort zone. It took some effort, but I managed to back away.

"I guess not."

Nick leveled a look at me. "If this is about Rella, maybe we should talk."

His ominous statement was like a punch in the stomach. "Maybe we should."

"You want to start?" Nick sat in one of the two chairs in my room. I took the other and tried to explain what I barely understood myself.

"When Rella answered your phone that night in Paris, it triggered something in me that I'd never experienced, and I didn't like it. I believed you had betrayed my trust and I was furious. It didn't occur to me that there was an innocent explanation, and Rella didn't offer one."

"Rella was drunk and groggy with sleep. But you already know this. What are you getting at?"

"Before, when you and I were together, I believed we were exclusive and committed to each other. After the misunderstanding, I realized that we had never talked about it; I had just taken it for granted. The point is that my first thought was that you had cheated. I felt like a naïve fool and reacted like one instead of trusting you and letting you explain. I need to be able to trust you completely if we're going to move ahead. It wouldn't be fair to either of us."

"But eventually you accepted my explanation about the hotel mix-up. That was two months ago. I thought we were making progress getting back on track, but obviously something has changed. Why didn't you talk to me sooner?"

"Because it's some kind of delayed reaction. I barely understand it myself, and I have to work it out by myself. I hate the doubts that creep into my mind."

"Hell, Aimee. We all have doubts. Do you think I liked watching your friend James O'Brien planting a kiss on you?"

"No, but did it make you wonder if I'd slept with him?"

"Of course not. That's not who you are."

"You're right. But don't you see? That's how I used to feel about you. I'm trying to get back there again, but it's taking time and I can't fake it." I felt tears sting with my next words. "And I can't ask you to wait much longer."

"How long I wait is up to me." He got up and came to me, taking my hands and lifting me from my chair. "You and I agreed to start over as friends with options. I get that the options are off the table right now. I'll accept that and I won't pressure you, but I'm not above testing you with a little flirting occasionally."

I felt myself smile. "I can handle that. But why are you being so understanding?"

"Because I like you and I like being with you. Even as a friend, you're more interesting than anyone else I know."

"Really? Why?"

He laughed. "Beats me. It must be because you're a librarian." He passed through the adjoining door into his room and I went to take my shower.

Half an hour later I had just pulled on jeans and a T-shirt when I heard a knock on the door between my room and Nick's. I opened it.

"Ready to work?" Nick asked.

"Yes, let's get started."

We listed everything we could think of about DeeDee and Cody O'Brien and the rest of the clan, including James, Keely, and Seamus—the patriarch with the pregnant wife. Then we added Laurie Popejoy, Phyllis Poole, and even Tucker Potkotter. We tried to draw intersecting circles on a page to see how their lives connected and ended up with something resembling a slinky toy with a broken belly.

"This isn't working," I said. "None of it suggests why Laurie might have come here, or why someone might have brought her here against her will. I think we're on a wild goose chase."

"Maybe, but let's keep going. We know she's mixed up in the cowboy's death somehow, and this is where his wife died. You were told Laurie Popejoy has family in Idaho, and you think you saw her leaving the wilderness in a pickup with an Idaho license plate. Cody

O'Brien skipped out on a surgery scheduled with the Poole woman, and James O'Brien told you he saw Poole at his sister-in-law's bedside here in Dunnsville. Chances are your missing nurse was headed this way. Let's find her and find out why."

Nick's pep talk didn't convince me we were going to succeed, but it did make me feel guilty for whining.

"I'm sorry," I said. "You're investing your time and Buck's money to help me, and I'm being a pain. Why are you even here? None of this has anything to do with you."

Nick reached out and took my hand. "Did you think I was going to let you have all the fun? We both have a sense of adventure, and we don't mind taking calculated risks. That makes us a good team. Besides, flying Buck Sawyer all over the world is boring compared to playing detective with you. Let's get back to work. Is anyone missing from our list?"

"There is one other possibility. Tobias Fausset."

"Poole's associate?" Nick jotted the name. "How does he fit in?"

"I don't know, but he and Laurie were in Code Blues together."

"TMC's music group? You think there was something going on between them?"

"I thought there might be, the way they sang together. The chemistry seemed so…."

"Powerful?" Nick asked. "Like it was with us?"

I swallowed. He said *was*. I hoped the past tense was only temporary. "They might have had a thing, but they never made it public."

Nick leaned back in his chair and stretched. "I need a break. Want a beer?"

"Where are you going to get a beer?"

"From the cooler in my room."

"Okay, just one."

He came back a few minutes later with two bottles, handed one to me, and took a pull from his.

"We need to make the most of our time tomorrow. When is your meeting with Cleo's contact at that hospital?"

"Ten o'clock."

"You think she knows about the bribes that waitress mentioned?"

"She has to know now, even if she didn't before." I took a sip of the cold beer. It made my throat tingle and soothed my frayed edges at the same time.

"You were told this woman you're meeting was working there back when DeeDee was hospitalized?"

"That's what Cleo said. She and Brenda McClurg met several years ago at a conference and hit it off."

Nick checked his notes. "In addition to Cody, we know James O'Brien and Phyllis Poole were in and out of DeeDee's room. Would your contact have any way of knowing what was going on?"

"That's what I'm hoping, but it's hard to know how much she'll remember."

"Or how much she'll be willing to tell." Nick drained the last of his beer. "It might be an outside chance, but DeeDee was a celebrity at the time—a big girl frog in a little pond. People remember things that stand out. A celebrity trick rider getting kicked in the head by her horse in front of a grandstand full of people would have made the news. Especially when she ended up dying."

"I agree." I yawned and looked at the digital clock

next to the bed. "It's almost midnight and we have a lot to do tomorrow. I need sleep."

Nick yawned back at me. "So do I. Anything else we need to go over tonight?"

"You haven't said what you're going to do tomorrow."

"After I drop you off at the hospital, I'm going to cruise around—see if I can spot a black F-150 with a crew cab and a dirty license plate."

"Wait a minute. I just remembered something."

I scrambled for my purse and pulled out the paperwork for our rental car. "Here, look at the license plate number. It starts the same way as the one I saw in the wilderness. The number 2, then the letter C. Do you think that means anything? Like what year it was issued?"

"Let me see that." Nick took out his phone and typed a few words. "Here it is." He pointed to the screen. "I'd forgotten about Idaho plates. They're all designated by county. We're in Canyon County; that's 2C."

"Then the pickup Laurie was in was licensed in this county."

"Definitely. We're on the right track if your friend Laurie has family around here. Now let's get some sleep. We have a lot to do tomorrow." He walked to the adjoining door and hesitated. "I'm locking this, so if you start to miss me, don't get any ideas."

I grabbed a pillow off the bed and tossed it at his back.

"Nice shot." He picked it up, walked over, and placed it gently on my bed. He turned down the covers and gave me a look full of meaning.

I felt a surge of longing and nearly gave in to it, but

just then his phone rang. He glanced at the screen and answered.

"Rella? What's up?" Nick walked to the door between our rooms with the phone to his ear. He turned to me, shrugged and mouthed *Sorry* as he went through and closed it behind him.

Perfect timing. I could spend the rest of my night wondering what might have happened if that call hadn't come.

While I sat staring at that door, I realized we'd left someone off our list. I picked up my pen and added another name: *Mystery Pat.*

I hung my outfit for the next morning in the bathroom and then turned on the TV. It boasted twenty cable channels, but I thumbed the remote until I found the local eleven o'clock news out of Boise. The scandal at Dunnsville Memorial rated a few minutes of air time and an interview with the administrator, who denied any wrongdoing.

I wondered if Brenda McClurg would be willing to tell me anything while the investigation was ongoing. Even after Cleo's intervention, McClurg could decide to clam up. She'd been at Dunnsville Memorial long enough to have a certain amount of loyalty to her employer. I turned off the set and lay there for what seemed like hours before I slept.

"WAKE UP. YOU'RE DROOLING." Nick's voice, but why was I hearing him in the middle of the night? I opened one eye and saw him sitting at the table in my room with two cups of coffee and two take-out boxes that smelled like bacon and toast. No wonder I was drooling. He opened the boxes. "Want to eat first or get dressed?"

"Dressed." I went into the bathroom and came out a few minutes later wearing black slacks and a white cotton shirt with short sleeves. A red linen jacket would dress up the outfit later when I went to meet with Brenda McClurg.

Nick watched me finish my last bites of bacon and jellied toast. "Did you have to make special arrangements to meet your contact on a Saturday?"

"No. It turns out she was already scheduled to work this weekend. I'm not sure why."

"I guess you'll find out. It's only eight o'clock. Want to kill some time riding around with me?"

"I might as well."

He dumped our empty cartons and cups in a wastebasket while I put on the red jacket and a pair of black Merrell Brios. They looked like Mary Janes—dressy enough for my outfit, but also practical. I could run like hell in them if I had to. I grabbed my purse, checking to make sure I had my cellphone and room key. "Let's go."

Outside in the crisp October morning, a few cotton-topped cumulus clouds with flat, gray bottoms rode a bright blue sky. Nick stared at them as he started the rental sedan.

"Reading the clouds?" I said. "They probably won't help you navigate the highway."

He pulled his gaze back to the dashboard in front of him. "Force of habit. There's a Ford dealership on the outskirts of town. Let's see if anyone there remembers selling a black F150 four by four with a crew cab. We'll have you back in plenty of time for your ten o'clock."

"They must sell a lot of those trucks out here. You don't even know the year model, do you?"

"Actually, I do. I'm pretty sure it was new. I've been looking at them myself."

"How are you going to explain interrogating the Ford dealer?"

"I'm just a potential customer looking for a good deal. And I'm not bashful about asking for references from satisfied customers."

I glanced at a billboard near the roadside in a weedy pasture populated by llamas and goats. It read: PARTY WITH PATTY: BIRTHDAYS, WEDDINGS AND WAKES. The paper was faded and torn, and it looked as if the party had been over for quite a while, but it jogged my memory. Nick and I had overlooked Mystery Pat in our brainstorming session the night before.

"Nick, we need to keep our eyes and ears open while we're here in case we come across anyone named Pat."

"Ah, Mystery Pat. You're right. Could be the guy in the black F150."

"You know, that would make sense if he really is her friend. Maybe calling him was the last thing she did before she went on the run."

Nick pulled into the dealership and parked near the sales office. Three salesmen emerged and the largest of them hot-footed it over to our rental car. He motioned Nick to roll down his window.

"Morning folks. I'm Morris. Welcome to Patterson's Premium Motors. Nice day, isn't it?" His hair was thick and wavy, and the sunlight gave it an unnatural sheen that suggested a do-it-yourself dye job.

Nick nodded. "You bet."

Patterson's! I nudged Nick in the ribs with my elbow.

"You and the missus here to do some shopping?"

Morris asked. "We have a fine selection of vehicles. You name it, we got it."

"We'd like to look around a bit," Nick said. "We're interested in the F150 crew cab. Word is you're willing to negotiate."

"Ah, fine choice. Your little woman okay with that? Maybe she'd like to take a test run in one of our new crossovers." Morris leaned down and peered at me through Nick's window. His cologne filled the little rental's small space with a pungent combination of musk and swamp grass. He caught a closer look at me and his eyebrows raised an eighth of an inch—registering us as an interracial couple. Nick saw it, too. He leaned over and kissed my cheek.

"What do you say, sweetheart? Pickup or crossover?"

"You promised to buy me a four by four." I lowered my eyes and tried to sound pouty and sultry at the same time.

Nick's mouth twitched, but he managed to keep a straight face.

"You heard my little lady. She wants what she wants."

Morris straightened up. "Then I'll put you together with Gary P. He's our expert on the F150." He signaled one of his colleagues over to our car.

"Hi folks, I'm Gary P," the new man said. He had a marathon runner's lean body and a shock of thick white hair.

"Are you Patterson, by any chance?" Nick said.

Gary P shook his head. "No chance of that. He passed on twenty years ago. New owner just kept the name. Why do you ask?"

"Your associate called you Gary P."

"That's me. Gary Podleski. We got another Gary. He's Sippowitz. So I'm Gary P and he's Gary S."

Nick and I followed Gary P around the lot to the area where the pickups were parked. Of the ten F150s on the lot, eight were black.

"Looks like black is popular," Nick said.

"Yeah, we do sell a lot of black." Gary peeled the wrapper off a stick of Doublemint gum and tongued it into his mouth. He frowned and looked down at his shoes. After a few chews, he squinted at Nick. "Buddy, you pick out one of these big boys and I'll give you the best deal in Idaho." His forced laugh scented the air with mint.

"You'll have to talk to my lady. It's going to be her ride, not mine."

I pointed to one of the black crew cabs. "I like that one."

EIGHTEEN

WE GOT OUT of the car and walked over to the pickup. Nick and Gary P did some verbal sparring about price, extras and all of the usual salesman-versus-buyer car lot talk. When Gary P said he couldn't offer the names of any of his satisfied customers, I piped up and whined, "Nicky, I changed my mind. I want a little car. Something cute, like a Porsche."

"Ah, no," Gary whispered to Nick. "You really gonna buy her a Porsche?"

Nick gave a rueful shake of his head. "Looks like I might have to. You wouldn't happen to have a used one here, would you?"

Gary P kicked at a pebble. "No, man. Can't you get her back to the 150?"

I walked back to the rental car. "Come on. Nicky, let's go look for a Porsche."

Nick put an arm around Gary P's shoulder and walked him a few steps away. I barely heard him say, "Hey, man. I like the 150, but you see what I'm up against. Maybe you could give me a couple of names. I might be able to persuade her if we get some good testimonials about customer satisfaction."

"Gimme a second," Gary P said. He walked toward the doors of the dealership. Nick slid into the rental and started the engine.

Gary P ran back out and thrust a sheet of paper at

Nick. "I'd lose my job if I gave you customer names, but here's another way for you to get what you need. You come on back now, hear?"

"Thanks, Buddy," Nick said. "I sure will."

Nick handed me the slip of paper then pulled out of the dealership and onto the highway.

"This will work," I said. "According to Gary P, you can get the dealership's buyer information by going online to the DMV."

Nick pulled into a minimart parking lot and read Gary P's instructions. He punched the DMV site into his iPhone and a few minutes later, had three names.

"Angela Winkle, Carson Littletree, and Lois McElroy."

"Two women?" Nick said.

"At least. We can't be sure about Carson."

"Think about the driver we saw with her in the wilderness. Any chance it was a woman?"

"I don't know. I just assumed it was a guy, but all I saw was a glimpse of sunglasses and a billed cap." I reached for my phone. "Maybe I can find something about Carson Littletree online."

I did an Internet search, but came up only with a Carson Little in Arkansas, a lot of Carsons who weren't Littletrees, and a couple links for *The Education of Little Tree*.

"Anything?" Nick said. "We'll be at the hospital in a couple of minutes."

"Not yet."

"Never mind, then. I'll look them up after I drop you off."

We reached Dunnsville Memorial just before ten o'clock. Nick stopped at the front entrance.

"How long do you expect to be here?"

"Probably no more than an hour, but leave your

phone on. I'll call you when I'm finished and wait for you in the lobby."

I found my way to Brenda McClurg's small, neat office, where she welcomed me with a firm handshake. Her *café au lait* complexion and Tina Turner hairdo made a striking first impression. She wore a flowing dress covered with hot pink and bright purple flowers.

"Welcome to Dunnsville Memorial Hospital." She took a seat behind her desk, gesturing an invitation for me to sit in a visitor's chair.

"Thank you for meeting with me on a Saturday," I said. "I hope it didn't disrupt your weekend."

"We have an accreditation inspection coming up in two weeks," she said. "You work in a hospital, right?"

"Yes, in the library."

"So you know the drill. With inspectors on the way, Saturday's just another day." I didn't envy her having an inspection just when the scandal broke in the media.

"I understand, and I want you to know how much I appreciate your time."

"No problem." She closed a calendar on her desk. "Now what can I do for you? Cleo said you were trying to help a woman in distress. I'm all for that."

"Did she say anything more?"

"No, she said you'd explain. I told her I'd do anything I could to help."

I chose my words carefully, telling her a nurse had disappeared from the hospital where I worked, and that I was worried about her.

"You think this woman came to Idaho for some reason?"

"It's possible. She may be from around here. I might be overreacting, but I'd like to be sure she's okay."

"I don't see how I can help with that," Brenda said.

"We think there's a connection between this nurse and a patient named DeeDee Dakota, who was admitted here two and a half years ago. Apparently the patient was here for about forty-eight hours."

"Ah, now I remember." Brenda rose from her desk and crossed the room to close the door of her office. She returned to her desk and sat. "Cleo mentioned the DeeDee Dakota case. And this has something to do with the missing nurse?"

"It might. We don't have a lot to go on."

"What's the nurse's name? Cleo didn't mention that."

"Laurie Popejoy."

Brenda's eyes widened. "Laurie? Laurie's missing? Oh, my heavens."

"You know Laurie?"

"She's my niece. My big sister's kid." Brenda picked up her phone.

"Then she *is* from around here?"

Brenda punched a button and held up a finger for me to wait.

"Maylene? It's Bren. Is Laurie there with you?" Brenda glanced at me and nodded. "Damn, why didn't you tell me about this?" She shook her head and the caramel curls bounced around her face. "Damn, double damn. Okay, okay, Laurie made you promise. I get it. Now listen. There's someone here who needs to talk to her."

IT TOOK TEN minutes for Nick to get back to the hospital and another twenty for us to find our way to the address Brenda had given me. On the way I asked if he had any luck with the three pickup buyers' names.

"I was just getting started when you called, but we

can probably eliminate Lois McElroy. She's almost eighty."

"Really? How do you know?"

"She's on Facebook. Neither of the others are. That's as far as I got."

We pulled up to a small stucco-sided house adjacent to a large field of pasture grass where half a dozen horses grazed. The clouds had multiplied since early morning, blocking the sun and leaving the air humid. The only vehicle in sight was a fifties vintage Plymouth Fury with sweeping tail fins and gleaming bronze paint. It was parked in front of a detached one-car garage. No sign of a pickup truck.

An older, more buxom version of Brenda stood guard in the open front doorway, wiping her hands on a dish towel. She wore a flowered bib apron over a short-sleeved white cotton blouse and gray slacks. Her white sneakers looked brand-new. I saw a curtain move at a window next to the door.

When we walked up, the woman turned and said over her shoulder, "Well, honey?"

Laurie stepped around her mother, waif-like in baggy blue jeans and a faded red sweat shirt.

"Yes, Mom, it's Aimee. It's all right." She reached out to me, and we shared a hug of mutual relief. "Thank God you found me. This is my mother, Maylene Popejoy."

Maylene threw a nervous glance toward where we had parked and beyond, as if searching for bad news. "Come in. I just put coffee on." She closed the front door and locked it as soon as we were inside.

Laurie led us into a small living room smelling of lemon-scented furniture polish. Crocheted doilies protected the arms of the comfy chairs and loveseat, and the shiny surface of every tabletop. Either Mr. Clean had just exited out the back door, or Maylene was one heck of a housekeeper.

I introduced Nick to Laurie and her mother, and before I could come up with an explanation for why he would fly me to Idaho to look for her, he interjected a reason of his own.

"I needed to log some hours to keep my pilot's license current, and Aimee needed a ride, so it worked out."

Laurie and her mother stood with expectant looks, as if there must be more to the story.

"Nick and I go way back," I offered. "He and my brother are best friends."

That satisfied Maylene, who waved us toward the spotless oak dining table. "You folks have a seat and I'll go get coffee." She hesitated, flipped the dishtowel over her shoulder. "Unless you'd rather have tea?"

"Coffee's fine," Nick said. I nodded.

Laurie took four placemats from the drawer of a china cabinet, arranged them on the table, and sat with us while her mother bustled in the kitchen. She put a finger to her lips and nodded toward the kitchen. Barely above a whisper, she said, "I can't believe you found me."

"I tried to call you back dozens of times after your first call." I kept my voice low. "What happened?"

"I'm so sorry. This will sound paranoid, but after I called you and Cleo, I realized someone might be able to track me by my cellphone, so I trashed it. I called you the second time from a payphone at Uncle Fudd's. I tried to call you again when I got here, but the only number I knew was your home phone and you didn't answer. I was afraid to leave any more messages."

"We were already flying here by then." I explained how Nick had heard Uncle Fudd's cuckoo clock and thought she might be hiding in the wilderness, and how we'd seen her in the black pickup with the Idaho plates.

"That was you, wasn't it?"

"Yes. But I don't remember seeing you. What were you driving?"

"A white pickup. We were hauling llamas in a trailer or we'd have followed you."

"The trailer...now I remember. At the Bunchgrass Trailhead road?"

"Yes. Who were you with?"

Laurie's glance darted toward the doorway into the kitchen. "Mama doesn't know about him. I'll have to explain later."

Sweet aromas of sugar and cinnamon preceded Maylene as she came into the dining room carrying a tray laden with hot rolls and a carafe of coffee.

"I thought a bite of something would do us all good." She tried to pour the coffee into my cup, but her hand shook so badly that Laurie took the carafe from her.

"I'll do that, Mama. You need to relax."

"I'm not infirm," Maylene said, "but I confess I've been shaky since Laurie came home."

"She's afraid for me," Laurie said with a guilty glance at her mother. "I shouldn't have brought trouble home to my folks."

"Nonsense," Maylene said. "Your daddy and I wouldn't have you in distress and us not knowing." She glanced down at her watch. "Speaking of Dad, I'd best put in a call. Let him know of this new development." She seemed to stumble as she headed for the kitchen, but righted herself and continued until she was out of sight.

Laurie picked at a piece of cinnamon roll. "I shouldn't have come here. She's just recovering from a bout of C.

diff that almost killed her. She's only been home from the hospital for a few days."

"*Clostridium difficile*?" I knew it was a serious diagnosis. "How did that happen?"

"She took a broad-spectrum antibiotic for a UTI."

Nick gave me a puzzled look.

"C. diff causes severe infection of the colon and life-threatening diarrhea. The antibiotic can eradicate the normal gut flora and allow the C. diff bacteria to take over. Put simply, it raises hell in the bowel."

"She would have been okay if she'd gone to a decent hospital," Laurie said, "but her family doctor admitted her to Dunnsville Memorial."

"Is there another hospital in Dunnsville?" I asked.

"No, that's what makes me so mad. She would have been fine at one of the larger hospitals in the area, but no, her doctor insisted she go to Dunnsville. He owns the hospital and Mom's sister works there. Mom trusts him, but I think he's way overdue for retirement."

"She seems to be doing okay now," I said.

"Only because I intervened as soon as I heard and got her transferred out of there. I just wish Auntie Brenda would resign from DMH. She says she's too close to being vested in her pension, but I don't believe she'll ever see it. They'll find a way to cheat her out of it." She tore off a piece of a cinnamon roll, looked at it for a moment and dropped it on her napkin. Her eyes glistened.

Nick cleared his throat. "Laurie, how much does your mother know about why you left Timbergate?"

Whispering, she said, "I told her I quit my job and came home because I was being harassed by someone at TMC. I had to tell them something, but I didn't want to say what's really going on. They'd be too worried."

"How long are you planning to stay with them?" I asked.

"I don't know. I hoped someone would have figured out who killed Cody by now."

"Wait," Nick said. "You mean you don't know who it is?"

"No." She frowned. "Is that what you thought? That I'd know who killed him?"

Maylene's soft conversational tones drifted from the kitchen. We didn't have much time to hear Laurie's story unless we could get her away from her mother.

"Can we leave here for a while?" I asked.

"Later, maybe, after my father gets home. I don't want to leave my mother alone. Dad's a mechanic at a potato processing plant. They called him in this morning to repair one of the machines. He's been insisting we call him every couple of hours."

Of course she wouldn't leave her recuperating mother alone, especially if there was a chance someone might show up looking to silence Laurie. But if Laurie didn't know what happened to Cody, why was she running?

Nick glanced toward the kitchen. Laurie and I looked at each other. Her mother had finished her phone call and we heard water running in the kitchen sink.

"How do you know Cody's death wasn't accidental if you didn't witness it?" Nick asked.

The water stopped running in the kitchen. Laurie shook her head. "No more now. We can meet somewhere later and talk. I'll explain everything then."

Maylene came back to the dining room, her face glistening with sweat. She held a large glass of water. "Daddy's reassured, honey. I told him your friends were here to help."

NINETEEN

L AURIE WALKED TO the car with us and gave me a hug.
When she grasped my hand I felt a scrap of folded
paper. "Take it," she whispered. I glanced back at the
porch, where her mother stood waving goodbye. I un-
folded her note as soon as we pulled out of the driveway.

Nick glanced over. "What's that?"

"A note from Laurie. She wants us to meet her at ten
o'clock tonight at the Blue Banjo."

"What's the Blue Banjo?" Nick said.

"She wrote the address." I pulled out my phone to
do a search. "Looks like it's a roadhouse. Take a left at
the next intersection."

We found the Blue Banjo on an isolated stretch of
road north of town just as a breeze split the oppressive
cloud cover. A shaft of sunlight cast a holy radiance on
a signboard at the entrance to the parking lot. It boasted
STEAK, BBQ, and DANCE FLOOR. A second sign,
attached below the larger one, advertised the evening's
entertainment as The Oakley Brothers.

It wasn't the rundown dive I'd expected. The gray
paint and red trim appeared fresh, and there were signs of
regular attention to landscaping. Cypress trees lined the
asphalt-coated driveway, and a red maple, autumn leaves
in full blazing crimson, shaded the entrance door. Nick
drove into the parking lot so we could get a closer look.

"Place looks empty."

A black pickup suddenly sped from behind the building and clipped our right rear fender, spinning the rental in a one-eighty. The driver laid a trail of smoking rubber on the asphalt. In seconds, he reached the highway and disappeared from sight.

"What the devil?" Nick got out, mumbling expletives, and checked the damage to the car. He came back shaking his head. "Taillight's smashed."

"Did you pay for rental insurance?"

He slipped back into the driver's seat. "Didn't think we'd need it." He slapped the steering wheel. "Damn fool."

"You, or the other guy?"

"Both." Nick tried the ignition. The motor turned over without a hitch. "We can drive it back to the rental place, but we're going to need another car."

"You think they'll let us take another one?"

"If not, we're on foot."

"Then drop me off at the hospital first."

"You want to go back there? Why?"

"I didn't get anywhere asking Brenda McClurg about DeeDee Dakota. Once she realized the nurse we were trying to find was her niece, the subject of DeeDee was dropped."

"I don't blame Laurie for keeping the truth from her family. If her parents are that upset about her being harassed, they'd be horrified to think a murderer was looking for her."

A hollow place opened in my chest. "You sound pretty sure that's the case."

"I'd rather be wrong, but I think it's likely."

"Nick, do you think the pickup that slammed into us back there is involved? Maybe it's the same one we saw in the wilderness."

"Maybe. When we found Laurie safe, I thought we could rule out the dude with the black pickup. I assume she'll tell us who he is when we get together tonight."

I called Brenda's office and her secretary told me she would be back from her lunch break in half an hour. She wouldn't guarantee an appointment but said she would let Brenda know I was dropping by.

"What are you going to do while I'm at the hospital?" I asked.

"I'll try to get another rental car, then I'll work on the other two names on Gary P's list. Call my cell when you're finished, and I'll get back as soon as I can."

Nick dropped me at the front entrance and I made my way to Brenda McClurg's office for the second time. I was fifteen minutes early when I reached her door. It was ajar and I heard a woman's voice inside, so I waited before entering. It took me a moment to realize the voice was not Brenda's, but her secretary's. She was carrying on a phone conversation.

"CJ, you'd better take care of this mess. I've kept my mouth shut about Caroline for a hell of a long time. Once we pass the inspection, I mean to have Brenda McClurg's job. You'd damn well better make it happen."

I was still early, so I headed for the women's room at the end of the corridor, where I pondered what I had just heard. The woman had told someone named CJ to clean up a mess. The scandal in the media? But she said she'd kept quiet about someone named Caroline, and that she wanted Brenda McClurg's job. I considered telling Brenda what I'd heard, but decided it wasn't my place to intervene.

I stepped into the corridor outside the women's room and called Brenda's office on my cellphone. The same woman answered. That didn't bode well for Brenda. Her secretary plotting to take over her job. I asked if McClurg was in and was told she would be back from lunch in ten minutes. I had passed a small cafeteria just down the hall. I thought I might find her there, but the only occupants were three women in black and white scrubs patterned like the hide of a Holstein cow. They huddled over some papers on the table, carrying on an animated conversation.

I bought a soggy tuna on white bread and fruit juice. Then I sat at a table and unwrapped my sandwich while snatches of conversation from the women drifted my way. I heard "cover-up" and "so what?" and "kids to feed." The working woman's dilemma.

The tuna sandwich was disgusting, but I was hungry enough to finish it. I returned to Brenda's office on time and found her alone. She invited me in.

"So you're back to finish our conversation," she said.

"I hope so, Brenda. Earlier I had just mentioned DeeDee Dakota when we got sidetracked about Laurie. It's important that I learn all I can about the time DeeDee spent here back when she had her accident at the rodeo."

"That was more than two years ago. Her record should have been copied and transported with her to Timbergate Medical Center."

"I realize that, but we've been unable to locate her chart."

"What name were you looking for?"

"We've tried her professional name and her married name, but neither of those pulled up her record."

"I can tell you why. She wasn't admitted here by either of those names. For legal purposes, she was Deirdre DeGraw. Most likely, that's how she was admitted at your facility."

"Why DeGraw?"

"That's how she was listed on all her ID, so that's what we used."

I'd have to call Cleo about the name confusion. No wonder she'd found no record of Deirdre O'Brien in the TMC records database.

"Brenda, is there anyone working here now who might have observed her care? A nurse who was assigned to her, maybe? It would help to know which doctors and nurses took care of her and who her visitors were."

"You're looking at her."

"You? Weren't you already in your current position?"

"You've got to remember what a small place this is. Lots of us did double duty. I have retrieved Ms. DeGraw's record from the Health Information office." She pulled a chart from her desk drawer. "Let's go through it and see if it will refresh my memory."

Brenda frowned at the page in front of her. "I remember being on duty in our ICU when they brought her in. My notes are here."

"You have an ICU here?" I tried to keep the disbelief from my voice.

"We have the basics. A mechanical ventilator, cardiac monitors, defibrillator, feeding tubes, suction pumps, drains and catheters. And the usual drugs."

"Was DeeDee on a ventilator?"

"Let's see." She flipped a couple of pages. "Yes. But not right away. She came in around nine o'clock at night, awake and alert. Same the next morning, so she was moved out of the unit to a room on the floor, and she responded well for the rest of the day. She slept normally through that night, but lapsed into a coma the following morning, just as she was about to be discharged. That's when she was moved back into the ICU and put on a ventilator."

"Then the coma was a result of her injury? Not medically induced?"

Brenda ran her finger down a page in the chart. "Not induced. You work in a hospital. You must know how common it is for a head injury to seem mild at first, then progress downhill rapidly."

"Yes. There was an actress a few years ago who made the news when she died after a skiing accident."

"Yes. Tragic, but we did what we could for Ms. De-Graw."

"What was her ratio of nursing care?"

"Three to one." She held my gaze with a hint of challenge.

"So you had other patients in ICU?"

"Two others. The unit only holds three beds. A couple of kids were brought in after a head-on. He was drunk and trying to impress his girlfriend by passing a semi on a two-lane road."

I understood her defensiveness. A ratio of two patients to one nurse is recommended for a medical ICU, unlike the ratio of four or five patients to one nurse on the medical floors. She was only slightly out of compliance caring for three at once.

"We saved both those kids," Brenda said. "And I *am* a registered nurse, in case you're wondering." If she got any more annoyed I'd be sent packing. I backed off.

"I'm sure you took wonderful care of DeeDee. It

sounds as if her injury was so severe she never had a chance."

"On the contrary, I thought she had a good chance. She seemed to be doing fine until those last few hours. Her husband thought the worst was over by the time his brother got here."

"Did you meet them? Cody and James O'Brien?"

"Oh, yes. More than 'met' them. They never left her side. At least the brother didn't. The husband left a few times to check on their horses and tend to some rodeo business."

"But his brother stayed with her?" I recalled James struggling with his feelings about DeeDee's death—the depth of loss he seemed to feel.

Brenda gazed past me, remembering. "Yes, James. That was the brother's name. He was with her constantly after she slipped into the coma that last morning. At one point, when the husband happened to be out, the brother-in-law was holding her hand and weeping. He seemed deeply affected, but it was none of my business."

TWENTY

BRENDA'S ACCOUNT OF James's behavior at DeeDee's bedside told me his feelings for his brother's wife went
beyond what was expected of a brother-in-law. James
seemed certain he'd seen Phyllis Poole in DeeDee's
hospital room. Had Dr. Poole really been there when
DeeDee was a patient? If so, why?

I chose an indirect approach. "Does the chart show
every physician who was involved in DeeDee's care?"
I stopped short of mentioning Dr. Poole's name.

Brenda flipped a page. "Only Dr. Carl Jasper."

CJ. The woman on the phone had been talking to
someone with those initials. "Is he still on staff?"

"Oh, yes." Brenda rolled her eyes heavenward. "He's
one of the founders of this place. The others are all dead.
Now he owns it outright. Been here since the dinosaur
age, and he'll be here until he becomes a fossil himself." Brenda closed the folder on her desk, sat back,
and crossed her arms. "I'm sorry. I told Cleo I'd try to
help you out, but I don't have anything else to tell you."
Brenda's body language and uncompromising expression sent a clear message. *We're through here.*

But I hadn't asked if Laurie was working at Dunnsville Memorial when DeeDee was a patient there. I
could try to exploit Brenda's concern for her niece—
tell her Laurie's life might depend on what I learned

about DeeDee's stay at DMH—but would she believe me? I decided it was worth a try.

"I understand," I said, "but there's something else...."

The door to Brenda's office burst open and a woman wearing a nubby pink Chanel suit stormed into the room.

"McClurg, you'd better come...." She put on the brakes when she saw me. "Oh, I didn't know you had a visitor." She stood rooted to the spot and leveled a look at Brenda that said I should be dispatched immediately.

A dark page-boy hairdo framed what had to be a surgically enhanced face. She appeared to be in her fifties and looked as if she'd last read a fashion magazine when Jackie Kennedy was First Lady.

"My executive assistant," Brenda said. "Jacqueline Poole."

"Aimee Machado," I said. "Pleased to meet you."

Now I had a face and a name to go with the voice I'd heard earlier. Her first name explained the fashion choices, but it didn't explain her surname. Was she related to Phyllis Poole? Or were the names an unbelievable coincidence? I was glad I hadn't mentioned Dr. Poole's name to Brenda before this woman arrived.

"What is it, Jackie?" Brenda said.

"I'd rather not say." She nodded toward me.

I took my cue and announced that I had to be going. I thanked Brenda for her time and left, wishing I could eavesdrop outside her door again. Unfortunately there was too much traffic in the hallway.

A call to Nick's cellphone went unanswered, so I left a message that I was waiting in the hospital lobby. I picked a chair by a window so I could watch the parking lot. The two other women in the room looked like elderly sisters and sat staring at a soap opera on a television set mounted high on the wall. I assumed they'd given up on real-life romance years ago until a steamy scene on the screen caused them to giggle and jab each other with their elbows.

Ten minutes passed, and no word from Nick. I pondered what I'd learned from Brenda. There was the revelation about James and his feelings for DeeDee, the intrigue at this little hospital involving Jackie Poole's resentment of Brenda McClurg, and most interesting, the possibility that Jackie Poole and Phyllis Poole were related. That gave some credence to James's claim that he'd seen Phyllis Poole in DeeDee's hospital room.

But why? Phyllis was working in New York back then, and Cleo said her CV didn't show any reference to Dunnsville Memorial Hospital. I desperately wanted to know about everyone who came near DeeDee while she was a patient at Dunnsville Memorial, and that was more than Brenda was willing to tell me. There had to be another way. I called Cleo to tell her that Dunnsville Memorial Hospital had used DeeDee's maiden name: Deirdre DeGraw.

"Then TMC must have used the same name to create her chart here," Cleo said. "That's why I couldn't remember her from the death review. I was trying to recall someone named O'Brien."

"Brenda seemed sure that everything in DeeDee's chart here in Idaho was copied and sent to TMC when DeeDee was transferred. When can you go down to the archives again?"

"I'm not sure when I'll have another chance. When will you be home?"

"Probably tomorrow. We're meeting with Laurie tonight, but after that there's not much more we can do here."

I finished the call just as a doctor in scrubs came into the waiting room. He approached the two waiting women, pulling their attention away from their television show. He spoke in low tones and they both broke into broad smiles and hugged him. One wiped a tear from her eye and the other blew her nose into a tissue. The doctor escorted them out into the corridor.

Alone, I glanced out the window and noticed a shiny black F150 pull up and stop. I saw Nick step out, and I raced outside to meet him at the entrance.

"Hi, what's going on? I left you a message fifteen minutes ago."

Nick put an arm around my shoulders. "Sorry, I was tied up. I would have called you, but I didn't want to interrupt anything in case you were sneaking around."

"Tied up doing what? Did you get this ride from the rental place?"

"No. The rental place didn't have another car for us. This is one of Gary P's fleet." Nick steered me toward the cab and opened the passenger door. "Hop in."

"So what's going on? This thing is brand-new, isn't it? Did they let you take it for a test drive?"

"Not exactly." Nick turned to me with a grin. "I bought it."

"You *what*? Are you serious?"

"We needed wheels on the ground, and I couldn't talk Gary P into letting me take it out alone for an overnight test drive. Seems car dealers are getting skittish these days. So I decided to buy it and have it shipped home."

"I can't believe you did this."

"Why not? It's a nice rig. I think Ginger would look good in it." He smiled. "And you can borrow it when your old clunker is at the car doctor. That seems to happen a lot lately."

"Tell me about it." Driving a shiny new pickup once in a while held major appeal. It was a pain to have to ask Harry or Nick for a ride every time my car was in the shop.

On the way to our motel, I filled Nick in on what I'd learned from Brenda and about DeeDee's name being DeGraw and not O'Brien. I described Jackie Poole's sneaky phone call with CJ, whose initials matched those of DeeDee's admitting physician. Nick thought the news about James at DeeDee's bedside was significant, and the Phyllis and Jackie Poole coincidence worth pursuing, but neither was proof of anything.

"Maybe we'll get the rest of the story when we meet your friend Laurie tonight."

Back in my room at the motel, I asked Nick about the other two names on our list.

"I think we can forget about Angela Winkle. She moved to Canada six months ago."

"Okay," I said. "We'll give her a pass for now. What about Carson Littletree?"

"I drew a blank."

"Maybe Laurie would recognize the name."

"Maybe. She might not know who killed Cody, but she knows something, and someone wants to get to her before she tells."

"Do you think that whoever is looking for her has figured out what we're up to?"

"It's very possible. Do you want to back out now?"

It was a good question. Why was I risking both our necks? For Cleo's sake? So we could protect her Siggy from Phyllis Poole, who might be completely harmless? Or better yet, whose surgical skill might save Sig's life?

"Not yet," I said. "Let's hear what Laurie has to say, then decide."

Nick responded with a quiet chuckle. "You're not fooling me. This riddle has you locked in a grip as tight as a pit bull's jaw."

THE SUN WAS down and stars were winking by the time we reached the nearly full parking lot of the Blue Banjo a few minutes before ten. Nick and I sat in the pickup inhaling the new car smell and wondering if any of the vehicles in the lot was Laurie's ride. The only one we'd seen at her parents' home was the vintage Plymouth Fury, and it was nowhere in sight.

Nick unlocked the glove compartment and took out his 22 caliber semi-automatic pistol. He slipped it into a shoulder holster I hadn't noticed under his windbreaker. A chill inched down the back of my neck, but I didn't comment.

At ten o'clock, a white GMC pickup with a camper shell pulled into the lot and parked. The driver's door didn't open, but Laurie stepped out on the passenger side. She glanced around the lot, gave a little wave toward the driver, who remained in the vehicle, then squared her shoulders and headed for the bar's entrance door. She had arranged for someone to wait for her—look out for her. Smart girl.

Nick and I waited for a couple of minutes then followed Laurie inside.

We stopped just inside the door to take in the room. A live blues combo was doing its rendition of Eric Clapton's "Stormy Monday." We spotted Laurie alone at a table in a dark corner as far away from the bandstand as possible.

"Go on over," Nick said. "I'll get a couple of beers from the bar."

I walked toward Laurie, trying to fake a bar patron's attitude and feeling like I was overacting. When I reached her table, she looked up at me as if we were strangers. I figured she must have a reason so I played along.

"Hi," I said. "Would you mind some company?"

"Sorry, I'm waiting for someone." Laurie kept her expression neutral.

Nick approached with a beer in each hand and I gave him a warning frown. "I thought we might share this table, but this woman is waiting for someone."

"No problem." Nick gestured with his elbow at an empty table across the room, and I followed him.

"Now what?" I asked.

"Let's give her a few minutes." Nick leaned over and nuzzled my ear. "Don't pull away," he whispered. "Fake it until we figure out what's going on with her."

"Do you think she's being watched?"

"Looks like she thinks so. Let's see if she gives us any kind of signal."

We watched Laurie make a call on her cellphone. She appeared to be in a heated conversation. After a minute she frowned, jammed her phone in the pocket of her jeans and walked toward the restrooms.

"Go," Nick said.

Laurie stood at the mirror inside the two-stall restroom. "Let's do this quickly while we're alone in here," she said.

"Okay, first question. Why did you try to reach me about Cody instead of going to the police?"

"I'm sure the horse didn't kill Cody, but I don't have proof. I needed to tell someone what I knew and thought of you because you have some knowledge of forensics and because I knew I could trust you to be discreet."

"Laurie, we don't have much time. Nick and I are

here to help you, but we need to know what happened the night Cody died."

"I was Cody's floor nurse that night. He was restless but when I asked if he wanted anxiety meds, he said he'd changed his mind and didn't want the surgery. He wanted to leave the hospital. I explained that he'd already waited too long to have his ruptured testicle repaired. I reassured him that Dr. Poole was an excellent surgeon."

I tried not to react to that piece of news. Apparently whatever Laurie knew had nothing to do with Dr. Poole. I wanted to explore that further, but I let her go on with her story.

"Cody said he wasn't afraid of the surgery, but he was afraid someone wanted to kill him, and he knew he'd be helpless if he was confined and sedated."

"Did you believe him?"

"Not until he told me someone had already made an attempt. He showed me a scab on his right shoulder where he said a bullet grazed him a few days earlier when he'd been out riding his horse in the foothills."

"Someone shot at him? Did he report it?"

"He said the sheriff's office took his report, but they thought it was a deer hunter's stray bullet."

"So you helped him sign out against medical advice?"

"Yes, but there's more." I could see doubt in her eyes. Could she really trust me?

"Laurie, I know you fled Timbergate because someone broke into your home."

"How do you know about that?"

"We went there looking for you and saw the broken door jamb. Do you know who it was?"

"Only that it had to be Cody's killer, and he must

think I know who he is. Do the police know about the break-in?"

"I don't think so. We didn't report it. Are you sure it was a man?"

"I assumed it was when I heard the door crashing in, but I didn't wait around to find out."

"You asked Nick and me to meet you here. Why are you pretending you don't know us?"

"We needed a place to talk, but now I think this was a bad idea. The bartender is a friend of mine. When I came in he told me someone who wasn't a regular had been asking about me earlier this evening."

"Did you ask for a description?"

"I did, but he said the guy was wearing a hoodie and dark glasses."

"Dark glasses in a bar? Sounds like he didn't want to be recognized." No wonder Laurie was nervous.

Laurie looked in the mirror, shook her head. "I thought I'd be safe in Idaho, but I made a big mistake. I left my laptop behind. Was it still there when you were in my house?" The image of her laptop, first there and then gone, came to mind.

"No, but whoever has it didn't think to take it for several days. That gave you a good head start. What kind of information was on it?"

"My Facebook profile. Hometown, that kind of thing. Damn. If someone decided to track me all the way to Idaho, I've put my family in danger." She opened the cold water tap and cupped her hands under the flow. She rinsed her face and dried it with a paper towel.

The restroom door opened and two blue-eyed blondes who looked like twins came in and went to the stalls. Laurie mouthed, *I have to leave*. She pulled out a pen, wrote a phone number on a piece of paper towel and handed it to me.

I waited a minute after she left, then went out to report to Nick. The combo was doing a rendition of "I Smell Trouble," and Nick was swaying on the dance floor with a red-haired amazon who had both arms draped around his neck and her body pasted against his. *Trouble, indeed.*

He spotted me and raised his eyebrows. I scanned the room for Laurie. We couldn't let her get away when we had only part of her story. I marched up to Nick and the redhead and did my best impression of a jealous girlfriend.

"Hey, sister, that's my man you're mauling. Get lost."

She looked down her nose at me without letting go of Nick. "You gotta be kidding." She looked at Nick. "Isn't she Mongolian or something?"

I narrowed my eyes and gave her a fierce glare that would have made both my Chinese and Portuguese ancestors proud. "Beat it, or you won't be able to dance for a year."

She looked at Nick again. "Is she for real?"

"You better believe it," Nick said. "She can kick my ass, so I'd hate to see what she'd do to you." He disentangled himself and walked me back to our table.

"What was that all about?" I said.

"Just trying to blend in."

"Great idea, Nick. Where's Laurie?"

"She took off out of here just before you came out of the restroom. Did you get her story?"

"Not all of it. We were interrupted, but she gave me this." I showed him the scrap of paper with the phone number and told him what Laurie said about Cody being grazed by a bullet when he was out riding. "He was afraid someone was trying to kill him."

"So he didn't lose his nerve about the surgery and the woman doctor? That's not why he left the hospital?"

"No, Laurie said he left because he was afraid he'd be an easy target if he was stuck in a hospital bed recovering from surgery."

"Let's go." He put an arm around my waist. "She's only been gone a few minutes. Maybe she's waiting outside. If not, we'll call her."

We scanned the parking lot looking for the white GMC pickup Laurie had arrived in, but it was gone. We went to Nick's new pickup and sat in the cab working out our next move. I wanted to call the phone number right away, but Nick wanted to wait while we watched the exit to see if anyone else left right away—someone who might be keeping track of Laurie. He rolled the windows down to catch any sounds from outside the roadhouse.

"What did she say about the black pickup we saw in the wilderness?" Nick asked. "Did she say who that was?"

"No, we didn't get to that before she left."

"Did you ask her if she knew someone named Carson Littletree?"

"No, there wasn't time. All I got was Cody's fear that someone wanted him dead. And her fear that the same someone is after her."

Then a piece dropped into place. *That's* why Cody called James from the hospital and asked him to come to California right away. He needed someone he trusted. He needed his brother. But I had to wonder if his trust in James was a mistake. Everyone in the O'Brien family seemed to have a hidden agenda. Why should James be an exception?

A sudden popping sound caught us off guard. It took a second before either of us realized a bullet had passed through our open windows and grazed the back of Nick's right hand, resting on the steering wheel.

"Get down." Nick shoved me toward the floorboard, turned on the ignition, and spun the truck around toward the road. Another bullet hit the rear window, which exploded into a million fragments.

"Damn," Nick said. "Stay down."

He pulled onto the highway and jammed the gas pedal to the floorboard. The truck's tires squealed in agony and the cab filled with the smell of burning rubber. I listened for the sound of more gunfire but heard nothing more than air rushing past our open windows. After several minutes of high-speed twists and turns, Nick finally eased up on the accelerator and stopped yelling at me to stay down. By then I was cramped and queasy.

"Can I come up now?" I said.

"Yeah. It looks like the shooter didn't follow us."

I managed to scramble up and fasten my seatbelt. "Any idea why not?"

"Hoping to scare us away, but not willing to risk being involved in a second murder, would be my guess."

"Your hand's hurt. It's dripping blood."

"It's just a scratch." He pulled a handkerchief from his back pocket. "Here, wrap this around it." He reached his hand out.

I wrapped it and tied it off, but blood still leaked through enough to stain the white cloth.

"What do we do now?"

"Call that phone number."

TWENTY-ONE

I PUNCHED IN the number from the scrap of paper towel. Laurie answered right away, asking where we were. I said someone had taken shots at us in the parking lot and we were headed north. When I assured her that no vehicles were following us, she gave me directions to a small church on the outskirts of Dunnsville.

Minutes later we spotted the church on a sparsely populated street. The parking lot looked empty. Nick pulled in and drove around behind the building. The white GMC pickup sat there alone. Nick pulled up next to it. A man with dark hair in braids sat behind the wheel. He rolled his window down and pointed a small handgun toward us.

"Tell me your names and be quick."

Nick pressed me back against the seat. "I'm Nick Alexander and she's Aimee Machado. Laurie Pope-joy's expecting us, so put the damn gun away or we're through here."

The gun disappeared. I ventured a guess. "Are you Carson Littletree?"

"My name's none of your business. Laurie's waiting for you inside. Use the back door. If you hear any commotion out here, you'd better make damned sure she stays safe."

There was sparse light inside the small building, but

we made out the shape of a woman sitting toward the front in a simple wooden pew. We walked over to her.

"Laurie?" I whispered.

She turned and pressed a hand to her chest. "Oh, God, I'm so sorry. I shouldn't have gone to the roadhouse." She spotted the bloody handkerchief wrapped around Nick's hand. "Are you okay?"

"It's not serious," Nick said, "but we don't want the shooter to find us and try again, so let's get this done. First, who's the guy outside in the white pickup?"

"He's my husband."

Nick and I exchanged astonished glances. It took me a minute to let go of my fantasy of Laurie and Tobias Fausset as a couple. Nick recovered faster.

"Jesus, lady, you'd better start explaining. And you can begin by telling us your husband's name. Is it Carson Littletree?"

It was Laurie's turn to be surprised. "No, his name is Daniel Littletree. Carson is his brother, the owner of the Blue Banjo." She looked from Nick to me. "How do you even know about Carson? He's so protective of his privacy, he even owns the road house under a fictitious name."

We explained about the black F150 and how we'd used the DMV website to search for the names of some of Patterson's Motors' customers. I wondered if Carson Littletree might have been in the black pickup that clipped our rental car earlier at the Blue Banjo. I told Laurie what happened and asked if she'd heard anything about it from Carson or her husband.

"Daniel and I saw Carson this afternoon," Laurie said. "His pickup looked as flawless as always. It's fairly new and he's a pretty careful driver."

"Then it had to be the guy who's after you. He was checking the place out like we were. How would he have known we planned to meet here? Did you tell anyone?"

"I can't think…. Wait, I did tell one person. My Aunt Brenda. But she wouldn't have any reason to tell anyone else. I trust her completely. She even knows Daniel and I are married."

"Why did you tell her about tonight?" I asked.

"She called just after you left, asking if everything was okay. I tried to reassure her that everything was fine, that the harassment issue had been blown out of proportion. I said Daniel and I were meeting friends for drinks tonight."

"Did you say where?"

"I might have mentioned the Blue Banjo. She knows Daniel's brother owns it, so she would have expected us to go there." Laurie shook her head. "But Aunt Brenda wouldn't betray me."

"Of course not, but we need to move on," I said. "Your husband is understandably short on patience, and we still have a lot of questions."

"First, who met you in the wilderness?" Nick asked. "That wasn't your husband's pickup."

Laurie drew a breath and released it in a heavy sigh. "I'll try to explain the whole story.

"I heard someone breaking into my house just before dawn on Tuesday morning. I'd only been back home from the incident involving Cody for about two hours. I climbed out my bathroom window and managed to get out of town without being followed. I headed up into the mountains as far as Uncle Fudd's Tavern. By the time I got there, I had heard on my car radio that Cody was dead. I watched the television news in Uncle Fudd's bar, hoping that someone had been arrested for killing Cody so I could go back and tell what I'd witnessed."

"Then why did you call in and resign from TMC?" I asked.

"I couldn't go to work, but I didn't want anyone at the hospital to think I was sick or missing. Nothing that would draw attention to me. I wanted an excuse to disappear, so I said I had a family emergency out of state. I rented a cabin across from Uncle Fudd's and spent Tuesday night there. That's when I called you and Cleo. Neither of you answered, so I left messages." She shivered. "Then I panicked and destroyed my phone."

"But you called me the second time from Uncle Fudd's phone on Wednesday night. How long did you stay in the cabin?"

"Only until Thursday morning. I decided I had to call Daniel. If he couldn't reach me on my cellphone, he'd be worried. I called him from Uncle Fudd's right after I called you, Aimee. He said his GMC had been sideswiped in an accident and was being repaired, so he borrowed Carson's pickup to drive to California. He said he'd meet me in the Thousand Lakes Wilderness as soon as he could get there."

"I have a question," Nick said. "How did you get to the trailhead after you left the cabin? Did you leave your car in the Bunchgrass parking lot?"

"No. I was afraid someone would recognize it. It was Daniel's idea to disable it. I thought of puncturing a tire, but Daniel said the tow truck driver would just put on my spare. He said to crack the driver's side windshield when I got close to the ranger station. Then I walked there and borrowed their phone. I called a tow truck to take the car back to a repair shop in Timbergate. No one would think to look for it there."

"I'm impressed," Nick said. "How'd you break the windshield?"

"I used a tire iron. The tow truck driver met me at the ranger station and took me back to my car. I told him a falling rock did the damage. He offered to let me ride back to Timbergate with him, but I told him someone was meeting me at the ranger station. He gave me a lift there."

"Is that where you met up with Daniel?" I asked.

"No, he was still on his way from Idaho, so I caught a ride to the trailhead with one of the rangers. When Daniel met me at Eiler, we decided to stay in the wilderness and let some time pass. We hoped whoever was after me would be arrested, or at least give up and quit looking for me. Except for an occasional fisherman, we had the lake to ourselves. After a few days, we decided to head home and hope no one would look for me in Idaho. The day you saw us was the day we decided to come home."

"Okay, my turn," I said. "Why do you work and live two states away and go by a different name when you're married to someone here in Idaho?"

"It's complicated."

"Try to keep it simple. We've already been shot at tonight. Nick's been hit. You wanted to tell me why you think Cody O'Brien was murdered. We need the rest of your story."

Laurie reached out toward Nick's injured hand. "I'm so sorry about dragging you into all this. My marriage has been a secret…except for Aunt Brenda. Daniel's family and mine didn't know about it until tonight. He's one-eighth Shoshone Indian, but without the braids, he doesn't look it. And I'm sure you've noticed that I'm black." She looked at Nick and me, then down at her lap.

"Your parents don't believe in mixed marriages?" I said. "That's not so unusual. Why didn't you just tell them to get over it?"

"You two probably think you understand the challenges of an interracial relationship, but take my word for it, Aimee, being half Asian isn't quite the same as being black. Our parents love us and want us to be happy, but they don't want us to be targets. Hate groups in this country aren't in the news as often as they used to be, but they're still out there. The only thing that arouses more rage in those people than a person of color is a mixed-race marriage. Especially between whites and blacks."

Laurie looked toward the church's entrance doors. Satisfied we were still safe, she explained that she and Daniel had eloped to Reno a year earlier. They traveled through northern California on their way home, thinking they might eventually relocate there. Both of them wanted to work in a hospital, so they stopped by the TMC personnel office and Laurie was offered a job. Two weeks later she started work at TMC. Daniel stayed in Idaho to complete the last year of his training as a physical therapist. They commuted back and forth as much as possible, and spent a lot of their time together camping in northern California.

"Which is why you chose the Thousand Lakes Wilderness when you went into hiding," I said.

"Yes. We spent our honeymoon there."

"Has Daniel finished his training program?" Nick asked.

"Yes, he'll graduate in December, and then he was going to move to Timbergate and try to get hired at TMC. We told our parents about our marriage tonight, but we've had to put our plans on hold until all this gets sorted out."

"Then let's hear your story about Cody's last night. Maybe we can help move things along," Nick said.

Laurie stared toward the simple altar in front of us. On a table covered in a white cloth stood a wooden crucifix that appeared to be carved out of mahogany. It wasn't clear what color Jesus was supposed to be, but the message seemed to be that it didn't matter.

She began her story with the night she was working swing shift on the surgery floor at TMC. Cody was one of the patients assigned to her. After dinner, he'd acted anxious and worried. She'd asked if he wanted something to calm him and help him sleep. He said he didn't want any sedatives, but he needed his cellphone and didn't know where it was.

The phone had been put away in a pocket of his jeans, which were stuffed into a bag and placed on a shelf under his hospital bed. She asked him if he wanted help making the call, and he said no, he wanted privacy. The other bed in his room was unoccupied, so she left him alone to make his call. That had to be when he'd called his brother, James, in New York.

Laurie said she checked back later and asked how he was doing. He still seemed agitated. Then she noticed what looked like a small spot of blood on the shoulder of his hospital gown and asked if she could take a look. She immediately suspected it was a gunshot wound. She'd seen enough of them in her training, so she asked him about it.

He told her about being grazed by a bullet while he was out riding and that the sheriff's deputy who took his report suggested it was a deer hunter's stray bullet.

"Hard to believe with his injured testicle that he'd want to be riding a horse," Nick said.

"I asked him about that," Laurie said. "He said it wasn't quite as bad then. His surgery was scheduled as an elective, not an emergency. But when he rode away from the shooter at a full gallop, he exacerbated the injury."

"Each time I checked on him, he seemed more anxious," Laurie said. "Finally, about half past ten, he told me he wanted his clothes. He wanted to check himself out of the hospital."

"What did you do?" I couldn't believe she would let him go.

"I knew his condition was serious. He'd been injured at a rodeo by a bull's hoof. Cody had put off having surgery until he was in severe pain."

"But he still went riding on Game Boy?"

"He said he wanted one last ride, just in case something went wrong during the surgery. I don't know how he managed, but by the time he rode out of the foothills at a full gallop to get away from the shooter, he knew he couldn't wait any longer. After he was admitted, he obviously had second thoughts. He felt he knew me well enough to ask me to help him leave the hospital."

"Wait, you're saying you and Cody knew each other?" Nick said. "How?"

"I've been working every other weekend at a pathology lab. Cody brought his father to the lab a few weeks ago for some blood work he has done on a monthly basis. That's why he recognized me when I introduced myself in the hospital."

Knowing what I did about Seamus O'Brien's medical condition, it didn't surprise me that he was having his blood checked fairly often.

Laurie went on, "I guess Cody felt he could trust me since I was a familiar face. He kept saying he had to get away, that someone wanted him dead, so I gave him an AMA form to sign."

"We know about the form," I said. "*Against Medical Advice*. It was found on his bed with his signature, but it wasn't signed by his doctor or a witness."

"Did he explain why he thought someone wanted him dead?" Nick asked.

"No. He said he wasn't sure. He asked me to keep it to myself."

"So he left the hospital. How do you know what happened after that?"

Laurie looked back toward the doors again, then put her head in her hands.

"Because I was there."

TWENTY-TWO

"You were there?" I was confused. Back at the Blue Banjo, Laurie had said she didn't know who the killer was.

Just then we heard the church's back door creak open. "Get down," Nick said. He spun toward the sound and crouched behind the back of the pew, pistol in hand.

"Hold your fire," came the voice from the doorway.

"It's Daniel," Laurie said.

We stood up and Nick holstered his gun. Daniel strode toward us. Laurie stepped out into the aisle and into his embrace. He kissed her forehead and kept an arm around her shoulders.

"You folks need to hurry. I've seen a couple vehicles pass by. No way to know if they're looking for us."

"Can you give us a few more minutes?" Nick asked. "We're almost finished."

"A few minutes, but I don't like it. If anyone else drives by, we're out of here." He headed for the door.

"Daniel, wait," Laurie said. "Bring me the first aid kit."

Daniel ducked out and quickly returned with the kit. "Hurry it up, folks. I'm running out of patience." The door closed behind him.

I trained the beam of Nick's pen light on his wound while Laurie cleansed and wrapped his hand. Satisfied with her work, she went on with her story.

Once she realized Cody was determined to leave the hospital, she decided to help him. She knew he could die of sepsis if he delayed the testicle surgery much longer, so she convinced him to wait until the end of her shift. She explained that he had the right to check out of the hospital against medical advice. She agreed to accompany him to a hospital a hundred miles north in Medford, Oregon, where she would help him arrange to have his surgery done.

Cody agreed, and Laurie drove him to the O'Brien compound east of Coyote Creek, dropped him off, and headed to her little house in town to change clothes. Cody hitched up his horse trailer, loaded Game Boy, and went to meet Laurie. She knew he wouldn't be able to park in the alley, so she waited for him outside the apartment house that stood in front of her little cottage.

When she asked him why he wanted to bring the horse, he said he'd be more comfortable knowing Game Boy was with him. Laurie knew the horse was worth a lot of money and figured it was probably Cody's greatest asset. He gave Laurie the name and phone number of a rancher friend in Medford and said he'd call and arrange to board the horse there until he recovered from his surgery.

"How did he manage to hitch up his trailer and load his horse?" Nick winced. "I'm in pain just imagining an injury like his."

"The pain meds. I made sure he had enough to keep the pain controlled until we reached Medford." Laurie glanced at me with a look between guilt and defiance. "I know he shouldn't have driven across town, but we didn't have much choice."

"Hey, I don't blame you," I said. "The poor guy must have been in agony."

"Sounds like the two of you had a good plan," Nick said. "What went wrong?"

"Everything. Oh God!" Laurie's voice broke. "It was so awful." She wiped at her eyes.

"Laurie, we know this is hard for you, but you heard Daniel," I said. "We have to get through this and get out of here."

"I know." She swallowed and continued.

They headed up I-5 in Cody's heavy-duty Dodge Ram, pulling the trailer. Laurie drove, and was just getting used to the rig after about ten miles when a raccoon ran in front of the truck and she hit the brakes. Cody wanted to check whether the sudden stop had caused any problem with the trailer hitch. He asked Laurie to pull over and park on the shoulder. He got out and walked back to the trailer.

Just then Laurie saw headlights in her rearview mirror. A vehicle pulled over to the shoulder behind them and stopped. Through her side view mirror she saw the driver get out of the other vehicle. She cracked her window and heard the other vehicle's engine still running. Then she heard Cody shout "No" and a thud, like someone falling. The horse gave a frantic sounding whinny. She came out of the cab, running back to the trailer and calling Cody's name. She saw someone jump back in the driver's seat of the other rig, flip a U-turn, and speed away.

The trailer door was ajar and when Laurie pulled it open, she saw Cody on the floor, unconscious, while Game Boy stood by. She ran back to the cab, spotted Cody's cellphone on the seat and used it to dial 911.

She claimed to be a passing motorist and didn't give her name. She put on the hazard lights and climbed in the trailer with Cody, keeping herself between his body and the horse's hooves. Cody was still breathing, but his pulse was barely perceptible—not a good sign. The horse stayed still, only moving occasionally to bend his neck down and sniff at Cody with a slight flare of his nostrils.

Laurie's breathing was rapid, as if she were reliving that night. "I heard a siren in the distance and recognized it as a Life Support Unit. I scrambled out of the trailer and dropped behind the brush alongside the road."

"Why didn't you stay?" I had to ask. "Why didn't you tell the paramedics what happened?"

"If there was hope for Cody, I knew the LSU team would keep him alive until they got him to TMC's emergency room. There was nothing I could do or say that would make a difference, and I was afraid. I didn't want whoever attacked Cody to know I was there."

"So you think someone followed the two of you up I-5?" Nick asked.

"They must have, but how did anyone know what Cody and I were doing? After we left the hospital I dropped him at his father's compound and drove home. It was nearly midnight. He told me that all three houses were dark and quiet. He went directly to the stables, loaded Game Boy, and drove to meet me. Someone might have seen us leaving the hospital in my car and followed us to the O'Brien compound, then followed Cody when he came to get me. Either that, or someone from the compound saw Cody load up Game Boy and leave. Either way, Cody must have been followed when he came to get me. It had to be the same person who shot at him in the foothills."

"And you didn't want to be the next target." I could relate to her fear, having just dodged the bullet that hit Nick.

"That's right. Whoever attacked Cody on I-5 knew he wasn't alone. When someone broke into my house, I barely got out in time."

"If the intruder knew where you lived, I'm surprised he didn't get to your place sooner," Nick said.

"Most people don't know about the cottage behind the apartment house. Maybe it took him that long to figure out that I lived there and not in one of the apartments. In any case, whoever killed Cody up on I-5 knows I was there and wants to make sure I never get a chance to tell my story."

"Why are you sure he was attacked?" Nick said. "Maybe someone stopped to help and Cody yelled *No* because he didn't need help. You didn't see what happened in that trailer. Maybe the horse kicked him while the other vehicle was driving away."

Laurie shook her head. "That's not the way it happened. While I sat with Cody, he came awake for a moment and whispered, 'It wasn't Game Boy.' He wasn't conscious long enough to tell me more."

It wasn't Game Boy. The same words Laurie left on my answering machine. Those words had started this convoluted journey that led us from Timbergate to the Thousand Lakes Wilderness and finally to Idaho.

"You were ten miles up the freeway on foot in the middle of the night," Nick said. "How did you get home?"

Laurie gazed at the crucifix on the altar in front of

us. "I said a quick prayer and started walking north, staying under cover until I was out of sight of the emergency workers. I reached a twenty-four hour truck stop and told the waitress my boyfriend and I had a fight and he forced me out of his car alongside the road. She vouched for one of the truckers, so I asked him for a ride."

"And he was okay?" Nick said. "Didn't make any moves on you?"

"No. He was great. When we came back down I-5, I saw a CHP unit and a tow truck there with Cody's pickup, but the Life Support Unit was gone. The trucker slowed, and I thought he might stop, but the officer waved him on." She shook her head, remembering. "It was a surreal feeling, passing by that scene, knowing I'd been involved and not knowing if Cody was dead or alive."

At that point Daniel pulled the back door open again.

"Time's up. Let's get out of here."

We started to follow him when I remembered we had another question.

"Wait, Laurie. Who is Pat?"

She gave me a confused frown. "Pat? I don't know. Why are you asking?"

"Here, this is what she's asking about." Nick pulled the piece of note paper from his shirt pocket and aimed his pen light at the marking he'd made by rubbing his pencil over the notepad we'd found on her desk. *Pat?*

"Oh, that. That's not a person. It's just a note I made after doing some weekend work at the path lab.

"What does it mean?" I asked.

"Paternity. I did the workup on a paternity test and a woman called me at home asking about the results.

I said I wasn't allowed to give out that kind of information. When I asked who was calling, she hung up."

"Who was the patient?" I thought of James's suspicion that Echo O'Brien was pregnant and my hunch that Seamus wasn't the father.

"I'm not allowed to give—"

"Please," I said. "If there's a chance it has something to do with Cody's death, tell us."

"Dammit Laurie," Daniel took her arm. "We've got to go. We've been here too long. Just tell them and let's get out of here."

"All right." Laurie gave a shudder. She was reaching the end of her rope. "It was requested by Seamus O'Brien. When Cody brought him in for his regularly scheduled blood test, he said his wife was pregnant and he wanted to make sure the child was his. He wanted it to be confidential. Only he and Cody would know the results."

"And you, of course. How long ago was this?" I glanced at Daniel, who scowled and worked his jaw, barely able to contain his impatience.

"About a week before Cody was admitted. I said we needed Seamus's wife's consent, but he didn't want her involved, so I suggested we just do a fertility test on him as a first step."

"And he agreed?"

"Reluctantly, but since that's all I offered, he accepted. He was barely able to produce any semen, but I told him I'd see what I could do."

"How did that work out?" Nick asked.

"I'd heard things about his wife." Laurie glanced at Daniel, whose nod seemed to encourage her to go on. "It wasn't a stretch to believe she'd been unfaithful, so

I decided to break the rules and do what I could to help Seamus. I remembered that we still had a vial of his wife's blood that had been drawn the day before. She'd been complaining of fatigue and her OB doc wanted a blood panel. There's a fairly new blood test that can establish paternity. It only takes about a week to get the results. Since I had blood from both the pregnant wife and Seamus, I ran the DNA comparison test."

"And is he the father?" I said.

"No. Seamus O'Brien definitely isn't the father. I called and told him, but I didn't elaborate about the DNA test. It would have gotten the lab in big trouble, and of course I'd have lost my part-time job there and maybe my license. I let him think the problem was infertility, which was most likely true. He had virtually no motile sperm cells."

"Did Cody know about this?" I looked at Nick. This news made our whole trip to Idaho worthwhile.

"Yes, Seamus told him," Laurie said. "The same day Cody was admitted to the hospital."

That's it," Daniel said. "We have to go."

Laurie leaned toward her husband and he held her close while they made their way to his truck.

I followed behind them. "Laurie, is there any chance you were working at Dunnsville Memorial when DeeDee was a patient there?"

"No, I was working at the hospital that spring, but I didn't get hired until mid-May, a couple of weeks after DeeDee was flown out to TMC. I do remember a nursing assistant, Caroline something, talking about being assigned to DeeDee's room."

Caroline. My pulse kicked up a couple of notches at that. The same name Jackie Poole had mentioned on the phone to someone she called CJ. What had she said? *I've kept my mouth shut about Caroline for a hell of a long time.*

"Do you know Caroline's last name?"

"I don't think I ever heard it."

"Do you know if she's still working at Dunnsville Memorial?"

"Not likely. I remember her complaining about emptying bed pans and bragging she was going to be rich before she was thirty. You could ask Aunt Brenda if there's a mention of Caroline in DeeDee's medical record."

Too late to try that. Brenda had already shut me out. I'd have to wait and see if Cleo had gotten her hands on DeeDee's medical record back at TMC.

"What about Dr. Phyllis Poole? Did you ever see her working at Dunnsville Memorial back then?"

"No, I would have remembered that," Laurie said. "I never met her until I started working at TMC."

"Okay, that's it. We're done here," Daniel said.

They got in the truck and he rolled down the window. "Laurie parents are going on a long vacation, and she and I are going to disappear until O'Brien's killer is locked up. Don't try to contact any of us, and don't bother calling that cellphone number again. It's a throw-away. She won't be answering." Daniel turned on the ignition, stepped on the gas, and they sped away.

While they headed in one direction, we went in the other, back to our motel.

Nick glanced at me. "What's wrong?"

"A throw-away cellphone. I can't believe he won't let us call her."

"Hey, the man's trying to keep his wife safe. I'd do the same."

Nick drove and I slumped down in the seat, wondering if we'd be drawing any more fire before we made it back to our rooms. We arrived at the motel without further trouble. Nick cut the engine and did a quick scan of the parking lot.

"Nick, there's something I need to tell you, but let's go inside first."

"I don't like the sound of this."

Inside my room I dropped into a chair. Nick stood with his arms crossed, blocking the door as if I might try to make a run for it. "Okay, what's this something?"

"I went back for the laptop the next night, and it was gone."

"Jesus, Aimee, you went back there alone?"

"Of course not. I took someone with me."

"Who was it? Harry? Why didn't he tell me?"

"Not Harry, someone else. A friend from work."

"Why would you do that? Who was he?"

"She. It was Cleo Cominoli. She's the reason I got into this mess. It was her idea to check up on Phyllis Poole."

"Start explaining. And this Cleo woman had better be an ex-Marine or at least one of your fellow black belts."

I gave him a quick recap of Cleo's fears about Sig's scheduled surgery under Dr. Poole's knife and how she and I went to Laurie's house for the laptop and found it gone. I implied that Cleo was tough as nails, which was true when it came to keeping the doctors at TMC in line. Nick didn't need to know she was a dud when it came to breaking and entering.

"You were asking for a bundle of trouble going back there," Nick said. "You could have damn well told me this a lot sooner."

"I'm telling you now because it could explain why Laurie was followed in Idaho."

Nick sat across from me. He looked down at the neat bandage Laurie had wrapped around his hand. "That may not be the only reason it was taken. She might have had files on it that related to her work at that lab—proof that Echo O'Brien is pregnant by someone other than Seamus."

"But that's not necessarily a problem for Echo. If Seamus dies before the child is born, she can simply claim she and Seamus agreed on a sperm donor."

"Maybe, but Laurie knew better. She said Seamus wanted the test and wanted it confidential. Only Seamus, Cody, and Laurie knew the truth."

"Not quite true," I said. "Echo O'Brien knows. Or at least she has a pretty darn good idea the father isn't Seamus."

Both of us sat lost in thought for a few minutes. My head was spinning with all the bits and pieces of information—what we knew and what we didn't. It seemed impossible to sort through the web of people and connections that stretched from Idaho to Timbergate. How did DeeDee's accident and her admission to Dunnsville Memorial link so many people to each other when there was no obvious connection? There was the mysterious Caroline, who might be the woman Jackie Poole had mentioned to CJ, who might be Carl Jasper, the sole owner of Dunnsville Memorial Hospital. So far, all conjecture, but there was at least one coincidence that might be possible to prove.

"Nick, what about Jackie Poole in Idaho and Dr. Phyllis Poole in California? Do you think that's a coincidence?"

"Seems likely. Poole's a fairly common name."

"I don't think it's that common. James is sure he saw Phyllis Poole in DeeDee's hospital room in Idaho. I think there is a connection. I was hoping Laurie could tell me if Jackie and Phyllis Poole are related, but I didn't get a chance to ask her."

"Does the Idaho Poole look like the doctor at Timbergate? Or at least like they could be related?"

"It's hard to tell." I told him how Jackie appeared to be surgically altered to look like the late JFK's wife. Who knew what she looked like before the plastic surgery and the hair dye? I didn't even know if her eyes were really brown, now that contacts came in all colors.

"You don't have much to go on."

"Maybe not, but I think we need to explore this. Jackie was scheming about something with someone she called CJ. She wants Brenda McClurg's job, but more important, the name of the doctor who admitted DeeDee Dakota to Dunnsville Memorial in Idaho is Carl Jasper. His initials are CJ, and he's the sole owner of the facility."

"Wait a minute." Nick went to his room and came back with two bottles of beer. "Want one? You're wound up pretty tight. It might take the edge off."

"Might as well."

"Now go ahead and tell me why Jasper and the Jackie Kennedy clone might have anything to do with Cody O'Brien being killed."

"I don't know. Do you realize how confusing all this is? We came here to find Laurie, thinking she'd tell us who killed Cody, and instead we found more questions than answers. Someone knows Laurie is on to something…and that we're trying to figure out who killed Cody. They came here to silence her…and us, too."

"You really think the two Poole women are involved?"

"If they're related, they must be mixed up in this somehow."

"Maybe I can find out for you," Nick said. "I do have the lady doctor's rain check."

"If she is mixed up in this, that rain check might be dangerous." I got up and moved the window curtain aside just enough to give me a view of the motel parking lot.

"Let me worry about that."

"What time are we taking off tomorrow?"

"As early as possible."

TWENTY-THREE

SUNDAY MORNING WE took the F150 back to the dealership, where Gary P and Nick had worked out arrangements to have a vehicle transport company pick it up. Nick explained the busted rear window by saying it had been vandalized during the night in the motel parking lot.

From there we took a taxi to the airport and were soon winging our way back to Timbergate.

On the flight home I made notes of everything we had learned in Idaho. I had already called ahead to fill Cleo in, especially concerning Echo's baby. I tried to reassure her about Sig's surgery, relaying Laurie's opinion that Dr. Poole was an excellent surgeon. Cleo wasn't convinced but agreed to wait a little longer before asking Sig to cancel. I asked if she'd been able to get her hands on DeeDee's medical record. She hadn't.

I turned Laurie's story over in my mind again and again. It bothered me not knowing whether Cody's wound had been compared to Game Boy's shoe. Had foul play been considered? Had the CHP officer even done a quick visual match? Apparently no photos had been taken at the scene. Quinn had said there were none in Cody's chart, but there was still a chance someone in TMC's morgue had photographed the wound.

A month after I was hired, I had talked Quinn into springing for two digital single lens reflex cameras—

one for the ER and one for the staff of TMC's morgue.
I supplied the staffers in both departments with books
and articles on forensic photography and gave them an
in-service, recommending they practice with the cameras whenever possible, even if a death appeared to be
accidental. If the crew in TMC's holding morgue took
photos of Cody, they should have been filed in his medical record. If not, there was a chance they were still on
the morgue's camera card.

Getting my hands on that camera would present a
problem, but it was worth a try. With a good, sharp
photo, I might find some way to compare Cody's wound
to Game Boy's hooves. But that presented other problems. The comparison would only work if the horse
hadn't been re-shod since Cody's death, and if the photos of the wound revealed enough detail for comparison.
There was also the question of where the horse had been
taken. Had Game Boy been returned to the O'Brien
ranch, or had he been impounded someplace else?

I made copious notes, glancing out the plane's window every few minutes at the varying landscape almost
30,000 feet below. I wondered if the sniper in the Blue
Banjo's parking lot was also on the way back to Timbergate. The bullets aimed our way told me Cody's killer
thought Laurie knew more that she actually did, and
that she'd passed that information along to us. I couldn't
help thinking time was running out.

THE CHANGE IN time zones shortened our flight home
by an hour, putting us down at the Timbergate Municipal Airport early Sunday afternoon. Nick executed
his usual smooth landing and did his post-flight check.
When the plane was refueled and locked in its hangar,

he drove me home. On the way I brought up my idea about finding a photo of Cody's wound and comparing it to Game Boy's horseshoes.

"Do you think it's worth pursuing, or does it seem too improbable?"

"It's a stretch. Wouldn't it be easier to report what Laurie saw to the sheriff's office?"

"If I did that, I'll have to give her name and disclose that she's hiding out in Idaho. That could put her at greater risk after all the trouble she and Daniel have gone through to keep her and her family safe."

"I think you can trust the sheriff's department to use discretion."

"Maybe, but I'm afraid my theory would sound so implausible that I wouldn't be taken seriously. I'd rather have something more concrete if we're going to convince law enforcement that Cody's death was murder. I want to try the horseshoe theory first. If that doesn't work, we'll have no choice but to report Laurie's story."

"How do you plan to get access to the horse? You don't know where it is, do you?"

"I'll bet James knows."

"You sure you want him to know what you're up to?"

"I won't tell him *why* I want to know. I thought I'd say I know of a potential buyer. The horse is worth a lot of money. The O'Brien clan would probably jump at the chance to sell it."

"Who's the imaginary buyer?" Nick said.

"I'll keep it vague. Say the buyer isn't ready to be identified just yet."

BACK AT THE RANCH, a late October shower had just swept through, leaving the sweet smell of freshly washed air.

As Nick drove down the lane to the barn, the llamas raised their heads from grazing to follow our progress. I counted seven adults and the white cria, now four months old and a fifth the size of an adult. They had gotten along fine without me, thanks to Harry.

Nick insisted on carrying my bag up the stairs to the deck outside my apartment. I unlocked my door and stood there feeling awkward about the next move.

"Want me to take this inside?" He nodded down at the bag.

"Okay."

Since he'd just been shot trying to help me, I wanted to know if I could count on him going forward. The bandage on his hand hadn't been changed since Laurie wrapped it the night before, and the blood that had seeped to the surface filled me with guilt. I'd drawn fire by meddling in the Cody O'Brien case, and I'd dragged Nick into it with me.

"Where do you want this?" Nick stood in my kitchen holding the bag.

"Anywhere's fine."

He put it on the floor next to my daybed and came back into the kitchen, where I had already filled the coffee maker with an industrial-strength load of French Roast. He pulled out one chair and pointed to another.

"Sit. I saw you making notes during the flight. Want to share with me?"

"Okay, but let me change that bandage while we talk. I didn't bargain for either of us getting shot in Idaho." I retrieved gauze, antibiotic ointment, and tape from my medicine cabinet.

"I don't call this being shot." Nick peeled off his bandage, revealing an inch-long abrasion across the back of his hand. "I've had worse scratches playing pick-up basketball."

I felt a warning sting of tears, tried to blink them away, and failed when they blurred my vision. I blinked and swallowed. "What if you'd been leaning forward just a few inches? God, Nick, I'm so sorry."

"It could have been you." He held his hand still while I cleansed the wound with a damp cloth. "Don't you get it? It's not me that guy was after."

"I know. It was Laurie."

"And now it's you. That guy's smart enough to realize Laurie told you everything she knew about Cody O'Brien. Right now you present a bigger problem to him than she does." He shook his head. "And that's just for starters. You know about the whole dysfunctional O'Brien clan, and now you know something hinky is going on in that sorry excuse for a hospital in Idaho."

"But I don't know how to put it all together." I applied antibiotic ointment and covered the back of his hand with gauze.

"The guy we're after doesn't know that, and he's not going to follow Laurie and her husband to some god-forsaken hideout in the Idaho wilderness. Hell no, he's going to come back to Timbergate where this started and shut you up before you blow his scheme wide open."

"What about you? You're in danger too, now that you know everything I know."

Nick smiled. "Honey, I know everything you know and then some. I've outsmarted a few bad actors in some pretty dicey situations, but that's because I'm not afraid to use a gun. You act like that black belt of yours is some kind of magic shield, but it doesn't make you bulletproof."

The coffee maker beeped the end of the brew cycle, giving me an excuse to ignore Nick's remark. I secured his wrapped hand with tape.

He got up and poured two cups of coffee while I scrounged in my snack drawer until I found an open package of peanut butter cookies. I dumped the mostly broken pieces on a paper plate and put them between us on the table.

"While we're on the subject, since when do you need a gun to fly Buck Sawyer around? You're supposed to be his pilot, not his bodyguard."

This was an area of our relationship that had caused strain more than once. Nick occasionally came back from one of his trips with Buck looking as if he'd been in a nasty bar fight. Each time I questioned him about it, he gave me a phony-sounding excuse. He either got mugged, or some thugs tried to steal the plane. Because he flew Buck to a number of South American countries involved in the illegal drug trade, it was always possible his explanations were true, but I had my doubts.

"There *is* more to my job description than flying, but it's complicated. When the time is right, we'll talk about it, but let's not go down that road right now," Nick said. "We're talking about keeping *you* safe. That scrape last summer was a perfect example of why Harry and I talked you into getting that snub-nosed .38 and a license to carry."

"I know that." I got up, topped off my cup, and held out the carafe. "Want more?"

"No. I want to know where your revolver is."

"It's locked in Jack's gun safe."

"Then let's go get it. It belongs with you until this is over."

We walked up the lane to the main house. In Jack's den, I dialed the combination and retrieved my gun while Nick did a walk-through and reported that all was okay.

Nick insisted on staying in my grandparents' house until they returned from Africa, but he was taking his temporary occupancy a little too seriously. Making himself right at home, he opened the refrigerator.

"Looks like Harry stocked the fridge. Want something to eat?"

"No thanks. I have a lot to do. I'm going back to the barn."

"Want me to walk you?"

"Not necessary. I'm armed now. I think I can make it across the pasture by myself." I heard myself sounding snarky and apologized.

I heard my cellphone ringing as I ran up the stairs outside my apartment. I rushed in and grabbed it. It was Harry checking in.

"Hey, Aimless, when did you get in?" He sounded tired.

"About two hours ago. Everything looks good. I guess you didn't have any problems while we were gone."

"Nothing I couldn't handle."

"I don't like the sound of that. What do you mean?"

"Had some unexpected company last night at the ranch. Keely O'Brien came by, high and pissed."

"How did she even know where you were?"

"She saw me leaving Four Corners Pizza and followed. Said she needed a shoulder to cry on. She was so messed up, it's a miracle she didn't wreck her car on the way."

"What did she want?"

"She wasn't easy to understand. Lots of crying,

swearing, and mumbling. At first she was muttering about Tucker. Some kind of lovers' quarrel, I guess. She kept calling him…let's just say it rhymes with his name. Then she switched to James and kept saying blood was thicker and he owed her. She was so incoherent I couldn't make sense of most of it. I took her car keys and made her stay on the couch and sleep it off, which is why I didn't get much sleep myself. She's so damned unpredictable…. I was afraid to close my eyes with her in the house."

I remembered what Keely said at the checkout counter in Coyote Creek. James owed her a part in one of his off-Broadway plays.

"Odd she'd bring that up with you, but it sounds like Keely when she's high. Did you get any useful information out of her when she woke up?"

"Nothing but a mess on the bathroom floor where she overshot the toilet bowl when she hurled. She wasn't talking this morning, but after coffee and toast, she seemed okay to drive home, so I gave her back her keys and let her go."

"Did anyone else show up at the ranch?"

"Not while I was there, and the motion sensor camera I rigged for the driveway didn't show anything suspicious."

"That makes sense, because our bad guy or guys were probably in Idaho the whole time Nick and I were there."

"True." Harry stifled a yawn and I ended the call by suggesting he get a nap.

I called James hoping to find out where Game Boy was stabled, but his phone went to voicemail. Rather than explain in a message, I asked him to call back.

Cleo was next on my list. I needed to get a look at Cody and DeeDee O'Brien's TMC patient charts, but I was wading into deep gray waters where confidentiality was concerned. Her access to patient information was less restricted than mine, so I needed her cooperation.

"You want to do *what*?" Cleo said.

"I need to go through their charts, but I don't want anyone at the hospital getting suspicious."

"Meaning Phyllis Poole? Then you're still apprehensive about her?"

"Enough that I'd rather she didn't know I was looking at those charts. I want to sneak into the records room and the archives, but I can't do it without your master key."

Cleo sighed. "I get that you need to see DeeDee's chart to look at her records from Idaho, but why Cody's?"

"I keep hoping a photo of his head wound will turn up. Maybe something has made it into his chart by now."

"You realize this could get us both fired?"

"This was your idea, remember?" I played my ace in the hole. "Is Sig's surgery still on for Thursday morning?"

"I'm afraid so. As far as he knows, Poole's a superstar urologic surgeon, and he's insisting on keeping that date and getting it over with." I heard a deep sigh, then she went on, "I still think it's a bad idea, but maybe I'm way off base. You said Laurie Popejoy thinks Poole is an excellent surgeon."

"Laurie did say that, but we both know an excellent surgeon can also be a psychopath. The two aren't mutually exclusive. You don't want a nut case operating on Sig's privates, do you?"

"That's not funny." Cleo's voice trembled.

"What's not...oh, sorry, no pun intended." I pressed

on. "Look, I'm not making light of this. We have precious little time between now and Sig's surgery, and I'm going to be swamped at work preparing for the Wednesday night CME program."

"I know. The urologic surgery case review. Most of the surgeons have finished their reviews, including Cody O'Brien's chart, but as far as I know, all of those charts are still set aside in the Health Information office."

"Have you heard any rumors about their findings?" I asked.

"No, but the urologists are all getting together Tuesday night to prep for the panel discussion."

"Another reason I need to go in right away. As soon as they've finished with Cody's chart it might be locked up again where we can't get to it. Do you have keys to the administration suite?"

"No, but I can get into everything else in the hospital."

"Even the morgue?"

"Sure, but why would you want to—"

"I'll explain later."

"When do you want to do this?" Cleo sounded skeptical.

"I'm thinking tomorrow night. Around midnight. When can I come by and get your keys?"

"Hold it a minute. My keys don't go anywhere without me. You said it yourself: I'm the one who got you involved."

"Then I'll come by your place around eleven." That would give me time to talk her out of coming along.

"Is the dress code the same as last time?"

"Not quite," I said. "Wear something you might wear

if you were called in after hours. We might have to convince someone that we have a legitimate reason to be
there in the middle of the night."

"Okay, but if that happens, keep in mind that I'm a
lousy liar."

"Then we'd better count on stealth and hope we don't
get caught."

I tried James again and left another voicemail message asking him to call. Then I texted Nick, telling him
I'd struck out so far with finding out where Game Boy
was being kept.

By the time I finished the afternoon chores, I felt a
nap coming on. The events of the past two days were
catching up with me.

TWENTY-FOUR

KNOCKING ON MY door pulled me awake. A glance at the time told me I'd slept for almost two hours. I checked my peephole and saw Nick.

"What's up?" I said, letting him in.

"I found the horse."

"You found Game Boy? How? Where?" Suddenly I was wide awake.

Nick pulled out a dinette chair and plopped down. "You can thank Harry. I was at his place when I got your text. It was his idea to search sites that sell high-dollar horses. It took longer than I expected. There are a lot of sites and lots of horses on each one." Nick held up his phone and showed me a picture of Game Boy. "Someone's already put the animal up for sale through a broker. It's got to be the O'Briens, don't you think?"

"Who else? But this is bad. If it sells right away, we'll never get a chance to examine the hooves." I looked again at his phone. Game Boy's asking price was listed as $250,000. "We need to pretend to be interested buyers."

"Already done," Nick said. "I contacted the broker and asked where I could see the animal in the flesh. I was told there's a legal issue regarding the death of the owner. The horse has been impounded at a veterinary clinic until a new owner is registered. The broker assured me it's just a formality, but he said I'd need an appointment to look at the animal."

"Good. If the horse is impounded, that implies Game Boy hasn't been re-shod, but we can ask about that. Did they say which vet?"

"Creekside? Does that sound familiar?"

"Yes, we use them for the llamas. It's a couple of miles up the road from the ranch. Did you already make an appointment?"

"No, there's not much point unless you can get a photo of the cowboy's head wound to compare with the hooves. I did convince the guy that I represent a very rich and serious buyer in Texas. That will explain my bringing a camera. I even mentioned we'd participate in an auction, so he's not going to sell out from under us."

"Okay, I'll see what I can do about the photo of Cody's wound tomorrow." I reached out and touched his arm. "Thank you."

"Like I said, thank your brother." Nick gave my forehead a quick peck and left.

I thought about Harry. He was always up for a little intrigue. I wanted to know more about why Keely was angry with Tucker, and why she felt James owed her. Harry would be the person to help me with that. I sent him a quick text asking him to call, but he didn't get back to me before bedtime.

MONDAY MORNING AT work I was buried in preparations for the Surgery Department's CME program. Dr. Fausset had confirmed that every urologic surgeon was required to participate in the panel discussion. I still needed to meet with him to get his input on the agenda. Time was running short, so I phoned his office asking for a call back.

By mid-afternoon Dr. Fausset still hadn't returned

my call, so I checked in with Cleo. We arranged to meet at three o'clock. When I walked over from the library, I met her coming out of her office on the first floor. We caught an empty elevator and punched the penthouse button. One of the few safe places to talk privately in a hospital is an uninterrupted elevator ride.

Cleo and I were set for our raid on the Health Information office. We decided one o'clock in the morning would be better than midnight. When the elevator opened on the penthouse floor, there stood Jared Quinn.

"Hello, ladies, what brings you here?" He stepped inside.

Cleo looked so guilty I pressed my hand to her back and gave her a little shove. "The painting I was telling you about is at the end of this hall. Thanks for taking a look."

I shoved a little harder and she lurched out into the penthouse corridor.

"Thanks, again," I said with a little wave. The doors closed, and Quinn arched his eyebrow. "Cleo has great taste in art," I said. "I'm thinking of buying a print by that artist, but it's kind of expensive. I always get her opinion before I buy."

"Huh," he said. He pressed the lobby button. "You, too?"

"Lobby. Yes. Busy day. I have to get back."

"Heard anything new on the Cody O'Brien situation?"

"Not really," I said. "How about you?"

"We may have some good news. James O'Brien called to tell me he's almost convinced the rest of his family to call off the lawsuit."

"That's great." *A good sign*, I thought, recalling James's promise. "Any idea how he accomplished that?"

"Something to do with his father's failing health," Quinn said. "Seamus is back in the hospital and it isn't looking good. He's in ICU."

"Oh, I didn't know."

I had been so busy with my workload I hadn't even checked the day's admissions list. That news spiked a new sense of urgency. If Seamus was near death, there might not be time to write his cheating wife out of his will. Unless James had already managed to take care of that sticky family matter while Nick and I were in Idaho. I needed to talk to James, and soon.

I was curious to know if someone in the O'Brien family had been granted power of attorney over the estate. The obvious choices were Echo, James, or Keely. Seamus knew Echo was pregnant with someone else's baby, and he knew Keely was struggling with drug dependency. Cody was dead, which left only James, whose career as a New York City producer may or may not be in financial trouble. My stomach went hollow at that thought.

Back in the library, I was about to call Nick when a man around my age came through the door pushing a housekeeping cart. He had shaggy dark brown hair and a soul patch on his chin. His ears sported hollowed-out gauges that created unsightly holes in both earlobes, a mystifying fashion statement that made me cringe every time I saw it. He parked the cart at the entrance and began emptying waste baskets into a large garbage bag. I didn't recognize him, so I walked over to introduce myself.

"Hi, I'm Aimee Machado, Librarian. You must be new."

"Cliff Weber," he mumbled. "Just fillin' in. Be outta your way in a minute."

When he had gone, I called Nick to see if he had set

up his planned rain check with Phyllis Poole. He told me they were meeting for drinks that night at one of Timbergate's popular singles bars. He sounded a little too enthusiastic, but I tried to tell myself it was for a good cause. If anyone could find out what she'd been doing in DeeDee Dakota's hospital room in Idaho, it was Nick. I had to know how her presence there fit in with Cody's death in Timbergate.

Harry finally called just before quitting time. He confirmed that his evening was open, so I told him I needed the answer to two questions: why was Keely so angry with Tucker, and why did James *owe* her? Harry had said she was vague about her reasons. I knew that Keely was sore about not being cast in one of James's shows. Was there something else? Something that might shed light on the complicated dynamic of the O'Brien family? Harry wasn't crazy about the idea of a date with Keely, but his love of intrigue won out, and he agreed to give it a try.

When I got home, I put in a call to James. He apologized for not calling me back, saying he'd been distracted by his father's failing health and had not been checking his messages. We arranged to meet and compare notes at Four Corners Pizza in Coyote Creek. Odds were good we wouldn't run into Nick and Dr. Poole there. I had to stay awake until one o'clock in the morning, so the impromptu date with James was a way to kill two birds with one pizza. I'd see what he knew about the status of his father's will, and with a little prodding he might even remember something more about Phyllis Poole. I didn't plan to tell him about my trip to Idaho with Nick.

Finally I checked my email and found a message

from Harry saying he'd called Keely to tell her he was
worried about her. He'd talked her into going out for
Italian food. Three dates arranged, and one to go. The
fourth was my post-midnight caper with Cleo, getting
into the Health Information office and the basement
archives, and if necessary, checking TMC's morgue
camera photos of Cody's head wound.

That made four chances to gather intelligence, but
with Seamus in ICU and failing fast, the whole thing
might fall apart before we could put the puzzle together. Meanwhile, we still needed a look at Game
Boy's hooves. I called Nick to see if he'd scored an appointment for us to see the horse.

"It's arranged for noon tomorrow," Nick said.

"Good. I'll meet you at Creekside tomorrow at noon."

I REACHED FOUR CORNERS PIZZA at eight o'clock that night
and spotted James studying the menu on the wall. He
seemed subdued, no doubt worried about his father. I
hadn't been able to coax my way into the ICU during
the workday to check on Seamus, so I had no idea how
critical he was. I held off asking James about him until
after we found an empty booth.

"I'm sorry to hear about your father," I said.

"Thank you. I'm glad someone is. I'm afraid the vultures are circling back at the compound."

The glow of the candle on our table made the moisture welling in his eyes glisten. Was his sorrow genu-
ine, or was I seeing an actor working his craft? He'd
been on stage plenty before he turned his hand to producing, so I couldn't be sure.

"I haven't had an opportunity to find out how he's
doing," I said. "Have you visited him this evening?"

"I don't know if you'd call it visiting. I sat at his bed-side in ICU for an hour, watching him sleep. The nurse assigned to him was in and out at least a dozen times. He's hooked up to all sorts of things. Those machines are intimidating as hell with all the wiggling lines and beeps and flashing numbers."

"Did his doctor come in while you were there?"

"You mean Dr. Poole? She came into the unit and spoke to his nurse, but I didn't hear any of that."

That threw me. I couldn't imagine why Dr. Poole was involved. This was a patient with a diagnosis in the realm of internal medicine and infectious disease, not urology. Unless he was having kidney failure. But why Poole? It should have been Dr. Fausset. Of course, Poole was Fausset's associate, and she would be on call for him if it was her turn in their call group's rotation. That mental exercise brought me back to square one, so I let it go for the time being.

"Jared Quinn told me your family might drop the lawsuit over Cody's death," I said. "Should I thank you for that?"

"The family lawyer deserves most of the credit. He says there isn't enough solid evidence against the hos-pital for malpractice or a wrongful death case. And I agreed with him. Suing was Echo's idea to begin with, and Keely would rather grow chest hair than go along with anything Echo wants to do."

"I guess that's two against one, since there's only the three of you left to make decisions."

"That's right. Tucker tried to put his two cents in, but the lawyer wasn't listening."

"Whose side was Tucker on?"

"It was kind of a wash. He seemed to side with Echo

at first. I guess he figured if he was to marry Keely, he'd benefit from any proceeds if they won the suit." James shook his head and seemed amused. "Keely shot him down. Said he could kiss her ass goodbye if he took Echo's side." That explained why Keely was angry with Tucker when she barged in on Harry.

"Sounds like Keely's developing a backbone."

"That's not all," James said. "Keely announced to all of us that she's going to fight for control of the O'Brien estate if Dad dies."

"Wow. What do you think about that?"

"More power to her. I didn't expect to inherit, and I sure as hell don't plan to hang around Coyote Creek stuffing dead animals for the rest of my life." He nodded at the pepperoni pizza on the table in front of us. "I can't even order white pizza in this godforsaken place."

"Again with the white pizza, James?"

I was sure his attitude had little to do with pizza and a lot to do with the collapse of his family. With his brother dead and his father most likely dying, all that remained would be two spoiled, dysfunctional young women.

"Do you think Keely can get her act together? She's going to have to stay sober if she's serious about taking over the O'Brien dynasty."

"She and I had a long talk last night. Turns out she's already enrolled herself in a rehab program and registered for business courses. Plus, she'd have an army of lawyers and financial consultants and all our father's employees to keep things running smoothly. It would be the first time in her life that she had a reason to grow up. I think she might surprise us all."

"Still, she seems pretty immature. Last I heard she

wasn't too happy with you. She said you'd never offered to give her a part in one of your plays, even though you owed her."

James looked away for a moment, seeming to search for someone across the room. "I do owe her. And I've been waiting for her to claim her reward, but it's not a part in a play. Do you remember her dancing when you were kids?"

"She wasn't too good at it," I said. "She didn't seem to feel the beat."

"That hasn't changed. She has no real talent as an actress or a singer, either."

"I don't understand," I said. "What else do you have to offer her?"

"My support if she takes on Echo in a fight for the family business."

"You'd give up your share just to help Keely? Why?"

"She's been keeping a confidence for me for a very long time. Even now, when it hardly matters anymore, she's kept her promise not to tell the rest of our family."

That was the last thing I'd expected to hear. "Is it something you can tell me?"

"I could, but I'd rather not. At least not just yet. Right now I'm more interested in keeping my focus on my father's health, and if he dies, on how to help Keely keep the bulk of his estate away from Echo."

"But how? If Echo is carrying an O'Brien heir, she's going to have a lot of clout when the estate is settled." I was torn with indecision. Should I tell him the baby's father wasn't Seamus? *Not yet.* "Have you told Keely you suspect Echo's pregnant?"

"No. I'm waiting to see if Dad pulls through. If he

survives a little longer, I'd like him to have the dignity of dealing with Echo himself."

That comment gave me the opening I'd been hoping for. "James, what do you mean about your father dealing with Echo?"

"This is tough." James rubbed the heel of his hand against his chest. "I promised Dad I'd keep his confidence, but I have to talk to someone about it."

"Only if you're sure, James." *Please let him confide in me.*

"Dad unburdened himself the morning he asked me to drive him to the hospital. He was fatalistic about the prospect of dying. Said it was time to let go of his pride." James cleared his throat and blinked away tears. "He told me Echo was pregnant, but he thought the odds were miniscule that he was the father, so he'd had some lab work done. Cody had helped him with the arrangements. It turned out he couldn't be the father of Echo's baby."

I didn't let on that I'd already learned the truth from Laurie Popejoy. "Is that why he wanted to change his will?"

"Yes, he was going to leave the bulk of his estate to Cody, but he was so weak and so ill that he'd barely begun the process before—"

"Before Cody died. So where do things stand now?"

"Echo doesn't know what Dad told me about the baby's paternity. She doesn't even know *he* knows the truth. I have Dad's power of attorney, but it dates back to before he married Echo, and she's already challenging that."

"Couldn't you block that by telling her you know about her baby?"

"Probably, but she's still Dad's wife, and we'd have

to put up a hell of a legal battle just to get her to submit to more blood tests."

"How long have they been married?"

"Less than two years. Not nearly long enough for her to take him to the cleaners in a divorce. She'd only get half of whatever was acquired while they were married. She's probably counting on the little heir giving her the leverage she'd need to fight Keely for the bulk of the estate."

James slumped back in his chair and suddenly looked so weary I couldn't bring myself to put him through any more questions. We walked to our cars agreeing to stay in touch, particularly about his father's condition.

When I arrived back at the ranch at eleven thirty, I called Cleo. She said she'd be ready at half past midnight for our attempt to sneak into the Health Information office. After I changed my clothes, I unlocked the file cabinet next to my computer. I stared at the snub-nosed .38 in the drawer, debating whether to take it along. I could almost feel Nick looking over my shoulder.

It won't do you any good in that drawer.

I picked it up.

TWENTY-FIVE

AT ONE O'CLOCK in the morning the TMC parking garage was deserted except for a few of the spaces reserved for doctors.

"Let me get this straight," Cleo said. "We go to Health Information first to look for Cody's chart. If there's no photo of his head wound in his chart, we go to the morgue and try to find a photo or a camera there. Then you want to search the archives for DeeDee's chart."

"That's right."

I locked my car and we walked toward the entrance. A few feet from the door, I hesitated. Cleo didn't realize I'd stopped, and she plowed into my back. The gun I had tucked into my waistband jarred loose and fell at her feet. Its shiny barrel caught the light of the harvest moon.

I heard Cleo gasp. "Aimee, is that yours?"

I grabbed the revolver and stuffed it in my purse. "Yes, it's mine, but we won't need it."

"Then why did you bring it?"

"Cleo, you don't have to do this. You can give me your keys and wait in the car."

For a moment I thought she'd agree, but she hung her head and mumbled something I couldn't quite make out.

"What?" I said.

"I said it isn't worth it. We should go home."

"You want to know if Sig's surgeon is mixed up in something devious, don't you?"

"I'll tell him to cancel. I'll beg. He can go to someone else. Someone in a different town, if necessary."

"That won't protect Poole's other patients, will it? She'll still be here performing surgeries."

"You said Laurie Popejoy thinks Poole's an excellent surgeon."

"And she's probably right, but what if she's wrong?"

The droop of Cleo's shoulders told me she'd given up arguing. "Okay, let's do this. But for God's sake, don't shoot anyone."

The basement corridor was empty and dimly lit, apparently on an energy-saving setting timed for the wee hours of morning. We made our way to the Health Information office and Cleo quickly unlocked the door. We slipped inside and closed it behind us. I pulled out a small flashlight for myself and handed another to Cleo.

"Do you need a password to get into the records database?"

"I have it," she said. "My security clearance allows me access to chart numbers, but I don't pull the charts myself during regular business hours. A clerk does that and notes in a log book the reason I need the chart. Right now, we're flouting the hell out of HIPAA."

She was referring to the federal protections for personal health information passed back in 1996. We'd be in serious trouble if anyone knew what we were doing.

I took a couple of long, slow breaths to ease the cramping in my neck. "Do you know where they've set aside the charts for the urology review?"

"They have a special nook for that." She led me to

a small recessed area and pointed to a stack of charts. "There they are." She began sorting through them.

I looked over her shoulder. "Is Cody's chart there?"

"Got it." She handed it to me.

I opened the folder and looked through the documentation related to his admission the night before his scheduled surgery. It was limited, since he'd only been in house long enough to be stripped of his clothes and have his scrotum shaved. His blood pressure and pulse were within normal limits, but his dramatically elevated sedimentation rate suggested a dangerous level of inflammation in his injured testicle and adjacent tissue. Nothing in Dr. Poole's dictated history and physical looked out of the ordinary.

The Emergency Room doctor's notes included time of death, and confirmed the patient was alive on arrival but died in the ER. No photo, but there was a sketch of the contusion on Cody's forehead showing that it resembled the partial shape of a horseshoe.

Cleo pointed at one of several photocopy machines in the room. "You want me to turn this on so you can make copies?"

"No. I'll use my phone. It's quieter." I took three shots of each of the few pages in the folder, then watched the door while Cleo put the chart back in its place.

"Now what?" she asked.

"Let's try the morgue next."

We listened for any sound of footfalls before sneaking out of Health Information and down the corridor to the morgue. Cleo's master key unlocked the door. In the beam of my flashlight I spotted half a dozen drawers in the opposite wall that looked large enough to hold corpses. An involuntary shudder rippled through me. When it passed, I led the way and Cleo closed the door behind us.

"Do you know where they keep the forensic camera?" Cleo whispered.

"No idea. I'll try the desk. Why don't you check the cupboards?"

"I can't. This crappy flashlight just died."

"Okay, then you guard the door and I'll search."

The desktop was clear: no file folders, no in or out baskets where I might find hard copies of photos. I pulled the handle of the deepest desk drawer, but it didn't open. I tried the top drawer with the same result. Just as I reached for another drawer, an urgent page blasted through the speakers in the ceiling of the dark room.

Code Blue, CCU, Code Blue, CCU.

Startled, I dropped my flashlight and it went out, pitching us into darkness.

"Cardiac Care Unit. That's not good," Cleo whispered from her post at the door. "You'd better hurry. That patient could die any minute now. The body would be stored here until it's transferred."

The room was cool, but sweat formed on my forehead as I crawled in the dark, groping for the flashlight. "How long before—"

"Half an hour, maybe less," Cleo said. "But the patient might pull through. Either way, make it quick. If we're caught in here, even you couldn't come up with a good enough excuse."

My fingers touched the flashlight, and when I shook it, it flickered. I turned it off and back on, and the beam held steady. But for how long?

The desk seemed like an obvious place to keep the

camera, but none of the drawers would open. I looked around for file cabinets, but there were none, so I crossed to the cupboards attached to one wall. After wasting precious minutes and finding nothing, I was almost ready to give up. Just then the speaker came to life again.

Cancel Code Blue, CCU, Cancel Code Blue, CCU.

I whispered to Cleo, "Does that mean they saved the patient?"

"No way to tell. It could have gone either way. Let's get out of here."

I threaded my way back toward the door, but the thought of leaving without finding the camera galled me. The only places I hadn't searched were the drawers used for storing bodies. I aimed my flashlight beam toward the nearest one.

"You've got to be kidding," Cleo said. "The camera would be ruined by the cold."

"No," I said. "They're fine in temperatures as low as zero Celsius. That's thirty-two degrees Fahrenheit and these refrigeration units are set at thirty-nine."

"How do you know this stuff?"

"Research. I'm a librarian."

"Still, who would put a camera in one of those drawers?"

"I wouldn't, but there's no place else to look." I walked over to the first drawer and tugged on the handle with my eyes closed. It slid open and a rush of cold air pimpled my arms. I squinted with my eyes half open, expecting to see a draped body with a toe tag. Instead, I saw what looked like someone's leftovers from lunch in a plastic container. I closed that drawer and tried the next one. Empty. The third and fourth drawers were empty, too.

"Aimee," Cleo hissed. "I hear someone coming."

In one of the last two drawers I saw what had to be a corpse. Just to be sure, I asked forgiveness from the deceased and gingerly picked up the shroud covering the face. It was a middle-aged woman. I repeated the process with the last drawer—another corpse. It was an elderly gentleman who seemed to be smiling in his sleep, as if he were communing with angels. I whispered, "God speed," and replaced his shroud, fighting back tears of apology for invading the privacy of these complete strangers.

I made my way to where Cleo stood near the door, listening.

"I think they went on by," she said. "We'd better get out now."

"Give me two more minutes." The sweat running down my back was making my revolver slip around in the waistband of my slacks, so I took it out and handed it to Cleo.

"Here, hold this for me, and keep your fingers away from the trigger."

"Jesus, Mary, and Joseph," she said, but she took the gun. "Aimee, this is crazy. You've already looked everywhere."

"Not in the desk. I can't give up without trying one more thing. Two minutes, I promise."

I trained my flashlight beam on the shallow top drawer running across the front of the desk. It was the only drawer with a lock. If I got it open, the rest of the drawers would unlock with it. A plastic container on the desk held paper clips in a variety of sizes. I wasn't particularly good at picking locks, but Harry had taught me how to do it when we were kids and wanted to snoop for Christmas presents our parents had hidden.

After a few jiggles and twists with the unbent clip, the top drawer popped open. It was empty except for a few pens and a roll of antacid tablets. The two drawers on the right were filled with the usual office supplies: stapler, sticky notepads, some letterhead, and envelopes.

I checked the deep bottom drawer next, and there it was. *The camera.*

"Cleo, I've got it." I turned it on and checked. There were a few practice shots of the morgue staff taking pictures of each other, and then I saw what I had hoped for. Three shots of Cody's wound. But how to get prints? Take the camera? How soon would it be discovered missing? Probably right away, since I was the one who encouraged them to practice using the camera as often as possible.

"Aimee," Cleo hissed, "your two minutes are up. Let's go."

"Not without the photos. This is what we came for." I turned on the computer, thinking I could attach the camera and email the photos to myself. But the computer was password protected.

"Pssst, look, Aimee."

I trained my flashlight on Cleo to see what she was trying to tell me, and saw her pointing my pistol toward me.

"Hey, watch what you're doing."

She looked down at the gun in her hand. "Oh, sorry." She pointed with her other hand. "Look at the printer. It should have a port for a memory card. See if you can wake it up and print the photos without the computer."

"Genius. I could kiss you." I printed all the photos then set the zoom to magnify the clearest photo at double its size. "That should do it."

"Then let's get out of here," Cleo said. "I'm about to vomit."

TWENTY-SIX

WITH THE PHOTOS stuffed in my purse, we left the morgue and hurried toward the archive room at the opposite end of the corridor to look for DeeDee Dakota's chart. We neared the door and saw that it was propped open with a housekeeping cart. Someone working the night shift. Cleo grabbed my arm and gestured back toward the way we'd come. She was right. We had to leave.

We made a clean getaway, but Cleo's nerves were so rattled that she held my car's little plastic trash bucket under her chin during the entire ten minute drive to her condo. She managed to keep her stomach contents down, and when I dropped her off around two thirty in the morning, she assured me we could still figure out a way to look at DeeDee's chart. I wasn't convinced but tried to hide my misgivings. Time was running out, and our chances of finding the answers we needed were slipping away.

I cut my headlights at the main house. No point stirring up the llamas and turkeys, and even more important, no point in waking Nick. He'd want to know where I'd been, and I was in no mood to listen to him rant. His car was in the driveway, so it was obvious his date with Dr. Poole had ended.

I knew I wouldn't sleep until I scrutinized the photos of Cody's wound, but I didn't want to risk turning on lights at that hour. If Nick happened to be awake, he might notice and show up wanting to know what was going on. I took my flashlight into my bathroom, closed the door, and trained the beam on each photo in turn.

The first one was out of focus, which I hadn't counted on. What if they were all blurry? I held my breath while I looked at the next one. Clearer, but part of the wound was out of the frame. I pulled out the magnified version of the clearest photo. It was in focus, and appeared as a purple, slightly crescent-shaped contusion on Cody's forehead. The skin was not broken, and there was no blood. The photographer had kept at it and finally gotten it right.

My first reaction was disappointment. The bruise could have been made by half of a horseshoe. At each end of it, I thought I detected small, deeper colored dots where the nail heads would be slightly elevated above the surface of the horseshoe. But most horseshoes take at least eight nails, four on each side. If what I was seeing was the nail track of half a horseshoe, there should have been at least four nails, and there were only two. Missing horseshoe nails on an animal as valuable as Game Boy? Cody would have taken care of that immediately.

I studied the image, hoping what I was seeing wasn't artifact or my imagination. Hoping I might have something to compare to Game Boy's hooves. If he hadn't been re-shod since the night Cody died, missing nails on at least one of his hooves would be obvious. If none were missing, there was at least a chance that Laurie was right and it wasn't Game Boy. But then how had Cody been killed by a blow from a horse's hoof?

I recalled Laurie saying another vehicle had stopped behind the trailer. She heard Cody shout, and whoever stopped had jumped back in the vehicle, wheeled around and taken off. Even if Laurie had stayed around to tell that story, there was nothing at the scene to suggest that it wasn't Game Boy's hoof that struck Cody. Could this photo convince anyone that the wound didn't match Game Boy's hooves? Maybe, but it would take the opinion of an expert forensic photographer. The opinion of a farrier might be a first step, but the only farrier who came to mind was Keely O'Brien's boyfriend, Tucker Potkotter. Not a good choice, since he was enmeshed with the O'Brien clan. I'd have to ask the vets at Creek-side Animal Care to recommend someone.

But first I wanted to see Game Boy's hooves. Nick and I were scheduled to meet at the vet's at noon, and since the digits on my alarm clock were approaching four in the morning, I forced myself to put the mystery aside and try to sleep.

JACK'S TOM TURKEYS took up a chorus of gobbling at six o'clock Tuesday morning, probably in response to the plaintive call of some lonely hen down in the valley. Leave it to the males to get all worked up over a new girl in town. Just as well. I needed extra caffeine to get me started, so I rolled out, put on the coffee pot, and took a quick shower.

As soon as I got to work, I started chipping away at the final details for the CME program. The Dietary Department needed a meal count, since the CME programs were always held in the evening and always included a banquet-style dinner.

The evaluation sheets had to be prepared. All CME attendees were given the opportunity to rate the program. Did it live up to its educational objectives? Dr. Beardsley was supposed to write up the objectives, but he was still in Aruba, so I had done that chore myself. It was mostly boilerplate; I'd reviewed past programs for the appropriate wording. *Attendees will gain insight into the appropriate indicators for urologic surgery...* and so on and so forth. With dinner arranged and evaluations done, all I had to do was confirm equipment needs such as microphones, speakers, and a projector.

The event was scheduled for seven o'clock the following evening, and I would have to be present to take attendance and then remain in the room playing sergeant-at-arms to make sure no one sneaked out early. Seemed kind of pathetic, since the room would be full of grown men and women. One of those women would be Dr. Phyllis Poole.

I wondered if the peer reviews of her cases would result in a recommendation that her privileges be suspended. I couldn't help thinking that if Cleo was right and Poole was involved in Cody O'Brien's murder, loss of hospital privileges would pale in comparison to a prison sentence.

My train of thought was interrupted by my phone. It was Harry, with news about his date with Keely, I hoped.

"What's up?" I said. "Any luck?"

"What? I don't even rate a polite *hello*?"

"Sorry. Hello. Did you score some useful information?"

"I think so. Do you want to do this on the phone?"

"Probably not. I can come by your job site for lunch.... No, wait, I have to meet Nick at lunchtime."

"Really? Since when?"

"We're going out to Creekside Animal Care to look at Game Boy's hooves."

"Maybe I can meet you there. Isn't there a taco stand somewhere nearby? We could grab a bite after you finish at the vet."

"Good plan. I also need to hear about Nick's date with…never mind. I'll call you back."

I had spotted Jared Quinn ambling toward me with his sensual big cat stride. Quinn was a first-rate hospital administrator and I liked to think of him as a friend, but I recalled his warning about snooping into the Cody O'Brien mystery. He'd take an extremely dim view of my nocturnal visits to the hospital with Cleo. And he wasn't stupid. If he caught wind that Nick was dating the hospital's top income-producing urologic surgeon, he'd smell trouble.

"How's it going?" Quinn asked. "Are we all set for tomorrow night?"

"We're right on schedule. All the peer reviews are finished. Now it's up to Dr. Fausset to decide how he wants to orchestrate the CME program."

"Have you talked to him recently?"

"No, but I put in a call to his office asking him to drop by sometime today."

"Well, good luck." Quinn frowned. "It seems no one's heard from him for several days. Code Blues has a gig this weekend, and he's missed a couple rehearsals without letting anyone know in advance."

Dr. Fausset missing? I felt something cold roll around in my midsection. No, I was letting my imagination run away with me. Not "missing." Just taking a few days off.

"Who's covering for him?" I thought I knew, hoped I was wrong.

"Dr. Phyllis Poole." Quinn chuckled. "None of Fausset's patients are thrilled about that."

So Fausset was AWOL, but Poole was present and accounted for. I shuffled some papers on my desk to hint to Quinn that I was busy and needed to get back to work, but what I really needed was time alone to process the possibilities his news presented.

"Unless you need anything, I'll be on my way," he said.

"No, I'm good. Thanks for checking."

"Don't mention it." He flashed his amiable smile. "Say hello to the llamas."

Always with the llamas. Quinn just couldn't resist. Half an hour later, Nick called to confirm what time to meet me at Creekside. I told him to plan on twelve thirty and said Harry might make it, too.

"I want to hear about your date with Dr. Poole and Harry's evening with Keely. Harry suggested we meet at the taco place and compare notes after we finish at the vet."

"Works for me. I'll see you at Creekside."

I wasn't looking forward to hearing about Nick's date with Poole, even if it was for a good cause. He was too darned good at turning on the charm. After seeing Poole behave like a love-sick teenager around Tobias Fausset, I knew the woman's cold exterior wasn't the whole story. She might burst into flame if lit by the right match.

I spent the rest of the morning trying to focus on my job. Lola's shift ended at noon, but she hesitated at my desk before leaving.

"Has the handsome Irishman been around lately?" The facial expression she was going for was mild curiosity, but her look was too steely for that and came closer to probing. She took a deep interest in my love life, or more accurately, the apparent lack of it.

"No, not lately," I said.

"That's all right, sweetie, you can't win them all. I hope you have a lovely afternoon."

"Thank you, Lola."

I watched her go, thinking she epitomized the zest for life I hoped to have at her age. I closed up and headed for Coyote Creek.

Most of the Creekside Animal Care staff was on lunch break when I arrived, but the large animal vet was busy stitching a mare that had tangled with some barbed wire. I took a seat in the waiting room and within a few minutes Nick arrived and joined me.

When Dr. Goodell finished with the mare, she invited us back to a small office where a tabby with a missing left eye sat guard on the corner of a desk.

I waited to see how Nick would handle the phony ploy about representing a buyer for Game Boy. He got right to it.

"As I mentioned when we arranged this visit, I'm representing a potential buyer for the O'Brien horse you're boarding. I invited Aimee along because you and she are acquainted. I hope that's all right."

"Certainly," Dr. Goodell said. "I recall you mentioning the buyer is from Texas."

"Yes. I'm not at liberty to give out the name just yet. For now, we want to get a good assessment of the animal's temperament."

"Are you comfortable with my opinion that the horse is physically sound?"

"Aimee assures me that I can rely on your evaluation."

"So how can I help you?"

I chimed in, "I'd like to spend a few minutes with the

horse. It's important to know how he reacts to touch, grooming, having his hooves lifted, that sort of thing."

"Let's get to it, then."

She led the way to a row of stables and stopped in front of one that was padlocked and posted with a sign that read: NO UNACCOMPANIED ADMITTANCE.

The scent of fresh hay mingled with the strong ammonia smell of a recently emptied bladder. Game Boy's golden Palomino head appeared over the door of his stall. He worked his nostrils, nickered, then tossed his head and backed away from the door.

Dr. Goodell entered the stall and clipped a lead rope to the horse's halter. She led him outside onto a patch of mowed grass and handed the lead to me. In my teens, I had often ridden the horses Jack owned back then. Now, being near a magnificent animal like Game Boy filled me with a thrill only an ardent horse lover could understand. I ran a hand down the white blaze on his face. He leaned in as if he enjoyed the touch. I tried scratching him behind his ears. He definitely wasn't ear shy. While I stroked his neck, Nick took out his camera and began clicking away, explaining that the buyer had asked for pictures.

"Aimee, do you want to try lifting his hooves?" Nick asked.

As I lifted the front hooves, Nick zoomed in on the horseshoes. The nail tracks of the shoes on both of the front hooves showed four nails on each side. None missing.

"Now for the hind legs," I said.

If Cody had been kicked by this horse, it most likely had been one of the rear hooves that left the mark. I walked to the hindquarters and reached down to grasp his left fetlock. He lifted his hoof with perfect manners, allowing me to brush away some dirt and get a good look at the horseshoe nails. All eight were present, four in each track. I heard Nick's camera capturing the shots we needed. The other hind hoof was the same. No missing nails. I had one last question for Dr. Goodell.

"I'm curious about the horseshoes. They seem new. Has he been re-shod since his owner was injured in the horse trailer?"

"Absolutely not. Game Boy is just as he was when he was brought here the day of the incident. Seamus O'Brien wanted him checked over for any possible injuries. Then he asked us to board the animal. He wanted no one else to have access to him. Seamus was quite grief-stricken about his son's death, so of course we agreed."

"Then payment will go to Seamus if the horse is sold?"

"Yes, or to the estate if poor Seamus should succumb. I understand he's hospitalized with a poor prognosis."

The prognosis for his estate wasn't looking too good either, unless we could find a way to keep it out of the hands of his scheming young wife.

TWENTY-SEVEN

NICK FOLLOWED ME to the taco stand a mile down the road from Creekside. The late October day was warm and sunny, so we walked to an outdoor picnic table with our food just as Harry drove up and parked. He gave us a wave and trotted over to the take-out window.

"Do you want to wait for him before we share intel?" Nick asked.

"Sure. We might as well eat first."

The spicy aromas in the air shifted my appetite into high gear. I bit into my fish taco; Nick cut into his tamale with a plastic fork. We had finished half of our meal by the time Harry joined us.

"Hi, fellow spies, is this seat taken?" He sat on the bench next to me and confronted a burrito the size of a football.

"Go ahead and eat," I said. "We'll fill you in."

Nick and I related our visit to Creekside, emphasizing the important details. All the horseshoes had eight nails present, and the horse had not been re-shod since the night Cody O'Brien died.

Harry swallowed a mouthful. "So there's a chance it wasn't Game Boy? Just like your nurse friend said?"

"A chance. But what does that get us?" Nick said. "It doesn't explain how O'Brien's head wound was caused by a horseshoe."

"Nick, why don't we let Harry finish his giant burrito while you report on your evening with Dr. Poole?"

"I did pick up an interesting fact," Nick said. "Did you know Phyllis Poole has a niece living in Timbergate?"

That news set my scalp tingling. "You're kidding! How did you get that out of her?"

Nick grinned. "You sure you want to know?"

Harry nearly choked, and I had to pat him on the back until he stopped coughing.

I glared at Nick. "Quit screwing around and just tell us."

"It seems Poole has a sister in Idaho—"

"Jackie Poole, right?" I slapped the table. "I knew that wasn't a coincidence."

"Hey, are you going to let me tell this story?" Nick glanced at Harry. "If she interrupts again, clamp a hand over her mouth."

Harry shook his head and swallowed. "And end up on the ground with her foot on my neck? No thanks."

"Okay, Nick. You made your point," I said. "Tell us about the sister."

"Older, by quite a bit. And you were right, she works at the hospital in Idaho where you met the McClurg woman. Seems Jackie Poole has a foster daughter who got into some kind of trouble with drugs when she was working as a nursing assistant at that same hospital. After that, she took off and no one knew where she was until the niece turned up in Timbergate, not long after Phyllis Poole joined the TMC medical staff."

"So what's the deal? Is Phyllis Poole keeping an eye on her foster niece? Helping her out? Keeping her sober, or what?"

"That was the plan, but the niece is married, and she's cut herself off from her Aunt Phyllis. Apparently they have little or no contact."

Harry swallowed the last bite of his burrito. "Did you get the niece's name? And what she has to do with Cody O'Brien?"

"Just her first name. Caroline. Poole wouldn't tell me who the niece married, but here's the interesting part. Poole says Caroline did a legal name change when she left Idaho. Something about making a fresh start. Poole stopped short of giving me the name. I don't think she realized name changes are public record. It didn't take long to find a Caroline Poole who had changed her name to Echo McCall."

I jumped up and nearly fell over trying to extricate myself from the picnic table. "Echo? Phyllis Poole's niece calls herself Echo? Oh my God, Nick! Do you know what that means?"

"I think so. Haven't I heard you refer to Seamus O'Brien's wife as Echo?"

"That's right. Echo must be the niece."

"If not, it's a hell of a coincidence." Harry crumpled his burrito wrapper and wiped his hands on a napkin.

"Nick, can we be a hundred percent positive that Echo O'Brien is the niece named Caroline?"

"Nothing is a hundred percent, Aimee. Ask any cop who works in identity theft."

"Come on, guys. Echo isn't a common name." I looked to Nick.

"I agree, but Harry's right. We can't be positive, and Phyllis Poole made it clear she isn't telling."

"Then let's move on to my report," Harry said. "It turns out Keely is more than a little suspicious about her boyfriend Tucker. She thinks he's fooling around. Want to guess with who?"

"With *whom*," I said, which earned me a big sigh from Harry and a laugh from Nick.

"Your sister can't help herself, Harry. Just tell us."

"Keely thinks Tucker and Echo have a thing going on. She woke up a couple of times in the middle of the night and he wasn't in their bed. The last time it happened, she stayed awake and waited for him to come back. When she confronted him, he made up a story about insomnia and claimed he was sitting up watching TV in the living room."

"Could be true," Nick said.

Harry nodded. "Or not."

"We have to know," I said. "Echo O'Brien is pregnant and claiming Seamus is the father. We know he isn't."

"And you think it's Tucker?" Harry said.

"Don't you?"

"I have to admit it seems pretty likely."

"Aimee?" Nick reached over to tap the face of my wrist watch. "When do you have to be back at work?"

"Now."

I hated to break up our brainstorming session. We had put together enough of the puzzle to know we were teasing out the truth, but I had to get back to the library.

As the afternoon wore on, I couldn't stop thinking about the Caroline connection. Jackie Poole told someone named CJ that she'd kept quiet about Caroline. Dr. Poole told Nick her foster niece named Caroline had worked at Dunnsville Memorial. Now it seemed likely that Caroline was Jackie Poole's foster daughter. But what did that have to do with the mysterious CJ who might or might not be Carl Jasper, owner of Dunnsville Memorial? I had no idea, but there was something more. Laurie Popejoy had mentioned a nursing assistant named Caroline who was assigned to DeeDee Dakota's hospital room. If Echo O'Brien *was* the mysterious Caroline, her life had followed a twisted trail. The hairs rising on the back of my neck told me it was a trail that might lead us to Cody O'Brien's killer.

A call from James O'Brien interrupted my musing. He said he had something to tell me and asked if I would meet him at Casa Loco after work. I agreed. He sounded unusually somber.

On the heels of James's call, I heard from Cleo saying she had something for me in her office. I closed the library and walked over to the main tower. I found her alone behind a desk piled with medical records and several of the black binders she used to organize minutes and documents related to various medical staff committees.

When I walked in, she looked up from her monitor and held her finger to her lips.

I kept quiet and mouthed, *What?*

She motioned for me to close the door. I did. Her office was in a heavy traffic area on the first floor where people often dropped in unannounced if they saw her door open.

Cleo reached across her desk and dropped a TMC medical record in front of me. I opened the cover and saw Deirdre DeGraw's name. *DeeDee Dakota's medical record, at last.*

"How did—"

Cleo shook her head and whispered, "Don't ask." She pointed at the chart. "You have ten minutes. Hurry up." No matter how she'd gotten it, she must have taken a big risk.

I felt blood rush to my face. I sat in her visitor's chair racing through the pages from the hospital in Idaho, looking for anything documenting people who had worked in DeeDee's hospital room. Particularly Phyllis Poole or her foster niece, Caroline.

Laurie Popejoy's Aunt Brenda turned up right away. She had told me she was DeeDee's primary nurse, so that was no surprise. There were a few other names, all unfamiliar. A neurologist, a radiologist, an orthopedist. She was admitted on a Saturday night around nine o'clock. Nothing in the early hours of her admission indicated a coma. The tentative diagnosis was concussion, but DeeDee was awake and responsive. Another twenty-four hours of observation in the hospital was recommended. She hadn't slipped into a coma until the morning she was due to be discharged.

"Aimee," Cleo hissed. "Five more minutes."

I scanned through more pages until finally a handwritten signature in a box under a checklist of duties performed by a nursing assistant jumped out at me: *Caroline Poole*. Alias Echo O'Brien?

I walked around Cleo's desk and pointed at the signature. "Look at this." She shrugged, and her puzzled look reminded me that I hadn't had a chance to tell her about Dr. Poole's foster niece, Caroline.

"Time's up." Cleo reached for the chart and I stepped back, holding it to my chest.

"Aimee," she whispered. "Give it back. I have to—"

Her office door opened and Jared Quinn walked in. I closed the chart and dropped it on Cleo's desk.

"Aimee, this is serendipity," Quinn said. "After I

sign a few forms for Cleo, may I walk you back to the library?"

"Yes, but I was just explaining a fine point of forensics to Cleo about the different types of autopsies. A medical autopsy is different from a medical-legal autopsy." I prayed she'd get my message. "The coroner may not require the full toxicology exam if the cause of death is not a sudden, unexplained death or an obvious homicide or suicide."

"Aimee's my forensics tutor," Cleo said. "I find it helpful."

"Good to hear," Quinn said. "Now let's see what you have for me."

Cleo pointed out the appropriate lines on several forms needing Quinn's signature. While he jotted his name on each, she gave me a look and mouthed, *Autopsy?* I nodded. She nodded back.

Quinn and I walked across the hospital campus toward the library under an overcast sky. He seemed thoughtful and I wondered what was on his mind. A brisk wind nipped the air. We picked up our pace, skirting around a Life Support Unit pulling in from the street entrance. Minutes later we were alone in the library.

"Any luck making contact with Tobias Fausset?" Quinn said.

The discovery of Dr. Poole's foster niece, Caroline, had pushed the whereabouts of Dr. Fausset to the back burner, and nearly off the stove altogether.

"No, but I'm sure he'll be in touch."

"His office manager implied he's taking personal time," Quinn said. "That usually translates to mean it's nobody's business where he is or why. I just don't like the timing. Seems odd, doesn't it?"

"It does. Almost like something unexpected happened."

"If we don't hear from Fausset by tomorrow noon, you'll have to ask the vice chairman of the Urology Department to step up and run tomorrow night's CME program. I'm not even sure who that is, but you'd better alert him just in case."

"I'll take care of it. Anything else?"

"That's all for now. Say hello—"

"I know. The llamas."

AT FIVE MINUTES to closing time, I called Cleo to see if she knew the name of the vice chairman of the Urology Department. I explained that I might need the vice chair to preside over the CME program.

"Well, that should be interesting." I heard a strange rasp in her voice.

"Why?"

"Because the vice chair of the Urology Department is Dr. Phyllis Poole."

TWENTY-EIGHT

JAMES WAS WAITING in Casa Loco's foyer when I arrived at five thirty. We took a booth with a window view of the cactus garden. The sight of the prickly needles reflected my state of mind. Our orders were taken, and drinks delivered—white wine for me, Dos Equis for James. Dressed in a black leather jacket over a pristine white shirt with a loose tie at his neck, he looked like what he was, a New York City producer. The lighting in the restaurant sparked red-gold highlights in his wavy hair.

James got right to the point. "Thank you for coming. I hope you won't be too shocked by what I'm about to tell you."

I didn't like the sound of that. Just then our waiter appeared to ask if we wanted to order dinner. We both gave him a quick negative. He seemed to sense the tension at our table and left without another word.

"You were saying?" I said.

"Damn, Aimee. This is going to be harder than any confession I ever made to a priest."

"I'm no priest, James. I can't absolve you, and I can't promise to protect your secrets. Keep that in mind before you bare your soul." My heart was beating so hard I seemed to bounce in my chair.

"It's nothing like that," he said. "I haven't murdered anyone, but I've carried a boatload of guilt with me for a long time."

The breath I'd been holding rushed from my lungs in an audible sigh. "I can't imagine you doing anything to trigger that degree of guilt. Not the James O'Brien I remember."

"The former altar boy? The good Catholic?" James asked. "Do you remember the ninth commandment?"

"The Catholic version? Sure. Thou shalt not covet thy neighbor's wife." It took a beat before I realized where he was going with this. "Oh, your *brother's* wife. DeeDee Dakota."

"I loved her, Aimee. God help me. I think I still do."

Was this how a priest felt hearing a confession? Obliged to wait for more information, but dreading what he might hear? Brenda McClurg had observed James at DeeDee's bedside in Idaho appearing to be more worried and more devoted to her than Cody had been. Where had that devotion led James?

"James, please look at me." I touched the back of his hand. "Loving your brother's wife is understandable. I'm relieved if that's your worst sin. You said you haven't murdered anyone and I believe you. Is there anything more on your conscience?"

James glanced out the window at the cactus garden. "There was more than coveting going on back then. DeeDee and I were in love. Waiting for the right moment to tell Cody."

"But they were the famous rodeo sweethearts. Was DeeDee going to ask for a divorce?"

"She didn't have to. They were never married."

"What?" I stared at James.

"It was an elaborate ruse that got out of hand. Cody was never husband material. He did a lot of drinking and partying. DeeDee put up with it for the first year or so because she was in love. Then she stayed with him, pretending they were married because of pressure from their agents. Their celebrity as rodeo sweethearts translated into big money in appearances and endorsements. DeeDee finally confided in me, admitting that she was unhappy. I commiserated, because my marriage was a disaster by then. From that start, we grew close, then fell very much in love."

I was getting in way over my head, but it was too late to turn back.

"Did Cody find out about your affair before DeeDee died?" Surely Cody hadn't been involved in DeeDee's unexpected spiral into a coma and death.

"No, Cody claimed he was scared straight by DeeDee's accident. He'd been flirting with a rodeo groupie there in Dunnsville. When DeeDee was hurt, he shut that down immediately."

"Flirting? Is that all it was?"

"Do I really have to spell it out?"

"It would help." I needed every detail James could provide.

"Cody swore it was a one night stand and told me he was going to marry DeeDee and be a model husband from then on. I figured he deserved one more chance, and so did DeeDee. I swallowed my bitter pill and vowed to step aside. I figured if Cody could man up, so could I. He never knew about DeeDee and me."

"Do you know who the woman was? Cody's fling?"

"No idea. There are so many rodeo groupies around that the cowboys are like kids in a candy store. Some women even follow the rodeo circuit and stalk their favorites. That's why the wives who care stick damn close to their men."

James had answered my most important question when he said he hadn't killed anyone. I had one more question. I waited while he ordered another round of drinks, then I plunged ahead.

"You said you saw Phyllis Poole in DeeDee's hospital room. Do you recall seeing anyone else on the hospital staff?"

"There was a black woman—the head nurse, I think. She was in the room several times a day." Brenda Mc-Clurg, Laurie Popejoy's aunt.

"Anyone else?" I didn't want to feed him Caroline Poole's name. If he had seen her in DeeDee's room, why wouldn't he recognize her as his father's wife?

"There was one young woman," James said. "She helped DeeDee to the bathroom and did simple tasks like refilling the paper towel dispenser. I didn't pay much attention."

"Do you remember what she looked like?"

"I usually left the room when any of the hospital staff came in, but I do remember that particular woman because she seemed so out of place. She had pink hair the color of cotton candy and glasses with big black frames. The glasses weren't a big deal, but the hair made me wonder how she got her job."

How she got her job, indeed. Jackie Poole was the answer to that question.

"You never heard her name?" I said.

"I don't think so. If I did, I doubt I would have remembered."

Was it really possible he'd seen Caroline Poole in that hospital and hadn't recognized her when she turned up as Echo O'Brien, married to his father? Had Seamus's young wife infiltrated his family like a cancer, spreading her malignant tentacles from Idaho to Timbergate?

I wanted so much to believe James, but his denial about recognizing Echo left a shred of doubt about his innocence. Until I was sure he wasn't part of a master plan about the O'Brien fortune, I couldn't tell him what I suspected.

"Why all these questions?" James gave me a puzzled look. "I have a feeling there's something you're holding back."

James was right, but what could I tell him that wouldn't jeopardize the progress Nick, Harry, and I had made? Something that wouldn't alert him if he was mixed up in a family conspiracy. I did a quick rewind of all the evidence we'd uncovered, scrambling for something to say.

"Nick and Harry and I have done a lot of investigating on our own, hoping to confirm that Cody's death was an accident. It seems pretty clear there's no evidence of foul play. It looks like both he and DeeDee were killed by their horses, and that's that." I reached for my purse, ready to leave.

"Wait," he said. "What about Cody's call to me from TMC? He said he had something important to tell me. We have every reason to believe it was about Echo's pregnancy and Dad's will. Now Cody's dead. You might think that's a coincidence and the shot someone took at him was a hunting accident, but I'm not convinced, and I'm not going back to New York while my father is in the hospital fighting for his life. Not while that cold, scheming… God, Aimee. Don't you see? We can't let Echo destroy my father's legacy while he's helpless to fight her."

"I'm sorry. I don't know what else to say."

James stood. "This isn't over, Aimee. You and

Harry and your boyfriend can think what you want."
He dropped some bills on the table and said again,
"This isn't over." He strode out of Casa Loco while I
sat watching his back, feeling eight years old again and
wanting his approval the way I had as a child. I wished
I could tell him the truth.

TWENTY-NINE

NICK'S CAR WAS parked at the main house when I reached Coyote Creek, so I pulled in next to it. I needed a sounding board after what I'd heard from James.

The door opened just as I reached out to ring the bell.

"I saw you drive up. What's going on?" Nick held a soup ladle in his hand. "I was about to sit down with a bowl of Jack's trout chowder. I found it in the freezer. There's plenty if you want to join me."

"No, thanks, not hungry." I had eaten some appetizers to soak up the wine before driving home. "I wanted to brainstorm, but I just realized it's almost dark and I haven't done the chores."

"No problem. I did the chores. The llamas and turkeys are already fed and watered. You might as well come on in."

Score a point for Nick. He could be so thoughtful and generous. But his thoughtfulness was part of our problem. Thanks to his generosity, Rella was still living in his apartment. After our talk about trust back in Idaho, it was hard to admit how that bothered me. *Get over it*, I thought. I wished I knew how.

"Thanks for doing that. Do you have coffee made?"

"Fresh ten minutes ago." He poured a cup and handed it to me. "You can talk while I eat. I get that this isn't strictly a social call."

"No. I'm on information overload. There are too

many pieces to this puzzle." I was counting on his help to sort out our newest evidence.

We sat across from each other at the antique oak table in Amah's kitchen nook. I told him everything I'd learned from James, starting with the fact that Cody and DeeDee were never married. Nick had finished eating by the time I got to the part where James admitted his love for DeeDee and their affair. Nick's eyes narrowed when I said I was almost certain James hadn't played any part in Cody's death.

"You're not the best judge of that, Aimee. He was your first big crush. Of course you want him to be innocent. He could be mixed up with either Keely or Echo in some plot to inherit the estate." Nick went to the sink to rinse his bowl. I watched his back and wondered if either of us was being objective.

"What you say is possible, of course, but I'm still convinced James isn't involved."

He dried the bowl and set it aside. "Come on. You're the one who told me about his financial straits. Combine that with his affair with Cody's wife, and you have a couple of strong motives."

"She wasn't Cody's wife, remember?"

"You're splitting hairs. She was his brother's woman."

"Okay, but James was in New York when Cody died."

"I'm not saying he did the deed himself. You don't want to know how cheap and easy it is to hire a freelancer."

"A hit man? In Sawyer County?"

"That term 'hit man' implies a level of professionalism. I'm talking about some low-life scumbag who needs a few thousand bucks to support his meth habit."

"What hired killer would have been clever enough

to make Cody's death look like a horse kicked him in the head?"

Nick came back to the table. "Good question. Not clever *enough*, since you seem to think the bruise doesn't quite match Game Boy's shoes."

"Right, the missing horseshoe nails. The problem is, I can't see how anyone could grip a horseshoe and whack it on someone's head hard enough to cause that kind of fatal wound. It would be too awkward."

"I agree," Nick said. "But according to Laurie Pope-joy, someone came up behind them while they were parked along I-5 that night. She insists Cody wasn't kicked by the horse, so whoever did the deed found a way to make it look like he was."

"Which means it was premeditated." I got up to heat my cold coffee. "That doesn't bode well for the culprit when he's caught."

The doorbell rang while my cup was in the micro-wave. I looked out the peephole. Harry stood on the porch. Good timing. We could use his input. I opened the door.

"You're just in time. Nick and I are comparing notes."

"That's why I'm here, big sister." He patted the top of my head, an annoying reminder that I might be two years older, but he was eight inches taller. "Nick called me when he saw you pull in the driveway." Harry sniffed. "I smell food. Am I too late for dinner?"

Nick filled a bowl with chowder and nuked it for Harry. While he ate, we filled him in on my conversa-tion with James.

Harry set his spoon and empty bowl aside. "Okay, since we know the when and where, why don't we start with the how and see if it tells us the who and the why."

He looked at Nick, and then at me. "Would one of you please write this down?"

Nick nodded at me. "You want to do the honors?"

I suppressed a comment about *women's work* and found paper and a pen in Amah's desk alcove in the kitchen. "Okay, go ahead."

"Horseshoe," Harry said. "Write that down." I wrote.

"Weapon." I wrote.

"Know-how." I wrote.

"Access." Again, I wrote.

"Something to gain." I wrote.

"Now let's look at the list," Harry said. "Do we know anyone who matches five out of five?"

"Holy shit." Nick said it; I thought it.

Harry grinned. "That wasn't so difficult, was it?"

What we had all concluded was the name of the person who had access to horseshoes and the cunning to figure out how to use one as a weapon. A farrier who was also a taxidermist. *Tucker Potkotter.* For him, a simple matter of attaching a horseshoe matching Game Boy's to the leg a taxidermist would use for constructing a full-body horse mount. *Trigger.*

"Harry," I said. "Are you sure? I thought you and Tucker were friends."

"Tucker's just a guy I know from the gym. He's friendly enough, but most psychopaths are, and I don't know a lot about him. Maybe he's not the guy, but he's sure sitting in a sweet spot if Seamus dies and Keely inherits." *Something to gain.*

"But don't forget," Nick said. "Echo's unborn kid is considered Seamus's under law, since she was married to him when she got pregnant. That means she still has plenty of leverage when it comes to a battle over the estate."

"It's more complicated than that," I said. "Remember Keely's suspicions about Tucker and Echo? We already have reason to believe he's the baby's father."

"What a soap opera," Harry said.

"Tucker's engaged to Keely, and he's probably the father of Echo's baby." I looked from Harry to Nick. "That's a sticky situation. Which woman is he going to latch on to if Seamus dies?"

"The one who gets the biggest piece of the pie," Nick said. "Looks like he's been playing them against each other."

"But were either of them involved in Cody's murder?" I had trouble imagining a woman capable of something that cold-blooded.

Harry waved a hand in the air. "Let's not get ahead of ourselves. We have five reasons to suspect Tucker's involved, but we have no proof."

We brainstormed for over an hour about how to build evidence against Tucker, but nothing short of his fingerprints on a murder weapon seemed likely to convince law enforcement that he was guilty. Or that there even *was* a murder.

"Remind me," Harry said. "How long ago was Cody found in the trailer?"

"It was a Monday, so it's been two weeks and two days. Why?"

"Any word on a coroner's report?"

"Not yet. Quinn told me some time ago that the coroner was taking his time because Cody was considered a high-profile case."

"But the coroner hasn't referred the case to law enforcement, has he?"

"No. Quinn said he would have been notified. I would have heard if that had happened."

"Then it's probably going to be considered an accident." He looked to Nick for confirmation.

"I think you're right. If the coroner thought the autopsy findings were suspicious, he would have alerted the sheriff right away."

"Then let's get back to Tucker," Harry said. "If he did use part of a full-body horse mount, it's probably on its way to Texas or Montana by now."

"Wait!" I raised my hand like a school kid. "Harry, remember that night you brought Keely by Amah and Jack's for dinner?"

Nick's eyebrows went up, but I quickly explained that it wasn't a date. Harry was driving her to the airport to meet James's plane as a favor to Tucker.

"What about it?" Harry said.

"That was two weeks ago, right? And we've all heard Jack talk about how long it takes to get a simple head mount done. He's waited months for some of his trophy heads. Imagine how long it would take to do a whole horse—especially with Seamus ill and trying to teach Tucker."

"She's right," Harry nodded at Nick. "If the horse isn't one of the jobs they're doing for the Safari Club International Convention in January, I'll bet it's been set aside."

"So you're suggesting Tucker followed Cody up I-5 that night and clubbed him over the head with a taxidermist's model of a horse's hind leg? How far would we get taking that to the sheriff?"

When Nick said it like that, it sounded worse than implausible, but what else would explain the horseshoe-shaped contusion on Cody's forehead?

"I agree with Nick," Harry said. "We'd be laughed out of the county if we went to law enforcement with a story like that. But for the sake of argument, let's say that's what happened. Was Cody's wound closed, or did it bleed?"

I reached for my purse and pulled out the enlarged morgue photo that I was still carrying around. "I don't think it bled. See for yourself." I handed it to Nick. He scrutinized it and handed it to Harry, who did the same.

Harry gave it back to me. "I don't know, Sis. That could be a photo of the surface of Mars." He turned to Nick. "What do you think?"

"I know this isn't what you want to hear, Aimee, but those marks you're attributing to horseshoe nails could be random blood clots under the skin."

"I'll admit that, but I've searched several databases and found dozens of images of trauma caused by horse kicks to the head, and not one of them looks like this photo. I've also looked at scalp contusions of all kinds, and many of them show a certain amount of recognizable detail."

"Sis, assuming you're right, Tucker would have ditched the weapon. Why keep it around? He's no genius, but he's not stupid, either."

"Maybe not," I pointed to the photo, "but is he smart enough to realize that no blood doesn't mean no DNA? The horseshoe could have picked up some of Cody's skin cells when it made contact. Or at least a few strands of his hair."

Nick exchanged a look with Harry. "Our forensic whiz at work."

"Give me a break." I put the photo back in my purse. "Anyone who watches TV would know that, but here's my point. If he used an essential part of one of Seamus's high-priced full-body mounts to kill Cody, he didn't dare ditch it or he would have been called on the carpet by Seamus. If he *is* Cody's killer, he couldn't risk drawing that kind of attention to himself."

Nick walked over to the coffee pot and refilled his cup. "Anyone else?"

Harry and I both waved him off. Nick came back to the table looking at me with apprehension before he spoke.

"There's something none of us have considered, but I think we have to put it on the table."

"If you have a theory, let's hear it," Harry said.

"Suppose Tucker is James O'Brien's hired hit man."

"To what end?" Harry asked.

"A bigger piece of the estate when his father dies."

I couldn't deny James had a motive, but I offered another possibility. "What about Phyllis Poole? She's the first person we suspected of being involved. Maybe she hired a hit man herself."

"Anything's possible," Nick said. "Can you give her a motive that sounds plausible?"

"To borrow your inheritance theory, maybe Phyllis Poole and her alleged niece are accomplices. Maybe Poole wanted both Cody and Seamus dead before anyone found out about the paternity of Echo's baby. Maybe Echo and Dr. Poole would love to inherit the multimillion dollar O'Brien estate and split the booty." Another thought came to me. "What about her missing lover, Tobias Fausset? Doesn't that make you wonder what was going on between the two of them?"

"Are you suggesting she talked Dr. Fausset into killing the cowboy and then killed Fausset herself?"

"It sounds crazy, I know, but he's missing and no one seems to know where he is."

"Hold it," Harry said. "This is starting to sound more like a pulp fiction plot than a brainstorming session. It's after ten o'clock. Why don't we break it up for now? Let's go to our corners, sleep on it, and touch base again tomorrow."

"We're running out of time," I said. "Seamus could die at any moment, and if he does, whoever inherits his estate may get away with murder. We have to pursue this horseshoe idea. What else have we got?"

"Sis, we'll get together again tomorrow. We'll get this figured out. Right, Nick?"

"Right. How about we meet here tomorrow at noon? Can you both get away from work?"

Harry agreed and so did I, but I wouldn't look either of them in the eye, which made Nick suspicious.

"You're up to something, Aimee." He turned to Harry. "She's your sister. Talk to her."

Harry frowned. "Don't even think of snooping around Tucker or the women. You'd be safer in a den of rattlesnakes."

He wasn't playing fair. I'd killed a rattlesnake with a pitchfork a couple of months earlier, and the sight of a length of coiled rope or a garden hose could still throw me off balance.

We agreed to call it a night and Harry headed out, mentioning that he had a late date. I drove down the lane to my apartment, mulling over the possibility that

Tucker Potkotter was Cody O'Brien's killer. How would we prove it? I had been in bed trying to read myself to sleep for half an hour when my phone rang. *Nick.*

"Hi, what's going on?"

"I'm going to have to make a run to the vet. Ginger mixed it up good with a coyote that found its way into Jack's backyard. She's lost a lot of blood and needs stitches."

"I'm sorry. I hope she'll be okay."

"She will once I take care of this, but I don't like leaving you alone. I think you should come with me."

"Really? It's past eleven. I'm already in bed. How long will you be gone?"

"I don't know. Dr. Goodell is meeting me there. I'll be leaving the dog overnight, so once the doc evaluates the injuries and gets to work, I'll be back."

"Then you won't be too long. Creekside is only a few minutes away. Don't worry about me. Just take care of your dog. If anything remotely alarming happens here, I'll call your cell."

"All right. That should work. Where's your gun?"

"Within reach. Go. Take care of Ginger."

Nick had fallen in love with that sweet dog. I knew how much it must bother him to see her injured. I watched out my kitchen window until he drove away a few minutes later.

That's when Cleo called.

THIRTY

"Aimee. Thank heaven you answered. Have you heard what's going on?" Cleo's voice was an octave higher than usual. Her panic set my left eyelid twitching.

"What more could be going on? We're already up to our—"

"It's Seamus. He's sinking fast and the whole clan is gathered around his bed in ICU."

I pressed a finger against my jerking eyelid. "How do you know this? Are you at work?" As part of her job, Cleo was sometimes called in after hours for special circumstances involving hospital privileges.

"Yes. I'm in my office. Dr. Poole requested a consult by an infectious disease specialist who isn't on the TMC medical staff. Dr. Beardsley's supposed to sign off on temporary privileges, but he isn't available, so I called Quinn. He can sign off if the chief of staff isn't around."

"Is Quinn still there?"

"No, he just left. He signed a few blank temporary privilege forms and said to call him at home for an approval if Poole requests anyone else who isn't on staff. That means I'm staying here until O'Brien either improves or expires."

"Why is Dr. Poole Seamus's primary? Doesn't he have an internist?"

"He did, but Seamus's wife fired him, so when the ER doc diagnosed renal failure, he called Dr. Fausset."

"Then why isn't Fausset there? Couldn't they reach him?"

"No, that's why Poole's in charge. She did the admit to ICU. Fausset's still absent and no one is saying why. The rumors have already started. Take your pick. He's either eloped or he's in rehab."

Or possibly dead.

Cleo went on, "Aimee, do you realize what this means? Poole is in a perfect position to make sure Seamus won't live to divorce her niece. If he dies, Echo O'Brien will use that baby she's carrying to cheat the remaining O'Briens out of their inheritance." Cleo choked back a sob. "We have to stop Poole. She's a cold-blooded killer and she's going to operate on Siggy Thursday morning."

"I thought you were going to talk him into canceling."

"He won't." Cleo sniffled and cleared her throat. "It's like he's bewitched. No matter what I say, he's going ahead with it. He claims he knows several men she's treated successfully. He says I've developed a paranoid obsession about her. He even accused me of being jealous." I heard her suck in a breath. "We have to prove she's treacherous, but there's no time."

"Maybe there's something I can do." I gave her a quick version of what Harry and Nick and I had come up with, including Tucker as a suspect and the possible weapon. "The only way to find it is to search the O'Brien compound. I promised Nick and Harry I wouldn't do anything reckless, but that doesn't matter now. If everyone who lives at the compound is at the hospital, there's no risk."

"You'd better take Nick with you. He's staying right there in your grandparents' house, isn't he?"

"Yes, but he isn't here. His dog got injured and he

had to take her to the vet. I don't know how long he's going to be gone."

"Then what about Harry?"

"Harry's off on a late date somewhere. I don't really need anyone to go along if everyone from the O'Brien compound is at the hospital. You can monitor that for me, but the sooner I get started, the better. If I can find what I'm looking for, I'll need to collect DNA from the horseshoe."

"How?"

"I have a kit. I ordered it for an in-service I gave last month up in Modoc County."

"Then why just the DNA? If you find a weapon, why not take it, if it isn't already attached to the rest of the fake horse?"

"If we remove the weapon, we can't prove where it came from. It needs to be left where it is. We're wasting time talking, Cleo. If I'm going to get this done, I need to get ready. You did say Tucker and all three O'Briens are there at the hospital?"

"Yes. James and Keely got here first. Then Echo and Tucker. As far as I can tell, none of the vultures wants to miss his last gasp. Then they can start picking his bones."

Cleo agreed to keep tabs on the O'Brien drama playing out in ICU. By eleven thirty I had changed into boots, dark jeans, and a black turtleneck. I put my phone in a small day pack with everything else I needed, including my pistol, and grabbed a lightweight fleece jacket.

The O'Brien compound was eight miles east of Coyote Creek. If we were right about the weapon, it had to be a section of a full-body horse mount. I hoped Tucker had decided his best option was to put it back where it belonged.

At the compound, I pulled my car around and parked a hundred feet from the gate. The moonlight made my flashlight unnecessary, so I dropped it in my pack and walked along the three-rail paddock fencing until I reached a spot where I could slip under the lowest rail.

The layout of the compound had not changed since I'd visited Keely there when we were children. There were three dwellings. Echo and Seamus obviously lived in the large main house, so I guessed Keely and Tucker shared one of the cottages and assumed James would be staying in the third cottage that would have been Cody's. The taxidermy shop, stables and barn were all set apart from the residences by about half an acre of cross-fenced corrals.

In a crouch, I followed the long gravel driveway to the taxidermy shop, stopping at any bush or shrub that offered cover. The closer I got, the more I worried about motion-sensor lights or other deterrents against prowlers or predators—attack dogs being high on the list. My pockets were stuffed with jerky just in case, but I wasn't sure guard dogs could be bribed.

Stress sweat had already soaked my turtleneck, and my fleece jacket held the moisture in, creating a sauna effect. My tense muscles and rapid heartbeat added to the mix, causing even more perspiration. I wiped a sleeve across my face to clear sweat from my eyes and called Cleo's cellphone for an update. She reported that Tucker and the family were all still there in ICU. I told her to text me if anything changed.

A few minutes later, I reached the taxidermy shop and worked my way to the outer wall that faced away from the houses. No lights or alarms so far, and no dogs, but the next problem was how to get inside. The entrance door was bound to be locked, and maybe alarmed. And it was visible from the main house. The only access on the side of the building where I crouched was a small window two feet above my head. I looked around for something to stand on and spotted a rototiller parked at the edge of a large plot of turned-up soil. A defunct garden was my first thought; then I spotted an incinerator surrounded by a chain-link fence and realized something had to be done with the offal and other detritus involved in taxidermy. *Cremation*. Burn and then bury the ashes was my guess.

Rototillers are heavy when they're running and almost immoveable when they're not. The process of dragging it the few feet to the window took ten minutes and more strength than I knew I possessed. Every muscle in my back and arms screamed for mercy by time it was in place. I had to sit on the ground and lean against the shop wall for a few moments to rest and catch my breath. I didn't make another call. Timbergate Medical Center was situated on the far side of Timbergate—easily a thirty minute drive, if not more.

Still no lights, no alarms, no dogs. Seamus would have been horrified. Where was his security? The mounts under construction in his shop had to be worth at least six figures. I could only guess that Tucker and the two women had either ignored or forgotten the usual security routines in their rush to go to the hospital. James was an outsider, so he wasn't likely to know whether security measures were in place.

I managed to find a few flat inches on the tiller's motor casing, enough for only one foot. It raised me up a good two feet. Moonlight glinted off the vicious inch-wide blades just below where I perched on tiptoe. The blades protruded on either side of the tiller. One slip and I stood a good chance of carving all the meat off my leg and probably bleeding to death. While I tugged at the window, my leg began to tremble. There wasn't enough space on the tiller to change feet and rest my right leg. I gave the window a desperate shove, and it slid open.

Did I have time to get inside and have a good look around? If I did, how would I get back out without slicing myself on the tiller blades? While I debated whether to abort or go for it, my phone vibrated. Cleo with a text? I stepped down and read her message. Tucker's leaving. Echo, Keely, and James staying. I had thirty minutes.

I stepped up on the tiller, grabbed the windowsill with both hands and pulled myself up until I hung there half in and half out. A work table below the window made it easy to drop down inside. I pulled latex gloves out of my pack and slipped them on.

The shop reeked of a foul mixture of musky animal hides and noxious chemicals. I used a pen light to scan the large space. As I suspected, the mounts nearest completion were all game animals. Deer, antelope, a wild boar, two black bears, even a wild turkey. I spotted some large forms stacked on a pallet in one dark corner. I went closer and saw a horse's head and neck formed from some kind of smooth ivory-colored sculpting material, and next to it, two horse's hindquarters made of the same material. Neither of them had hooves attached. They were much larger that I'd envisioned. I tried to lift one, to judge whether it could be used to strike a blow, but it was too heavy and probably too awkward even for someone much taller and stronger.

A glance at my watch told me I had fifteen minutes. I looked around in confusion. I'd been so sure, and so wrong. There had to be something smaller with a horseshoe attached. My only hope was that some part of the murder weapon was hard to replace. Had Tucker used one of the hooves destined for the full-body horse mount? If so, he would have dismantled the weapon and put the hoof back where it belonged. I went back to the pallet and looked around. I spotted a box on a nearby table. Inside it were three hooves. Where was the fourth? Tossed along the freeway the night Cody died? Or hidden somewhere until the hoof could be put back in the box? Or was I making desperate assumptions about something that didn't exist?

A closed door at the back of the room was the only place I hadn't checked. It was worth a minute to take a look. It opened into a hallway with a bathroom on the right and a closed door on the left marked with an orange flame. I trained the beam of my pen light on a chart on the door marked with a grid. Hand-entered dates indicated when the incinerator was fired up, once a month. The last date had been three weeks earlier—a week before Cody died.

I pushed the door open. The room felt refrigerated, but it smelled like death. A large stainless-steel cart was piled high with flesh and bones, cartilage, and other animal parts I didn't want to think about. It had to be where they stored the waste headed to the incinerator. I was still wearing my latex gloves, so I clenched my teeth against nausea and began shifting the mass around to see what I could find.

After a few long minutes I uncovered a plastic garbage bag and inside it, found what I was looking for.

The makeshift weapon looked like an old wooden hatchet handle about eighteen inches long with a horse's hoof attached. It was the perfect size to use as a club, and there was a horseshoe attached to the hoof. The shoe was a perfect match to Game Boy's, except for two missing horseshoe nails.

I pulled the DNA swabs from the kit, but decided not to use them. With luck a legitimate forensics tech would process the weapon and find evidence of Cody's skin cells on the shoe. I didn't want to chance wiping them all away. I dusted the handle for prints, expecting it to be wiped clean, and it was. But Tucker had forgotten about the plastic bag he had used to wrap the weapon. I managed to tease up a few prints there and took half a dozen quick photos of both the prints and the weapon. With a small magnifying glass from my kit, I inspected the horseshoe and hit pay dirt—a few human hairs partially wedged between the horseshoe and the hoof. *Cody's hair*. I took two of the hairs and left the others. With the hair samples secure in my kit, I stuffed it in my day pack, along with my phone. I put the horseshoe club back in the plastic bag and shoved it back under the offal pile.

I closed the door to the waste disposal room and checked the schedule on the door one last time. Another week before the incinerator was due to burn. If it was Tucker who hid the club there two weeks ago, he must have been confident it wouldn't be found before he could get back to it. Despite the week remaining before the scheduled burn, that critical evidence could disappear at any moment. Hoping the truth of what had happened to Cody would come out before it did, I hurried back to the table in the shop and lowered myself out the window. If I didn't fall against the tiller blades, I was home free.

"Hey! What the hell do you think you're doing?"

The man's shout came from somewhere inside the shop, but it couldn't be Tucker. He hadn't had time to drive home. And James was still at the hospital. Who else could it be?

Hanging outside the window, I managed to touch the flat surface of the tiller with the ball of one foot. I pushed off and threw myself clear, landing on all fours. I took off running a zigzag line toward my car.

"Stop or I'll shoot." The voice sounded raspy and the words were slurred, but the shot that rang out wasn't a warning. The bullet nicked a Juniper bush inches from my head.

I pulled off my day pack as I neared the fence, tossed it over and dove under like a ball player sliding into home base. I scooped up the pack and dashed the hundred feet to my car. In spite of my shaking hand, I got the key in the ignition on the first try. The engine turned over and I stomped the gas pedal, leaving a cloud of smoking rubber in my wake.

So the O'Briens had a security guard after all. One who wasn't expecting an intruder to wake him from what was probably an alcohol-induced slumber. He hadn't even chased me to my car—bare feet, I guessed. Would Tucker suspect it was me in the shop? I'd been wearing a black ball cap with my hair twisted up inside, and the guard hadn't heard my voice. I hoped he would assume the incident was an attempted burglary, something all too common in Coyote Creek. A look in my rearview mirror confirmed I wasn't being followed. At least not yet.

THIRTY-ONE

HALF A MILE from the O'Brien ranch, I spotted head-lights coming toward me in the distance. Would Tucker recognize my car? Maybe. Coyote Creek was a small community. A gravel road came up on my right. I turned in and kept going, but slowly, watching my rearview mirror. The vehicle kept going toward the compound. When it was out of sight, I pulled out of the side road and headed home.

My cellphone rang as I approached Jack and Amah's driveway. Their house was dark and Nick's car was there. I cut my headlights and drove down the lane by moonlight. My cellphone kept ringing, but I wanted to get inside my apartment before I answered. When I reached for my doorknob, the door swung open.

"This had better be good." There stood Nick. I felt my jaw drop, but I couldn't seem to close my mouth.

"Sit down," he said, "and start talking."

Nick sat at my dinette table with his arms crossed over his chest. My cellphone rang again. Cleo calling. I answered, expecting the worst about Seamus.

"What is it?"

"Nick knows," Cleo said. "I'm sorry, I got worried about you and called him. I wanted to warn you before you got home."

"Too late." I glanced at the storm clouds riding across

Nick's face and nearly broke out in hysterical laughter. "Are you still at TMC? What's the status on Seamus?"

"I'm home. Seamus is responding to treatment for the time being."

The world felt lighter for a moment. "Really? That's amazing." I told her I'd call her first thing in the morning.

Eager to tell Nick what I'd found at the compound, I put my phone down and dropped my day pack on the table. He started on me before my bottom hit the chair.

"I won't waste my breath telling you how angry I am." He reached out and brushed something off the shoulder of my jacket. *Bits of a juniper bush?* "Cleo claims you weren't in any danger, but you don't look like a walk in the park. What happened out there?"

"Wait. First, how's Ginger?"

"She's going to be fine. Don't change the subject."

I told him most of the story, including the part about finding the makeshift club buried in offal destined for the incinerator, but I left out the part about the man who fired at me. I ended with how I was certain Tucker was behind the whole scheme, including chasing Laurie Popejoy all the way to Idaho and shooting at us in the Blue Banjo parking lot.

"There's a problem with that theory," Nick said. "Tucker never left Timbergate."

"What? That's impossible. It had to be him. Who else is there?" Then it dawned on me what he was implying. "Don't tell me you think it was James."

"James never left Timbergate, either." Nick looked down at a piece of paper on the table in front of him. "This is a report of their activities during the time you and I were in Idaho. They never left town."

"What? You had them under surveillance?"

"Something like that. The point is, we *were* being targeted by someone in that parking lot, most likely whoever was after Laurie, but it wasn't Tucker or James."

"Then it was someone working for Tucker, right?"

"Or James," Nick said.

"Or Phyllis Poole," I countered. "Maybe she hired the guy out at the O'Brien compound who—" I nearly choked trying to hold back the rest of my sentence. The gunshot wasn't something I wanted to blurt out, but it was too late.

Nick's face clouded. "The guy who what?"

"Okay, if you'll stay calm, I'll explain." I told him the rest of the story.

"Someone shot at you tonight? Were you going to leave out that little detail?"

"It was just a warning. I didn't want to worry you."

I showed Nick the photos on my phone of the makeshift club and the fingerprints from the plastic bag. "I think that club is the murder weapon. There were strands of hair on it. I'm hoping it's Cody's hair."

"You *think* and you *hope*." Nick wasn't one to see the glass half full. "How do you expect to use it? You can't just waltz into the Sawyer County crime lab. As soon as you told them where you got your evidence, you'd be charged with breaking and entering."

I refused to think I'd gone through the ordeal at Seamus's compound for nothing. The forensic evidence was in my kit. It might be worthless in court, but maybe there was another way to use it.

"What about Harry?" I said. "Maybe Keely mentioned something to him about a grounds man or caretaker at the compound. Should I call him?"

Nick yawned and ran his fingers through his hair. "Might as well."

Harry sounded sleepy and annoyed. "You realize it's almost two in the morning?" he said.

"Sorry, but this can't wait." I gave him a rundown of the evening's events, ending in someone firing what I described as a warning shot while I fled the compound. He was silent so long I thought he'd gone back to sleep.

"Harry? Any ideas?"

"Give me a minute. I'm so furious with you for going out there alone I can't think straight."

"Sorry, but I didn't have time. The window of opportunity was too narrow. I went alone because it seemed quicker and perfectly safe. Let it go and just tell me if Keely mentioned any hired help working at the compound."

"No, but I could probably call her tomorrow and ask."

"Okay, please do that before we meet with Nick at noon."

I filled Nick in on Harry's half of the conversation. There was nothing we could do to identify the new man at the compound before morning, and it looked like Seamus might make it through the night. We both needed sleep. I had to be at work in a few hours, and with the CME program on the calendar, my work day would last well into the evening.

Out my kitchen window I watched Nick walk alone up the lane to the main house. My throat tightened at the memory of all the times I'd walked by his side. I wondered what it would take to find the right balance between independence and mutual trust that would set us back on course. I hoped it would be soon, and wondered how many other couples faced the same struggle.

THIRTY-TWO

CLEO AND I arrived at work early Wednesday morning so we could meet in her office before the day kicked into high gear. We sat at her desk munching granola bars and sipping coffee while we compared notes. I had finished telling her about my visit to the O'Brien ranch. It was her turn.

"As of six o'clock this morning, Seamus is still alive."

"That's great news. Is there any word on Tobias Fausset's whereabouts?"

"Not a whisper. It's creepy," she said. "Like he's vanished into thin air. Sorry, but it looks like you're stuck with Dr. Poole running the CME program tonight."

"Yeah, the fox presiding over the hen house, except reverse the genders."

"Exactly. A hungry female fox in a room full of roosters." Cleo's forehead was etched with worry lines. "There's no way she'll have her privileges suspended in time. Siggy's going under her knife at nine o'clock tomorrow morning."

"Why don't you attend the program tonight? You have clearance for all medical staff meetings, don't you?"

"I do, but Continuing Medical Education is your bailiwick. I wouldn't want anyone thinking I was there to coach you because Beardsley's out of town."

"Don't let that stop you. This isn't about my ego."

"I might show up before it's over, but there's something else I want to check on, and I won't have a chance until after work."

"Does it involve Poole?"

"I don't know about that, but something you said about autopsies just before you left my office with Quinn has been bothering me. I looked through DeeDee's chart again before I returned it to the archives. She died here at TMC under a physician's care, and there was no suspicion of foul play, so you were right, when her autopsy was done, no blood was drawn for toxicology tests. Her case was classic. A delayed coma isn't uncommon if head trauma causes bleeding into the brain. Her death certificate showed cause of death consistent with the head trauma."

"Then what is it that's troubling you?"

"There should have been lab work done by TMC's lab when she was admitted here. Her chart shows it was ordered, including a tox screen, but there was no lab slip of any kind in her chart." Cleo drew an asterisk on a notepad on her desk, then circled it. "Doesn't that seem odd? She was admitted to the ICU, for God's sake."

"How long was she here?"

"Not long, why?"

"Maybe she died before her blood could be drawn."

"I didn't think of that." She tapped the notepad with her pen. "But there's another possibility. What if lab work *was* done? What if it was misfiled?"

"Maybe you're right, maybe—"

"What?"

I scooted to the edge of my chair. "Remember, she had two different names. Deirdre DeGraw and DeeDee Dakota. Maybe some Health Information clerk messed up and two charts were made."

"No, I looked for a chart for DeeDee Dakota when I couldn't find her as Deirdre O'Brien. The only patient record made for her was Deirdre DeGraw. But there's a chance her lab work was misfiled in someone else's chart. Someone with a similar name who was a patient here back then. I'm going to see if I can find any names that look promising. If I do, I'll go back into the archives tonight."

"You're serious? You'll go back to that cave?"

"I will if I have to. Sig has already been admitted to the surgery floor. He's on the schedule for six o'clock tomorrow morning. It's my last chance to see if there's anything connecting that hospital in Idaho with DeeDee's death here at TMC. If I can convince him that Poole's a criminal or a psycho, he won't go through with the procedure. And tonight is ideal. The basement will be deserted. I don't know how long it will take, so if I don't show up at the CME program, meet me here in my office when it's over."

Cleo's office door opened and we both stopped talking. It was one of the housekeeping staff, the man with the ghoulish ear gauges who had introduced himself to me in the library as Cliff Weber.

"Sorry to interrupt, ladies, just here to empty your trash." He walked over to the shredder sitting next to a row of metal file cabinets, dumped the contents into his cart, and replaced the liner. He nodded toward the wastebasket near her desk. "Need that one, too."

Cleo pushed her wastebasket toward him with her foot. "What happened to Louise? She usually comes by in the morning."

"Vacation, I guess. They told me to cover this floor

today." He dumped the basket, replaced the liner, and giving us a salute, went out the door whistling softly.

Cleo shook her head at the closing door. "I hope Louise gets back soon. I'd hate to start every day looking at those ghastly ears."

I laughed. "I know what you mean. He's been in the library a couple of times and I always try not to look. He must fill in wherever the Housekeeping Department needs him."

"Looks like it," Cleo said. "Let's get back to DeeDee's lab work. I'm going to drop by Health Information right away to see if I can come up with any names similar to Deirdre DeGraw. I'll let you know what I find."

I left Cleo's office after she said again that she would try to drop by the CME program when she was finished in the basement archive room. It was a last-ditch effort, but she was determined to see if she could find a misfiled lab report for DeeDee. I figured she'd be finished with that well before the CME presentation ended at ten o'clock.

In the library I checked my cellphone and spotted a text from Nick telling me that he and Harry had decided the three of us should meet at Harry's job site trailer at noon instead of driving out to the ranch in Coyote Creek.

My last-minute preparations for the CME program were almost complete. Every member of the Surgery Department was required to attend, so the hospital's banquet room would be prepared, including audiovisual equipment set up by the IT staff. The Dietary Department would arrange banquet tables for nearly a hundred meals. After I checked in with IT and Dietary, I had to make sure I had enough evaluation sheets.

Every doctor who attended was supposed to grade the program.

By noon, everything on my list was finished. I locked the library and headed to the mall construction site to meet Harry and Nick. The three-story complex was no longer just a skeleton, but even with exterior walls taking shape, Harry estimated another two years before the project was finished. Nick's F150 that had caught a bullet in Idaho was parked near Harry's trailer. I parked next to it, noticing that the damaged window had been replaced. The day had warmed nicely after a chilly morning and the door to Harry's trailer was open.

"Come on in, Sis." Harry and Nick sat at opposite ends of the dinette, each with a bottled sport drink and a submarine sandwich. Nick scooted around the bench to the back of the table to make room for me.

"Did you bring anything to eat?" Harry said.

"No. I forgot about eating. I'm not really hungry." But the sight of their sandwiches set off a tummy rumble they both heard.

Nick looked at Harry. "Got a knife?"

Harry pulled a knife from a drawer next to the sink and a bottle of green tea from his fridge. He handed me the bottle and they each trimmed off a third of their sandwich. My lunch.

"Who's first?" Harry looked at me.

"Not me," I said. "I don't know anything new, except Seamus is still alive, or was a few minutes ago." I looked at Nick. "I saw the pickup, by the way. When did it arrive?"

"Two days ago. I dropped it off at the glass shop yesterday. They work fast."

Harry looked puzzled for a moment, then caught up.

"Oh, yeah, the Idaho incident." He glared at me. "I hope we aren't going to hear about any more shots being fired before this is over." He turned to Nick. "What about you? Anything to report?"

"Maybe. It looks like we might get a match on the prints Aimee pulled at the compound."

I swallowed a mouthful of corned beef and cocked my head toward Nick. "Really? How?"

"I called in a favor and emailed your fingerprint photos to a contact in Sacramento. He'll run them through AFIS, but pretend you didn't hear that. And remember, we can't legally use anything we get back from him."

"If the prints are in the system, at least we'll know who they belong to," Harry said. "How soon?"

"Don't know. He's only agreed to try."

Harry tossed his napkin and sandwich wrappers in a wastebasket by the door. "Okay, I'm next. I called Keely this morning. She was visiting Seamus in the ICU, but Echo, James, and Tucker were all there, too. I asked her to step outside where they couldn't hear."

"And?" I said.

"She said Tucker needed someone to help with the mounts when Seamus got too sick to work. They brought in a guy from out of state who's had some experience. She said he's bunking in the old groom's quarters in the barn."

"Did she tell you his name?"

"No. She said she'd probably heard it but couldn't remember. She did say he and Tucker don't get along."

Nick leaned back and gave me a sideways glance. "Looks like you're the only one with nothing to report. That makes me wonder if you're up to something again."

"No, I promise. No more heroics." Then I thought

about Cleo's plan to go hunting in the archives after work while I was at the CME presentation. I told Nick and Harry what she had in mind and the possibility that DeeDee's lab work had been misfiled.

"Wait a minute," Harry said. "Are you saying Cleo suspects foul play in the death of the cowboy's wife?"

"It's unlikely, but possible. Except DeeDee wasn't Cody's wife." I told Harry what James had said about Cody and DeeDee's relationship.

Nick pushed his paper plate aside. "Even if the trick rider's death was suspicious, it's a stretch to think there's a link to what's happening now."

"Maybe so, but you have to admit that if there *is* a link, we're a step closer to solving this thing." I reminded him that Echo O'Brien might be the link if we could be certain that she was Phyllis Poole's niece, Caroline.

"Unfortunately," Nick said, "Poole made it clear that she's not saying."

Harry opened his laptop. "Then let's try something else. I wish I'd thought of this sooner." His fingers were flying across the keyboard. "There she is," he said. "God bless Google images."

I got up and looked over his shoulder. There were dozens of photos of Echo O'Brien, all with Seamus by her side, and most of them posed with big game hunters at various outdoor sportsmen's conventions.

"Okay, what's the other name? Poole's niece?"

"Try Caroline Poole," I said. "That would have been her name when she was working at the hospital in Idaho."

Harry entered the name and dozens more photos appeared. Some obviously too old, or black, or Asian, or just the wrong body type or facial construction. He kept scrolling until a young woman appeared with cotton candy pink hair and thick glasses with black frames.

"That one," I said. "James talked about a nursing assistant with pink hair and glasses like those who was in and out of DeeDee's hospital room in Idaho."

"It looks like some kind of mug shot," Harry said. "Maybe for an ID badge."

Harry pulled up the photo and went back and pulled up one of the photos of Echo. He used his photo editing program to switch Echo's dark brown locks with Caroline's pink do.

"Can you take off Caroline's glasses?" I said.

"Yep." Harry erased the frames and we all agreed there was no doubt about it. Both photos were of the same face.

"Print them," Nick said. "One copy for each of us." He turned to me. "Okay, she's definitely a link to Phyllis Poole, but we still need to figure out what it means."

"Right," Harry said. "Echo's married to Seamus and wants to inherit his estate. We also know she's pregnant with someone else's kid, but what's that got to do with DeeDee Dakota's death?"

"And where does Phyllis Poole fit in?" Nick said. "She's a woman who clearly gets what she wants, but from what I can tell she's too smart to throw it all away just to protect her conniving niece."

"What if there's more than conniving going on? Someone killed Cody O'Brien, and now Seamus is near death. What ties them together?" I tapped the photos looking up at me from the table. "It has to be the paternity of Echo's baby. Cody knew and he's dead. Laurie Popejoy knows and she was stalked and forced into hiding. That leaves Seamus. He knows too, and his survival depends on Phyllis Poole."

"But we don't know how much Phyllis Poole knows," Harry said. "I'm not taking sides here, but Nick's right. She's just as innocent as you hope James is until we know more about those prints you pulled from the bag the murder weapon was wrapped in."

"Hell," Nick said. "We don't even know if that thing you found at the compound *is* the murder weapon. Maybe it's just a piece of taxidermy that went wrong."

"No," I said. "I've called more than one taxidermy business asking about horse mounts. They use actual horse's hooves. They're attached to a mold of the full hind quarter, and most often, there are no horseshoes attached. That club had a hoof attached, and a horseshoe nailed to the hoof. Someone went to a lot of trouble to make that weapon, and to use the same kind of shoe that's on Game Boy's hooves. I think it was made for one purpose only."

"Premeditation," Nick said. "The cowboy was doomed."

I nodded. "Keely was considered too unstable to manage the estate, and James said he didn't want to inherit. If we believe him, then Cody was the main obstacle to Echo's claim on the estate. Someone, most likely Tucker, took a shot at Cody, but he was only grazed. A hunter's stray bullet could be explained away once, but not twice, so they had to think of another way."

Harry closed the laptop. "Let the horse take the blame. And it worked."

"So far," I said.

THIRTY-THREE

Jared Quinn strolled up to my desk in the library at five o'clock looking like he'd just stepped off the cover of *Esquire* and smelling like the Garden of Eden. It seemed improbable for a hospital administrator to be good-looking and a decent human being, but he made it work.

"How's it going, Aimee? Are you ready to fly solo tonight?"

"I am. Will you be there?"

"That's why I dropped by. I'd like to attend, but since Dr. Beardsley left you on your own this time, I didn't want you to think I'm keeping an eye on you."

"Not at all. I'd like to have you there."

"Fine, then. I'll save you a seat. I know you'll be busy until the last minute."

"Thanks." If things went south where Phyllis Poole was concerned, it would be handy to have Quinn there.

I locked the library and headed across campus to the main tower with my briefcase full of notebooks, pens, and program evaluation forms. Before heading up to the banquet room on the second floor, I stopped by Cleo's office.

"Aimee, I was just trying to call you."

"Why? Is Seamus—"

"No, he's still hanging on." She lowered her voice. "I wanted to touch base about tonight."

"Good. Have you had any luck finding names similar to DeeDee's?"

"I have two possibilities who were hospitalized back then. Both records are in the archives now: Deana De-Graw, and Delores McGraw."

"Wow. They *are* close. Do you have their chart numbers?"

"Yes. I just hope the charts are shelved where they belong, or it could take a while to find them."

"Okay, good luck. The Dietary staff starts serving dinner at six o'clock, and the program begins at seven. Do you want me to call you with an all clear when Poole shows up?"

"Definitely. I'll be here catching up on some paperwork."

I didn't like the idea of Cleo sneaking into the archives in that gloomy basement alone, but she was determined.

"Come up to the banquet room as soon as you're finished in the basement. You should get there in time for the panel's recommendations."

"I hope so. If Dr. Poole gets raked over the coals, I don't want to miss it." Cleo smiled. "I'm going to look in on Sig before I go to the basement, but I'll get to the program as soon as I can."

"Remember, Poole's running the show, so don't get your hopes up." I left her to her paperwork and headed for the elevators.

Dinner in the banquet room was cleared away by the Dietary staff at six forty-five. Phyllis Poole arrived minutes later, a dead ringer for C.S. Lewis's Ice Queen—except for the light gray business suit and sensible shoes. Poole walked over to where Jared Quinn and I were sitting, thanked him for coming, and asked me if I'd done a sound check and whether the media equipment was cued up. I assured her everything was ready.

"Good." She frowned, looking around. "Since Beardsley isn't here, who'll introduce me?" She turned to Quinn. "Jared? Is that your task?"

Quinn shook his head. "That would be Aimee's task, Dr. Poole."

Poole's frown deepened for a moment, but she recovered quickly. "All right, then. Let's get to it."

"We'll start promptly at seven, Dr. Poole." I excused myself, walked out into the corridor and called Cleo. She picked up on the first ring.

"Cominoli."

"She's here," I said.

"Thanks. I should be there within the hour."

Cleo broke the connection and I checked the time on my phone. Five minutes to show time. I went back inside and sat next to Quinn. I had asked him to read over the introduction I'd prepared.

"Looks good." He smiled and nodded at the podium. "Break a leg."

I introduced Poole as Vice-chair of the Urology Department and moderator of the program. She walked to the podium accompanied by a smattering of applause. The head table was set up to accommodate all ten members of the Urology Department, but Dr. Tobias Fausset was conspicuously absent. Poole explained by saying he had been called away on a family-related matter.

His family or Poole's? I hoped he hadn't been called away for good.

Each urologist took a turn discussing the cases he or she had reviewed. No patient names were given, and their doctors' names were not revealed. The medical history, indications for surgery, treatments, and outcomes were reported. The cases with complications were first, then the death cases. Even without a patient name, the circumstances of Cody O'Brien's case gave his identity away. The reviewing doctor stated that the patient left AMA and was discovered dead the next day of an accident unrelated to his medical problem. I caught a shift in Quinn's posture at that point. This was the case that both he and I had been waiting for.

The circumstances of Cody's case and the justification for his admission and planned surgery were presented. A disturbingly graphic photo of his injured testicle flashed on the projection screen. I heard a few muffled groans from the audience. Quinn blinked and wiped a hand across his forehead. No one would have argued with the need for a surgical repair. I was amazed Cody had managed to walk out of the hospital, load up his horse, and drive across town to meet Laurie Popejoy, no matter how much pain medicine he had on board.

The evening closed with the panel of urologists who reviewed the cases giving their opinions about the quality of care. All of them gave their colleagues high marks. Members of the audience who asked questions seemed satisfied with the panelists' answers.

The final topic was a call for a review of procedures involving patients who leave the hospital against medical advice. Dr. Poole took the microphone to thank everyone for attending, and that was that. No disciplinary actions were recommended. The presentation wound up at nine o'clock, and Cleo had not arrived. The whole thing felt so anticlimactic that I was almost glad she hadn't been there to see it. I hoped that she had found something important in the basement.

I reminded everyone to fill out their evaluation forms before leaving, and by the time I collected them, it was past nine thirty. The room was empty, and Cleo still hadn't arrived. I called Security to let them know it was time to lock up the banquet room, then caught the elevator to Cleo's office, eager to learn what had kept her away.

Her office was dark and locked. I knocked, but got no response.

Great. I had to go down to that dismal room in the basement to look for her. I hurried over to the library, dropped off the CME documents, then ran back to the main tower. I didn't have a key to the archives, but with Cleo still there, that wouldn't be a problem. As I approached along the dimly lit, deserted corridor, I saw that the door was open and the light was on.

I peered inside but didn't see her. "Cleo? Are you there?" No answer.

I wound my way through several rows of metal shelves, getting closer to the far end of the room, when the lights suddenly went out and I heard the door close. *Damn. Not good.* Probably a security guard making rounds, thinking someone forgot to lock the room. With the dim screen light of my phone, I spotted a shape on the floor. I knelt closer.

It was Cleo, lying deathly still with a bloody head wound. My breath caught for a dizzy moment. Praying she was alive, I checked her breathing and pulse. They both seemed normal. A hopeful sign, but she still didn't respond.

"Cleo, can you hear me?" Her eyes seemed to move beneath the lids, but they didn't open.

"Cleo, please, if you can hear me, open your eyes." No reaction. I punched the number for the ER, hoping the call would go through. I thought I heard someone answer, but before I could speak, my phone was knocked to the floor and I was jerked backward by a powerful arm circling my neck.

I yelled toward the phone on the floor. "Dr. Strong to basement stor—"

"Not another sound out of you, bitch." My attacker clamped his hand over my nose and mouth, cutting off my breath. I raised my hands in a gesture of defeat, but his grip didn't relax. I jammed my heel down on his arch and reached up at the same time, trying to grab one of the fingers covering my mouth. I hoped to jerk it back hard enough to break it. Instead, my finger caught in something. I yanked as hard as I could to free my hand, and the attacker howled in pain, shoved me aside, and limped toward the exit door to make his escape.

I felt something strange in my left hand as I reached down to pick up my phone. With the light from its screen I saw a torn earlobe with a hollow metal circle still attached. The bloody mess was stuck on my ring finger like a ghoulish wedding band from a grade B zombie movie.

Cleo had not moved, so I illuminated her face. Her eyes remained closed. I redialed the ER while I walked to the exit door and flipped on the room light. I was told that a security guard and an ER doctor were both on the way. I hurried back to Cleo, patting her cheeks and rubbing her hands, desperate for a response.

"Cleo. Can you hear me? Please, wake up!"

Her eyes opened. "I *am* awake. I was awake the whole time. Is he gone?"

"Yes. Thank God." Relief left me speechless, but not for long. I was puzzled by her deception.

"You scared me silly. Why did you fake being unconscious?"

"I knew he was still in the room. I was afraid he'd hit me again if I tried to warn you, so I thought I'd play 'possum and let you take him down with that jujitsu black belt thing you do." Cleo touched at the blood drying on her forehead. "You had me worried there for a moment, though. I was just about to bite him on the ankle when you stomped on his foot."

I actually laughed at the thought of fastidious Cleo chomping down on the thug's hairy leg. She glanced at my left hand.

"What's that ghastly thing on your finger?"

"Part of his ear."

"Oh, my God, Aimee. That's disgusting. It's like the guy from housekeeping. That looks just like those ugly things that made holes in his ears."

"You're right." It took a moment to sink in. "You think he's the guy?"

"He'd be pretty easy to identify if he's walking with a limp and missing part of an ear."

I started giggling and she did, too. By that time the doctor and the guard arrived. They both seemed a little put out because the more we tried to stop snickering the worse it got.

It only took a few minutes to get Cleo transferred upstairs to the ER to have her head examined. While she was there, I went to the restroom, where I wrapped the ear gauge and the attached flesh in a paper towel.

After scrubbing my hands with hot, soapy water, I went back to the ER. Cleo's doctor agreed to discharge her when I told him I'd drive her home and stay with her overnight to watch her pupils for signs of a concussion or a brain bleed.

On our drive she told me what had happened. Before searching for the records, she'd decided to stop by Sig's hospital room. When she got to the storage room, she searched for almost two hours before finally finding both the charts she was looking for. As we suspected, DeeDee's tox report had been misfiled. Cleo spotted it as soon as she opened Deana DeGraw's chart, but before she could remove it, she was assaulted by the intruder.

"So you didn't have a chance to read it?"

"No, but it was definitely done by the Timbergate lab after DeeDee was admitted here."

"So where is the chart?"

"I don't know. It flew out of my hands when I was attacked."

We reached Cleo's condo at ten o'clock, but it felt like midnight. Cleo refused to go to sleep. Just as well, since I wanted to keep checking her pupils. My report of the urology panel's conclusions had not reassured her. She hated knowing that Phyllis Poole was still scheduled to take a knife to Sig's prostate in the morning.

Cleo insisted I call both Nick and Harry to fill them in. Harry's reaction was typical. Anger, then concern, and finally a demand that I lock myself in with Cleo and stay put for the rest of the night. Nick's response was different, and a distinct improvement from what I expected. He listened calmly, then asked what I planned to do about finding the chart with the tox report. My first impulse was to lie and say I was going to do nothing, but he wouldn't have believed me.

"The man in the basement didn't have anything in his hands when he attacked me, so maybe the chart is still there."

"You're going back to that storage room, aren't you?"

"If it's there, I want to find it, and it has to be tonight."

"But you can't leave your friend home alone."

"No." I glanced at Cleo, lying on the couch and fading fast. "I'm stuck unless I can get someone to watch her through the night."

"Give me the address where you are. I'll see what I can do."

I jumped at the offer, and when the doorbell rang ten minutes later, I raced to open it, ready to throw my arms around Nick in a full-on hug. But he wasn't alone. Beside him was Rella, his ex-girlfriend and current co-pilot, looking down at me from her near six feet in height. I froze in place with my mouth open and my hand still on the doorknob, trying to accept the fact that she was doing me a favor. Doing Nick a favor, at least.

"Are you going to let us in?" Nick said.

"Oh, sure." I stepped back.

"We don't have a lot of time, do we?"

"No, we don't, but—"

"Rella's going to stay here with Cleo while we take care of that urgent matter at the hospital." From the sound of that, he hadn't given Rella a lot of details.

Cleo had dozed off, so I covered her with a comforter from her bedroom. Rella assured me she had a solid background in medicine from her years in the military and could monitor Cleo's status until Nick and I returned. She went to Cleo, felt her pulse and adjusted her comforter in a gentle but competent way that reassured me. I thanked her and realized I meant it when I said I was glad she was there.

I hadn't been issued keys to most of the hospital's offices and departments, but Cleo had keys to everything except the administration suite. I dug them from her purse. Nick raised an eyebrow at me.

"She'd give them to me if she was awake," I said. "This whole thing was her idea in the first place."

"Fine," he said. "Let's get going."

THIRTY-FOUR

WE LEFT NICK'S car at Cleo's in case Rella needed it. Visiting hours were over when we reached TMC near midnight, so I parked in a corner of the visitor's lot where my car might not be noticed. I led the way to the same employee's entrance Cleo and I had used before on our late night incursion.

"What's your plan?" Nick said.

"When we get to the archive room, you can stand guard while I search the area where I found Cleo on the floor. She said she had the chart and dropped it. I don't think the thug took it, so it should still be there somewhere."

"Let's do it."

I couldn't get over the feeling that he was being too darned cooperative, but it was working to my advantage, so I let it go.

We reached the storage room without encountering anyone in the corridor.

"No crime scene tape yet," Nick said. "Better hurry."

I unlocked the door and we slipped inside. Nick stayed near the door while I flipped on the overhead light and hurried to the spot where Cleo had fallen. My stomach pitched for a moment when I saw the dark patch of her blood on the floor. There were only a few inches of clearance from the floor to the bottom shelf in each four-foot section. I had to lie on my stomach with my cheek pressed to the gritty cement floor to peer under the shelves on both sides of the narrow aisle. I wondered how far a dropped chart might slide. I spotted nothing except several generations of dust bunnies. After a few minutes, I heard the scuff of footsteps near my head.

"Any luck?" Nick was standing above me with his phone in his hand.

"Not yet."

"Keep at it. I'll step out in the hall and try to check in with Rella. I doubt if I can make a call from inside this cave."

He was right about checking with Rella. We needed to know if Cleo's condition was still stable. While he was gone, I checked under the shelves in the opposite direction. I saw a disturbed path running through the dust under one of the shelves. Already flattened down on my stomach, I stretched my arm under the shelf, trying not to sneeze and straining until I felt what had to be a chart cover. I got a grip on it and pulled it out. I stood up and brushed the dust off myself and the chart. Inside the folder was the misfiled lab report Cleo had seen.

The toxicology report documented the presence of barbiturates. That would account for DeeDee's sudden coma after showing no complications from her head trauma. The barbiturates would not have been ordered when she arrived at TMC in a coma. She must have been drugged at the hospital in Idaho by someone who knew phenobarbital could be used to induce a coma. But who? And why? What possible reason could anyone have for wanting her dead? And why would the same person kill Cody O'Brien? Or *was* it the same person? I removed the report and jammed it in my purse.

Nick hadn't returned, so I turned out the light and found him in the corridor with his phone to his ear.

"Okay," he said into his phone, "he'll be there in ten minutes." He turned to me. "Any luck?"

"Got it."

"Good. Let's get going. Rella has to go home. One of her nephews is breaking out in something the baby-sitter thinks is chicken pox. Harry's on his way over there to keep an eye on your friend."

"How's Rella getting home without a car?"

"She has mine," he said.

"How will you get it back?"

"You can drop me off at her place to pick it up." Her place, meaning his apartment, loaned to her for an un-determined interval.

"Why don't I drop you off there right now?"

"Not gonna happen. I'm not letting you out of my sight."

"What?" We had reached my car and I slipped be-hind the wheel.

"You're taking too many chances." Nick slid in on the passenger side. "You sneaked out to the O'Brien compound and nearly got shot, then you sneaked into that storage room and got mugged."

"So you're not only here to help, you're also here as my bodyguard?"

"I'm afraid it's a little of both. I'm trying to respect your independence, but sometimes the buddy system is safer than flying solo. Do you mind?"

"No. I appreciate the help, but you're the one that bullet grazed in Idaho. I don't want you getting hurt again on my account."

"I take full responsibility for my own safety. You

should know that by now." He reached out and touched my cheek with his fingers. "Now that we've cleared that up, what's your next move?"

My cheek tingled where he'd touched it, reminding me of long-ago butterfly kisses. I rubbed the sensation away with the palm of my hand.

"I want to go back inside and visit the ICU. That should be safe enough."

"All the same, I'm coming along."

"I stand a much better chance of getting in to see Seamus O'Brien if I'm alone."

"There must be a waiting room." He pointed at my purse. "Is that lab report in here?"

"Yes. I had to take it. Why?"

He shrugged. "Someone knows it exists and wants it pretty badly, or Cleo wouldn't be on the injured list. Do you have any idea who her attacker might be?"

His question reminded me that I hadn't mentioned the gory details when I told him about my scuffle with the man in the basement. I showed him the gruesome little morsel.

"So you're carrying your attacker's earlobe around in your purse?" Nick leaned his head back and started to laugh.

"It's not funny. It's evidence. What else could I do with it?" I told him about Cliff Weber, the man from housekeeping with the ghastly earrings.

"Sorry, you're right. But you have to admit, even for you, that's pretty weird."

"I agree, it's disgusting. Now, if you're through laughing, let's get going."

We got out of the car and went back inside the hospital. I walked with Nick to the ICU waiting room. From there I used an in-house phone to call in to the ICU nursing staff and identify myself. The nurse in charge was a regular library patron who knew me well. I explained that I was a close family friend of the O'Briens and asked if I could come in and speak to Seamus's nurse. She told me to go to the entrance doors and wait there.

The door to the unit opened halfway and the nurse I had just spoken to stood there looking apologetic. Behind her, the usual banks of ICU machinery hummed. Artificial lighting and the lack of windows did away with any sense of day or night. The recycled air wafting toward me through the open door seemed to hold a faint scent of hope.

"I'm sorry, Aimee. We can't bend the rules, even for you. All I'm allowed to say is whether his status is stable or unstable."

"Which is it, then?"

"The latter, I'm afraid. I'm sorry, I really can't say more."

"I understand, but I thought if his son James was there, he might step out and talk to me."

"I'm afraid he isn't here. The wife has requested that she be his only visitor."

"What about his daughter, Keely?"

The nurse worked her lower lip. "I feel bad about it, but the wife is on record as his next of kin, so we have to respect her wishes. The son and daughter haven't been in since this morning."

I didn't like the sound of that. Echo sure as heck wasn't grieving. What was she up to?

"Is his wife with him now?"

"No, I believe she's taking a restroom break. Maybe you can catch up with her there."

I thanked her and hurried back to Nick, telling him I needed a bathroom break. No point getting him involved until I knew what was going on.

I pushed the restroom door open, expecting to see Echo primping or having a smoke, but she was nowhere in sight. I checked for feet under the three stall doors. In the middle stall, I spotted black leather boots with silver toe tips. The other two were empty, so I opened the first stall, closed and locked the door, then quietly climbed up on the toilet to peek over the top of the partition. It was Echo, and she was filling a syringe from a vial. I couldn't read the print on the vial, but it could only be one thing: *phenobarbital.*

Just as I tried to get down and sneak out of the stall, my foot slipped and slid into the toilet bowl. My shoe was stuck, and by the time I got my foot loose and my stall door unlocked, she was headed toward the restroom door.

"Wait!" I shouted.

She stopped and turned. Her eyes widened and she ran for the exit. I lunged after her and grabbed the purse strap slung over her shoulder, dragging her backward. She yanked her arm free and the purse dropped on the toes of my shoeless foot, shooting pain up my leg. I figured the only thing heavy enough to do that had to be a gun. She bent down to grab the purse, but I kicked it out of reach under one of the toilet stalls. She growled like a feral cat and lunged for the exit, but I grasped a handful of her hair and jerked her backward.

"Let go of me, bitch." She wheeled around and stuck my left arm just below the elbow with the needle attached to the syringe.

I grabbed her hand before she could depress the

plunger all the way and jerked my arm free, but she'd already injected me with some of the drug. How much would it take to put me out? How soon? I bent her wrist forward until I heard a pop and the syringe dropped. She shrieked and stumbled out the door with her right hand dangling oddly from her wrist. I had to look away, not sure if it was the sight of what I'd done to her or the drug coursing through my veins that was making me dizzy and nauseated. I felt myself sink to the restroom floor, then somehow Nick was there, exploding with a string of profanities. I heard most of it, but it seemed to be coming from a faraway place.

"Don't let her get away," I said. "Get Quinn."

Then I took a little nap.

THIRTY-FIVE

I woke up in the ER with an IV drip in the back of my hand, a pulse rate monitor clipped to my finger and a blood pressure cuff on my arm. I wondered why I was there and why Nick was sitting next to my bed holding my free hand. Then I remembered.

"Where is she?" I heard myself speak, but the words seemed to come from someone else.

"The police are looking for her."

"She got away?" I propped myself up on my elbows.

"Hey, relax," Nick said. "You're supposed to lie flat until the doctor comes back to check on you."

I lowered myself down. "We need to tell the police about Seamus. Echo was drugging him."

"Already done." Nick gave my hand a gentle squeeze. "As soon as Quinn showed up I told him I'd found you on the bathroom floor along with the vial and syringe Echo left behind. It didn't take him long to put the pieces together. The police have the evidence. If she wasn't wearing gloves, her prints will be easy to recover."

"Seamus?"

"They've checked his blood for barbiturates and posted a strict no visitors order. No one's allowed near Seamus, especially none of the O'Briens, until this is sorted out."

"I need to talk to the police. Echo must have killed DeeDee. And she had to be involved in Cody's death, too.

And the earlobe guy must be in on it. If it's who I think it is, his name is Cliff Weber. He needs to be found."

"They're already on it. I got his name from Cleo and gave it to them, along with the grisly little package you had in your purse and the lab report you found in that storage room. I told the police I'd take you to the station to be interviewed, but they want to make sure the drug is out of your system before they talk to you."

Nick helped me try to stand. I felt off balance and realized I was missing a shoe. Probably still in that toilet.

"Nick, they're going to get away. What time is it?"

"Four thirty in the morning."

"I need to get out of here."

"Take it easy. The police have Weber's name and the photo from his hospital ID badge. If he's missing part of an ear, he's going to be pretty easy to identify. I'm guessing he's hunkered down somewhere, licking his wounds."

"And Echo has a broken wrist, so neither of them is in good shape for a getaway."

"You broke her wrist?" Nick actually laughed.

"I had to. If she'd pumped that whole syringe into me, you'd be having this conversation with a corpse."

Nick's laughter died away. "Damn, don't even say that."

An ER doctor came over and introduced himself. I reminded him that I worked in the hospital library and that we'd met. He seemed to take that as a good sign that my brain was functioning. He told me the amount of barbiturate in my system wasn't enough to cause any severe damage. My discharge orders were to go home, rest, and monitor my heart rate and blood pressure for the next twenty-four hours. I was to report any residual dizziness, headache, or confusion. I agreed, and once I was unhooked from the monitoring equipment I signed the discharge papers put in front of me.

"Okay, let's get you home," Nick said.

An attendant propelled me out to the parking lot in a wheelchair. It seemed like overkill, but I didn't have the energy to argue. Nick drove us to Coyote Creek in my car. He suggested I try to rest on the way, but I had more questions.

"Has anybody talked to James or Keely? Do they know what's been going on?"

"Quinn gave the police their names and contact information. Last I heard, no one has been able to contact them. They checked all three houses on the O'Brien compound right after I found you. That was just a few hours ago. No one was there."

"What about Tucker? Do you think he was part of it?"

Nick glanced at me. "Same as James and Keely. No one's heard from him, either."

"Maybe they were all in on it. Maybe they've all taken off somewhere. Does anyone know if Phyllis Poole is around?"

"You're not going to let go of this, are you?"

"How can I? I don't even know how Cleo's doing. Her fiancé is supposed to go under Phyllis Poole's knife in less than two hours, and we're not sure the doctor's innocent in all this—or if Poole will show up to perform Sig's surgery. Do the police know about her relationship to Echo?"

"Cleo's fine. Harry's taking her to the ER later this morning for a checkup. She's hoping to work the rest of the day if she gets cleared. I don't know what the police know about Dr. Poole, but we can hash this out after you've had some sleep. Quinn isn't expecting you to show up at work today."

Nick insisted that I stay in the guest room in the main house. He said I wasn't ready to climb the stairs to my apartment over the barn. It seemed like a good plan, and once we got inside, I felt another nap coming on.

As I drifted off, a kaleidoscope of characters whirled through my mind. Echo O'Brien with the enraged face of a killer. Phyllis Poole, a pale and serene vision who might have orchestrated the whole thing. Charming James O'Brien. Was he as innocent as he was charismatic? Keely O'Brien and Tucker Potkotter floated by. Were they in on the plot, or just two hapless bystanders? Even Tobias Fausset appeared for a moment, then vanished as he had in real life. Where had he gone? Next came Laurie Popejoy. The only witness. Had she gone far enough, hidden deep enough to survive? Or would she be silenced by a pregnant black widow and a fugitive thug with a mangled ear?

THIRTY-SIX

A SCRATCHING SENSATION on my chin pulled me out of a restless doze. Fanny was licking me with her raspy little tongue. With one eye open, I peered at the wall clock in Amah's guest room and discovered it was noon. No wonder the cat wanted me to get up. *Breakfast.*

I stood up, waiting a moment to check for vertigo. My balance seemed okay, so I walked to the bathroom down the hall. All systems seemed to be working. I wandered out to Amah's kitchen, where I found a pot of hot coffee and Nick reading the paper.

He looked up. "Chores are done. How are you feeling?"

"Good as new."

"I doubt that, but you look a whole lot better." He poured a cup of coffee and put it on the table in front of me. "If I leave, will you stay put?"

"Where are you going to go without a car? Or were you thinking of borrowing mine?"

"No need." He nodded toward the window facing the driveway. "Here's my ride."

I looked out and spotted Rella stepping out of Nick's car and walking to the front door. Nick explained that Rella needed to practice take-offs and landings in the newest plane in Buck Sawyer's fleet. They had made the arrangements at the municipal airport before my run-in with Echo O'Brien in the hospital restroom.

"It'll only take about an hour, but we can postpone

if you'd rather not be alone." Nick looked to Rella for agreement.

"Yes, of course," she said. "How are you feeling?"

"I'm perfectly fine. There's no reason to change your plans. And Rella, I haven't had a chance to thank you for stepping in to watch my friend Cleo the other night. Is your nephew with the chicken pox feeling better?"

"Yes. Apparently it was poison oak and not chicken pox. The nanny will watch him and his brother until I get home." The brief, awkwardly polite exchange with Rella was the only conversation we'd had since Nick and I broke up, but it was a start.

Nick made me promise to call if I needed him. I watched their easy camaraderie with mixed feelings as they walked to Nick's car and drove away together. They needed that bond to work together as co-pilots, but it still presented a hurdle for me to overcome. I heard an echo of my earlier self-admonition.

Get over it.

Food seemed like a good idea, so I made myself an omelet and washed it down with V-8 juice and another cup of coffee. While I ate, I thought about Cliff Weber of the missing earlobe. Echo must have worked some angle to get him a job in TMC's Housekeeping Department. If I was right, he'd been a busy boy. Helping Tucker with taxidermy, playing security guard at the compound and spying via his job at TMC. Then a new twist occurred to me. What if the father of Echo's baby *wasn't* Tucker? What if Cliff, the jack-of-all-trades, had performed that duty as well?

The food worked its magic. I found my purse and keys in the guest room and drove down the lane to the barn. Climbing the stairs outside my apartment was a good test, and I passed. No dizziness or weakness, and once inside, I checked my pulse rate. It was steady and normal, which was all I needed to know. I had things to do, and it was almost one o'clock. I remembered that I hadn't answered when Nick asked if I would stay put, so my conscience was clear.

I showered, pulled on a pair of black jeans and laced up my light hiking boots. The day was cool and overcast, so I chose a dark gray pullover sweatshirt.

Nick was right. It was up to the police to capture Echo and whoever else was involved in the murders of DeeDee and Cody and with the attempted murder of Seamus. So why was I so invested in this mystery? Because the O'Brien family was part of my past. James and Keely had both been important to me as a young girl. If they were being victimized by Echo O'Brien and some thug, I wanted to help. But first I had to know if my childhood friends were part of the scheme.

Then a new thought took hold. Dr. Poole had been scheduled to operate on Cleo's darling Siggy this morning. I needed to know how that turned out—whether patients at TMC were safe under Phyllis Poole's care, including Seamus O'Brien.

I called Cleo. She picked up on the second ring, sounding stressed.

"Hi, it's me," I said. "Are you okay? You sound terrible."

"I'm tired and I have a monster headache, but I couldn't stay home. I thought Sig would want me here while he was in surgery." I heard a weary sigh. "What about you? I heard you were attacked by Seamus's wife. Are you all right?"

"I'm fine, but I wanted to know about Sig. Did Poole do his surgery this morning?"

"No. The poor guy got bumped by an emergency. Another surgeon needed the OR. He was rescheduled for half an hour ago, but Poole didn't show up, so he was sent home again."

"Why didn't Poole show?" I braced myself for news I didn't wanted to hear.

"No one knows. Her service called to say she couldn't make it and that she wouldn't be available for the rest of the day. Fausset's still out of touch, so the third associate in their group is fielding everything."

That spun me in another direction. Poole's niece had a broken wrist, and Cliff Weber had a torn earlobe. Neither could risk going to an emergency room. Phyllis Poole was a doctor. Maybe they went to her for medical help. If she was involved in their plot, that would be an obvious move.

"Cleo, do you have a home address for Poole?"

"Hold on while I pull her file." She came back with an address in Silver Hills, an exclusive neighborhood of luxurious homes. "If anyone asks, I didn't give this to you."

"Give what to me?"

"Exactly. But promise me, if you're going to her house, don't do anything dangerous."

"I'll drive by, that's all." I stuffed my ponytail inside a black baseball cap, put my .38 in my fanny pack along with my Leatherman, and headed west to Timbergate.

As soon as I spotted Echo's black Hummer parked in the driveway at Poole's address, I called 911 to say I had sighted a vehicle used by two fugitives the police were trying to locate. I gave the address and the license plate information. It was the same plate I'd seen at the market in Coyote Creek when Keely and Tucker were there with Echo: TAXDMY2.

The dispatcher asked me to stay on the line, but I didn't want to tie up my phone. I said I'd call back right away. Next I called Harry for backup. He didn't answer, so I left a message, and then called Nick. I was relieved when he answered, until he reminded me that he and Rella were at the municipal airport ten miles away. I told him I'd spotted Echo's car and that I'd called 911.

"Dammit, Aimee, I knew you'd pull something like this. Get away from there, then call me back." Nick ended the call before I could respond.

I parked down the street two houses away from Poole's. The afternoon sun skidded in and out behind clouds as I approached the house on foot. I crept along a fence bordering the property, ducking behind shrubbery until I made my way to a window with half-closed blinds. I peeked inside and saw Weber, with a bandaged ear, holding a gun on a grim-faced Phyllis Poole while she attempted to splint Echo's injured wrist. There was no sign of Keely, James, or Tucker. Where were they? Holed up somewhere waiting for Weber and Echo to join them in a getaway? Or were they tied up in Poole's house? Or, worst case, were they collateral damage in Echo's contemptible scheme?

I called 911 again, asking why no one had shown up. I was told all units were on high-priority calls. I said the situation had escalated. A gunman was holding someone hostage. The dispatcher ordered me to stay on the line, then put me on hold. She came back on to say a unit would arrive as soon as possible.

She asked if I was in a safe place where I could observe. I said I was, but I was afraid the fugitives would leave any minute.

"They might take the hostage with them," I said. "What should I do?"

"Stay on the line with me. Don't put yourself in danger. Stay out of sight until help arrives. If necessary, leave the scene."

There had to be something I could do. Disabling the Hummer came to mind, but I didn't tell her that, because she would tell me not to interfere. A glance in the window told me it would take several more minutes for Poole to finish with Echo's wrist. I left the phone on, but dropped it in my fanny pack, where my pistol beckoned.

The gun was tempting, but I couldn't shoot out a tire without drawing attention. Instead, I pulled out my multi-tool Leatherman, hoping I could puncture one of the tires with its heavy duty blade. I made my way back along the fence until I reached the street where the Hummer was parked. I crept around the driver's side to the front of the car.

When I braced myself against the fender, the car alarm exploded in a blast that nearly knocked me over. I dropped flat and slid underneath the Hummer on my belly while deafening blasts assaulted my eardrums. I barely heard the muted voice of the 911 dispatcher from inside my fanny pack, "What's going on?"

I tried to jab at the sidewall of the closest tire with the Leatherman's blade, but my leverage was all wrong. The blade didn't sink in. If Weber came out to check on the car, I needed both hands for my gun. I blessed the Hummer's design for the maximum ground clearance that let me roll over. I slid the pack around and switched the Leatherman for my gun.

Someone inside must have found the remote, because the alarm suddenly went silent. I froze when I heard the front door of Poole's house open. Weber poked his head out, looking toward the Hummer.

"Some damn kid must have hit it with a bike. Let's get the hell out of here. We'll take the doc with us." He pulled his head back inside and closed the door.

I rolled out and made a break for the shrubs along the fence. Weber had said, *We'll take the doc.* If they were taking only Phyllis Poole, that didn't bode well for James and Keely—or for Tucker. Still, there was a chance they were alive.

I listened for the sound of sirens, but heard nothing to suggest help was on the way. I hung up on 911 and dialed Nick's number again.

"Where are you?" He sounded furious.

"At Poole's house." I gave him the address but didn't give him a chance to yell at me. "I'm leaving my phone on. Don't hang up." I stuffed the phone back in my pack.

The door opened and Phyllis Poole stood there, rigid, hands tied in front of her with some kind of twine. Weber stepped to her side and quickly covered her hands with a jacket. I spotted the gun he held close against her back. She winced as he gripped her elbow and forced her outside.

Echo followed with her right arm in a sling and her left hand holding a set of keys. She pulled the front door closed, and the threesome started toward the street where the Hummer was parked. The affluent neighborhood was deserted, which would be a good thing if the police arrived and shots were fired. That was unlikely, because the trio was already halfway to the street. I was still Dr. Poole's only hope.

Should I shoot Weber or wait until they were in the car and try to shoot out the tires? I came up with a third option. As Weber tried to force Poole into the backseat, I fired at the Hummer's front fender and set the alarm blasting again. Weber spun away from Poole to see where the shot had come from. Echo froze in confusion, long enough for Poole to lunge at her, knocking her to the ground. Just then a TPD cruiser pulled up with lights flashing and siren blaring.

I stepped out from behind the shrubs, pointing at Weber, yelling, "He has a gun."

The first officer out of the car aimed his weapon at Weber and yelled, "Drop the gun, sir. On your knees. Hands on your head." Weber obeyed, tossing his gun across the lawn. The second officer cut the cruiser's lights and sirens, but by that time, the street began to fill with people.

The first officer yelled, "Drop the gun, lady. Down on your knees, hands on your head."

It took a moment to realize he was yelling at me, but the gun he pointed my way made it clear. I tossed my .38 out of reach.

"I'm innocent. I called this in." I nodded toward Weber and Echo. "They're killers. They were taking a hostage—"

"Sit down on the ground and wait, lady."

I didn't argue, but I did keep track of everyone. Weber was still on his knees, but by now Poole and Echo were standing. Poole had her hands on her head, still tied with the twine. Echo managed to comply with her good arm, but the other stayed secured at her side in the sling.

"She's telling the truth." Poole nodded toward me and shouted over the blasts, "She was trying to help me."

"You too, keep quiet. On your knees." He pointed toward the ground and both women dropped. He kept Poole, Echo, and me covered while his partner struggled to cuff a violently thrashing Weber.

"Just get him locked in the unit," the older officer said.

"I don't have him cuffed yet."

"We don't have time right now. Just lock him in the unit. We'll get to the cuffs as soon as we can."

When he saw that Weber was secured in the cruiser, he shouted, "Now take care of that damn car alarm." Then he nodded at the gathering crowd. "All of you, go home. Get off the street." The curiosity seekers scattered toward their homes.

The second cop shouted, "Who owns this vehicle?"

"I do," Echo cried out, pointing at me. "That crazy woman was going to shoot me. I was trying to get away from her. My husband is in the hospital. I have to go to him." The conniving felon even managed to work up a tear.

"She's lying," I shouted over the blasting alarm. "She tried to kill me. You have to arrest her."

The second cop nodded at Echo. "Turn off that friggin' alarm."

Echo got up, took a step toward the Hummer. The cop blocked her. "Stop right there. Use your remote."

"I can't, officer," Echo said. "I'm sorry, the remote doesn't work. I have to get in and start the car to turn off the alarm."

"She's lying," I called out. "She used her remote from inside her house."

"Lady." Cop two glared at me. "You were told to keep quiet."

"Yes, sir," I said. I glanced at Weber in time to see him smirk, but I didn't care as long as he was still locked in the cruiser.

The second cop looked at the sling on Echo's disabled right arm and made his decision. He motioned her toward the Hummer with his gun and followed her to the driver's side door. Hope sank when I saw cunning in Echo's expression. Once she got behind the wheel, she would make a run for it, disappear, and become someone else.

THIRTY-SEVEN

ECHO CLIMBED BEHIND the wheel, started the Hummer, and slammed the open driver's door against the officer's arm, knocking his gun to the ground. She peeled out, laying a strip of rubber and leaving behind a cloud of smoke. The red-faced officer grabbed up his gun while his partner blistered the air with a string of curses, ending with, "Get on the damn radio and call it in. And get some backup out here."

The second officer spoke into the radio clipped to his shoulder. He waited for a response, and his face fell. "They'll get a BOLO out for the Hummer, but it looks like we're on our own."

"Then let's get this done." The older cop turned to Poole. "You stay right where you are. Officer Blake is going to question your friend while I get the injured man's story. Understand?"

Poole nodded.

Officer Blake motioned to me to join him where he was standing near the back of the cruiser. The older officer opened the back door of the unit with his gun trained on Weber.

"Step out of the unit, sir."

Cliff Weber was already big and mean, but seeing Echo take off without him had thrown him into a rage. As soon as the door opened, he lunged out, bellowing like a mad bull, and tackled the older officer, knocking his gun out of reach on the lawn. Then both men fell against Officer Blake, and all three fell on the hard cement sidewalk like dominoes. Blake's weapon landed in the gutter. The older cop groaned, then went limp. Officer Blake was conscious, but still on all fours. Weber was struggling to his feet.

Poole and I read each other's minds. She leapt up and scrambled across the lawn for my gun and Weber's while I raced to retrieve both of the policemen's guns.

"Get down or I'll shoot," Poole screamed at Weber. With her hands still tied at the wrists, she managed to hold a gun in each hand, both pointed at Weber's chest. I did the same.

As we stood there like two-fisted gunslingers, an intoxicating rush of power surged through my body. Was this what Poole felt in the operating room when she used her fine mind and her surgeon's hands? Or what Rella had felt in the pilot's seat of a fighter jet? For just a moment, I understood both of these women and even felt kinship with them. My musing quickly faded when I saw the malicious glint in Weber's eyes. Poole saw it, too, but it was too late. Weber grabbed the still dazed Officer Blake in a choke hold, using him as a shield.

"Don't be foolish," Poole said. "I'm a doctor with a good grasp of anatomy, and I'm also a very good shot." She glanced at me. "How about you, Aimee?"

"Just tell me where to aim."

"Go ahead, ladies, take your best shot." Weber laughed. "You hit a cop, you'll have to tell it to a judge. This guy is dead if you don't toss me one of those guns and put the others down."

I believed him.

Poole swore, looked at me. Her hands were still tied.

I put both my guns on the ground. She put one on the ground and slowly walked toward Weber, holding the other gun by the barrel. I watched, desperate to help, my mind racing through possible jujitsu moves that could break Weber's hold on the policeman. But how to get close enough?

A small airplane suddenly streaked toward us, flying too low. The pilot had to be in trouble—the plane coming at us was surely going to crash into Poole's house. Then I saw the tail number and realized it was one of Buck Sawyer's planes. I expected to see Nick at the controls, but the pilot was Rella. She pulled the nose up just in time, circled, and came at us again. Weber craned his neck to see what was going on. He still had his arm around the officer's neck, but between reaching for the gun in Poole's hand and leaning back to watch the plane, he was doubly distracted.

While he stared at the sky, I lunged behind him, grabbed the collar of his shirt, and crouched down, giving a vicious yank. Weber lost his grip on the cop and flipped backward over me, landing face-first on the sidewalk. I looked up from his bloody nose just in time to see Rella tip her wings and fly away. I expected to see Nick and Harry appear any minute, but neither of them arrived before Officer Blake had arrested and cuffed Weber and locked him in the backseat of the TPD cruiser.

By then the older cop had regained consciousness, and a stunning goose egg had sprouted on his forehead. Dr. Poole told him to lie still, that she had called for an ambulance. While we waited, the enraged Weber, with blood bubbling from his nose, shouted obscenities through the partially open window of the cruiser.

He screamed about police brutality, ranted that he was innocent, that he wanted a lawyer. While he worked himself into a frenzy, Officer Blake stood at the window, and despite Weber's tirade, calmly recited the Miranda warning.

"Sir, you have the right to remain silent...."

THIRTY-EIGHT

DR. POOLE and I were not placed under arrest. We both volunteered to go to the police station to give our versions of the incident. There we were placed in separate interview rooms. I'd been alone for an hour when a woman with a droopy face and close-cropped blond hair came in looking far more real than the glamorous actresses who play lady cops on TV. Her maroon pantsuit had been in style when I was in middle school. She peered at me through thick lenses with dark red frames.

"Hello, I'm detective Wooten. I brought you a bottle of water, but before we begin this interview, can I get you coffee? Maybe a soda?"

"I'm fine with the water," I said. "I'd rather get started. But first, isn't there something about a Miranda warning?"

Wooten smiled. "No. That's a common misunderstanding. Since you're not under arrest, we have no need to Mirandize you. We simply want to hear your version of the incident involving our officers. Are you willing to help us out with that?"

"Yes, I'd like to do that. But first, can you tell me if the officers who were attacked are okay?"

"They're being checked out. Thank you for asking." She uncapped her pen and held it over a notepad. "Now I'd like for you to tell me everything you can remember about the incident that brought you here today. I'll take notes, but your statement will also be recorded."

I told her I knew the police were looking for Cliff Weber and Echo O'Brien and that I had reason to believe they might have gone to Dr. Poole's house.

"I knew both of them were injured, and since one of them is related to Dr. Poole, I thought they might go to her for medical care. I went to her home to see if I was right. When I spotted their vehicle, I called 911 right away."

"Interesting." Wooten was jotting quickly on her notepad. "Go on."

I gave her a blow by blow account of everything that happened from the time I arrived until a second TPD unit finally showed up and Weber was taken away. I stopped to sip from my water bottle.

"That's all I can tell you, Detective Wooten. Are we finished?"

"Not quite. We have been informed that you assaulted Mr. Weber on two occasions—on the first occasion tearing his earlobe and on the second, breaking his nose."

I was so glad to hear his nose was broken that I almost smiled.

Detective Wooten went on. "We've also been told that you broke the wrist of Mrs. O'Brien." She leaned back in her chair. "What can you tell me about those allegations?"

"Mr. Weber attacked me in the basement of the hospital where I work on the first occasion, and I injured his ear trying to free myself. His nose was broken during today's incident when I used a jujitsu technique to force him to release the police officer he was threatening with a chokehold. I'm sure the officer involved will verify my account."

"He's being interviewed. We'll see if your stories match. What about the woman with the broken wrist?"

"That also happened at the hospital where I work. She tried to kill me with a syringe filled with phenobarbital. I had to disable her to save myself. Again, I was forced to use a martial arts technique. I hold a third degree black belt. If you'd like to verify, I have my ID from the dojo where I'm a member."

"Maybe later. Tell me more about why this woman would want to kill you with the syringe. Does it somehow pertain to today's incident?"

"Yes. I suspect that the woman who calls herself Echo O'Brien has already committed one murder, and I found evidence that should prove Cliff Weber is also a killer."

I related the entire story, starting with how I found the club used to kill Cody O'Brien, and how hospital records led to the discovery that Echo had almost certainly killed DeeDee Dakota two and a half years earlier. Detective Wooten left me in the room at that point, asking me to stay until she returned.

While I waited, I wondered what had kept both Nick and Harry from showing up at Poole's house. I had called Nick and left my phone on, then later Rella showed up in the plane, but Nick never appeared. And where was Harry? I had no idea if he'd even seen the message I left for him.

Detective Wooten finally came back into the room. "We're finished here. Please come with me." She escorted me to the lobby, where Nick and Harry stood smiling.

"You're free to go, Miss Machado." The detective gave me her card in case I thought of anything else to tell her.

Nick, Harry, and I headed for Coyote Creek, where we hurried through the outdoor chores so we could unwind in the main house and compare notes.

Nick filled us in first with his account. He and Rella knew what was going on, because his phone and mine had been connected. He knew Echo had escaped and he knew Poole's address. They agreed that Rella should fly over to assess the situation while Nick went in pursuit of Echo. He guessed correctly that she might head down the freeway to Sacramento and try to catch a flight to parts unknown. Nick was able to station himself along the freeway and watch for her Hummer. As soon as he spotted it, he called in her location to the CHP. Meanwhile, Rella flew by Poole's house, saw Weber restraining the officer, and put her skills to good use.

Next, Harry told his part of the story. He hadn't checked his messages right away, and by the time he did, I'd already called Nick and left my phone on, so he couldn't return my call. Nick's phone was tied up, too, so Harry was in the dark. He assumed Nick and I were handling some kind of situation, so he waited awhile, but after an hour passed and he still couldn't reach either of us, he got curious and called Rella.

"Wait a minute," I said. "How did you happen to know her number?"

"Remember, she had to call me to take over the night she was watching Cleo for a possible concussion. After that, her number was in my phone."

"Oh, right. The night she thought her nephew had chicken pox."

"Right. Turned out the kid only had poison oak. Anyway, Rella had already buzzed the scene. She filled me in and I figured I'd drop by the TPD office to see what was going on. Nick showed up at about the same time."

"Meanwhile," Nick added, "Jared Quinn had filled in the blanks with the police about your tussle with Echo at the hospital, and Cleo had told them what she knew. It became obvious that Weber and Echo were two very bad characters, and that you and Dr. Poole were only trying to save your own skins. Tucker confirmed that the incinerator hasn't been used since you were out at the O'Brien compound, so with a search warrant, that club Weber used on Cody should be easy to find."

"Search warrant," I said. "Did anyone say whether I'm going to be in trouble for breaking into the taxidermy shop?"

"None of the O'Briens will want to see that happen. Especially since you found the weapon that proved Cody was murdered. At most, some judge might feel obliged to give you a lecture and a slap on the wrist."

Harry broke into a broad grin. "Looks like your pal Game Boy is no longer a suspect."

"I'm glad, but there's one more thing that has me confused. Keely, James, and Tucker weren't allowed to visit Seamus in the ICU, but the police didn't find any of them at the O'Brien ranch. Where were they?"

"I know that one," Harry said. "The three of them were in Sacramento with Seamus's estate lawyer. Apparently Seamus gave them instructions about writing Echo out of his will. He wanted it done immediately in case he didn't recover."

"But she's still legally his wife and pregnant. How

will they get around that? The baby will be his legal heir, won't it?"

"Turns out Echo—or Caroline Poole, or whoever she is—was never legally married to Seamus," Harry said. "She was already married to Cliff Weber when she walked down the aisle with Seamus. Once bigamy is tacked on to her other crimes, not the least of which are murder and attempted murder, she'll probably be a guest of the state for the rest of her life."

"But she's pregnant. What's going to become of that child?" God help it if Jackie Poole got custody.

"Apparently, even with her lack of qualifications for motherhood, Echo still has a say in that, and she hasn't decided."

"There's one more thing that puzzles me," I said. "Why did James think he'd seen Phyllis Poole in DeeDee Dakota's hospital room in Idaho?"

Nick answered that one. "Poole was cut loose a couple hours ago and went straight to Cleo. They had an interesting and very private chat. Cleo knew you'd want to know, so she filled me in right away."

"Cleo and Poole? This should be interesting."

"It is. It turns out Poole was in Dunnsville on some kind of family business at the time of DeeDee's accident, so one of DeeDee's doctors asked Poole to do a renal evaluation."

"But Poole's CV had no mention of her connection to Idaho, and there was nothing in DeeDee's chart showing Poole had been involved in the case."

"That's because her foster niece, Caroline Poole, was implicated in a drug theft scandal at that hospital about that time, and Phyllis Poole didn't want her own reputation tainted by association. She managed to purge any reference to herself from DeeDee's chart, and she eliminated any reference to Idaho or Dunnsville Memorial from her CV."

"Wow, a falsified CV? If that comes out, she could lose her privileges at TMC."

Nick smiled. "It won't come out if Cleo has her way. She's had a major change of heart about the lady doctor."

"I said it before…what a soap opera." Harry stood up with a stretch and a yawn. "It's getting late. I need to get home and do a couple loads of laundry."

"Since when do you care about laundry?"

"I'm way behind." He gave us a salute and headed out the door.

Suspicious, I asked Nick if he'd arranged that so we would be alone.

"No, I swear. But just so you know, I'm not leaving you here by yourself tonight. You've had a few tough days."

There was no fight left in me, so I poured each of us a glass of wine. I took Nick's to him and started down the hall with mine.

"Where are you going?" Nick asked.

"I need a shower."

"So do I." He picked up his glass and followed me.

THIRTY-NINE

NICK AND I arrived for a special evening at Margie's Bean Pot exactly one month after the stand-off at Phyllis Poole's home. As we walked to our table, I was congratulated by several fellow employees who had heard about Beardsley's retirement and my promotion.

We were just in time to hear Laurie Popejoy's sublime version of the classic Etta James song, "At Last." The entire restaurant was reserved for Timbergate Medical Center employees and guests, including Laurie Popejoy and her husband, Daniel Littletree, who sat at our table. The absence of Tobias Fausset and Phyllis Poole from the Code Blues combo seemed strange, but everyone knew why they weren't on stage that night.

Rella sat next to Harry at our table, often leaning close to him and whispering. He wore an expression I couldn't decipher, but I planned to interrogate him later. Cleo and her darling Siggy held hands like teenagers. Since Sig's remarkably successful prostate surgery, Cleo had become Dr. Phyllis Poole's biggest fan.

Keely O'Brien and Tucker sat at the table next to ours, along with James and Seamus. Much to the relief of his remaining heirs, the elder O'Brien had survived his ordeal with tick-borne infections. Cody's horse had a new lease on life, too. Keely had always loved horses, and when she begged her father to keep Game Boy, Seamus agreed, on the condition that Keely stay clean and sober. It appeared to be working when she proudly announced she had just entered her first cutting horse competition. It seemed fitting that the horse that had witnessed Cody O'Brien's death now had a chance to redeem Keely O'Brien's life.

The O'Brien table was rounded out by Laurie Pope-joy's parents and her Aunt Brenda, former employee of the recently closed Dunnsville Memorial Hospital in Idaho. The owner, Dr. Carl Jasper, and his business partner, Jackie Poole, both fled to Ecuador when the FBI began investigating their hospital.

It turned out that Caroline Poole, alias Echo O'Brien, was the result of a fling Jasper had years earlier when he was a married father of several young children. Jackie knew the truth, and in return for keeping quiet and raising the girl as her foster daughter, she became a silent partner in the hospital and a co-conspirator in Jasper's illegal schemes.

Amidst the applause for Laurie's song were calls for an encore. She took the mic again and began singing "Sentimental Journey." That's when James stood and came to our table.

"Mr. Alexander, do you mind if I borrow Aimee for a dance?"

"Of course not," Nick said. What else could he say?

James had flown out from New York two days earlier and had to catch a flight back the next morning. We hadn't been in touch in the month since Echo and Weber's plot unraveled.

We swayed to the gentle rhythm of Laurie's song, and after a moment, James said, "Hey, Little Aimless, a penny for your thoughts."

"Sorry, they're not for sale."

"Can't blame me for asking, but there is something I need to know. I didn't ask this before I left last month, so I'm asking now if that's okay."

My throat went a little dry, but I managed to answer, "Okay."

"Then here goes." He leaned close and spoke quietly in my ear. "Is Nick Alexander the right guy for you?"

In James's arms, I was reminded of our steamy dances at Margie's almost two months earlier when he had come back into my life. He still smelled like lemon meringue pie, and I still cherished the precious memories of my girlish crush. Laurie's vocal treatment seemed to seep into my pores, and I wanted her song to go on and on, but it ended and the spell was broken. I gave James the only answer I could.

"You were the love of my life when I was a child, but I'm pretty sure Nick is the love of my grown-up life. It's just that we still have things to work out."

"Good enough, Little Aimless. Be happy, okay?"

James walked me back to Nick and returned to the O'Brien table, where he and his family were getting on with their lives, relieved to finally know why DeeDee and Cody had died.

The truth had finally come out. It had been Echo, back in her days as Caroline Poole, who was the pink-haired one-night stand Cody had brushed off in Idaho. Her revenge was to drug Cody's wife. Simple to do, since Caroline was a nursing assistant with access to DeeDee's room. A couple of months after DeeDee died, Caroline left Idaho and reinvented herself. She ended up dealing cards in Reno, where she met and married Cliff Weber.

Seamus O'Brien's fate was sealed when he was in

Reno for a Safari Club International convention. He enjoyed gambling, but made the mistake of flirting with Echo while he played blackjack. That's when she and Weber cooked up their plan. Their long con would have worked once she got pregnant, even though the baby's father was Weber, but they got nervous when Cody showed up injured and retired from rodeo. He thought Echo looked familiar—in spite of her nose job, different hair color, and cosmetic dentistry.

Echo figured it was just a matter time before Cody figured out who she was, and she was right. When she overheard Cody talking to Seamus about a paternity test, she and Weber decided Cody had to go. The rifle bullet missed, but the horseshoe club got the job done. Seamus would have been the third victim if Echo hadn't been stopped in time.

All of that was tied up in a neat bundle by the TPD. Echo and Weber were going to spend the rest of their lives behind bars, but there was some good news. The unborn baby boy Echo did not want had already found a family.

Laurie stepped up to the mic again with a sweet rendition of an old R&B song, "The Boy I'm Gonna Marry." It set the mood for the rest of the evening. The occasion for the gathering at Margie's was unexpected, but it was one everyone wanted to celebrate. Laurie's song ended, and after a rush of applause died away, Jared Quinn stepped up to the mic.

"Ladies and gentlemen, most of you are aware that Tobias Fausset spent some time away from Timbergate recently." He nodded to a table near the bandstand where Tobias was seated. All eyes turned toward Tobias and Phyllis Poole. There were whispers and some soft laughter, then Quinn went on speaking.

"We know now that Dr. Fausset took time off to visit his mother and father in Rio de Janeiro and to accompany them back to Timbergate for an extended visit. Tonight, his parents are here to join the rest of us in celebrating as their son begins a new chapter in his life." As Quinn took his place with the combo, the audience applauded and cheered.

Code Blues played a soulful version of Richard Wagner's "Bridal Chorus," while Dr. Tobias Fausset and Dr. Phyllis Poole stood and walked arm in arm toward the bandstand.

The room went quiet as the Timbergate Medical Center Chaplain, with Bible in hand, performed a wedding ceremony for the couple already making plans to adopt their first child.

* * * * *

Photo courtesy of Lowell Martinson

SHARON ST. George had the good fortune to spend an idyllic childhood in a small northern California town, riding horseback and camping with her family in the nearby mountains. One of her favorite pastimes was reading fiction, and a trip to the library was always an occasion of great joy. She's traded horses for llamas, but she still treks to the high mountain lakes near her home—always with a mystery novel in her backpack.

Sharon's writing credits include three plays, several years writing advertising copy, a book on NASA's space food project, and feature stories too numerous to count. She holds dual degrees in English and Theatre Arts, and occasionally acts in, or directs, one of her local community theater productions. *Checked Out* is her second novel and the second book in the Aimee Machado mystery series, which began with *Due for Discard*.

Sharon is a member of Sisters in Crime and Mystery

Writers of America, and she serves as program director for Writers Forum, a nonprofit organization for writers in northern California.

For more information, go to www.sharonstgeorge.com.

Get 4 FREE REWARDS!

We'll send you 2 FREE Books **plus** 2 FREE Mystery Gifts.

FREE
Value Over
$20

Both the **Romance** and **Suspense** collections feature compelling novels written by many of today's best-selling authors.

YES! Please send me 2 FREE novels from the Essential Romance or Essential Suspense Collection and my 2 FREE gifts (gifts are worth about $10 retail). After receiving them, if I don't wish to receive any more books, I can return the shipping statement marked "cancel." If I don't cancel, I will receive 4 brand-new novels every month and be billed just $6.74 each in the U.S. or $7.24 each in Canada. That's a savings of at least 16% off the cover price. It's quite a bargain! Shipping and handling is just 50¢ per book in the U.S. and 75¢ per book in Canada*. I understand that accepting the 2 free books and gifts places me under no obligation to buy anything. I can always return a shipment and cancel at any time. The free books and gifts are mine to keep no matter what I decide.

Choose one: ☐ **Essential Romance**
(194/394 MDN GMY7)

☐ **Essential Suspense**
(191/391 MDN GMY7)

Name (please print)

Address   Apt. #

City   State/Province   Zip/Postal Code

Mail to the **Reader Service:**
IN U.S.A.: P.O. Box 1341, Buffalo, NY 14240-8531
IN CANADA: P.O. Box 603, Fort Erie, Ontario L2A 5X3

Want to try two free books from another series! Call 1-800-873-8635 or visit www.ReaderService.com.

*Terms and prices subject to change without notice. Prices do not include applicable taxes. Sales tax applicable in NY. Canadian residents will be charged applicable taxes. Offer not valid in Quebec. This offer is limited to one order per household. Books received may not be as shown. Not valid for current subscribers to the Essential Romance or Essential Suspense Collection. All orders subject to approval. Credit or debit balances in a customer's account(s) may be offset by any other outstanding balance owed by or to the customer. Please allow 4 to 6 weeks for delivery. Offer available while quantities last.

Your Privacy—The Reader Service is committed to protecting your privacy. Our Privacy Policy is available online at www.ReaderService.com or upon request from the Reader Service. We make a portion of our mailing list available to reputable third parties that offer products we believe may interest you. If you prefer that we not exchange your name with third parties, or if you wish to clarify or modify your communication preferences, please visit us at www.ReaderService.com/consumerschoice or write to us at Reader Service Preference Service, P.O. Box 9062, Buffalo, NY 14240-9062. Include your complete name and address.

STRS18

Get 4 FREE REWARDS!

We'll send you 2 FREE Books plus 2 FREE Mystery Gifts.

Love Inspired® Suspense books feature Christian characters facing challenges to their faith... and lives.

FREE
Value Over
$20

YES! Please send me 2 FREE Love Inspired® Suspense novels and my 2 FREE mystery gifts (gifts are worth about $10 retail). After receiving them, if I don't wish to receive any more books, I can return the shipping statement marked "cancel." If I don't cancel, I will receive 4 brand-new novels every month and be billed just $5.24 each for the regular-print edition or $5.74 each for the larger-print edition in the U.S., or $5.74 each for the regular-print edition or $6.24 each for the larger-print edition in Canada. That's a savings of at least 13% off the cover price. It's quite a bargain! Shipping and handling is just 50¢ per book in the U.S. and 75¢ per book in Canada*. I understand that accepting the 2 free books and gifts places me under no obligation to buy anything. I can always return a shipment and cancel at any time. The free books and gifts are mine to keep no matter what I decide.

Choose one: ☐ **Love Inspired® Suspense**
Regular-Print
(153/353 IDN GMY5)

☐ **Love Inspired® Suspense**
Larger-Print
(107/307 IDN GMY5)

Name (please print)

Address   Apt. #

City   State/Province   Zip/Postal Code

Mail to the **Reader Service**:
IN U.S.A.: P.O. Box 1341, Buffalo, NY 14240-8531
IN CANADA: P.O. Box 603, Fort Erie, Ontario L2A 5X3

Want to try two free books from another series! Call 1-800-873-8635 or visit www.ReaderService.com.
